Reviewers acclaim T. Davis Bunn's novel
The Maestro

"*The Maestro* is a wonderful story of God's hand bringing spiritual and creative seeds to full fruit. All of us struggle with how to best offer our talents to God. This is a powerful story of that struggle, and will encourage anyone dealing with these questions. It is truly a book with vision."

MARTY McCALL
First Call

"In *The Maestro*, T. Davis Bunn shows a fine gift for story-telling. He weaves together the external events of a person's life with an inner spiritual journey, and combines a seriousness of theme with a splendid sense of humor."

REVEREND PAUL S. FIDDES
   Principal Director
Regents Park College
(Baptist Seminary)
Oxford University

"If a fiction book can get an 'A' rating, this one does."

PATTY ECKARD
Choice Books

"The story is powerful, carefully researched, and well-developed. Gianni's personal struggle mirrors those of many young people, and the guidance he receives is guidance for the reader as well. This book would be an excellent choice for persons for whom music is a priority. It is one of the best novels I've read in a long time."

JOAN RAE MILLS
Provident Book Finder

"*The Maestro* does a very rare and beautiful thing—it lays bare the tenuous relationship between a man's gift, and the God who placed that gift in him. The world in which these characters move is as real as any that Dickens ever created."

GILBERT MORRIS
Author of the House of Winslow Series

"You are a very good writer. Your descriptive passages are poetic!"

JAMES G. MARTIN
Governor
State of North Carolina

Selected as one of the twenty "Essential Reading" novels—along with books by Bunyan, Milton, Austin, Dickens, and C. S. Lewis— by Colin Duriez for the European Christian bookstore journal.

Books by T. Davis Bunn

The Quilt
The Gift
The Messenger
The Music Box

The Maestro
The Presence
Promises to Keep
*Return to Harmony**
Riders of the Pale Horse

The Priceless Collection
Secret Treasures of Eastern Europe

1. *Florian's Gate*
2. *The Amber Room*
3. *Winter Palace*

Rendezvous With Destiny

1. *Rhineland Inheritance*
2. *Gibraltar Passage*
3. *Sahara Crosswind*
4. *Berlin Encounter*
5. *Istanbul Express*

*with Janette Oke

The Amber Room

T. DAVIS BUNN

BETHANY HOUSE PUBLISHERS
MINNEAPOLIS, MINNESOTA 55438

Cover design by Koechel Peterson & Associates
Minneapolis, Minnesota.

Published by Bethany House Publishers
A Ministry of Bethany Fellowship, Inc.
6820 Auto Club Road, Minneapolis, Minnesota 55438

Printed in the United States of America

Library of Congress Cataloging-in-Publication Data

Bunn, T. Davis, 1952–
   The amber room / T. Davis Bunn.
     p.   cm.
Sequel to *Florian's Gate*.
   I. Title.
PS3552.U4718A8   1992
813'.54—dc20   92–24828
ISBN 1–55661–285–0   CIP

T. Davis Bunn is a native of North Carolina. His former international business career took him to over forty countries in Europe, Africa, and the Middle East. Researching the trail of the Amber Room led him from the glamor of London's West End to Hitler's underground bunkers in former East Germany, and from there to the ancient Monastery of the Black Madonna in Poland. He drew on insights gained from interviews with Eastern European government and church officials as well as from yellowed war-time files and recent exposés of former East German secret police documents. He and his wife, Isabella, currently make their home in Oxford, England.

This book is dedicated to
my father

Thomas D. Bunn

with love
and thanks for the divine grace
that has made us friends.

"My son, if you accept my words and store up my
commands within you,
Turning your ear to wisdom and applying your
heart to understanding,
And if you call out for insight and cry aloud
for understanding,
And if you look for it as for silver and search
for it as for hidden treasure,
Then you will understand the fear of the Lord
and find the knowledge of God."

PROVERBS 2:1–5

"Until a man has found God and been found by God,
he begins at no beginning, he works to no end.
He may have his friendships, his partial loyalties,
his scraps of honor. But all these things fall
into place, and life falls into place, only with
God."

H. G. WELLS

AUTHOR'S NOTE

As with *Florian's Gate*, antiques described in these pages, including the medieval chalice, do indeed exist. Prices quoted here reflect either recent purchases or estimates.

Information on reliquaries was garnered from a number of sources, and fashioned to suit this story.

As to the Amber Room, all information given in these pages leading up to the end of World War II—including its label as the Eighth Wonder of the World—is true.

The search continues . . .

CHAPTER
1

Jeffrey Allen Sinclair worked hard at maintaining his calm. This bank vault was the closest he had ever come to being entombed.

"You oughtta give me some room for maneuvering, kid." The buyer was a silver-maned gentleman whom Betty had introduced only as Marv. His accent was New Jersey, his manner brash. "One point one mil plus change is kinda steep."

The Swiss bank's central underground vault was tucked discreetly behind the safety-deposit chambers, and reminded Jeffrey of a fur-lined cave. Plush maroon carpet, toned to match the thousands and thousands of burnished metal boxes, covered every available surface—floors, walls, ceilings, private inspection booths, even the wheeled tables used for carting security boxes back and forth. This padding sucked sound from the air, leaving a brooding oppressiveness, a sensation that human passage here was barely tolerated.

The Rubens portrait of Isabel of Bourbon was a splash of life in the deadened chamber. Recessed lighting fell with vivid clarity on the painting, leaving the viewers and the rest of the room in shadows. That and the painting's obvious mastery of execution lent the portrait a singular power.

"That was the agreement," Jeffrey said, feeling as though

the walls were eating his words. "We've done our part. We've had an expert authenticate and appraise the painting, and we've sought no competing bids. In return, as we told Betty, we expect no negotiation on the established price."

The painting had been entrusted to him by Dr. Pavel Rokovski in Cracow, to be smuggled out of Poland. Jeffrey was instructed to sell it as quietly as possible to someone who would respect the Polish government's need to keep the sale very private.

"Buy it, Marv," Betty said. An antiques dealer who had done business with Jeffrey on a number of occasions, she projected a polished self-assurance unaffected by their surroundings. "If you don't, I will."

"Yeah, yeah, okay." Marv sighed, reached into his coat pocket, and drew out a single-page banker's draft. "Can't shoot a guy for trying."

Jeffrey accepted the draft, counted the zeros, read the words, resisted the urge to kiss the document. "Maybe you two could decide on the transport arrangements."

Betty inspected the tall young man with evident approval. Since Jeffrey had begun working at Alexander Kantor's antique shop in London eighteen months before, she had taken great pleasure watching him grow in the trade. She replied, "That's already taken care of."

"Yeah, the lady said you were for real; she did all the detail work before we got here." Marv shifted in his leather-lined seat. "Got something I wanna ask you, kid."

"Jeffrey," Betty corrected. "The young man's name is Jeffrey. He's just done you a great favor, Marv. The least you could do is try to remember his name."

"Taking over a mil offa me is a favor?"

"Giving you the right to buy a Rubens at any price is a favor, and you know it."

"Okay, Jeffrey, then."

Betty rose to her feet. "Well, Jeffrey, I owe you one."

"Seems to me it's mutual."

She shook her head. "You took me at my word."

"I trust you, Betty."

"I'm sure someone else has paid me such a nice compliment, but I can't remember when. Can I buy you lunch?"

He glanced at his watch. "I don't think there's time. I've got a plane back to London at two. Alexander's expecting me."

"I'll walk you out, then, if that's okay."

"It'd be great."

"You've already taken care of the export documents?"

He nodded. "They're with the bank manager. He'll get a confirmation on this check and hand them over."

"That's it, then." She turned toward the automatic door, asked, "You ready, Marv?"

"We're right behind you," Marv replied. He waited for the door to sigh shut behind her, then said, "You're okay, kid."

"Thank you, sir."

"No muss, no fuss, just like the lady said. I like that." He was a well-groomed man in his fifties, with the look of a silver-maned wolf. Not a fox—a fox was too sleek an image, too polished. But a winter wolf, yes. Jeffrey could easily picture Marv emerging from snow-covered woods to howl at the moon. "The lady tells me secrecy's top on your list with this one, am I right?"

"It would help us a lot if the painting effectively disappeared, yes."

"Say no more, kid. And don't you worry. Where this painting's gonna go, it might as well stay buried down here in this vault." He gave the portrait another long look, nodded once. "Okay, that's enough. Let's get outta here. This place is giving me the heebie-jeebies. Tomb of Crazy Eddie the Carpet King."

On their way past the long rows of gleaming metal drawers, Marv asked, "You got anything else like this hanging around?"

"This is the first painting of world-class standing I've ever handled," Jeffrey confessed.

"Who said anything about paintings?" He stopped their forward progress by jabbing two fingers into Jeffrey's chest. "Look, you're a good kid. You're smart, you got class, you keep your ear to the ground, am I right?"

"I try."

"Sure you do. Okay, here's the thing. My wife, she likes paintings. Personally, I don't have all that many that keep me interested. This one, yeah, maybe I'm gonna put it in my study—don't worry, kid, that's one place nobody but nobody ever goes. But like I said, my wife's the one who's nuts over paintings."

Marv touched the knot of his tie with a manicured hand. "What I'm after, personally speaking, is *unique*. You with me? One of a kind. Stuff a museum'd take one look at and start picking their jawbones up off the floor. Something like the Wright brothers' first airplane."

"I think that one's in the Smithsonian."

"Yeah, I wrote 'em a while back. Offered to do my patriotic duty, help bail the government out, take the sucker off their hands. Didn't even get a reply. They got some nerve."

"You're looking for the kind of item that nobody else has," Jeffrey interpreted.

"See, I said you were a bright kid. Not just anything, though. No miniature Disney castle made outta silver-plated tongue depressors, you with me? It's gotta be unique, and it's gotta be *class*."

"How about historic?"

"Yeah, sure, history's okay. But *mystery* is better. Like the long lost treasures of the great Queen Smelda. The solid gold throne of the ancient fire-worshiping king of Kazookistan. Stuff like that."

"Last I heard, solid gold thrones don't come cheap."

"Listen, kid. You bring me unique and class and mystery all tied up in one little bundle, the sky ain't high enough for how far I'd go."

The Union Bank of Switzerland straddled the Paradeplatz, Zurich's central square, and was connected to the main train station by the mile-long Bahnhofstrasse. This central pedestrian boulevard was lined with the most expensive shops in all Switzerland. Jeffrey took great draughts of the biting winter air as he walked beside Betty and enjoyed playing the wide-eyed tourist. Fresh snowfall muffled sounds and gave the ancient facades a fairy-tale air. Streetcars clanged and rumbled, roasting chestnuts perfumed the air, passersby conversed in guttural Swiss German. It was a good time to be alive.

As they walked, Jeffrey told Betty of his conversation with Marv. She was not surprised. "Marv was born about six hundred years too late. He imagines himself sitting in his mountain fastness, surrounded by suits of shining armor and all the treasures from his crusading days."

"More like a prince of thieves," Jeffrey offered.

"As it is, Marv has had to make do with thirty dry-cleaning businesses and half the garbage-collection companies in New Jersey. He sees himself buying respectability with his art." She shook her head. "On second thought, he's probably better off living now. He can twist the secret knob and walk down the stairs that nobody but a builder, fifty or sixty stonemasons, and half of Princeton know about. Then he can sit in front of his latest acquisition and dream about a time when he'd have ridden off into the sunset in pursuit of stolen treasures and damsels in distress, and forget the fact that he'd probably have gotten himself killed. Romantics tend not to survive in romantic times."

"I didn't know you were a cynic."

"Cynic? Me?" Betty laughed. "I just don't like losing clients with more money than sense. They're too rare to sacrifice to the call of the wild."

"Personally, I think the times we're living in are about as romantic as they can get."

Betty arched an eyebrow. "You don't mean to tell me you're in love."

"Afraid so."

"How utterly charming. Who is she?"

"You'll meet her the next time you're in London."

"Not the beauty you've hired as your assistant."

He swung around. "How did you hear about that?"

"My dear Jeffrey, the price of success is that everything you do becomes the stuff of rumors. Is she as beautiful as they say?"

"I think so."

"Marvelous. Tell me her name."

"Katya." Speaking the word was enough to bring a flush of pleasure to his cheeks.

"How positively delicious. A hint of mystery even in her name. You must tell me all about her very soon."

"When are you coming back to London?"

"That depends on you. Do you have anything to show me?"

"We just got in a new shipment last month. No Jacobean pieces, but some excellent early Chippendale. I was going to give it over to another dealer. You know we don't often keep the English stuff. I could hold it for you, though."

"Don't ever let an English dealer hear you call Chippendale 'stuff.' They'll hand you your head. But I must say you are tempting me."

"There is one other item. I have a friend, well, a dealer in London who comes as close as any dealer I know to being a friend—except you, that is."

"How very kind you are, sir."

"Andrew has a piece I really think you'd like. It looks like an early Jacobean sideboard. American."

That stopped her. "You're certain?"

"Reasonably. I think it was originally done as a church altar."

"Then hold it for me." She resumed her stroll. "If you're right, Jeffrey, you may have yet another excellent find to your credit."

"And if I'm not?"

"Then there is no harm done, none whatsoever. Jacobean from either side of the ocean is still a highly sought-after commodity."

"How high should I go?"

She shook her head. "I believe this is an admirable opportunity to raise our level of trust another notch or two."

"You want me to bid on it for you?"

"I want you to secure it for me," she replied firmly. "All I ask is that you use your best judgment."

Jeffrey was visibly rocked. "Thanks, Betty. A lot."

"You are most welcome, my dear. I believe we are marking the beginning of a long and beautiful friendship. I do not count many as true friends. I'm pleased to include you among them."

They walked on in companionable silence until Jeffrey asked, "Was there any special reason why Marv hit on me about the big-ticket items?"

Betty smiled at him. "You'll be pleased to know that Alexander's mystique is now being attached to your name."

"You're kidding."

"Where did you go for almost a month this past summer?"

"I can't answer that."

"Of course you can't," Betty answered smugly. A puff of ice-laden wind funneled through the closely packed buildings and painted frost on their cheeks. She pulled her fur-lined collar tighter. "It certainly is bitter out here, don't you think?"

"You're changing the subject."

"Marv is what you might call perpetually hungry. He is far from dull, despite the impression he might give. You don't rise to the top of the New Jersey garbage heap without being remarkably agile and intelligent in a rather base way." Betty pointed toward an art gallery's front window. "Do you have time for me to pop in here for a moment?"

"Of course."

The shop's interior was stifling after the icy air. They shed coats and mufflers, stamped warmth back into their feet, denied the attentive saleswoman's offer of assistance, strolled around the spacious rooms.

"They occasionally come up with some real prizes in here," Betty explained. "I like to stop in whenever I can."

"Marv treated my discovery of another new find as a real possibility," Jeffrey persisted.

"Lower your voice," Betty said softly. "There have been rumors. All of a sudden, everywhere I go I'm hearing tales right out of my children's storybooks. Nazi spoils popping to the surface. Bankrupt Eastern European countries selling off things the world hasn't heard of for centuries."

"What kind of things?"

Betty turned a sparkling gaze his way. "Treasures, Jeffrey. Mysteries in gold and silver. Hoards of legendary kings and queens."

She patted his sleeve. "You will remember your friend if you ever stumble across one, won't you?"

CHAPTER
2

The place held that certain smell of an all-night tavern, one distilled to an ever-stronger proof the closer the hour crawled toward dawn. The establishment had no name—bars such as these in former East Germany seldom did. It was a single vast chamber in a run-down district of Schwerin, and possessed all the charm of a subway.

Everybody smoked. Many patrons stayed with the cardboard-tipped Russian fags said to be packed with sawdust and droppings. Others bit down on acrid-smelling cigarillos fashioned by wrapping shreds of Black Sea tobacco around straw as crooked as the fate that drew the patrons here. They spoke from throats filed down with metal rasps. Laid over the fumes like plaster off a trowel was the smell of unwashed bodies packed too closely together for too long.

The only Western import was Jägermeister, a foul, seventy-proof brew of roots and herbs meant to soothe an overstuffed belly. Here it was sucked from tiny one-shot bottles wrapped in coarse paper, taken between drafts of good East German beer. Jägermeister was the perfect companion for boilermakers, since it both numbed the belly and zapped the head with lightning-bolt accuracy.

The crowd kept itself carefully segregated. Hotel porters, security, police, and prostitutes all gathered up by the counter, where the coffee machine blew clouds of steam like a patient locomotive. The professional drunks huddled together at the two tables flanking the door; they were blasted by icy wind and snow flurries every time someone entered or left. The tavern's far side was held by the taxi and truck drivers, either off duty or on break or unable to sleep beyond the routine of catching naps between rides. They kept their backs turned to the rest of the world and talked in the tones of those most comfortable with secrets.

The one they called Ferret sat as usual between the two others, his head buried in a sheaf of papers. His eyes were so poor he read with his nose almost touching the page. Those who knew him said it was because he rarely saw the light of day.

He had the body of a worm and the mind of a camera—whatever the eye scanned the memory never lost. In days gone by he had used this mind to protect his body, shielding himself behind the strength of others who used his abilities for gaining and holding power. Now the power holders were disgraced, either in hiding or in prison. It was only a matter of days before the investigators started working one rank further down and came upon Ferret.

The majority of the Communist overlords had held on to power so long they had not believed the cowed East Germans would dare take it back. Ferret had watched the first mob gather before the Stasi headquarters in Leipzig and had known differently. He had listened to the mob sing freedom songs and spent the long night hours stuffing files with any possible importance into boxes and bags and wastebaskets. Hauling them down to the loading platform and stuffing them into the city maintenance van had been the most strenuous exercise Ferret had done in his entire life.

He had driven the entire next day, stopping only when darkness and exhaustion forced him to pull off the narrow, rutted excuse for a road and sleep. Every passing car had jerked him awake, foggy-brained and panic-stricken, but his hunch had paid off. The police had been too overwhelmed with concern over their own future to worry about a dilapidated van and a few missing files.

The second day of driving had brought him to Schwerin, the capital of the former East German state known as Mecklenburg-Vorpommern. Ferret had used a set of false identification documents, prepared years before for a contingency just such as this, to check into a lakeside resort with a walled-in parking area. The following day he had bribed his way into a filthy cellar storage room turned into an illegal studio apartment—no ventilation, no windows, a one-ring cooker plugged into the overhead light socket, bathroom one floor up via an outside stairway. With the eleven-year apartment waiting list, this was the only room available anywhere and his only because he had Western marks to slip the landlady.

In the old days, Ferret's official title had been that of *Prokurist* for the Local Workers' Council in Leipzig. It was as high a position as the Ferret could manage and still maintain his invisibility, but *Prokurist* was pretty high indeed. The *Prokurist* was the man with power to sign—that is, the power to approve checks, authorize contracts, organize budgets. Ferret had kept his position by making no decisions at all, only furthering the decisions of those who knew the value of a Ferret and courted him with the dedication of a love-addled Romeo.

What the title did not say was that the Ferret was also the Stasi's local mole.

It had been a perfect match—the secret police whom everyone feared, hated, and refused to speak of, and a man who preferred invisibility to all other powers. Ferret had fed Stasi the information it used as fuel. The Stasi had shielded Ferret with its might.

Until the night Ferret saw his carefully constructed world go up in the flickering flames of a hundred thousand candles.

"Had the belly pains again this morning, I did." Kurt, the man at Ferret's right, was a former Stasi spy, and Ferret's contact in the secret police. He and numerous other mid-level henchmen remained safe from the West German prosecutors simply because there were so many of them. Those who were being picked up tended to be the targets of strong grudges, and those who could be found. Kurt was not immune to grudge holders, but a set of false documents and a different name kept him safe. For the moment.

"Spent three hours sitting in line at the clinic," Kurt complained. "Probably caught the plague or something. You should have seen the lot in there. Pathetic."

The third person at their table was not impressed. Erika, as she was now known, was the former assistant chief jailer at the notorious Dresden women's prison. Like Ferret and Kurt, she was now just another bit of flotsam washed up on the new tide of democracy.

Erika pinched the Russian cigarette's filter, pressing the cardboard tube into a tighter hole to restrict the bitter smoke. She motioned toward Ferret, speaking as if the little man were not there. "Take a look at those old papers. What's he working on?"

"Our freedom." Kurt had obeyed the Ferret's frantic midnight call and left town with a second van loaded to the hilt with stolen Stasi files. "How did it go last night?"

"You see the creep at the end of the bar, no, don't turn around. The blue suit with ice for eyes. He'll be over in about three seconds for his touch."

"The cops saw you?"

"Not me." She punched her cigarette into ashes. "Your buyers didn't have a clue."

"They're not mine." Kurt swung one arm over the back of his chair, risked a casual glance toward the bar, waved at somebody who wasn't there. "The one with the rug on his head?"

"He's been my contact," Erika replied. "Until yesterday it all ran smoothly. But he's got a lever now, and he's going to use it."

The police who frequented the tavern were those who valued the universal language and pocketed a percentage of every deal cut on the tavern's far side. For them a regular visit to its crowded depths was necessary—they had to keep a careful eye on their egg-laying taxi-driving geese.

The routine was well known. Truckers brought the black-market wares in from all over the globe, but mostly from the faltering East. Taxi drivers found the local buyers. In the tumultuous days since the nation of East Germany foundered off the maps and into history, cities like Schwerin had taken on the smell and feel of the Wild West. This left a lot of room for policemen unsure of future paychecks to increase their pocket change.

Contact with the undercurrent of gray goods was far from difficult, especially since most of the newer taxi drivers were former comrades in one guise or another. These days, each new face behind the wheel of a cab brought a new story— one entire table in the taxi drivers' corner this evening was made up of former army colonels, another of air force pilots. Communist Party henchmen formed a good solid block, most of them from the innumerable middle levels—the paper pushers and wheel greasers and slogan shouters who had neither the clout nor the foreknowledge to protect themselves when their house of cards came crashing down.

Another contingent of new nighttime taxi drivers, as well as street sweepers and bricklayers and every other job where identification papers were not too carefully inspected, were former Stasi mid-level spies. Stasi was the popular nickname given to the MFS, or *Ministerium für Staats Sicherheit,* the Ministry for State Security. The East German secret police had provided a model for numerous smaller nations around the world, wherever money was tight and security was deemed of far greater importance than human rights.

And now it was gone.

The police who huddled by the counter and kept a money-lender's eye on the nighttime traffic had seen what happened to the Stasi—four hundred thousand jobs gone in the blink of an eye. They knew the prevailing opinion of cops; since the Wall's collapse they were universally known as Honecker's Henchmen. They saw the West German police flash by in their Mercedes patrol cars, and sneering contempt for Ossie cops—Ossie was slang for a citizen of former East Germany, Wessie for those from the West. They heard about the Bonn government's refusal to upgrade either their salaries or their equipment. Ossie coppers who were willing to stop living on false hopes and face up to Western reality knew it was only a matter of time.

The straight-edged fools in police uniforms who had crossed over to Bonn's side could say what they wanted— *nobody* could do away with forty-six years of Communist laws overnight and understand what the West Germans wanted to put in its place. Not the police, not the lawyers, and not the people. The uncertainty of life under a new system nobody comprehended or, if truth be known, really cared much for, was enormous. The chance for gain was even greater.

Kurt swiveled back around and murmured, "Here he comes."

The cop's joviality only touched the bottom half of his face. He pulled over a chair and sat down. "Any reason for sitting next to the window?"

"It keeps away the flies," Kurt replied. "Most of them, anyway."

"It's so cold over here it burns. Ferret here must have a frozen back." He twisted his head around. "What's that you're working on, Ferret?"

The Ferret raised his head, squinted in confusion through bottle-bottom glasses, murmured, "Oh, hello, Inspector." The head dropped back to an inch or so from the page.

"Not inspector anymore," the man replied. "Just policeman now. And how long at this job is anyone's guess."

"Tough," Erika replied.

The dead smile returned. "You probably heard, they brought in your colleagues from the Zoo this morning." The Zoo was the name neighbors had given the central prison in East Berlin. It was named for the sounds that rose from its confines, particularly at night.

"I heard."

"Yes, thought you had. Well, in times like this it certainly is nice to have friends who can cover for you, yes?" He leaned forward. "Since when did you work with the Viets, Kurt?"

"I don't know what you're talking about."

"No, of course not. And you don't have any connections to the vodka trade out of Poland, either, I'm sure."

"I wish I did."

"Yes, I suppose so. Did I mention that they've raised the bounty on nailing Eastern bootleggers? Five thousand marks it is now, with vodka top of the list. Five thousand marks. Almost enough to make a man go legal."

Unification had brought a flood of West German marks

into the defunct East German economy. Traders from the poorer Eastern lands flocked over the border by thousands of ill-defined paths, bringing anything they could buy cheaply and sell for more—Chinese T-shirts available in Cracow for fifty cents, Pakistani sweaters, prime Polish vodka that went for two dollars a liter in Poland and five times that in Germany.

The worst of the illegal traders were Vietnamese, invited over to study or work or simply visit as friends of the former Communist regime, and now refusing to go home. The new Wessie bureaucrats were denying them residency visas; they lived with the constant threat of deportation and a growing hatred of the new authorities. Their tightly knit community slid daily toward overt violence and blatantly illegal activities.

The policeman rose to his feet and nodded to the group. "I'll be on my rounds tomorrow if you need to see me."

Kurt watched him move away, asked, "How much does he want?"

"Half," Erika replied.

"Too much."

"He saw the buyers unload the van, Kurt. Chaing told me. Stood and watched them."

"That's impossible."

"Not if they did it behind the all-night gas station."

Kurt scoffed. "Nobody's that stupid."

"Your traders are."

"I told you, they're not my anything."

"They're going to be our noose if we don't pay the man."

Ferret chose that moment to raise his head. "I don't think we will," he said. "Pay him, I mean."

Kurt turned his way. "Why not?"

"We'll need that money."

"You've found it?"

The bulbous head dropped once more. "Perhaps."

"Perhaps isn't good enough."

"More than perhaps." Ferret lifted his gaze. "My freedom is resting on this as well, you know."

"What are you two going on about," Erika demanded.

"Ferret's been hunting for something," Kurt replied, his

eyes remaining on the strange-shaped man. "Something big."

Erika twisted her head to examine Ferret's folder and saw handwriting on a yellowed sheet. "How old is that?"

"Old," Ferret replied, placing a possessive hand across the page.

"Forty-seven years, to be exact," Kurt replied. "Ferret and I have been talking. We need a third."

"A third for what?"

His eyes still on Ferret, Kurt asked, "Do you have any contacts left in the Dresden archives?"

Erika showed the world her best poker face. "I might. What's in it for me?"

"Freedom," Kurt replied. "Papers. Money. Lots of money."

"So what is it you're looking for?"

"Can you keep a secret?"

Erika snorted. "I should. I've had a lifetime of practice."

"A treasure, then," Kurt replied. "One called the Amber Room."

Erika thought it over. "What do I have to do?"

The Ferret raised his watery eyes and said quietly, "We are looking for a certain man."

CHAPTER
3

Jeffrey stepped farther back into the Cafe Royale's entrance hall as the front doors admitted several well-dressed patrons and a blast of freezing wind. "Meeting Dr. Rokovski the day after my return from Zurich is a little too much coincidence for me."

Located just half a block off Piccadilly Circus, the Cafe Royale had been a hub of the London social whirl for over a century. It was one of the few public haunts of Victorian England that had managed to remain financially afloat since World War II. The bars and restaurants displayed typically Victorian proportions—an almost endless series of overdone rooms set on seven floors.

"You know full well that I absolutely must speak with Pavel now," Alexander replied. "I need his blessing on this gala business. I should have already requested it, if truth be known, but it was something I wished to do in person."

"It'd be a lot nicer if we could have this meeting after the check is cleared and the Rubens deal over and done with."

"Don't be so nervous," Alexander replied. "Rokovski is not in London on our account, of that I am sure. He is here for a conference and is meeting us because I invited him."

"I still don't like it. What if he's upset because the sale took so long to go through?"

Alexander shook his head, his own calm unruffled. "The

gentleman is a professional, and a professional will understand that in a sale requiring absolute discretion, patience is of the utmost importance."

"You're sure?"

"See for yourself." Alexander pointed through the glass portals to the street, where a taxi was depositing the Dr. Pavel Rokovski, director of the Polish Ministry of Culture's Cracow division and Alexander's primary contact for his export of Polish antiques. "Does that look like the face of a worried man?"

"Alexander. Mr. Sinclair," Dr. Rokovski effused, striding forward with an outstretched hand. "How wonderful to see you again."

"Please call me Jeffrey."

"Of course, thank you. I am so sorry to be late. I decided to take the tube because I was warned that traffic is terrible here in London, and I found the right line, but I am afraid that I took it in the wrong direction. The next thing I knew, I was in Hendon Central."

"That's quite all right," replied Alexander. "It was nice to have a moment to catch our breaths at the end of the day." He gestured them forward. "Come, gentlemen. Our table awaits."

They were led to a table in the front bar, where paintings in elaborate gilt frames fought for space on richly brocaded walls. Rokovski settled into a French settee upholstered in red velvet, took in the ornate high ceiling, heavy drapes, and rich carpeting. "Some of our castle's royal chambers are not as fine as this."

"I quite enjoy the ambience," Alexander agreed. "And its location makes the cafe an excellent rendezvous point."

"I'm sorry that my schedule is so tight," Rokovski said, "but the conference planners do have us on a treadmill."

"I quite understand," Alexander replied.

"I would love to stay and explore London by night," Rokovski continued, "but instead I must be back at the South Bank Center for a reception by seven. You know I am here to make contacts for a variety of traveling exhibits we hope to lure to Cracow in the coming months."

"It is wonderful that you would take time for us at all,"

Alexander said. "I am delighted that we could meet even briefly, as I have some very good news for you. We can now confirm that the Rubens has been sold. The price, even in this difficult market, was at the high end of our preliminary estimate."

"Splendid, splendid," Rokovski said, his eyes dancing from one to the other. "Would it be indelicate to ask the figure?"

Alexander nodded to his assistant. Jeffrey replied, "One point one five."

Rokovski showed momentary confusion. "One point one five what?"

"Million," Jeffrey said. "Dollars."

"So much," Rokovski breathed.

"The transfer will go through tomorrow, less our commissions and the payment for the initial information," Alexander said. "In accordance with our arrangements."

"This is wonderful. Just wonderful. It will mean so much for the preservation and expansion of our religious art collection."

"This service has brought me great satisfaction," Alexander assured him. "I am indeed grateful for the opportunity to be a part of this transaction."

"When may I use these funds?"

"Immediately," Alexander replied. "That is, as soon as the bank has finished with its paperwork."

"Excellent." Rokovski showed great relief. "You see, in anticipation of the sale's being a success, I have already committed our museum to urgent repair and restoration work for which we do not have the money. I can't thank either of you enough. I am only sorry that others cannot know of your extraordinary contribution."

Alexander nodded his formal thanks. "Speaking of contributions, Pavel, it has occurred to me that your project to house the nation's collection of religious art requires both more funding and wider public support. I have therefore taken it upon myself to lay the groundwork for a fund-raising gala to promote your efforts."

Rokovski was baffled. "What means this, gala?"

"It is a quite well-known event in Western circles," Alexander replied. "Various charities organize deluxe receptions or dinner parties, charge an outrageous amount per plate, and invite hundreds of people."

"And these people will come?"

"Given the proper mixture of exclusivity and good cause," Alexander replied, "not only will they come, but they will pay for the privilege. I expect to sell these tickets for two hundred pounds."

Rokovski gaped. "Per person?"

"You're quite right," Alexander smiled. "Two hundred fifty would be much more appropriate for such a worthy cause."

"You see, Dr. Rokovski," Jeffrey explained, "not only do you raise money for your cause through selling tickets, but you also attract the attention of celebrities and the media."

"Call me Pavel, please."

"Thank you. This leads to further private donations and sometimes even bequests."

"I see," Rokovski nodded. "So this must be a very special party for all such special people."

"I intend to hold it at the Ritz," Alexander replied. "I have booked the grand ballroom, and I expect no fewer than six hundred would-be patrons of Polish art."

"Incredible," Rokovski breathed. "And what are you going to showcase?"

It was Alexander's turn to show confusion. "What do you mean?"

"Is that not the correct word? Most conferences I have attended have some type of centerpiece to excite the participants' imagination. An example you can show the people of what you are trying to do. Some photograph or brochures, perhaps even the real thing."

"The real thing?" Alexander leaned forward. "Bring an example of Polish artwork over for the event? That would be extraordinary."

"I have an idea," Rokovski said. "There is a collection of exceptional religious artifacts within the Marian Church. We should find you something small yet beautiful, an article that would represent the wonder of Polish religion and heritage. Something easily transportable—perhaps a medieval chalice. I know the curate, Mr. Karlovich, quite well."

"This is a splendid proposition," Alexander said. "This would help our project immensely."

"Of course, I will arrange all the necessary export documents," Rokovski said, writing in a small pocket notebook. "I suggest we extend to you three pieces. First, the article from the Marian Church—but I do not have direct control over the church, you understand. Approval must be given by the curate."

"I understand, and am indeed grateful."

"As for pieces within the national collections, well, of course, those are within my jurisdiction." He thought for a moment, nodded to himself. "Might I suggest a small oil painting of the Madonna and Child? And there is a splendid miniature altar in the Czartoryski Collection. An exceptional piece, I promise you."

"The three together would comprise an extraordinary exhibit," Alexander enthused. "Such treasures would go far to convince the guests to become true patrons of our cause."

Rokovski glanced at his watch, rose to his feet. "Then I will call you from Cracow the day after tomorrow. We can ship the altar and the painting, there is no difficulty at that point. I must warn you, however, that Curate Karlovich would insist on a personal envoy to transport whatever article he loans you to London and back."

"I had planned to travel to Poland on other business next week," Alexander replied. "I will see to this matter and give Mr. Karlovich my personal assurances."

CHAPTER
4

London's East End was a completely different world, run by a different sort of people and held in place by different laws. Jeffrey loved the feeling of passing through alien gates and was thrilled to find Katya enjoying it as well.

He motioned toward a bakery whose front window displayed nothing but opaque frost and several dozen icicles. "Sorry about the cold."

"It's too early to worry about little things like that." She snuggled happily against him on the taxi seat. "Some people haven't even gone to bed yet."

"Some people do this every day."

"Not me." She prodded his shoulder into a more comfortable shape. "I should have brought my pillow."

He reached into his satchel, poured coffee from the thermos, held it toward her. "Maybe this will help."

She tasted the cup and gagged. "What is this?"

"Coffee. What did you think?"

"It goes down like tar." She looked at him with eyes cleared from the slightest hint of sleepiness. "I'm glad you're better at antiquing than you are at making coffee."

"You woke up in a hurry."

"This is too exciting to worry about things like sleep," she replied. "My first antiques market. How much can I spend?"

He showed genuine alarm. "Nothing."

She smiled. "Got you."

He sank back in the taxi seat. "Be still my heart."

"What are we going for, if not to buy?"

"Sometimes we find bargains or smaller pieces for the shop," Jeffrey explained. "But less often in the London markets than in those out in the country. Usually, I just like to come and look and learn. Today, though, I've got to see Andrew about a piece I want to take from his shop. He's been away for a week, and his assistant said he'd be back in time for today's market."

They crossed over Tower Bridge, with its soaring ramparts and trademark red brick keeps. Their taxi passed block after block of small businesses and corner cafes and derelict warehouses before letting them off in front of a tumbledown building marked by piles of refuse and crowds of people. Jeffrey paid the driver and steered Katya around the gossips and sharp-eyed thieves and runners and sniffers. Runners owned items but could not afford their own shop, he explained as they walked, while sniffers looked for price discrepancies and borrowed. Jeffrey stopped her by a burly young man squatting beside several flung-open boxes of goods.

"Go in a High Street shop with ten quid," the street hawker called to the jostling, friendly throng. "They'll throw you out on your ear. 'Ave a look at this then. Atomizer spray, 'ave a gander at the brochure, sixteen quid for the large size. And the perfume, twenty-two fifty for the blokes with more wallet than sense. Goes on the top like that. Bath soap and men's cologne, all top o' the line, right? And what am I gonna do for you, then?" Smack went the broad-bladed hand on the top of one box. "Not seventy quid as they'd take you for on the High Street." Smack! "Not sixty." Smack! "Not even fifty nor forty nor even thirty." Smack! "Ten pounds is all I'm askin'."

He hefted the half-dozen gaudy boxes between two grimy hands.

"Ten quid for the lot. Who's got a lady or two waitin'? Not to mention a posh cologne for yourselves, gents. Ten quid, price of your cab ride home after she thanks you proper. And you ladies, how's about a gift for yourselves, then? All right, who's willing to part with a tenner?"

Satisfied with the show, the crowd moved forward with money outstretched as the hawker hastily stuffed his wares into shopping bags. Jeffrey took Katya's arm and led her inside.

Bermondsey Market was a rabbit warren of plywood booths and rickety stalls with whitewashed pegboard walls, crammed in what once had been a warehouse for the river traffic. The gathering began each Friday morning at four o'clock and ran until noon. Rents were outrageous, considering the surroundings.

The first buyers to arrive were always the professionals, in and out with time left over for a hot cuppa before winding up their shop shutters. By nine o'clock the pointed banter of the dealers had been replaced by a babel of languages. Well-heeled aficionados from a dozen countries paraded in furs and jewelry, looking for a buy on the cheap. Their dollars and francs and liras and yen and marks kept the stallholders well fed.

Across the street was the outdoor spillover market, crowded with shopkeepers who were on the waiting list for a stall in the building. On cold days like this they cursed and suffered and lowered prices to draw customers out into the winter weather.

The market's interior was warmer only by degree. Jeffrey could still see his breath as they strolled around the stalls closest to the wide-open entrance. Stallholders either wore layers of sweaters under voluminous greatcoats or stood around in sweatshirts and jeans and pretended not to feel the cold. Many wore old woolen mittens with the fingers cut out for having a feel of the goods.

Jeffrey strolled and nodded at familiar faces and inspected wares and listened to the swirl of talk. Hearing a familiar voice, he turned to find Andrew leaning across a glass-topped jewelry case, talking to a young stallholder with a street-hardened face. Andrew wore a camel-hair overcoat and cashmere scarf against the chill, but the stylish clothes did not erase the marks of tougher times from his face and bearing. He had been the first to admit Jeffrey into the inner circle of London's antique dealers, a gift of confidence that Jeffrey had never forgotten.

"You don't mind if things come to market by different routes, then," the stallholder asked Andrew.

"No, of course not," Andrew replied, his casual tone belied by the gleam in his eyes. "Long as it hasn't grown wings and flown out somebody's window with half the local force tailing it, I'm quite pleased with a good piece, however it arrives."

"This is the fellow I came to see," Jeffrey said to Katya, pointing toward Andrew. "Why don't you have a look around, then come find us out by the tea wagon when you're done."

"All right." She gave him an excited smile and wandered off.

Jeffrey inched closer to the pair.

"How's it going in Albania, then?" the young man demanded of Andrew, motioning with his head toward the unseen stalls across the street.

"Cold," Andrew replied. "Let's have a look at the emerald. Is that Indian?"

"Victorian, more like. Done up to suit somebody arriving home after playing tourist out with the natives." He slipped the gold floral design with an emerald heart into Andrew's hand. "Anybody buying anything?"

"What, outside?" Andrew slipped a jeweler's loop out of his pocket and screwed it in. "Too cold to tell. I put this eyepiece in to have a look at a bit of merchandise and it froze to my skin."

"Scares people off, the cold. I was out there for eight years, next to that old duffer propped up in the corner behind you. Used to give me nightmares, hearing the weather report for a day like this."

"Shows how soft you are."

"Easy for you to say, isn't it? What with the posh West End shop and six little helpers all in a row. Open at ten, close at four, with a two-hour lunch in between. Stretch out in back for a quiet kip after tea."

Jeffrey sidled up. "Sounds like a good life to me."

Andrew turned and showed genuine pleasure. "Hello, lad. Out for a gander, are you?" He handed back the piece to the stallholder, adding, "Let me know about that other little item, will you?"

"Right you are."

"Come on over here, lad," Andrew said, drawing Jeffrey out of the stream of buyers. "Now, what can I do for you?"

"I passed by your shop the other day. Your salesclerk said you were up north at an auction," Jeffrey said. "I might have a buyer for that piece in your window."

"Oh, I couldn't bear to part with that one," Andrew replied automatically. "Was actually thinking of taking it home."

The piece in question was the seventeenth-century oak sideboard Jeffrey had described to Betty. "Do you think it was made in America?"

Andrew's gaze turned shrewd. "You had more than just a gander at it, didn't you?"

"I thought it might be, from its size," Jeffrey replied. "My buyer is from the States, I think she'd go for it in a big way."

"Really?" Andrew brushed at his sleeve in a calculated display of disinterest. "Pity they couldn't clean this place once a year or so, wouldn't you say?"

"She'd probably be willing to offer upward of thirty thousand for it."

"Dollars or pounds?"

"Pounds."

Andrew shook his head. "I'm so taken with it myself, lad. Tragic, it is. Really don't think I could part with the item."

Jeffrey refused to be driven higher. "But you have to eat."

Andrew sighed his agreement. "I suppose you'll want it carted around to your place, then."

"You don't think I'd send her around to you, do you?"

"No harm in hoping, is there?" The business done, Andrew permitted himself a grin. "Come on, then. I'll let you buy me a cup of tea. Strongest thing we can get around here, this time of day."

They walked out the back entrance and over to a trailer-stall that sold steaming cups of tea. Andrew accepted a cup and stepped into the relative warmth of an unused loading dock. "You remember our friend Sydney Greenfield?"

"Purveyor to the would-bes and has-beens, sure." Jeffrey

permitted himself a smile. "Sydney's all right."

"In a manner of speaking," Andrew replied. "Saw him the other day. Passing strange it was. Sydney was fitted out in a whole new wardrobe, Saville Row by the looks of it. I asked him what was the occasion, know what he said?"

"I couldn't imagine."

"No, nor I. Stood right there and told me he'd come into a bit of the folding stuff."

"More than a bit, by the sounds of things."

"All right for some, I told him. Was it legal?"

"What a question."

"Swore up and down it was legit. New clients, he said." Andrew sipped, sighed a sweetened steam, sipped again. "Mate of mine, next shop down but one, said he saw Sydney down Portobello way last week."

Portobello Road was another of the famous weekly London markets. In recent years it had become much more of a tourist event, and therefore much pricier, than the other two. Portobello was on Saturday, Covent Garden on Monday, and Bermondsey on Friday. All others were pretenders to the first ranking.

"Shocked him no end, it did," Andrew continued. "Sydney's been going through some hard times, you know, owed money to half the dealers down there. So happened he was paying them off."

"And he said this new business of his was legit?"

Andrew shrugged. "There he was, my mate said, yapping away with everyone, peeling notes off this roll he couldn't hardly get out of his pocket, it was so big. My mate strolled over and got the big grin, the back slap, like Sydney hadn't been playing a ghost for the past couple of months. Anyway, my mate asked him, where's my five hundred quid. In my pocket, Sydney said, and it's yours on one condition. It's mine anyway, my mate told him. Wait, Sydney said, you'll like this. Spread the word about, I've got a truckload of goods to unload."

"Sydney?"

"Not what you'd call top-quality stuff, Sydney told him." Andrew's face settled into bleak lines. "Heard some tales toward the end of last summer, from a bloke I use sometimes for ornamental work. Told me Sydney came in with a crate of odds and ends, asked him to see what he could do with it. This bloke did a load of patching, came up with a sort of Sheraton-Empire-Chippendale-Florentine bit of old rubbish."

"Is that legal?"

"Long as the seller declares the item for what it is, lad, there's no harm in working puzzles. This bloke's just as hard hit by the recession as the rest of us. Anyway, Sydney started coming in every few days with another patchwork job, been at it ever since. Now he's out about town with money to burn."

"Something smells funny," Jeffrey agreed.

"Yes, well, it's been hard times for the likes of our Sydney." Andrew tossed his cup into a nearby rubbish bin. "Problem is, I'm afraid he's stepped over the invisible line on this latest caper. Gone from a bit of malarkey to something out and out crooked."

"You sound worried."

"I am. I've always had a soft spot for old Greenfield."

"Me, too."

"Yes, thought you did. But it's a short road he's traveling, if he's turned to dealing in the false bits. I don't like the idea of one of our own going down in flames."

Katya chose that moment to look out the back door. She walked toward them, carrying a slender package wrapped in brown paper and bound with twine. Andrew rose from his worried stoop and touched the knot of his tie. "Hello, what's this, then?"

Jeffrey waved her over. "Sorry this has taken so long."

"That's all right." She raised her package. "I found a present for Gregor." She then turned and smiled a greeting to Andrew. "Hello. I'm Katya Nichols."

"You most certainly are." He bowed over her hand, straightened, and said to Jeffrey, "Mount Street's bringing in a different sort of clientele these days, is it?"

"Andrew's a dealer in Kensington," Jeffrey explained to her.

"*The* dealer in Kensington," Andrew murmured, letting her hand go with reluctance.

"Katya works in my shop."

"If that's all you could think to do with this one, lad, then my estimation of you has just plummeted." Andrew turned back to Katya. "Salaries are much higher over Kensington way, my dear. Shorter hours, much nicer working conditions, better lot of goods, five-hour lunch breaks highly recommended."

She treated him to the sort of smile that did not need to descend from her eyes. "And what is your specialty?"

"Any odds and ends the lad here leaves for the rest of us to handle."

"Andrew loves to give me a hard time," Jeffrey explained.

"Hand on my heart," Andrew insisted, "I've never put the lad down. Had enough of that when I did my apprenticeship as an electrician's helper."

"You never," Jeffrey said.

"Straight up. Put paid to that as soon as I could, too, and never looked back. Gave me all sorts of trouble, that did. Proved a total ruddy disaster."

"So why did you go into it?"

Andrew shrugged easily. "The old man said if it was good enough for him and all that. My first day on the job, walked into this house where they had a dog the size of my car. Gave me a bit of a whuff, it did. I played like the space shuttle, shwooosh. Took me thirty seconds to get my feet back on solid ground."

"A bit of a whuff," Jeffrey repeated, smiling at Katya.

"Second job," Andrew went on, "we had this lady offer to take me and my mate upstairs. I was married by then, knew the old dear would have me guts for garters if I was to go and try that. I thanked her kindly, said there were some pleasures I was meant to forgo in this life." Andrew shuddered at the memory. "Decided then and there I wasn't made for hard labor. Too dangerous."

Jeffrey asked Katya, "Would you like a cup of tea?"

"Love one, thank you."

"How about you, Andrew?"

"Chip off the old concrete, you are."

As he made for the wagon, Jeffrey heard Katya say behind him, "So then you moved into antiques?"

"Well, no, there was a bit more to it than that. What happened was, a couple weeks later I bought the wife a birthday present from a neighbor, a lovely little bit of gold and such. Cost me upward of a hundred quid, it did. That night I started worrying that maybe I'd been took, so I stopped by a mate of mine who worked in this jewelry store. Told me it was early Victorian, offered me nine-fifty on the spot."

Jeffrey returned, handed out the cups, and asked, "What did you end up giving your wife?"

"A brand-new kitchen, can you imagine? 'Course, that was after I spent all I made from that sale and all we had left from the dole going around the neighbors, buying up whatever they had they didn't need. Got took a few times, of course, but did right well in the end."

"So you stayed with jewelry?" Katya asked.

"Bits and pieces, now and then," Andrew replied easily. "I've kept my passion, Victorian mostly. That's what brings me around here."

"You mean you collect for yourself?"

"Oh my yes. Fact is, lot of dealers start off as collectors. Once they're good and hooked, they find themselves with too many lovelies and strapped for cash. Then along comes something new which they absolutely must have, and they sell a piece they've grown tired of. If they're careful and don't get taken, they find themselves shocked to the very core at how much they make. It hits them then, doesn't it? How maybe here's a way of making pleasure pay off."

"Don't let Andrew fool you," Jeffrey said. "Very few manage not to get taken in this business. He also happens to be a very successful dealer of French Empire furniture and accessories, among other things."

"Why the interest in Victorian jewelry?" Katya asked.

"It was a fussy period, the Victorian era," Andrew replied, with the enthusiasm of a true collector. "It was proceeded by the Georgian, and a very severe style that was indeed. All straight lines and hard angles, nothing for the feminine or the foppish. Soon as the Victorians came, jewelry and furniture and houses all went in for a great load of foppery."

"I heard the railroads had something to do with this change," Jeffrey said.

"Well, perhaps not so much on the style itself, but certainly on its rapid spread. Before, you see, most people had a ten-mile radius which was their entire world, cradle to grave, as it were. All their lifelong, that was as far as their purses and their work would allow them to travel. The railways changed all that. Everyone, right down to a simple carpenter or jeweler or purchaser of a new home, could travel right into London-town and see the sights and learn about the latest fashion. Suddenly they could get ornaments from anywhere in the kingdom."

"Or designs," Katya offered.

"Exactly. Queen Victoria was a marvelous one for jewelry. She wore tons of it herself, yellow gold in the day and white gold at night. After her beloved Prince Albert died, she went in for funeral jewelry in a big way as well. That's done in dark stones, you see, often with strands of hair either enameled or set in lockets, lots of inscriptions, in loving memory of the old so-and-so, what have you. Rings and brooches and great pendants dangling down."

Jeffrey glanced at his watch. "We need to be getting back. I'm opening the shop today."

"Where's your man Kantor, then?"

"You know better than to ask that."

"Right you are, lad. And about that other little item, you didn't hear it from me."

Jeffrey smiled. "What other item?"

Jeffrey saw Katya off to classes with a kiss before placing the call to Poland. Conditions were improving; it took less than a half hour to obtain a line to Cracow, and once made the connection was fine.

"Is that you, Jeffrey?" Gregor's heartfelt pleasure could be sensed even over the telephone. Gregor was Alexander's cousin, a deeply religious gentleman who had escaped from Poland during the war, only to heed what he felt was the Lord's call to return and serve the poor. He also operated as Alexander's primary contact in Cracow. He financed numerous charitable efforts through locating long-stored antiques to be sold in the West. "How are you, my dear boy?"

"I'm fine," Jeffrey replied. "It's great to speak with you again."

"I, too, have missed your questing voice. When do you plan to visit with me again?"

"I'm not sure. Alexander should be arriving tomorrow to see about something from the Marian Church for—"

"I know all about the article and the gala. Alexander spoke with me the other evening. I am glad to say that my dear cousin has wisely decided to forgo the exertions of further purchasing trips after this one."

This was news. "He hasn't said anything to me about it."

"He has so much on his mind just now, I doubt seriously if he can remember his own name. But never mind. This will most likely be the last antiques shipment he will arrange for himself. And why not, when he has a perfectly able assistant to see to such matters?"

"Then I guess I'll be seeing you sooner than I thought."

"As soon as possible after the gala," Gregor replied. "And nothing could bring me greater pleasure, I assure you. As a matter of fact, I thought that was why you were calling."

"No. I have some news." Jeffrey found it necessary to take several breaths before the band across his chest eased. "I wanted you to know that I'm thinking about asking Katya to marry me."

"My dear Jeffrey," Gregor effused. "How marvelous for you both. Are you asking for my advice?"

"I guess so."

"Do it!" Gregor shouted the words. "There. Have I done my duty well?"

"You're sure this is the right thing?"

Gregor laughed. "Ah, my boy, you make me feel young again."

"I guess that means yes."

"Indeed it does. When will you ask her?"

"In about three weeks, after she's completed her exams. That is, I'll do it unless my nerve gives out between now and then."

"I shall pray that it does not. As I shall for your peace of mind and for your joyful life together."

"Thanks, Gregor. Thanks a lot. It helps just to know I'm not going into this alone."

"My dear young friend, we are never alone."

"I know that." Jeffrey hesitated, then continued, "At least, sometimes I know it."

"Yet there are other times, moments when you feel most alone," Gregor finished for him. "You wonder who the Father truly is and where He is to be found."

"That's it exactly," Jeffrey agreed, and felt immense relief to have his doubts and fears pushed from the confining space of his heart. "Now that I've started looking, the fear that I won't find God is enormous."

"Do you read the Bible?"

"Every day."

"Do you pray?"

"I try," Jeffrey replied. "I feel as if I'm talking to the wall."

"Have you discussed this with Katya?"

He nodded to a man a thousand miles away. "She tells me to be patient and keep looking."

"Wise advice from a wise woman."

"She says it's a problem a lot more common to new Christians than the quick-fix preachers would have me believe."

"That's what she called them? Quick-fix preachers?" Gregor laughed delightedly. "You shall make a worthy couple for His work."

"I don't see how I can do much if I can't find Him."

"He will find *you,* my dear young friend. Never fear. If you search in earnest, then He would withhold His gift of the Spirit only for a purpose. It will all be clear to you soon enough."

"You're not just saying that to make me feel better?"

"My dear Jeffrey." Gregor sounded genuinely shocked. "I would never dream of doing such a thing. When you find your doubts rising, try to remember that the Lord Jesus did not tell His disciples to go out and *look* for the Spirit."

"He said wait and He will come," Jeffrey finished. "I read about that the other night."

"Perhaps it would also help you to speak to others whose faith you admire. Ask them how they came to find the Father, what special moment stands out in their memory. Learn from their experiences."

"All right. Thanks."

"I thank you. It is always a delight to teach someone who truly seeks to learn. Now, when do you think you will be in Cracow next?"

"A couple of months, I suppose. Right after Alexander's gala."

"Excellent. Anything of utmost urgency my dear cousin can see to while he is here. We will speak more upon your arrival. In the meantime, seek out those who hold fast to faith. Ask them to share the moment of their illumination."

The moment of illumination. Jeffrey liked that phrase. "I will."

"Splendid. And take care of our dear Alexander."

"I'll try. This gala is either driving him crazy or making him happier than he's been in years," Jeffrey said. "It depends on when you catch him."

"The gala, yes. Well, either it is a worthy activity or a harmless pastime."

"You don't mean according to whether or not it makes money?"

"Of course not. Listen to me, Jeffrey. A man can rebuild an entire nation, but if his eyes and ears and heart and mind are tuned to the clamor of his fellowman, his works are empty of eternal blessing."

"So what happens if you can't find God? Do you just stop working?"

"Not at all. You must do three things *while* you work. First, you must earnestly seek the Lord and never, ever believe that worthy action is a substitute for a daily walk in faith. Second, you must always dedicate your efforts to the Lord and seek His acclaim only. And third—can you guess what the third action is?"

"Love."

"The most crucial element of all," Gregor agreed. "Without love, your greatest effort is but dust blowing in the wind."

"It's great talking with you like this again," Jeffrey told him.

"Make Christ your teacher, search for a knowledge of divine love," Gregor replied. "And give your darling fiancée my heartfelt best wishes."

CHAPTER
5

Erika found her former colleague, Birgit Teilmacher, fairly comfortable in her position as file keeper in the Dresden archives' new location—an abandoned underground bunker system left over from World War II. Birgit had served as secretary to the director of the women's prison, and anyone who held such a job was both Party member and Stasi informant. But no one had time to investigate secretaries— not yet, anyway. Birgit's punishment for the moment was simply to be relocated and forgotten.

Erika entered the concrete-walled room with, "How does it feel, spending eight hours a day underground?"

If she felt any surprise at the unannounced visit, Birgit masked it well. "I wish it were only eight. They've got me doing the work of five people down here." She inspected the other woman's solid girth. "You haven't been sticking to your diet."

Erika shrugged off her knee-length black-leather coat. "It doesn't pay for people in my new profession to be too petite. Gives the jokers ideas."

"Set it down over there." Birgit motioned to a corner filing cabinet. "You really should get another coat. That one makes you look as feminine as a tree trunk."

"It so happens I'm attached to that coat," Erika replied. "It's the only thing I have left from my old life."

"You should have chosen something else." Birgit hefted a vast sheaf of papers. "I'm kept busy these days making records of change. Know what these are? Statistics on abortions. These are the latest hospital records. Abortions are up by over five hundred percent since the Wall came down."

"People get to choose between a new child and a new car," Erika replied. "The new car wasn't available before." She took a seat and asked, "How are you?"

"Enduring." Birgit's features took on a thoroughly bleak cast. "What other choice do any of us have these days?"

The Ossies were coming to resent the Wessies and resent their economic invasion in ever-stronger terms. Companies that had been the lifeblood of small Ossie communities were being bought up for pennies, with the new owners showing nothing but horror over the factories' condition. The best machines were stripped and often taken back to Western factories, or so the rumors went and the pulp newspapers accused—accusations most people were only too happy to believe. Ossie management and workers had been fired wholesale, with the remaining few required to retrain under Wessie technicians. Wessie workers, brought in at breathtaking salaries to work the best jobs, showed with every word and gesture their scorn for the East—people, land, factories, the lot.

Other companies, now controlled by the West-dominated behemoth called the Treuhand, had been declared wasteful or polluting or decrepit or junk and closed down overnight. A land that had never known even half a percent of unemployment now had forty-three percent of its work force on welfare—at a time when rents had risen by six hundred percent and food prices had jumped almost twentyfold.

On the other side of the vanished border, the West German government leaders faced a nightmarish dilemma. They knew beyond the slightest doubt that unless the situation in the East stabilized before the next election, they would be ousted. Their only answer was to spend as much as possible as fast as possible, and haul the new eastern states up by their bootstraps. Yet in the first two years alone, unification had cost the German people five hundred billion marks—

over three hundred billion dollars. Inflation had been capped only by introducing a temporary income-tax hike and by raising interest rates to twice the highest level they had been since World War II. A nation of Wessies listened and wondered at the black hole called former East Germany that was bleeding their wealth.

But the Ossies themselves felt they were seeing only the tiniest trickle of all this wealth. Their wage levels, when they could find jobs, remained frozen at forty percent of that of Wessie workers on the same jobs—and Ossie prices were now at Wessie levels. The Porsche 928s and Mercedes 600s they were seeing with increasing frequency on their newly repaired roads bore Wessie license plates and were driven by their new Wessie bosses.

The Ossie tabloid press took great glee in throwing out infuriating little snippets about who was really growing rich on all this supposed rebuilding. They greeted the Ossies each morning with the news that there was now a five-year waiting list for the hundred thousand dollar BMW 850i. That the West was seeing a boom for new luxury housing like nothing in the country's history. That Cartier jewelers sold more gold and diamonds and emeralds in the former West Germany than in the rest of the world combined.

While this went on, they stood helpless in the face of public shame. Every day, another lake in former East Germany was declared dead from overpollution. Each night, commentators monitored reports on another twenty thousand, thirty thousand, two hundred thousand Ossie employees who had been fired from jobs found to be totally profitless, totally without value to the new German federation. The Ossies sat in their little rooms and felt themselves growing smaller, their lives ever more meaningless. They watched, helpless and failing, as their entire way of life was slowly strangled away.

The Ossies knew what was happening. Years of Communism did not make them dumb, only bitterly suspicious. To their eyes, everything pointed toward the fact that the Ossies were being doled out crumbs, like beggars at a rich man's table.

And daily their resentment grew.

"It was one of the things we learned best, wasn't it," Erika replied. "How to endure."

Birgit did not deny it. "They arrested everyone who worked at the Berlin prison. Everyone. Right down to the," she hesitated, then settled on "guards."

"I heard," Erika said, probing softly. "It worries you, does it?"

Birgit shrugged. "So what is this new profession of yours?"

"Driving a taxi."

"Where?"

"Best not to say," Erika replied.

"A different name, I suppose."

Erika nodded. "And here you are," she said, "down in a hole."

The Dresden archives used to be kept partly in the Stasi's city headquarters, partly in the Communist Party building, and partly at City Hall. Nowadays, however, the Stasi building was a cultural center, the Communist Party building housed the new regional Ministry of Economics; and the City Hall's archives were being scrutinized by imported Wessie investigators.

This investigation was no easy task. The one product the Communist regime had produced in greatest amounts was paper, and nothing had *ever* been thrown away. Wessie investigators for one region, when asked to give an approximate date for completing their inquest, laughed and took the reporters on a tour of the two hundred *rooms* filled with uninspected files. They then told the reporters that more than half the people who should be charged with criminal offenses would escape trial by dying of old age.

There was also a rising tide of Ossie resentment over how many were being hurt, and how badly. The public was now permitted to inspect their own Stasi files, and surprises were frequent and harsh. One woman discovered that her husband of twenty-six years had been a Stasi informer since their engagement. The governor of the state of Thuringen was deposed on accusations of having informed for Stasi, although more than two-thirds of the populace thought he had done an excellent job. A new Ossie member of the German parliament was found to have informed for the Stasi after graduating from college over twenty years ago; the shame of this discovery caused him to commit suicide.

Initial studies suggested that over a third of the Ossie population had informed for Stasi at one time or another. Out of a population of eighteen million, almost six million had at one time or another fed the Stasi's endless appetite for information. Did this mean they all would be threatened with exposure and punishment? Would all families and friendships and working relationships be seared by the light of this new day?

"How can we be treated like criminals?" Birgit was not a large woman, but her wiry form crackled with an energy that made the room seem too small to contain her. "I did what I was told. I followed orders. I pledged my life to the Party. Is this what I deserve?"

"Let us hope you never have to ask those questions of a Wessie judge," Erika said.

Birgit deflated. "I have nightmares."

"Don't we all."

"Not of the past. Of the future."

"What is there for us to fear of the past?" Erika leaned across the desk. "I am working on a way out."

Birgit inspected her former colleague. "You mean money."

Erika nodded. "A lot of it."

"Enough for me?"

"Perhaps."

Birgit inspected the paper-clouded desk, the rough walls with their plastering of clammy concrete, and asked quietly, "What must I do?"

"Are we safe here?"

Birgit gave a humorless laugh. "These walls are half a meter thick. There are seven meters of earth between us and the road overhead. Why would the Wessies bore holes just to bug the archives? They haven't even bothered to give me new ventilation."

Erika said, "I need help locating a certain man. He changed his name after the war, of that we are fairly sure.

He was born and raised here in Dresden. Where he moved afterward, I don't know."

"That's all?"

"I have his name. An old picture. His rank in the army during the war."

Birgit grimaced. "Gestapo?"

"No. Transport corps."

"Ah, of course. For movement of treasure. That's it, isn't it?"

Erika remained silent.

"Of course," Birgit repeated. She raised her eyes to the bare bulb overhead. "I could try and find fingerprints, match old records. Everyone had to have prints taken for the new identity cards issued back in the late forties. He was born here?"

"Yes. And lived here until enlisting. The records would still be here?"

"Here or Berlin. You'd be surprised how many survived the bombings. Leave that with me. I still have a few friends."

"How long will it take?"

"As long as I need," Birgit replied. "How much do you pay?"

"Four thousand marks now, more later."

"How much more, how much later?"

"A lot more, hopefully not long from now. We are all feeling the pressure these days."

"It would be nice to receive more now."

"It would be nicer still if we had it."

Birgit examined her. "Can I trust you?"

"You know who I am, you know," Erika hesitated, then finished with, "you know."

"Let me see your new identification," Birgit demanded.

Erika thought about it, then reached into her shoulder bag and handed over the green Wessie identity card. Birgit examined it carefully, compared it with the professional taxi license Erika also supplied, and made note of Erika's new name and address. "First-class product."

"It ought to be. It cost enough."

"But it will work only so long as you don't try to leave the country."

Erika nodded. This was well known. Stasi had issued over thirty thousand false West German passports during the last year before the Wall fell, as well as about the same number of American passports, and it had proven immensely difficult to determine who owned them. In the early weeks of transition, many files had been lost to a sudden spate of fires. Other paper piles had been fed to the compost heaps of newly avid gardeners, and honey had been discovered coating hard disks in several central computers.

The Wessies were aware of the traffic in false papers, as many Ossies sought to grow new faces and leave behind old lives. The Wessies instituted a policy of checking ID papers at all border crossings. Before, this had been done on a random basis only. Nowadays, even the border guards on trains were equipped with hand-held computer links into which every name and ID number was punched.

"We will need to cross only one time," Erika replied. "I hear the Dutch border is full of holes."

"You think you will make enough from this to disappear forever?"

"Forever is not my concern," Erika said. "A year or two of comfort is as far as I care to look just now."

"Four thousand marks," Birgit said thoughtfully. "Think of what comfort four thousand Wessie marks would have brought under the old regime."

"Under the old regime," Erika replied, "I would not have been asking."

"No, I suppose not." Birgit toyed with her pen. "What if he's dead?"

"Then," Erika replied, "we spend our remaining days dreading every knock at the door, every ring of the phone, every unmarked letter in the post."

Birgit nodded, expecting nothing else. "I will see what I can do."

CHAPTER
6

The day of Alexander's return from Cracow, Jeffrey received a call from Frau Reining, an East German attorney based in Schwerin. She had first contacted them the previous summer, while defending families who had been victimized by the former Communist regime. Since then, she had become a valuable ally in their hunt for rare antiques. The line rained a constant barrage of static as Jeffrey yelled a hello.

"Fräulein Nichols, she is there?"

"In fifteen days," he shouted. Frau Reining spoke a truly awful English. They normally relied on Katya and her fluent German for translation. "She prepares for her exams. You call her apartment?"

"Ach, nein, I wait four, five hours for this line. We try, yes?"

"We try," Jeffrey agreed.

"Have three *Stück* for you. You understand *Stück*?"

"I think so. Big schtukes or little?"

"Big. Wood. Old."

"Right. Antique furniture."

"Very beautiful. You buy, yes?"

"I'll have to check them out first."

"What?"

"Yes," Jeffrey surrendered loudly. "I buy."

"Good. Also have other seller. In Erfurt. South. He needs honest man."

"Thank you," he yelled.

"Find one honest man, no need to look for other. You understand? This man, he too is honest. I know."

"I believe you." He cleared his throat, shouted, "You want me to come to Schwerin?"

"Not here. Erfurt. You know?"

"No, but I'm sure I can find it on a map."

"What?"

"I find."

"Fräulein Nichols, she know it. Capital of Thuringen." Through the static he heard the sound of a match being lit, of smoke being drawn. "Man is Herr Diehl. Spell Dieter-Igloo-Europa-Heinrich-Ludwig. Siegfried Diehl. Godly man. You understand?"

"I think so," he replied.

"He suffered much. The Communists made him pay much. Too much. More than, how do you say tenth for church?"

"Tithe."

"Yes. Communists no stop at tenth. Or half. They take all. Job. Pension. School for children. Home. He pay much for religion. Good man. You see."

Jeffrey scribbled, hoped the spelling was close enough for Katya to figure out. "All is ready for me now?"

"Yes. You go with Fräulein Nichols. Siegfried, he has no English." She coughed, shouted over the static, "When you go?"

"We have a lot going on right now. I'll have to speak with Mr. Kantor, but I—"

"What?"

"Four or five weeks, maybe."

"Not sooner?"

"I don't think so."

"So. I tell Siegfried."

"You're sending your antiques to," he hesitated, not wanting to name the town, "Siegfried's shop?"

"Pliss?"

"Your schtukes." Jeffrey was growing hoarse.

"Ah. Yes. With Siegfried. You go, look for shop on bridge."

His hand hovered over the page. "He works near a bridge?"

"Not near. On. On bridge. Shop on bridge. Called *Glock,* means bell in German. Look for Bell Shop on bridge."

That evening Jeffrey made his way on foot to the Grosvenor Apartments, a red-brick Victorian structure overlooking Hyde Park. The floors had been converted into luxury apartments that rented by the week or month. Three weeks before departing for Poland, Alexander had let out his Geneva apartment and made this building his permanent residence. It was Jeffrey's first visit to Alexander's new home. The old man had insisted on being allowed to, as he put it, let the dust settle before inviting in guests.

Alexander answered the door with, "My dear young friend, come in. Come in."

"Thanks. Welcome back." Jeffrey took a step and pointed to the delicate French commode decorating the entrance hall. "I know that piece."

"Don't go around pricing the furniture, that's a good boy."

"I was wondering what happened to it. I thought I had a buyer lined up, then I come in one morning and, poof, it's gone. You took it to Switzerland, didn't you? And now it's back here."

"Yes, well, that's one of the benefits of ownership, isn't it."

"And the sofa there. Isn't that part of our Biedermeier set? Yes. I see the secretary in your living room."

"My dear young man, I'll thank you to turn off the calculator in your eyes and drop the urge to call a moving van. Now come in."

Jeffrey silently took note of the two late medieval tapestries adorning the walls where the foyer opened into the living area. He had a client who was still asking about those.

Two long steps separated the white marble foyer from the living area's split-beam floor. The furniture was sparse, each piece set on silk Persian carpets and spaced to be viewed individually, like fine jewelry displayed on beds of multicolored velvet. Tall windows at the room's far end overlooked Park Lane and the park beyond. Noise from the constant traffic speeding by seven floors below was reduced to a steady hum.

"This is beautiful," Jeffrey declared.

"I'm so glad you like it. Sit down. Can I offer you anything? A coffee, perhaps?"

"Coffee's fine, thanks." Jeffrey selected an eighteenth-century Dutch high-backed chair upholstered in white silk. "I'm sorry you wouldn't let me meet you at the airport."

"The older I become, the more I am inclined to suffer through my little foibles in private," Alexander replied. "And how is your dear lady?"

"All right, as far as I know. I talk to her every evening, but we won't be seeing each other for another two weeks."

"Yes, she has exams, doesn't she? How are they progressing?"

"All right, she thinks. She sounds very tired, though."

"I'm sure she must be."

Jeffrey cleared his throat, decided to have it out while his nerves were still intact. "I'm thinking about asking her to marry me."

"My dear boy!" Alexander's face lit up with genuine pleasure. "What absolutely splendid news."

"If she'll have me."

"Of that I have no doubt. I am most pleased with this excellent decision on your part, as well as with all that lies behind it."

"A queasy stomach," Jeffrey offered. "Clammy hands. Unsteady legs."

"Divine inspiration, true love," Alexander countered. "A joining for life. I wish you every success."

"Thanks, Alexander."

"Now then." Alexander lowered himself into a chair. "As a pre-wedding gift, you must allow me to bestow upon you an engagement ring."

"It's too much," Jeffrey objected.

"Nonsense. I have the perfect item in mind. It was one of my very first purchases after the war, and I have held on to it for sentimental reasons."

Faced with the old gentleman's positive delight, Jeffrey swallowed his protests. "You did the same thing when my grandparents became engaged."

Alexander's strong eyes glimmered. "How very kind of you to remember."

"My grandmother told me about it when she heard I was coming to work for you." Jeffrey faced the old man squarely. "That was one of the best things that's ever happened to me, Alexander."

"You do me much kindness." It was the old gentleman's turn to pause and taste from his cup. "Such a mood should not be dampened by the mundane. I propose we leave our business affairs until later."

"Fine with me."

"Excellent. I do have something rather fascinating that you might care to hear about this evening."

"The pieces for the gala," Jeffrey guessed.

"Exactly. The altar and painting from Rokovski are indeed splendid. The chalice from the Marian Church, however, is something truly unique."

"Chalice is another word for the cup used in the Communion, isn't that right?"

"Ah, that is your Protestant upbringing." Alexander topped up his and Jeffrey's cups from a sterling silver coffeepot. "The development of the chalice is a story steeped in two thousand years of mystery and intrigue."

"Great," Jeffrey said, his enthusiasm undisguised. "I love the stories in this business almost as much as I do the pieces themselves."

"Do you indeed?" Alexander nodded approval. "I am indeed happy to know that you share my love of mystery."

"Sometimes it wakes me up at night," Jeffrey confessed. "I'll lie there and see pages of the books go through my head. I think of these incredibly beautiful pieces, and feel as if I'm reaching across the centuries to talk with the makers, learn their secrets, share with them the pleasures of creation."

"It is a passion that has never failed to ignite the fires in me," Alexander agreed. "I have wondered if this is what fuels the desire of acquisition for some. For myself, it has never been necessary to hold on to any particular item. To *find* is more than enough. To watch it pass through my hands, and for a brief moment to be a part of its history, that is adequate.

I suppose my earlier experiences have left me too aware of the brevity of life and the transient nature of all possessions. But of that we shall not speak tonight." He smiled at Jeffrey. "Tonight we shall revel in the mysteries."

"Sounds good to me."

"Excellent. Then tell me of your favorite piece, my boy. Make it live for me."

"Favorite." Jeffrey settled into his chair, leaned his head on the back rest. "That's a hard one."

"Do not speak of the mundane. Reach back into the shrouded mists of time and describe what has so held you enthralled."

"There's a piece in the shop's basement right now that I'm holding for Betty," Jeffrey said. "Ever since it arrived, I haven't been able to get it out of my mind."

Alexander stripped the foil off a long Davidoff, snipped the end, struck a long match. "Some of my vices have proven more difficult to leave behind than others. I do hope you won't mind."

"You know I enjoy the odor," Jeffrey replied. "As to somebody else's vices, if I ever reach perfection myself, maybe I'll feel I've got room to criticize."

"Thank you." When the cigar was well lit, Alexander leaned back in his chair, set his feet on the stool, and retreated behind his fragrant cloud. "Carry on, Jeffrey."

"The piece was made in America," he began. "I'm almost positive of that. But it's an exact replica of an altar table I found in a book on the Cambridge churches, only smaller. The Cambridge altar was made in the days of King Henry VIII, when the Church of England was formed by a king who wanted a son and heir so badly he was willing to break with Catholic Rome and force an entire country to accept a new doctrine."

"Excellent," Alexander murmured. His only feature which showed clearly through the fumes were his eyes, colored like the smoke and lit bright as the cigar's burning tip.

"The way I imagine it," Jeffrey went on, "there was a man who lived then. A truly gifted man, who could take the hardest of oaks and feel the veins and trace the patterns buried within the wood. He was a man of faith who tried to follow the Word, and he was troubled by the goings-on in the house of God."

Alexander leaned forward. "His name?"

Jeffrey thought a moment, decided, "Matthew."

Alexander settled back. "Go on."

"Matthew was an artist of wide repute. In fact, he became so well known for the quality of work that even the great bishop in Cambridge heard his name. He was called in to make this new altar table in commemoration of some great earthly event.

"Matthew knew that the church was notorious for declaring artists' work as donations and paying poorly and slowly. He was also aware that to refuse someone as powerful as the bishop was to court death. But more importantly, Matthew wanted to contribute his work to such a great and holy place as the Cambridge Cathedral. Matthew accepted the task. And he put his very best effort into this work.

"He sat there day after day, praying and meditating on the structure that would house his work, the building with which his work would need to wed. He sketched the church's medieval stained-glass windows. Then he sketched the cathedral's great cross, which was made around the year eleven hundred. And as he worked, he listened to the talk that swirled around him.

"He heard the church officials whisper gossip in his ears, tales and politics and subterfuge and things of this earth, which he felt had no place in the worship of his Lord. In time he began work on the actual cabinet, but as a very troubled man.

"He carved the front panels as a series of reminders, calling all who served from the table to remember the One they served. He harkened back to the earlier days, when faith was the reason for their gathering, not the words of earthly kings. He carved the cross. He carved the apostles as they appeared in stained-glass windows made when the church was young. And when the piece was done, he stayed to see Mass celebrated upon his creation, and then he left the cathedral, never to return."

"My dear Jeffrey," Alexander said quietly. "You surprise me."

"Mathew had a son," Jeffrey went on, "who took his father's name and trade. In time he passed both on to his own son, along with the story of the Cambridge altar. The grandson grew in stature and talent to match that of his grandfather, and shared with him his dislike for the church's earth-bound concerns. As he grew older, his dislike for the church's tainted ways grew so strong that Matthew decided to leave the world behind and take his family to America. But before he left, he traveled back to the Cambridge Cathedral and made careful sketchings of his grandfather's altar.

"Throughout that long voyage, the storms raged and threatened to consign him and his wife and his children to the bitter depths. He suffered during that trip. There is no question of that in my mind. He suffered badly. The food was terrible, the cold almost unbearable, the wet and the stink their constant companions. He and his family were not oceangoing folk, and at times their seasickness made them wish one of those huge waves would swamp their little boat and put an end to their trials.

"Matthew and his family arrived in the Virginia colony just as a new church was being built. One much smaller and simpler than the Cambridge Cathedral, but filled with the Spirit that had called to his grandfather's heart. Matthew had no money, only his tools and talent and the desire that burned in his breast. His contribution to the new church was yet another altar table, one miniaturized to fit the smaller surroundings. But the panels were exactly the same, Alexander. Exactly the same cross, the same cup, the same apostles.

"And when Matthew looked upon his finished work, he knew peace in his heart. He knew then that his decision and the voyage and the new beginnings were right. Here he and his family had found a home where their lives could be dedicated to worshiping God, not to men's unending struggle for power."

Jeffrey leaned back, went on, "There's one more thing. The legs of this piece were carved with a symbol of the man's own struggle. An interlocked series of fish traced down each leg, but set on the inside face, where few were likely to see them. The secret sign of the fish, first used by the Christians of the Roman labyrinths."

The room was silent save for Alexander's occasional puffs. Then, "I congratulate you, Jeffrey. You have made it live for me."

The old gentleman stood. "Come. I have made reservations for us at the Connaught. Over dinner I will share with you a mystery of my own."

CHAPTER
7

A biting wind kept them company during the walk from Alexander's apartment to the Connaught. Yet it was a clear night, and the air tasted dry and clean. Jeffrey delighted in the city and the companionship. Alexander walked alongside him, puffing contentedly on his cigar, eyeing the buildings and the passing people with a lively interest.

As they turned the corner onto South Audley street, Jeffrey asked, "How is Gregor?"

"All right, I suppose." Alexander fanned his smoke with an irritated motion.

"What's the matter?"

"My dear cousin does not approve of my activities."

"You mean, the gala?"

"I'm sure I don't know," Alexander replied peevishly. "I have not asked, and he has not said. All I can tell you is that he continues to challenge me with what he leaves unsaid."

Jeffrey could not help but smile. "I know what you mean."

"Do you? How positively reassuring. I thought it was perhaps the voice of my conscience that was nagging at me."

"Maybe that's why Gregor gets under your skin," Jeffrey offered. "Because he says what you're already thinking on a deeper level."

"Whatever the reason, he is positively the most unsettling man I have ever met." Alexander tossed his cigar aside.

"He is typically so blunt about matters dealing with the state of my soul. This new reticence of his has been most disturbing."

"Disturb." Jeffrey nodded agreement. "That's exactly what he does to me."

"Does he indeed?"

"Every time we speak. He's always saying what I least expect to hear. And what unsettles me most."

"And still you turn to him?"

Jeffrey sought a way to express what he felt. "Somehow just being around him gives me the confidence to take the next step."

Alexander stopped on the Connaught doorstep and stared at Jeffrey a moment. "It is reassuring to hear that I do not face these unanswered questions alone."

"There's a world of difference between knowing what I need to do and doing it," Jeffrey replied.

"There is indeed," Alexander agreed. "Nonetheless, it pleases me immensely to know that I face this quest with a companion." He opened the door, motioned Jeffrey through. "Come. Let us dine."

The Connaught occupied a corner of Carlos Place, which stood a mere jot and tiddle away from the clamor of Berkley Square. Its view was of nothing more appealing than a pair of city streets and a matchbook-sized patch of green flanked by waiting taxis. The hotel's interior was all ancient wood and rich decorum. The public area was a dozen rooms laid out as a series of tastefully decorated formal parlors. Guests of the hotel and restaurant, many of whom had continued to frequent the establishment for decades, walked across creaking floorboards and spoke in quiet, cultured tones. Ties and jackets for gentlemen, and appropriately refined dress for ladies, were required at all times.

The restaurant reminded Jeffrey of the leather-and-wood lined study of a very wealthy man; the original oils adorning the walls were worth millions. The bill of fare was unabashedly English and leaned heavily toward succulent roasts, platters of steamed vegetables, ruby-toned clarets, and thick treacly desserts.

Once they had ordered and were again alone, Alexander

confessed, "I have known a growing pressure within me to come to terms with these new demands of faith—and yet, so often, I feel that I am groping in the dark."

"I find faith mysterious, too," Jeffrey admitted.

"Well, then," Alexander replied, "perhaps we shall have the pleasure on other cold nights of comparing our walks in the mists of misunderstanding. But for now, I need to speak of other matters."

Alexander lowered his voice. "In recent days, I have recognized that my strength and days are precious commodities, and health a gift that must be harbored. I therefore intend, as time goes on, to leave an increasing amount of the purchasing and travel to your capable hands. I shall reserve my time and strength for those pursuits that have not received the attention they should during earlier years. That is, if you do not object."

"I'm deeply honored," Jeffrey replied.

"On the contrary, it is I who am grateful to the Lord with whom I am just beginning to have a nodding acquaintance for gracing my latter years with such a friend as you." He took a brisker tone. "I shall remain increasingly in London, minding the shop while you are away. Thus the reason for my new flat. As you accept these new responsibilities, I should hope that you would take advantage of my experience."

"And wisdom," Jeffrey finished for him. "Of course I will."

"Excellent." Alexander leaned back as the waiter set down his plate. "Now, let us turn our attention to something more in tune to this splendid repast."

"The chalice," Jeffrey said. He nodded his thanks to the waiter and took a first whiff of perfumed steam.

"Precisely. The chalice has a most interesting history," Alexander said. "It is one of the few elements of Christianity that has fascinated me over the years."

Jeffrey could not help but smile. "We're talking about an antique. Of course you liked it."

Alexander did not deny it. "Part of the joy of collecting is the wealth of legends that spring up around the items. The older the piece, the more enchanting the stories. Imagine, if you will, that some magnificent object has stood in one corner or another, protected by nothing more than its owner's greed or love of art—"

"Or both," Jeffrey offered.

"I will thank you not to interrupt the flow of history," Alexander said crossly. "Now look what you've done. I've forgotten what it was I wanted to speak about."

"Greed?"

"Ah, yes. History. Thank you. This object has stood surrounded by intrigue and wars and power struggles, heard secrets spoken from lips whose commands sent hundreds of thousands into mindless battle, observed the endless march of time."

"If it only had eyes," Jeffrey murmured.

"You have the romance of a horse's nether regions," Alexander snapped.

"Sorry," Jeffrey said, hiding his grin behind his glass. "Just slipped out."

"It must be something they put in American baby formula. Saps away the ability to wax lyrical about anything but the color green."

"This was interesting, it really was," Jeffrey soothed. "You were going to say something about the chalice?"

"Are you sure you can stay awake for another few moments? Keep your mind off your bank balance?"

"I try not to think on that too much. Red ink scares me."

"The legend of the chalice is as old as Christianity itself. It began with Joseph of Arimathea, the wealthy Jew who was granted care of Christ's body after the crucifixion. The story goes that Joseph was also given the cup that Christ had used at the Last Supper, the one which held the wine that Jesus declared was His blood, and from which the apostles all drank. As Joseph washed the Lord's body, some blood flowed from His wounds, and Joseph caught this blood in the vessel.

"When the Jewish authorities discovered that Christ's body had disappeared from the tomb, they frantically began a search for a scapegoat. This makes perfect sense, you see— that's why I think there might be a grain of truth to the legend. An essential element of their desire to kill Jesus was to end the turmoil caused by His claim to be the Messiah.

Now, if His body had disappeared, then His followers could easily either proclaim that He had not died, or that He had risen.

"At that point, therefore, the authorities were not looking for answers; they had no time for such niceties. They were looking for someone upon whom blame for this misdeed could be publicly laid. And Joseph was the perfect scapegoat. He was rich, he had been identified as a follower of Jesus, and he was as well known in some circles as are the rich of today. In other words, he was not some nobody just pulled off the street—perhaps that is why the Lord's body was entrusted to him in the first place.

"Whatever the reasons, Joseph was seized by the authorities, accused of stealing the body, thrown into prison, and denied food. After several days of this harsh treatment, according to the legend, Joseph received a visitation from the risen Christ, who was said to have entrusted the cup to him, along with instructions to share the secret of the communion with all believers.

"Joseph remained in the cell for forty years, fed by a dove that came every night and dropped bread into the cup. When he was finally released, in A.D. 70, he immediately left Jerusalem on a trip that was positively filled to the brim with adventures. He made his footsore way to England and finally settled in Avalon, the Celtic name for the heavenly otherworld, located in what today is known as Glastonbury.

"Joseph then received another vision, which instructed him to establish a church on that site and spend his remaining days sharing communion with all who came seeking truth. And it is there, my young friend, that the shroud of time falls over the legend until it is revived in the days of King Arthur."

"The Grail," Jeffrey said. "You're telling me about the Holy Grail, aren't you."

"Precisely. In very early medieval times, the idea of the Grail fell into disfavor with the church. Alchemists, as magicians of that day were known, began to say that the Grail was not a cup at all, but rather a hollowed-out piece of stone called *lapis exillas,* or *lapis lapsus ex caelis,* which translates as 'the stone fallen from heaven.' This stone was said to have remarkable properties, healing anyone who touched it and stopping the aging process for anyone who kept hold of it. Great wizards were said to remain unbounded by time through tying a portion of this grail stone around their necks. So long as it remained upon their persons, the only sign they would show of passing years was the whitening of their hair. Their bodies would remain locked to the age they had been when first touching the stone.

"Naturally, the church was less than pleased by the rise of such heretical nonsense, especially when it was supposedly connected to the person of Christ. So they split the concept of the Grail, and all the legends attached to it, from the concept of a chalice, or the cup used in taking Communion."

Alexander folded his napkin and set it beside his empty plate. "And now, if you would be so good as to come with me, I have something back in the apartment that I wish to show you."

Jeffrey rose to his feet. "You left the Polish pieces in your apartment?"

"Just the chalice, and just until tomorrow," Alexander replied, and led him from the room. "The other pair will arrive closer to the gala event. Security in my building is quite good, I assure you. But in any event, I will settle the chalice into one of our shop's display cases. That is, after it has been photographed by a professional. I have decided to use it as the centerpiece for my invitations."

The wind had abated by the time they left the restaurant. After the chamber's overly warm confines, the dry, crisp air was invigorating. They strolled at a comfortable pace along quietened city streets, the streetlights' golden glow splashing against centuries-old facades and creating an aura of different evenings and other eras.

"The curate at the Marian Church was decidedly one of the strangest characters I have dealt with in years," Alexander told him as they walked.

"How so?"

"He had quite the most remarkable eyes I have ever seen. Almost fanatical in their brilliance."

"You didn't call him weird just because of the way he looked at you."

"I did not say weird at all, and no, it was not just his eyes. There was an aura of strangeness about the man. Something I can't quite put my finger on. As though he dwelled in worlds that no other mortal could fathom."

Jeffrey smiled. "I hear another story in the making."

"Indeed. My entire encounter with the gentleman was quite remarkable."

• • •

The Marian Church's rectory was a centuries-old stone cottage, connected to the cathedral and to Cracow's main plaza by a broad cobblestone way. Alexander used his umbrella handle to rap sharply on the stout oaken door, which was swiftly opened by the curate himself.

Curate Karlovich was a wild, Rasputin-like figure. A man of astonishing intensity, he was tall and slim, with thick black hair disheveled as the beard that cascaded in unruly curls down his front. He was dressed completely in black— black sweater, black trousers, black thick-soled shoes. On his left hand he wore an enormous gold ring, which he tapped on whatever surface was nearest in accent to his words. There was a disturbing aura about the man, evident from the first moment of their contact.

"Mr. Kantor! Greetings, greetings!" He bustled forward with outstretched hand. "Dr. Rokovski told me I should expect you this morning. Indeed, I cannot tell you how very opportune your visit is."

"Thank you. I imagine Dr. Rokovski explained—"

"Yes, of course! I am sure a man of your discernment will very much appreciate what I am about to show you. Please follow me." The curate turned and hurried through an arched wooden door, down an ancient stone-lined hallway, and into the Marian Church. He led Alexander to the center of the nave, genuflected slightly, and waved Alexander toward a massive pillar in the left corner.

An elaborately carved staircase encircled the front half of the pillar, leading up to one of the church's three medieval podiums. Karlovich unlocked a small door that had been hollowed from the back of the same pillar, the wood bowed so as to fit the pillar's gradual curve. He switched on a dim light and pointed Alexander down a set of very steep, very narrow stairs. Alexander lowered his head and made his way gingerly downward. Above and behind him, Karlovich slammed the door with a resounding boom, locked it, and hastened down to the cellar landing.

"Please come this way," Karlovich announced. He moved swiftly along a cavelike passage carved from the solid stone upon which the church stood.

"How old is this tunnel?" Alexander asked, struggling with the too-small confines, the coffin-still air, the meager lighting, and the strangeness of it all.

"A thousand years, perhaps two. Perhaps more. Its age is a mystery as complete as the reason behind its first being carved." The ancient stone bounced and jumbled words that were spoken in electric haste. "I suppose it goes without saying that this place is closed to the public. In fact, very few of our church officials have access here. We cannot be too careful with these treasures."

"I quite agree," Alexander replied, walking with one shoulder twisted slightly back in order not to rub against the passageways' narrow confines.

"I have worked on my own here for nearly twenty years," Karlovich said. "Sometimes I think I am alone in my appreciation of these things—their beauty and their value."

"Dr. Rokovski has told me your collection is most impressive." He was immensely relieved when the tunnel widened and ended against a gate of iron bars.

"Yes, Rokovski would understand. But most people, they think the job of a church curate is to keep the candlesticks counted and the pews dust free." His keys jangled as he fitted one into the gate's lock and twisted. "Here we are."

Alexander peered beyond the elaborate wrought-iron gate and made out a crude but spacious semicircular gallery. "This place has quite an eerie feeling to it."

"Indeed. Some centuries ago, this chamber served as a crypt." The gate shuddered its protest as Karlovich shouldered it aside. "There may still be a few bones around here, for all I know."

Karlovich pointed toward a sarcophagus no more than five feet long, its time-worn stone top carved with the image of a medieval knight. "Come have a seat on my little bench."

Reluctantly Alexander did as he was instructed, saying a silent apology to whoever's remains rested within.

The curate approached a series of crude wooden panels that covered the three opposing walls. They were made of ancient oak planking, banded together with long iron bars whose ends made up hinges on one side and locks on the other. It required a pair of skeleton keys, each almost a foot long, to unlock the central double panel, and all of Karlovich's strength to move the two massive doors aside.

Alexander squinted through the dust raised by Karlovich's effort and saw an expanse of rusting wire-mesh screens. Karlovich reached into the upper recesses and flicked an unseen switch. At once the cages' interiors were illuminated.

Alexander leapt forward at the sight.

Karlovich was clearly pleased with the reaction. "I did not think you would be disappointed with my little display."

"Disappointed?" Alexander said, his voice catching. "This is such treasure as dreams are made of."

The hollow enclosure held hundreds of gold and silver items. Each was worthy to be a centerpiece for a major museum's religious art collection, yet here they were crammed together like cheap souvenirs in an Arabic bazaar. Alexander saw crosses and carvings and statues and reliquaries and icons and chalices. Most were heavy with jewels—pearls and coral and amber, emeralds the size of grapes, giant rubies carved in the crudely uneven facets of very ancient times. Many were adorned with intricate patterns of semiprecious stones.

"You are looking for one special item, yes?" Karlovich unlocked one of the smaller wire-screen doors. "Something very special for your fund-raising efforts in London."

"That is correct," Alexander replied. His breath came in short bursts, as though a giant hand had clamped itself around his chest.

"Something that would capture the imagination, symbolize the sacred, and impress upon these potential benefactors the importance of collecting and preserving such works. A chalice, perhaps." Karlovich reached into the recesses. "We are not just talking about art. We are speaking about our religion and our tradition."

"I find these chalices incredibly striking," Alexander agreed, striving to keep his voice level, to keep the pleading from his tone. "Perhaps not as fragile as the other pieces."

"Then a chalice it shall be." Karlovich pulled out a heavily carved chalice of solid gold, almost eighteen inches high. "Might I present you with a personal favorite. This dates from the end of the fifteenth century, when Cracow was the royal capital of the great Polish-Lithuanian empire and this church was the seat of worship for the patriarchs and kings of the age."

"A splendid choice," Alexander said, fighting the urge to reach forward, hold the chalice in his own hands, examine it more closely.

"It is, of course, made of hammered gold. The filigree at the base here is exquisite, wouldn't you agree? We believe it was made here in the vicinity of Cracow. At one time there were rumors that it originated in an Italian city-state, but nothing substantiated so far as I know. Fifteenth century, that much is certain. The shape and size is very typical for that era."

Rising from the octagonal base was a slender pillar whose lines gracefully joined with a wreathlike central carving. Above this, an inverted crown was fashioned into the base of the cup itself. The rim held a smooth, highly polished finish.

Karlovich held the chalice up before his dark, gleaming eyes and stared at it as though hypnotized. "A chalice," he murmured. "Yes. The Holy Grail. The circle of the sun, of wholeness, of completion. The mystical symbol of man's search for continuity and perfection. Yes, it is all here in a chalice. Here the wine is placed for the mystery of Communion, that we might drink and share in the eternal promise and thus come full circle."

Reverently he handed the chalice to Alexander and said, "Guard it well."

CHAPTER
8

"I still don't see why you put so much stock in what that little mole says," Erika said.

"Not mole," Kurt replied. "Ferret. He's the most ferocious man I've ever met."

Erika laughed at that. "You want to sell me for an idiot."

"It's the truth, I tell you. He gets his teeth into something and he never lets go. Never. He'd take on an elephant, know it'll probably kill him in the end, and still never let up."

"Sounds suicidal."

"You don't understand," Kurt said with unaccustomed patience. "There's method to his madness. Ferret built himself a reputation, see. Nobody took him on. *Nobody*. Maybe they didn't like him or want to work with him, but even then they left him alone. The Ferret stayed safe and dry no matter which way the winds blew."

"Until now."

"Yes, well, these aren't winds, are they. More like an eruption."

They were driving the Schwerin-to-Berlin autobahn in a nondescript rental truck. Their progress was slowed to a crawl by the snowy slush and by the two emblems of East joining West—perpetual roadwork and traffic.

"Ferret and I," Kurt went on, "we've been together fourteen years. I've never seen a mind like his, not even in the snakes at the top. He wants to stay out of the light, though. He's fanatic about that. That's why I know I can trust him. He pushes me to the front, so I keep him hidden."

"What about me?"

"We thought you'd fit in, or we wouldn't be driving out here together."

"Speaking of which, I don't see why you need me tonight."

"Let's just say helping out with matters like this is part of the deal."

"An obligation."

Kurt shook his head. "Think of it as a favor."

"A favor is something I can turn down."

"Not if you're smart."

He was doing it again, hinting at something without ever saying anything outright. She kept her voice casual. "So, what does Ferret have his teeth into now?"

Kurt took his time replying. "He's been going through those old records ever since I met him. I thought he was crazy, just a weird little guy spending all night reading garbage files from just after the war. Called it his hobby. Said he was putting together puzzles."

"Booty," she guessed. "He's after the Nazi booty. I heard it was all myth."

"Some of it was. Most of the real goods went with the ones who survived and fled to South America. The Odessa, that's no fable. Ferret traced a dozen or so of these puzzles, followed them all the way to Argentina or Paraguay. A couple of times he found something he'd been searching for in auction catalogues, maybe traced the seller back to a Gomez Schumann in Montevideo. Crazy how all those old Nazis gave their children Spanish first names."

"The treasure," Erika reminded him.

"Soon as one piece was identified," Kurt went on, "Ferret called the puzzle finished and moved on. He used his title to send off for other such records and start a new search. He spent all his free time searching. His flat was a kitchen, a fold-up table, a mattress, and three rooms of papers."

"Why not just blackmail the old Nazis living in South America?"

"No future in that. They have a reputation for nailing

anybody who gets too close. Stuck to their old ways. No, Ferret's been after something *clean*. Something with a future."

"After all these years." Erika shook her head. "You really think there's something left?"

"Something big." Kurt smiled his grim, bloodless line. "Big enough to relocate us permanently."

Erika examined his face. Sweeping lines of rain-flecked light streaked Kurt's face from shadow to parchment yellow and back again. "You don't know what it is, do you?"

"I know enough."

"The Amber Room, that's all," she pressed. "I heard him the same as you. I looked it up, know what I found? Amber is petrified tree sap. That's what you're looking for? A room made from old resin?"

Kurt shook his head. "We're looking for freedom and the money to enjoy it with."

"How can you sound so sure about something that's nothing more than rumor? If it's real, why haven't the Russians found it already?"

"Palm trees," Kurt said. "I've always wanted to live where I could catch my own fish and drink rum all day."

Erika leaned back in her seat, stared out at the slush-lined autobahn. "I don't believe this."

"Sleep on the beach," Kurt continued. "Watch the stars through swaying palms. Hear strange bird calls."

"I've gotten hooked up with a pair of clowns."

"Turn the color of old leather and grow a beard. Be a legend to the tourists," Kurt said. "Watch sunsets and strolling girls in small bikinis."

"Who is in charge of this circus, you or Ferret?"

"Drinks with bunches of fruit stuck in the top. You remember the fruit we used to get? Oranges from Cuba the size of olives and stuffed with seeds. I was ten years old before I saw my first banana."

"Where are we going anyway? Can you tell me that much?"

Kurt signaled his exit, took the snow-covered ramp slow and easy. "It doesn't matter," he replied. "Just look ferocious and keep the boys honest. You're probably real good at that."

It was amazing, Kurt thought as he watched the guy stomp and slip over frozen muddy ground toward him. Put a red star on his cap brim and he could be coming straight from the other side.

"I ain't no spy," the guy growled in greeting. He had the slightly seedy look of quartermaster sergeants the world over. His American uniform was crumpled, his boots loose-laced and grimy. An enormous beer gut was held in place by a strained webbing belt. A two-day growth of beard peppered his face. Teeth the color of old ivory chomped on the shreds of an ancient stogie. A bluish web of spidery veins spread out across flabby cheeks from a dedicated drinker's nose. Knuckles were scarred by the same fights that had chipped segments from his trio of heavy rings.

But what kept Kurt from worrying about his own health, standing in a frozen empty clearing in a stretch of forest halfway to Berlin, was the avarice gleaming in the quartermaster's eyes.

"Ain't got nothing against unloading the butts." The cigar was unplugged long enough for the quartermaster to spit a long brown stream onto the iron-hard earth. "But I ain't no spy."

The clearing was turned a whitish silver by headlights from two trucks. Behind the lights, ghostly half figures moved in stealthy haste, slipping and cursing on the icy earth and sending long plumes of frozen breath into the starry sky.

Kurt stood with all the patience he could muster. The quartermaster's accent was so thick that he could barely make out the man's words as English. And he knew from experience that the man wouldn't understand anything Kurt tried to say in return. Kurt's English was rudimentary at best, learned from books and not from practice. In his former life, there had been few opportunities to converse with native English speakers. He just stood and waited for the quartermaster to finish his grumbling protests so they could get down to business.

The collapse of the Berlin Wall was beginning to show effects in areas further and further afield, like ripples spreading out from a stone dropped in a pond. Or a meteorite.

Or a bomb. Something big enough to uncover the rotting muck at the bottom of the pond.

The Soviet empire, with its iron girdle of vassal states, no longer posed a threat to the free world. The Americans, therefore, were pulling out of Berlin in a very big way. Orders came down the line two or three times a week, whittling away at what once had been the greatest concentration of American military anywhere outside the States. Some garrisons had been stripped to the bone. Others had been shut down entirely.

The entire spy apparatus, listening stations and all, was being torn down and packed up and shipped a thousand miles to the east, sometimes much farther. Stations were being planned for formerly unheard-of places, borderlands in Poland and Czechoslovakia, even inside Russia, and pointed toward China. Old hands read orders containing their new postings and shook their heads in amazement as their universe was redefined—then got busy with their packing.

Some items, however, were not to be removed in the mass exodus. It was decided, for instance, that it would be easier to restock a minor item like cigarettes at the new locations than to move the supplies already in Berlin. But this relatively minor decision was more complex than it seemed. American soldiers were per capita the largest group of smokers in the United States. Added to that was the fact that there were somewhere around half a million American soldiers, diplomats, agents, and dependants in and around Berlin, and *all* of them bought their butts at the PX's vastly reduced prices.

Given these facts, a minor logistics decision took on somewhat larger implications.

Like how to liquidate two *warehouses* full of cigarettes. Just in Berlin.

Suddenly the official German channels became swamped with offers of cheap smokes. Supermarket chains found faxes waiting for them each morning, the quoted prices dropping at a panic rate the closer it came to pulling-out day. Yet no matter how low the offers dropped, these legal channels could absorb only so many cigarettes.

So when supply officers arrived in the mornings to learn that a hundred thousand packs or so had disappeared into the frozen night, the hunt for thieves was perfunctory. After all, the whole shebang was due for closure in less than three months.

Overnight, therefore, a new product began appearing on the black markets of Poland and the Ukraine—even as far away as Moscow, Budapest, and, if rumor was to be believed, Istanbul. Enterprising traders offered cigarettes that had actually been made in the United States with top-quality American tobacco—and at prices which were equal to or slightly less than the local imitation.

For it wasn't just the Berlin-based warriors who were being shipped Stateside; the same post-Cold War demilitarization was taking place all over Europe, with the same loose trail of cheap tobacco flooding the markets. Polish border guards were eating well these days, their meager income supplemented with bribes from dealers like Kurt.

But that wasn't why the quartermaster continued his foot-stomping inspection of the frozen ground at his feet.

"I read the file three times," he grumbled. "Can't figure out what you guys want this junk for. I mean, the guy's been dead for forty-seven years! He some friend of yours?"

Kurt made do with a nod, knowing a question had been asked but not at all sure what the man had said. Kurt had decided the quartermaster's blustering was all show. He was going to hand over the documents; he was just easing his conscience. So Kurt waited, stifling his need to shiver. He could feel the freezing air grab hold of his face and pull the skin taut.

He himself did not know what was so important about these records of an interrogation in a World War II American prisoner-of-war camp of a German soldier who had died of dysentery four months later. All Kurt knew, in fact, was what Ferret had told him—the man's name, his date of birth, date of capture, and date of eternal release. That much was included in the official record Ferret had plucked from his ever-present pile of yellowed documents. It was a copy of the death certificate that should be on top of the file Kurt was bargaining for. It was Kurt's only way of authenticating what was to be passed over.

A shout rose from the darkness behind the trucks. The quartermaster signaled to his men. He stomped across the frozen earth, reached into his inside pocket, and drew out a thin manila envelope. "Let's see the money."

Kurt pulled out two envelopes and hefted one in each hand. "Cigarettes," he said, raising the right. Then, raising the left, he specified, "File."

Erika emerged from the shadows long enough to wave one impatient hand. Kurt handed over the right-hand packet.

With a final oath, the quartermaster gave in to greed and passed over the envelope. Kurt backed off before the money could be grabbed, opened the envelope, drew out the slip of paper from his pocket, and compared it to the top paper in the file. They were the same. He flipped through the aged papers. Three additional pages. Not much for almost the entire profit they would gain from this shipment.

"Read it on your own time, buddy," the quartermaster said and gestured impatiently for the money.

Reluctantly Kurt handed it over, and wondered at the waste. The man slit the packet with a practiced motion, counted swiftly. Another shout came from the trucks. "Inna minute," the quartermaster called back. He finished counting and stuffed the packet in his coat. "Don't ever ask me for stuff like that again."

Kurt nodded. "Next week, more cigarettes?"

"Maybe," the quartermaster growled. "I'll be in touch." He turned and stomped away.

CHAPTER
9

Jeffrey and Katya celebrated the end of her exams by traveling to her mother's home in Coventry. It was a strangely silent trip. Jeffrey found it impossible to do as he wished—to caress the dark, wayward hairs spilling across her forehead, or kiss the line of her neck, or confess that her weeks of absence had positively wounded him. Too much was trapped inside him to come out just then. Even to say he had missed her remained an elusive goal. He made do with brief glimpses into those violet-gray depths, an occasional squeeze of her hand, and fleeting conversation about anything but that which filled his heart to bursting.

"I received a letter from my brother yesterday," he told her. "The first ever."

"I'm glad," she answered, her voice little more than a sigh, a velvet breeze that wafted gently by him. "It's time you two made peace."

He nodded agreement. "He wrote like there hasn't been any break at all, like it was yesterday the last time we were together. He's going to AA every night, and he's been sober for two hundred days. That's the way he said it, counting it one day at a time. He says he rewarded himself with three chocolate sodas and this letter. And he's started writing poetry."

"Your grandmother must be very happy," Katya said.

With that expression of quiet understanding, the dam controlling his emotions and his thoughts threatened to yield. But he could not do it, not then, not without saying it all. And he was determined not to rush, not to push himself upon her when she was still so tired from her studies. So he settled back and said nothing more the rest of the trip.

Once inside the Coventry train station, he gave Katya's gloved fingers a quick squeeze. "I'll be right back."

When he came running back a few minutes later she asked impatiently, "Where did you go?"

"I remembered something important."

"What are you trying to hide behind your back?"

"A bag of switches."

"No, they're not. They're flowers. Did you get those for Mama?"

"Don't tell me she's allergic or something. Breaks out in hives at the sight of a bloom."

A look from the heart and to the heart passed for a fleeting instant across her features, the first since her return. She raised up on tiptoe and kissed him soundly. Dropping down, she grabbed his hand, swung him around, and said, "Time to go."

"You're blushing."

"I said it was time to go, Jeffrey. Mama's waiting. Look, there's a taxi."

Magda's place was just as he had last seen it—cluttered and hot and overly close. The old woman opened the door, grimaced her greeting, accepted Katya's kiss. Then she hobbled back to her seat on feet swathed in stretch bandages and covered by lumpy support hose. Her dress skewed to starboard, her head was a mop of disorderly gray. Once seated, she said, "Good evening, Jeffrey."

He was suddenly very shy. "I wanted you to have these."

She showed genuine surprise. "You brought flowers? For me?"

He made do with a nod.

She accepted the bundle, peeled back the paper, looked a long moment. "Orchids in the middle of winter. And carnations. Did Katya tell you they were my favorites?"

"No, I didn't," Katya replied, her eyes resting on Jeffrey. "They're beautiful."

"Yes, aren't they?" She lifted them up to her daughter. "Be a dear and put these in water, won't you?"

When Katya had disappeared into the kitchen, Jeffrey eased himself into the chair nearest Magda and ventured, "I owe you an apology."

"I don't recall being offended, young man."

"It wasn't for anything I said."

She inspected his face. "My daughter was correct. You are indeed an honest man." A bony hand covered with age spots reached across and patted his arm. "The flowers are a splendid peace offering. Thank you."

His heart hammering in his throat, Jeffrey forced himself to say, "I need to ask you something, Mrs. Nichols. Well, two things, if I may."

"Mrs. Nichols, is it?" She raised her gaze as Katya entered the doorway. "Please leave us alone for a moment longer, daughter."

"What's the matter?"

"Go see to Ling. He's probably getting lonely out in the back room. The poor thing sings all the time nowadays, and there is no one to listen except me." Since being deposited in Mrs. Nichols' care last summer, the little bird had become a permanent member of the household. "We won't be long, will we, Jeffrey?"

He shook his head, not willing to look in Katya's direction, and waited for Magda to say, "Very well, young man. I am listening."

He swallowed. "I love your daughter very much, Mrs. Nichols. I want to ask your permission to marry her."

"I see." The piercing gaze did not waver. "And how does my daughter feel about this?"

"I think she agrees. I hope she does."

"You're not sure?"

"I've learned to take nothing for granted with your daughter, Mrs. Nichols." He swallowed again. "And I decided that I wanted to ask for your permission first."

"So. You do me much honor." The sharp gray eyes crinkled slightly. "Wise and honest and honorable besides. Very well, young man. You have my blessing. You may return to calling me Magda now."

He permitted himself a shaky breath. "Thank you." The words seemed totally inadequate. "I'll try—"

"Yes, yes." She silenced him impatiently. "I know you will, Jeffrey. Do not embarrass yourself. It is not necessary. Polish women are good nurturers, and my daughter has enough Polish blood in her to make a good wife." She looked at him a moment. "Katya is most fortunate to have found a man such as you. I hope she realizes it."

"You're very kind."

"Not at all, young man. I simply seek to answer honesty with honesty," she replied. "Now what was the other thing you wished to speak about?"

"May I ask you how you came to faith?"

"What a remarkable question." The piercing gaze returned. "What an exceptional husband you shall make. Young man, I would have to go back many years and many miles to answer that question."

"I'd really like to know."

"Yes, I see that is true. Very well, I shall tell you." Magda grimaced and shifted one leg. "Would you please be so kind as to place another cushion under my feet?"

"Sure." He selected a pillow from the pile by the settee, then helped her raise her feet and set the pad in place.

"Thank you so much. Do you know, my very first memory is of pain in those feet." She stared down at them. "I have not thought of that in years."

Jeffrey settled back in his chair, immensely glad to have his first question behind him, but too full of the strain to feel any elation—yet. He inspected the sagging, wrinkled features and decided he had seldom seen a more unattractive face, nor one with more determined strength.

"It was around the time of my third birthday. I know because of what my mother told me years later. It is the only memory I retain of my earliest years. Yet it is so clear that all I have to do is close my eyes and I can still see it, hear it, and feel the cold. We were walking, you see. Or rather, my father was walking. He carried me on his back. He and my mother had lined his knapsack with blankets and placed me inside it. Once I was strapped into place, they began their trek.

"There were seven families on this journey, mostly German Volk who had been hired by distant landowners to come and work on their vast estates. My mother was Polish, from a small village near what then was the German border. I remember that she made the most beautiful lace I have ever seen. My father was a skilled tanner and leather worker. They had worked for a landowner in what today is Hungary, on an estate so big it contained eleven whole villages. But the First World War wiped out much of landowning families' wealth, and the Depression finished them off entirely. Whole regions were starving, cities throughout Europe were filled with bread riots, Communists battled Fascists for power, and peace was nothing but an empty word.

"In 1935 my father and mother, along with six other families related by blood or marriage, decided that if they stayed where they were, they would perish. My mother had a sister who was married to a Polish farmer, a landowner with many serfs, who said in a letter that he would offer us roof and bread and a warm hearth. My father was not pleased with leaving behind a home he had built with his own hands, but a starving man cannot afford the luxury of argument.

"They set off in late October, a week after the letter from Poland arrived. If you have never tried to gather seven men and seven women, along with their children and their grandparents and even a cousin and great-uncle or two, and point them toward an unknown destination, with no money and very little food, you will not understand the arguments and indecisions and hesitations that filled their lives. They were leaving behind the only life they knew, risking everything for a future that was utterly unknown. Still they went, because as they looked around them they were impressed with the fact that to stay meant to die.

"That week of indecision almost cost them their lives. An early snowfall blanketed Europe, and rumors swept their village of signs and portents pointing toward the century's worst winter. It was this same snowfall that silenced the arguments and finally pushed them to move, for there was no fuel in my father's village. The train of wagons bearing coal for their stoves had never arrived.

"The morning my family set off for Poland, others began the trek to Budapest, where later that month more than six hundred thousand people rioted for bread and heat. It was a very bad winter, young man. There were riots in cities and hamlets from Berlin to Paris, from Königsberg to Constantinople. We heard rumors of war in Spain—and speculations that the war would spread. Women gave birth to babies and cried when tiny mouths first sought the breast, for they didn't know if a world would exist where the little ones might live and grow strong.

"But all of these things were told to me much later, long after we arrived in Poland, and after my father had learned of the madness that swept the land of his forefathers. My father hated the Fascists with a loathing that frightened me as a child. He was a gentle, caring man, with great strong arms and a warm lap and a barrel of a chest. The only time I ever recall hearing him curse was when he would speak of the Fascist regime. No doubt he would have viewed Stalin and the Communist lies with the same contempt, but by the time the Communists arrived in Poland my father was already dead, killed by a Nazi bullet in the Warsaw Uprising, fighting for a country he had come to call his own.

"My father sought out the good people in Poland, and what he found in them he loved. The Poles are a great people, Jeffrey. They truly are. Their sense of honor and duty and love of God is very great, great enough to sustain them through a century and a half of military occupation, followed by two world wars, the Nazi demons with their death camps, and fifty years of the Communists. Ask yourself this, young man. If two hundred years of such hardships had befallen the United States of America, would your people—those who survived—still be capable of calling themselves a nation?"

"I don't know," he replied softly.

"Well, on to my story. The estate where my parents settled lay in Upper Silesia, and that region was soon to be the flash point kindling the German invasion. You see, Poland had ceased to exist as an independent nation in the eighteenth century. It remained parcelled out between the Austro-Hungarian, Russian and Prussian empires for one hundred and fifty years. At the end of World War I, when the Austrian kings were vanquished and the empire was destroyed, the boundaries of Europe were redrawn. Upon this new map Poland once again existed, and it included a portion of what once had been the Prussian empire. There were many, many Germans still living there, some of them landed and titled gentry. So the Fascists claimed this land as their own, a part of the Fatherland usurped by foreigners. But it was nothing but an excuse, you see. The Fascists intended to rule the world, and Poland was simply a good place to start.

"My father hated lies of all kind. To him, truth was the bond that held the world in place. It was the gift that one man of honor offered to another without expecting anything in return. For him, the Fascists were transforming Germany into a land built upon lies, cemented into place with hatred. It was evil spawned and evil bred, and if truth had no place there, neither did he.

"I grew up knowing only Polish friends, speaking Polish except in our home, where I spoke German. My father was very proud of my ability with the difficult Polish language. He never did learn the language very well, but he made friends even in those suspicious times by the fervor of his hatred for the Fascists. Everyone in the area could see his horror when Germany invaded. He joined the local underground, and he spent the war years helping to hide and transport Jews seeking to escape the Nazi massacre. Because he was German, you see, there was less suspicion cast his way by the local military authorities.

"My childhood memories are all of faces appearing in the darkest night. Frightened faces. Exhausted faces. Faces who looked as though they never expected to see the light of day ever again. They were hidden in a secret cave my father dug beneath our coal cellar. Sometimes they stayed in that dark, airless hole for as long as a week, until the next stage of their passage was prepared. They came and they went, and I would scarcely ever hear them or see them unless I helped my mother take them food. I knew without anyone telling me that I should never speak of the ghost people living in my cellar. Even at nine and ten years of age, I knew that to speak of them would be the death of us all. And I burned with pride for the bravery of my dear papa and mama.

"It was in those days that I learned to pray, sending off these silent families into the darkness of an evil-laden night. Hard times and hatred allowed bad people to take over our homeland, my father often said to me. These new rulers were intent on killing all who challenged their ideas of racial purity or political loyalties. We had only one recourse, he told me every night as he opened the worn Bible and sought out a passage. We had only one refuge, in faith. Over and over he said to me, we must climb the stairway of prayer and enter into the most Holy Place."

The kitchen door creaked open and Katya's face emerged. "Mama?"

"What is it, daughter?"

"Do I have to stay in here all afternoon?"

"We won't be much longer," Magda replied, her eyes remaining on Jeffrey.

"Can't I join you?"

"Your young man and I are just getting better acquainted," Magda replied. "Give us just a few more minutes, daughter. I am almost done." She waited until the door had closed, then asked, "Have I bored you, young man?"

Jeffrey leaned back in his chair, felt as though he had been holding his breath. "Not at all. I have a thousand questions, though."

"You must save them for another time. We cannot keep my daughter cooped up all night." The eyes crinkled once more. "You are an excellent listener."

"There's a lot to learn."

"I see you mean that. Very well, I shall await your questions with pleasure. For the moment, let me simply tell you what I intended, which was my very earliest memory. It was of our trek to Poland. We moved mostly at night, you see. The woods were often safer than the roads, for the roads were ruled by thieves. In the woods there were only wolves, and the animals were said to be much kinder to those they caught than the thieves.

"My mother used to talk of that walk, of how she trod endlessly behind my father as he broke a path and flattened the snow. Many times she wanted to stop and go to sleep, she said. It was only looking at my tiny face that kept her upright and marching onward.

"Mama used to say that I only thought I remembered what I did. She said I heard her speak of it so often that the memory became my own. But that is not true, young man. I can still see the icy nighttime landscape with the great shadow-trees and their dark branches cutting jagged edges through the sky overhead. Many nights there was a bright moon, our only light, and it transformed the forest into another world, one I have often returned to in my deepest dreams.

"Only my head rose from the knapsack's confines. I remember clearly the way blankets were wrapped securely around my arms and legs. It would be so very hard at first, when we set off each day at dusk, not to squirm and complain at being trapped. But then, ever so slowly, the icy fingers of cold would begin to claw their way into my papa's leather satchel and wrap a steely grip around my little hands, and it would grow steadily easier to remain still and drift in and out of wakefulness. I knew what the cold was trying to do, you see. I had seen in my dreams how death sent the beasts of winter in to snatch me away from my body. After a few hours of traveling, I would be rocked to sleep on my papa's strong back, and then I would see the beast of cold there nibbling at my fingers and my feet, trying to cut the cords and let death draw me up and away.

"Then I would start awake, and there would be my mother's face, drawn and exhausted and worried, and I knew, as little as I was, that I had to be strong for her. When we were bedded down for the day in some kind farmer's barn or an empty house or if necessary in a riverbank cavern, I often heard my mother ask why I remained so quiet. Not even a whimper of sound, my mother would say, how is that possible for a girl of her age? And my father would look at me, and somehow I knew he understood, because instead of answering he would bend over and caress my forehead and tell me over and over that I had to be strong, and that when I could not, I had to ask God to be strong for me. That was my first lesson of faith, young man. I have carried it with me all of my days, and it has served me well. When I found that my strength was not enough, I turned and let God be strong for me. And He has never let me down. Never.

"The trip took twenty days. We lost six of the people who started off with us, two to thieves, one to a wolf, the rest to the beasts of hunger and cold. I lost both of my little toes, and no matter how my parents and the doctor might blame it on frostbite, I knew."

Magda nodded her head slowly, holding Jeffrey transfixed with glistening eyes. "Oh yes, young man, I knew. I had slept and dreamed and watched the beasts of winter gnaw them off."

On the train ride back to London, Jeffrey remained silent and reserved. A half hour into the journey, Katya asked him, "What are you thinking?"

"Something your mother said."

"Are you going to tell me what you talked about?"

"Later I will. Right now, it's still a little raw."

"Yes, I see it in your eyes. Mama's stories have a tendency to do that sometimes." She reached for his hand. "Just tell me what you were thinking of, then."

"I was just wondering how it was possible for Poland to keep such a strong sense of identity over such a long period. Two hundred years, Katya. I know you told me about how the church became an anchor for the people, their language, and their heritage. But it seems to me that it wouldn't be enough. There must have been a *lot* of strangers who moved in, people who after a while started calling themselves Poles. And what about all the Poles who went overseas?" He turned and looked out the window. "I tell you the truth, when I think about the dreadful things your people endured, it feels as if somebody is stabbing at my heart."

She bent over, kissed his open palm, raised it and set it upon her cheek, totally unmindful of the stares gathering from other parts of the train compartment. "Thank you for caring, Jeffrey."

"The more I learn about all of this, the more I am amazed at who the Poles are."

"You're as much a Pole as I am, Jeffrey. One grandparent, the same as me."

"Just in blood. I don't speak the language. I don't understand the culture, I've never even traveled there before last year. When she was young, my mother reached this stage where all she really wanted was to fit in with her friends. She wouldn't even admit that her father had been born outside the United States. The whole idea of being half Polish embarrassed her." He shook his head. "I wish there were some way I could go back and meet my mother when she was growing up, and tell her that she *must* hold on to her heritage, to learn the language and keep contact with the family. If not for her, then for her unborn son."

"I heard a story once," Katya said. "A group of cows had gathered in a barn, and a flock of sheep were grazing on a nearby meadow. It came time for one of the sheep to lamb, so she went into the barn for shelter. By the time the lamb was born, a heavy snowstorm had started falling. Several of the other sheep, those with young offspring and a few of the weaker ones, also moved into the warm, safe barn."

She gazed at him. "Now tell me, Jeffrey. Does the lamb become a cow simply because it is born and spent its first days in the warm, safe barn, or is blood more important?"

"Your stories are as harsh as your land. Where did you hear them?"

"When we were still living in Baltimore, my father got into financial trouble. I was very little, but my mother went to work in a ceramics factory," Katya explained. "Mama was in her late thirties when I was born. They had tried and tried for years to have children, and they couldn't. Then they gave up, and a couple of years later I came along. Before I was born, Mama had started painting designs on pottery that a friend was casting. She had always painted, and she enjoyed applying her skills to ceramics.

"Mama left me with a neighbor, an old Polish woman I called Chacha Linka. *Babcha* is the word for grandmother or old woman, and Halinka was her name. Chacha Linka was as close to pronouncing it as I could come. She never learned much English, and she only spoke to me in Polish. I don't remember ever actually learning the language, but

Chacha Linka talked to me in Polish all the time, so I must have picked it up. I can still remember coming home one day and saying something to my daddy and being so amazed that he couldn't understand me. It just didn't make any sense. How could I know something my daddy didn't?"

She turned to the window for a long moment, seeing out beyond the industry-scarred landscape to the world of remembering. "Chacha Linka had more stories than anybody I have ever known. A lot of them were about the Bolsheviki. That's what she called the Russians until the day she died. Bolsheviki. Even though the revolution had been over for seventy years, she still called them that."

"Sounds like a name out of some old black-and-white movie."

"Not for her. *Bolshoi* means large or big, like the Bolshoi Ballet—the Grand Ballet. Bolsheviki meant members of the Great Party, although the Communists weren't really so numerous. Lenin used that name to make it sound as if they represented all the people. It was propaganda appeal, making it appear bigger than it really was."

"All that doesn't sound like the makings of a kiddie's fairy tale."

"Some of the stories scared me," she agreed. "Some of them were awful. Really gave me nightmares. But some of them were beautiful."

"There's so much I don't know," Jeffrey said quietly. "So much to learn. It's like a treasure trove. You make me feel so *enriched.*"

She turned back from the window to give him a look of pure gratitude. "There's something I've wanted to speak with you about for a very long time. I wonder if maybe now is the time."

"We won't know unless you try."

"Do you know what it means to tithe?"

"Sure, I know the word. Ten percent of what you make."

"Ten percent that is dedicated to the Lord's work." She hesitated, and in that heartbeat's span was transformed into a shy little girl. "I was wondering if you would like to tithe with me."

The way she said it brought a burning to the back of his eyes. "It sounds fine, Katya."

"You don't have to if you don't want to."

"No, I'd like that. Really."

"I just thought." Again she paused and searched, her cheeks touched with a rosebud of blooming red. "I thought it might be a nice part of joining our lives together."

He reached across for her hand. It was on his tongue to ask her, but he checked the words at the very last moment. Not then. Not there.

"I was thinking maybe we could find something, a project or a need the next time we're in Poland together, and dedicate our work together on it to our Father." Violet-gray eyes peeked out from beneath the protection of long, dark lashes. "Do you like the idea?"

It was hard not to say what was on his mind, hard to hold to his original plan, hard to bring out the simple words, "I like it very much, Katya."

She looked at him with eyes that were never spent. Katya held his hand with both of hers and blessed him with her gaze for the remainder of the trip back to London.

CHAPTER

10

The farther from the main highway Kurt traveled, the more treacherous the road became. Four lanes dwindled to two, then the asphalt gave way to brick. Ice and snow packed between the stones created tiny, unseen deathtraps. Wrecks littered the roads, usually where slow-motion Ossie plastic cars met Wessie speed machines too intent on showing off to pay attention to the road and the weather. Kurt's neck throbbed from the tension of trying to keep a fixed appointment time under impossible conditions.

Kurt slowed for a truck entering a factory gateway, corrected a momentary skid, slowed even more. Near the Arnstadt city limits the road became flanked by the Karl Marx Industrial Estate, the high nameplates over each entrance now crudely whitewashed out. Chemical works gave way to cement factories, then to steel mills and a power station. On the other side of the street, high-rise workers' barracks marched in endless rows. Not a tree could be seen in the more than seven miles of factories and tenements.

He passed through the utterly charmless town and started climbing hills along a bone-jarring road. The radio kept him company with a mixture of American sixties' pop, Wessie rock, and a clear-speaking, carefully neutered Wessie announcer. Every trace of the old regime had been wiped from radio and television. No one listened to the Ossie musical groups anymore. No one talked about them. No one even admitted that the music had ever existed.

Kurt had eyes the color of dried mud. His face was as scarred and battered as a building site, marked by early bouts with various poxes. He tended toward gray in everything he wore—gray suits, ties, striped shirts, socks, dark gray shoes. It left him looking like a lump of angry mold.

Kurt considered himself an out-of-work spy, which he was, but not with the dangerously glamorous past as he would have liked. His spy trips abroad, the ones he referred to in mysterious half tones when chatting up bar girls, had been as overseer to trade missions visiting industrial fairs; they had been boring as only a trade fair could be for someone who had not the first clue about the subject on display. The other East German delegates had immediately pegged Kurt for a stooge, and shunned him throughout the trip. His only company had been other Stasi stooges, most of whom spent their time either shopping or drinking or touring the local porno houses. Kurt had found their company worse than being alone.

The fact that Kurt treated every trip abroad as an all-important mission earned him kudos from the home office and a reputation among traveling technicians as the ultimate pain. His presence on a technical trade mission meant that each morning at breakfast, every mission member had to submit a report on the previous day's activities—what they had learned, whom they had visited, what technology they had managed to pry loose from suspicious Western salesmen. But the Stasi bureaucrats liked Kurt's thoroughness. While his efforts never granted him his sought-after position as either an embassy staffer or a Western-based agent, they allowed him to travel at least twice a year to the West. In a country as tightly controlled as East Germany, this freedom was nothing to sneeze at.

But for Kurt it was not enough. He had always wanted to be an international spook, always seen himself as made for a dangerous life. He took whatever self-defense courses were offered. He wore a full-length black-leather overcoat long after warm weather transformed it into a mobile sauna. While shaving he practiced heavy-lidded expressions, and imagined himself squeezing information from a suspect with his gaze alone. He refused to marry, avoided any long-term connection that might close the book on overseas assignments. He slaved nights over correspondence language courses, though he had no aptitude for foreign tongues, and proudly slaughtered both Russian and French and Spanish— for some reason, English had always baffled him. Every report he submitted featured a tone of overblown intrigue.

Yet Kurt was never allowed to make the transition to full-time international spy. The hierarchies were distinct and separated by light years; international spies were normally chosen while still in university. In later life, the transition was possible only with that most treasured of possessions— a Party patron. Someone so high and so mighty that rules could be completely ignored, stomped upon, transgressed, and leave the receiver unbruised by having done the impossible.

Kurt had no such connections. He was too harsh in attitude, too abrupt in speech, too lacking in the ability to fawn and grovel. Kurt rose within the national hierarchy by sheer brute ability. His dream for a last-minute transfer remained unquenched. His bitterness knew no bounds.

Kurt's contact was standing where he had promised, beneath a glaring sign sporting a death's head, a crude picture of an explosion, and the ominous words: "Deadly Danger of Bombs and Mines. Do Not Enter." Kurt pulled into the narrow gravel pathway and stopped. The man was barrel-chested and short and powerfully muscled. He was dressed in the lightweight clothes of one who has learned not to feel the cold—denim overalls and unbuttoned jacket and a battered construction helmet. He thrust out one grimy hand, said in greeting, "The money?"

"It's here," Kurt replied, climbing from the car.

"Let's have it, then." When Kurt handed it over the contact counted carefully with stubby, blue-cold fingers. He pocketed the bills and said, "There's only ten minutes of light left. Let's go."

Kurt cast a nervous glance back at the sign. "I don't see why we can't talk this over in the car." When the man did not stop, Kurt swore under his breath and started up the gravel slope.

"Talk all day and it still wouldn't be clear," the man said, pausing by a second sign that proclaimed, in bold red letters, *Lebensgefahr*, Life-Threatening Danger. The man went on, "Yeltsin made his little speech and walked off with almost half a billion marks. Those fools in Bonn should have come up here and checked it out before handing over the money."

"Checked out what?" When newly elected Russian Premier Boris Yeltsin made his first official visit to Germany, he stated at the opening press conference that he knew where the Amber Room was buried. The news captured the headlines of every newspaper and magazine in Germany, and many in the rest of Europe. Yeltsin said that his researchers, in their investigation of newly uncovered postwar files, had unearthed clear evidence of where the Nazis had stored the most precious of their plundered treasures.

Yeltsin promised that he would disclose this site in return for additional emergency aid to his ailing nation. The Bonn government took his proclamation in stride, determined to allow nothing to upset relations so long as Soviet troops remained stationed on German soil. They replied that, in celebration of Yeltsin's visit, they had already decided to give an additional four hundred million marks in emergency aid.

Yeltsin's lackeys then identified the site as the caves bored into the Jonastal, the Jonas Valley, outside Arnstadt. The caverns had been dug during World War II by prisoners brought from the neighboring Buchenwald concentration camp.

After the first flurry of activity and official investigations, there had been nothing from Bonn except stony silence.

Kurt's eyes cast another glance at the sign's warning. "Shouldn't we find a safer place to talk?"

The man snorted. "We've had droves of fat Bonn politicians come parading up here for months. Not to mention trucks and bulldozers and backhoes and even sonar equipment. I doubt if you'll find anything they haven't."

"So why the signs?"

"The same reason all the Wessie fat-bellies left empty-handed." He pointed to veined white cliffs rising above frozen pines. "Yeltsin said the treasures were buried in a cave. And then one of the researchers in Moscow admitted that it wasn't the Amber Room that was mentioned in these records they found, but other treasures the Nazis hauled off from that same area around St. Petersburg. Hah. We *know* that. Everybody within fifty kilometers knows that."

Kurt showed exaggerated patience, hoped the man would come to the point before his feet froze to the ground. "So why isn't everybody out digging?"

"Because we like living more than we like golden caskets." In one sweeping motion he took in the tall pines rising up between them and the steepest cliffs, and the bone-colored stone looming up beyond them. "Look. The SS brought Buchenwald prisoners up here, had them dig caves. Not cave. Caves. Hundreds of them. Thousands, maybe. Nobody knows, see? Not how many, not even where. Some were used to store bombs from the munitions factory in Arnah. Why? Because bombers can come and find a building and bomb it. Harder to target a seven-kilometer-wide cliff face.

"Some caves for bombs, and some for treasures. At least, that's what the legends say. My father used to talk about the truck convoys that came through Arnstadt after the night curfew forced everybody indoors. Truck after truck after truck without lights, grinding through our city, all headed for the Jonas Valley. Official propaganda said all the trucks were full of bombs, and there was less danger of air raids hitting the trucks at night. But there were stories. Still are. Too many to be just smoke, for my mind."

He stabbed the air with an angry gesture. "But which caves were for bombs? And which for treasures?"

The faint breeze stopped. In that moment of utter stillness, snowflakes drifted down from a leaden sky. Kurt searched the cliffside. "So why don't I see any cave openings?"

"Because when they pulled out, the SS set off dynamite charges along the crest of the cliffs," the man replied. "See all those hills of rubble behind the pines? Man-made avalanches, the lot. Covered over all the cave openings."

Kurt nodded. "So you don't know where to dig."

"Not so fast. See how white the cliffs are? Chalk. Softest

stone there is. The Nazis' dynamite shifted the *mountains,* not just the openings. The caves are rubble."

The man lifted his white construction helmet, wiped at the stress that knotted his brow. "While the Wessies were all crowding around down here, making speeches for the press and getting in the way, we pounded steel rods fifteen meters long into the cliff face at likely looking places. Three men getting paid five times normal wage and sweating bullets, holding the rods in place, while two men with hammers took turns banging the rods in five centimeters at a time, and all the while waiting for a bomb to turn the rod into a giant's spear.

"They found three caves. In two and a half weeks. Three caves from how many, a thousand? All empty as far back as they could go, which wasn't far." He shook his head. "We cleared out the openings with shovels and a backhoe, a bottle of schnapps between each team before they started and another two when they stopped. They sent in bomb demolition experts with maybe fifty kilos of lead clothing and equipment per man. The experts got in about ten meters, and the rock overhead shifted a little—they shift all the time, these cliffs. They're permanently destabilized by the dynamite. There was this little rumble and a little puff of dust out the cave mouth, then screams and six men in lead blankets came running out so fast they didn't hardly touch earth."

Kurt was truly sorry he had missed that. "What happens now?"

"They stop, what else? You can't bulldoze a cliff filled with half a million tons of forty-five-year-old unexploded bombs in caves that could shift any minute."

"Buried forever, then."

"Until we develop something that can see through solid rock, that's my guess."

"If it's here at all."

"Oh, something's here. They didn't go to all that trouble just to hide some bombs." The man shook his head. "Raise a tombstone to the Nazi treasures, let the SS have the last laugh; that's my answer. There's already been enough blood spilled over whatever's buried there."

Kurt drove back into the worn-down drabness of Arn-

stadt and called Ferret from the safety of one of the new
telephone boxes the Wessies were planting in every city
square. "It's impossible to tell," he reported.

"No matter," the little man replied in his flat, childlike
lisp. "What did you find?"

Kurt relayed the events of the afternoon. "The chalk cliffs
stretch for maybe seven, eight kilometers. It's an impossible
task. It'd take years to sift through a tenth of the area."

"But as yet they have found nothing?"

"Three empty caves." Kurt admitted to doubt with, "How
can you be sure that this Amber Room of yours is not buried
there?"

"I'm sure," came the quiet reply.

"Then why must I travel to Weimar?"

"To be even more certain. As long as they have not found
the first treasure, we can proceed with the knowledge that
our treasure is elsewhere."

Our treasure. Kurt felt the thrill of sudden wealth. "So
where is elsewhere?"

"That we shall soon discuss upon your return," Ferret
replied. "And remember what we discussed before you departed Schwerin."

"I haven't forgotten."

"The first order their workers will receive," Ferret went
on, "once something has been found, is to deny everything.
So don't listen to their words. Watch their eyes. Their eyes
won't lie."

CHAPTER

11

Jeffrey made his way down Mount Street from the printer's, barely able to see above the boxes stacked in his arms. He kicked at the shop door until Alexander emerged from the back to usher him in.

"Thank you, thank you. Another trip and I do believe my back would have sought refuge in traction."

"Don't even joke like that." Jeffrey dropped the load and looked around the shop. Engraved invitations in matching envelopes were stacked like ivory mountains on two Empire side tables. "Those are ready to go?"

"Nine hundred," Alexander replied with tired satisfaction. "Your four are all that remain."

"I bet you'll be glad to see the last of this."

"On the contrary, I've quite enjoyed the effort." Alexander gave a weary smile. "Several times I've caught myself wondering why this aspect of godly service was not granted more attention."

"That service is fun?"

Alexander shook his head. "No, that it is fulfilling." He bent over one of Jeffrey's boxes, slit the tape with a practiced motion, and held one of the cards up to the light. "Marvelous," he declared. "Simply marvelous quality, wouldn't you say?"

The invitation was a large folded card of textured ivory

with gilt edging. On the cover was a splendid color photograph of the chalice. Alexander opened the invitation and read in dramatic tones, "Patrons of the Religious Heritage of Poland request the honour of your presence at a gala banquet on Saturday, the twenty-fifth of February, in the Main Ballroom of the Ritz Hotel, Piccadilly, London W1." He tapped out the smaller type with the edge of his pen. "Black tie, R.S.V.P., et cetera, et cetera."

He separated the reply card, read off, "Kindly reserve so many places for the gala banquet hosted by the Patrons of the Religious Heritage of Poland. Enclosed is our cheque for so much at two hundred and fifty pounds per reservation."

He replaced the card. "I think our response will be very good indeed. Just today I received word that some royalty expect to attend."

"That's great."

"Minor royalty, mind you. But their presence will certainly add a nice touch to the program, don't you think?"

Jeffrey followed him into the back office, where every seat but one was covered in a deluge of papers and forms. "The Brits sure love their royals."

The sound of the doorbell brought a moan from Alexander. He raised his head from the pile of documents, printouts, address lists, and menu forms, and threw his assistant a harried look. "For the next three weeks, until this gala is behind us, you shall have to deal with all but the emergencies. Except for your trip to East Germany, of course, which I am beginning to regret."

Jeffrey looked to the corner mirror that afforded a view of the shop's front door. "It's Sydney Greenfield."

"Not an emergency by any stretch of the imagination," Alexander replied, dropping his head back to his work. "He's all yours."

Sydney Greenfield owned no shop of his own, yet managed to eke an income from offering the goods of others to buyers in and around London. Jeffrey had not seen him since hearing news of his changed fortunes. As he walked toward the entrance, he observed that Sydney had replaced his shiny broadcloth for an elegant outfit whose hand-tailored lines did much to mask his girth. Sydney entered with his usual panache, yet looked oddly unbalanced without his sidekick, a little parrot of a man known to the world simply as Ty.

Jeffrey shook hands and led Sydney to a pair of eighteenth-century walnut armchairs. Once his guest was seated and had been offered coffee, Jeffrey asked, "Where's Ty?"

"Down with a case of the throat, poor man." Greenfield sipped from the delicate porcelain with his little finger cocked at a ridiculous angle. He waved a careless hand toward the back of the shop. "Might have a buyer for that little item there in the corner. That is, if the price is right."

The piece in question was a French side cabinet made in Paris around 1855, the interior lined in fragrant cedar and the exterior in highly polished ebony. What made this cabinet so extraordinary was the high-quality *boulle*, or brass and tortoise shell inlay, that adorned the facade. The pair of front doors were bound with shining hinges and corners and keyholes, their central panels decorated with shimmering maidens playing lyres. The top and central pillar featured trios of angels fashioned of such gentle hues as to vanish and reappear with the passage of light.

"That's a rather pricey item," Jeffrey warned.

"I'm sure it is, lad," Greenfield replied easily. "But if the article was going into the home of an old and trusted associate, I imagine you might be willing to lop off a nought or two."

Jeffrey lifted his eyebrows. "Andrew told me you were on to something big."

"Oh yes." Greenfield showed vast pleasure. "It's amazing how many people are out there with more money than taste."

"He was wondering if you'd actually crossed the line."

"Andrew's a fine man, one of the few I'd take such a question from without getting my hair up. I haven't, lad, and that's the truth. On my honor, I haven't." He drained his cup, held it aloft for a refill. "No need to, as a matter of fact."

"People will buy your creations knowing they're rubbish?"

"Pay good money for them in the process," he replied. "You see, lad, I've spent donkey's years dealing with people who've scrabbled all their lives for the filthy lucre, as it were. Never had time to learn taste, they didn't. So here they are,

finally striding along the top of the muck heap, and some
bloke comes by and offers them a pretty bauble for their
living room at sixty thousand quid. They go right through
the ruddy roof, they do."

"I'm with you," Jeffrey said.

" 'Course you are. Always knew you for a sharp lad. So
up I pop with a pretty little dresser or chaise lounge or what
have you, maybe not quite so pretty but not bad all the same."

"And the price is half the other."

"Not even, lad. Not even. Both are old, though, you see.
Both have that scent of class to them."

"After a fashion."

Greenfield waved at the words as though swatting flies.
"Details, lad. Mere details, in their eyes at least, and that's
where it counts. Dealers in the genuine articles and people
in the know aren't likely to be invited into homes of such as
these, you see. So they look from one item to the other, and
most times decide they'd just as soon have what I'm selling
and pocket the extra."

Jeffrey thought it over, decided, "Smart. Very smart
idea."

"I agree," Alexander called from his alcove.

"Thank you both. I take that as high praise, indeed, coming from professionals such as your good selves." Greenfield
set down his cup, glanced around the shop, went on, "Mind
you, if I'd been given the choice, I'd much rather spend my
days surrounded by such beauties."

Alexander emerged to walk over and shake Sydney's
hand. "You are always welcome here. Always."

"You're a real gentleman, you are, Mr. Kantor. And I've
said the same to anyone who listens."

Alexander accepted the compliment with a solemn nod.
"We don't always have a choice as to which cards life deals
us, though, do we?"

"No, Mr. Kantor, we don't. And more's the pity."

"Of course, if you are as successful as it sounds, you might
have an opportunity to fill your own life with the genuine
articles."

"Just what I'm hoping to do," Greenfield replied, eyeing
the cabinet.

Alexander smiled briefly. "You yourself are certainly one of those able to appreciate works of art for what they are."

"Kind of you to say so, Mr. Kantor. I try to be."

"Well, if anything in this shop ever takes your fancy, I believe we could make you a special offer of twenty percent off our price." Frosty gray eyes twinkled. "Don't you think that would be appropriate, Jeffrey?"

"A special dealer's discount," Jeffrey agreed.

Greenfield looked from one to the other and said gravely, "I'm touched, gentlemen. I truly am."

"Now, you'll have to excuse me. I am literally over my head in preparations for this gala."

"Of course, of course." Greenfield stood and shook the proffered hand, hesitated, then pointed toward the glass-sided Art Deco display case where the chalice stood in solitary splendor. "I hope you gentlemen won't mind me saying this, but it seems passing strange that you'd leave that article on display in your shop like this."

"What makes you say that? Our security is exemplary." Alexander had already turned and retreated to his alcove. "Besides, everything here is heavily insured."

"Maybe so, but this isn't your own goods, now, is it?" Greenfield walked over to the cabinet. "It's one thing to run a risk with something that's here to be sold. Holding a priceless item you're supposed to return is another kettle of fish, far as I see it."

"We've never had any trouble before," Jeffrey said.

"But these ads and the invitations you've done with the chalice in all its glory," Greenfield objected. "You're announcing to all the world you've got this medieval artifact here in your shop. Sounds dodgy to me."

Jeffrey turned to where Alexander stood by the alcove's entrance. "Maybe we should arrange for a night security guard."

"No good, lad," Greenfield replied. "You'd just be erasing all doubt that the chalice is here. What I'd suggest is, lay it low in a vault. Myself, I use Barclay's up by Charing Cross. Best security in the business, by my vote. They know how to deal with works such as these."

"Coutts is our bank," Jeffrey said doubtfully.

"We're not talking about banking business, now, are we? This is security. Offer it to the biggest museums, they do. Make a professional job of it. They'll rent you guards, armored security display cases for the event, cart it over in an armored car, bring it back, no muss, no fuss."

"Another problem." Alexander wiped a weary brow. "Just when I need it least."

"Handling it that way would be a load off our mind," Jeffrey pointed out.

"What you've got here is priceless, irreplaceable," Greenfield said, bending down for a closer look. "An incredible risk. If you allow, I'll have them come by to collect this beauty and put it in storage until your gala evening. Armored car would take it both ways, set you up with a portable alarm system, display case, guards for the evening. Just say the word."

"Maybe we ought to move it," Jeffrey agreed.

"See to it, then," Alexander complied.

"That's the spirit," Greenfield straightened. "Be a pleasure to help out gentlemen like yourselves, take part in a worthy deed. I'll just go have a word with the men in charge and get back to you."

Once Jeffrey had ushered Greenfield out of the shop, he returned to Alexander. "Did you mean what you said, about regretting this East Germany trip?"

Alexander did not raise his head from the sheaf of papers. "You must admit, it does come at a rather inopportune time."

"Do you want me to put it off?"

"No, of course not. I simply wish for the impossible, to have you go and at the same time have you stay and help."

"I suppose I could call and put them off."

"No, you cannot," Alexander replied firmly. "Business like this simply cannot be postponed. You are building what may prove to be lifelong business relationships."

"I'll be back as soon as I can."

"Take whatever time is required," Alexander said. "I'll muddle on along here quite adequately, I assure you."

"Is there anything I can do to help out now?"

"There is, as a matter of fact." Alexander hefted a ream of faxed pages. "I've received these menu suggestions from the Ritz, but I have so much going on I can't seem to decide on anything. Could you and Katya possibly meet with the banqueting manager and take care of it for me?"

"Any chance we could ask for samples?"

But Alexander was already buried once more in his work. "Just no heavy sauces, that's all I ask. I would rather our guests go home inspired than bloated."

Jeffrey reached for his coat. "No problem."

"Oh, and chocolate. We must have some chocolate for dessert. I've already been forewarned that one of our honored honorables throws quite a tiff unless indulged with a chocolate finale."

Jeffrey walked over to where Katya waited in the Ritz Hotel's marbled foyer, watching the bustling scene with bright eyes. He told her, "Even the bellhops in this place sound as if they've graduated from Cambridge."

"I've spotted two film stars in the past five minutes." She gave herself an excited little hug. "I almost forgot there was a world out there beyond my exam papers, and now look at me."

"Yes, look at you," Jeffrey agreed. "Come on. The banqueting manager's been held up, so we're his guests for tea."

The Ritz Tea Salon was in the middle of the hotel, up three stairs and through an entrance adorned with floral trellises. The chamber itself was done as a fairy queen's garden. Little marble-topped tables dotted a pink and gold salon adorned with gilded cupids and hanging flower arrangements. Waitresses whisked about in starched crinoline and petticoats.

Tea was served in delicate porcelain and poured through a silver strainer. Tiny sandwiches and scones and muffins arrived on a three-story circular silver palaver. Clotted cream and strawberry jam in little silver bowls completed the repast.

Katya watched with wide eyes as Jeffrey poured her tea. Leaning over, she said in an awestruck whisper, "I feel as if I'm inside a box of valentine chocolates."

Jeffrey whipped open the banqueting menus, said, "Okay,

now to business. I think we should go for steak and baked potato. No, on second thought, how about a real treat—barbecued baby back ribs and coleslaw. I'm sure this crowd hasn't ever seen anything like that before."

Katya gave him a horrified look. "You can't be serious."

" 'Course I am. Get them some bibs, sure, and we'll need something great for starters." He pretended to read down the page. "Here it is. A paper plate piled high with boiled shrimp."

She reached across and plucked the menu from his hands. Katya studied the pages, a frown of concentration puckering her features. Then she brightened. "Oh, look at this. Lobster mousse on a bed of spinach and wrapped in strips of smoked salmon. Doesn't that sound wonderful as a starter?"

"Personally, I'd rather have the shrimp," he replied, loving her.

"Then for the main course, yes, stuffed pheasant in a sorrel and peppercorn sauce with a frou-frou of vegetables." She smiled. "When I was a little girl, I used to think that if I ate a peppercorn I'd grow a mole."

"What?"

She returned to the menu. "It made perfect sense to me."

"A frou-frou of anything doesn't sound very appetizing to my ears. I think we'd be a lot better off going with corn on the cob."

Katya turned the page. "And what to drink?"

"We'll just stick some wash buckets full of ice and bottles in the middle of the tables," Jeffrey replied. "Let everybody grab whatever they like."

She lifted her head to reply, then focused on someone behind him. "We've got company."

Jeffrey swiveled in his chair and caught sight of the Count di Garibaldi, a real-estate magnate who was both a friend of Alexander's and a long-time client. The old gentleman was bent over the hand of a ravishing young woman less than a third his age. She wore a clinging bit of nothing and a king's ransom worth of jewelry, and had two giant Afghan hounds in tow.

Katya made innocent eyes. "She must be his niece."

"One of many," Jeffrey agreed, rising to his feet. When

the Count had finished following the young lady's swaying departure with frank admiration, Jeffrey waved him over.

"Jeffrey, Katya." The Count approached them with a regal air and a genuine smile. "This is indeed a great pleasure."

"How are you, sir?"

"Utterly splendid. And how is Alexander? Not waning, I hope."

Jeffrey smiled. "Practicing his dance steps the last time I saw. He wants to have his jig down properly for the occasion."

"He's teaching you his odd brand of humor, I see." The Count glanced at his watch. "I'm a bit early for an engagement. May I join you for a glass of sherry?"

"It would be our honor."

"I received something quite remarkable in the mail this morning," Count di Garibaldi said, pulling Alexander's invitation from his coat pocket. "Of course I would be delighted to attend and offer whatever support you might require."

"Alexander will be very happy to hear that. Thank you."

"And this chalice. Lovely, just lovely. But do you know, what strikes me is how Italian in appearance it seems. Yet you say this is Polish?"

"It came from a Polish collection," Jeffrey replied. "And Alexander was told it was probably made in the Cracow region."

"Interesting. Most interesting." The Count slipped on a pair of reading spectacles, pointed at the picture. "You see this filigree work at the base, that appears very Florentine to my eye. In fact, the whole thing appears somewhat familiar, as though I had seen it before. I don't suppose that is possible."

"Extremely doubtful," Jeffrey said. "The whole collection's been locked in a crypt for ages."

The Count was clearly not convinced. "I don't need to tell you that I am quite well connected in Rome, and I feel that I have . . . Well, no, I suppose I am mistaken if you say this is definitely a Polish piece."

"It is definitely from a Polish collection," Katya said.

"That is the whole point of this event," Jeffrey added. "To

show the beauty of Polish religious artifacts and to create a fund for their preservation."

"Well." The Count folded his glasses and placed them with the invitation back in his pocket. "I am so looking forward to seeing you on the evening. I am quite sure it will not only be a great success, but a splendid fete for all present."

CHAPTER
12

Dinner that night was a most intimate affair, prepared in Jeffrey's minuscule kitchen, a place so narrow that to pass each other gave them excuses for gentle contact and sweet caresses. They ate, and tasted nothing but each other. They drank, and knew little beyond the flavor of their love. They shared silences that transcended all need for words, and they spoke simply to enjoy the sound of each other's voice.

After dinner, Jeffrey led Katya the brief distance to Park Lane, then through the underpass and into Hyde Park's dark confines. It was a cold, clear night. From their unlit path winding through ancient trees, the stars appeared to rest just overhead, silently flickering friends set there to keep them company.

"I'm really excited about our trip to Erfurt," she said, snuggling deeper inside her coat. "It's an unexpected gift, a reward for these past months."

Jeffrey nodded, not able to think of such things just then. He stopped her by the lake's edge, checked in all directions to make sure no one was near.

Then he looked at her. In the silvery light, her eyes were expanding, growing, drawing him in.

She pointed to where the lake ended. "That was where we found Ling."

He nodded. His heart had swelled to the point that it blocked his words.

"I've always thought it was a gift from God, finding that little bird." She gazed unblinkingly up at him. "Keeping us together. Showing me that love can overcome all odds, all fears, all reason."

She did not drop her gaze as she slipped one hand into his. "I've never thanked you for that lesson, have I?"

There's no need, he thought, but could not speak. He remained immobile, mute. Now that he was here, the words would not come.

Katya retrieved her hand, slipped off her glove, ran her fingers down the side of his face. "The answer is yes, Jeffrey."

"I haven't asked you yet," he said, his voice a bare whisper.

"This is my gift of thanks," she said. Frozen smoky veils billowed around her face in time to her soft-spoken words. "I love you, Jeffrey Allen Sinclair."

"Will you marry me?" The words did not come from him. He stood at a distance, his heart hammering a frantic pace, and watched a stranger speak for him. Again. "I love you, and I want you to be my wife. Will you marry me, Katya Nichols?"

She wrapped her arms around him, said to his chest, "I have loved you since the very first moment I saw you."

"Is that a yes?"

"Yes for now, yes for tomorrow, yes for all the tomorrows God grants us."

She looked up at him with eyes as luminous as two earthbound stars. "You may kiss the bride."

CHAPTER
13

The bar was on a small side street two blocks from Schwerin's official Soviet Officers' Club. As surrounding old-town structures emerged from construction scaffolding all bright and shiny and renovated, the officers' club had sunk to ever-greater depths of obscurity. The front facade, the only portion of the club that had ever been painted, was now gray and grimy and flaking. The remaining exterior was crumbling brick and black-veined plaster. The double entrance doors no longer closed entirely and had to be chained shut at night. To either side were shattered marquees featuring brawny men and women on smudged, fly-blown posters.

The back-street bar where Kurt stood and drank and waited was little more than a hovel, its planked flooring scuffed and seldom swept. Huddled in the dimly lit depths were hard-drinking men and women who felt far more at home in such remnants of the old regime. Here gathered those who were shunned by the new democracy, and who in turn eluded the attention of new masters they neither knew nor welcomed. As the city's renovation crept farther and farther, they retreated in grumbling hostile throngs and watched helplessly as the noose of new laws and alien changes settled around their necks. Kurt waited in the smoky bar and sipped his beer and sighed at the irony of it all.

Kurt's position at the bar's back corner offered him an excellent view of all who entered and left, including the Russian who stepped into the gloomy depths. Kurt remained hunkered over his drink, watching from the corner of his eye.

Iron discipline kept the Russian's advancing age in check. The body was ramrod straight, the gaze as direct and unbending as his spine. The uniform was neat and pressed in rigid lines. His officer's cap bore the gold stars of senior rank. Kurt straightened slightly. Immediately the colonel's gaze swung his way. Kurt waited to breathe until the piercing eyes continued their careful sweep of the room.

The colonel walked to the bar, set his cap to one side, spoke quietly to the bartender. Russians were not an uncommon sight in this bar—either aides waiting out their superiors' stay in the officers' club or officers seeking less public places to do their drinking. Yet this man was very different from the others lost in the convenient shadows. He did not even unbend when drinking his beer. His hair was gray and short-cropped, his face lined but unsagging. Kurt moved closer, wondering what it must have cost such a man to come here.

The officer did not raise his eyes from his glass as Kurt sidled up beside him and asked in very poor Russian, "Buy you a drink?"

"My glass is full," the officer replied, his German heavily accented but exact.

"You are allowed only one beer?" Kurt pressed on in Russian.

The officer turned and held him with eyes the color and temperature of a Siberian winter sky. "I'll not stand here and listen to you desecrate my mother tongue."

Kurt switched to a venomously soft German. "I have money and I'm buying. But that doesn't interest a man of principle like you. Of course not. No doubt you come here to mingle with the locals. Show off your medals." He turned and stomped off to a corner table.

Reluctantly the officer picked up his cap and his beer and followed Kurt. He stood over the table and announced, "We speak in German."

"We can speak in Swahili for all I care," Kurt muttered to his beer.

The officer remained standing. "I will not be insulted with offers to buy my coat or my boots."

"I wouldn't have to kill time in this dive waiting for an officer, if that was all I was after," Kurt snapped. "A hundred of your soldiers are standing on the street corners selling everything from their belts to their guns to their commandant's medals. I could dress and arm a platoon in five minutes out there."

It was true. Stricter punishment had removed weapons from display at the roadside stands, but all could still be had for a price. In recent weeks, enterprising Wessie journalists had exposed the depths of the crisis by purchasing one hundred automatic weapons, a case of grenades, fifty land mines, twenty kilos of plastic explosive, a rocket launcher, and a late-model tank. All from broke, hungry Russian soldiers hanging around Ossie city squares. All for pennies on the dollar. They even filmed a negotiation to buy three jet fighters from disillusioned pilots.

Kurt reminded himself of his purpose and offered a truce. "Why do we quarrel? It wasn't so long ago that we were almost as allies."

"True, true," the colonel subsided. "Perhaps because I am so angry with my own fate, I strike where there is no need."

"I know the sentiment," Kurt admitted, "all too well."

"Problems are mounting," the colonel said, "here and at home." With a deft motion he raised and drained his glass and set it on the table. "Perhaps I will have that drink after all."

Kurt was on his feet at once and headed for the bar. He returned swiftly, carrying a pair of vodka shots and glasses of beer. Russian boilermakers for them both. He motioned with the beers for the colonel to be seated. "Join me."

The iron-hard man fought briefly with himself, nodded agreement. "My men are hungry," the colonel replied, and sank heavily into a chair. "Our salaries have remained the same, while the ruble has been devalued to *one-fifteenth* of its former worth. Our shipments of supplies from Russia have almost stopped. There is no food. No coal. No money."

"Yes, well," Kurt said with feigned nonchalance. "That's why we are here, I suppose."

"We serve a nation that no longer exists and has no barracks to return us to," the officer persisted. Muted earth tones of browns and deep reds colored his uniform, from heavy wool greatcoat to carefully tended boots. The only bright splashes were the gold stars of rank on his shoulders and cap. "We have a dozen new masters, and no masters at all. Every night there are screams and fights among men who have lost their esprit de corps."

"With that I cannot help," Kurt said. "With the food, perhaps. But not the fact that you are now a federation at war with itself."

"I was a good officer," the soldier replied. "My men were good men. We had a duty and we did it well."

"You were an oppressor," Kurt flashed, his control momentarily snapping. "You were never wanted here. Never."

The frosty eyes narrowed. "Our task was not to be loved."

Kurt backed down. "Yes. Well." He raised his vodka. "To the past."

"Much safer than the future," the colonel agreed, and tossed back his glass. He breathed fumes, blinked hard, asked, "You heard of the Kazakh riots?"

"Yes." Seventeen thousand soldiers at the Biakanur Space Center in Kazakhstan had rioted, leaving three dead and countless wounded, many fatally. Earlier, their officers had bartered their services as common laborers to the space center authorities in exchange for food and cigarettes. The space center no longer had money to pay employees, and the soldiers were slowly starving. It had been a good agreement, except for the tragic fact that the soldiers had never been paid; the space center had not received their own promised provisions, and had been left with less than enough to feed themselves. The troops had responded by burning down all they had built and several other buildings besides.

Kurt sipped his beer. "Now perhaps we can get down to business."

The flat tones of a defeated soldier returned. "To business."

"I need information," Kurt said. "Nothing sensitive or

harmful to your precious nation." He grinned coldly, corrected himself. "Nations."

The officer let it pass. "What kind of information?"

"About a German soldier. He was captured by Red Army soldiers as they invaded Poland—"

"The correct term is liberated," the officer corrected.

Kurt waved it aside. "He was questioned and sent to a POW camp, and he died in Siberia in 1946. We wish to know what he said during his interrogation."

"Forty-seven years is a long time to carry a grudge," the colonel ventured.

"He was a doctor," Kurt persisted. "No SS horror. Nothing involved with state security. You break no code."

The colonel bridled. "I break every code just by being here."

"Uncertain times," Kurt soothed. "They call for special measures. Would you not rather search this out for me than sell your guns?"

The colonel subsided. "This will cost you."

"Of course it will."

"Even before I know if it is possible, I will have to make payments of my own."

Kurt frowned. "It would be far better to promise payment upon delivery."

The officer snorted. "We have had our fill of promises. We have warehouses full of promises instead of food."

"There is that," Kurt admitted.

"I will be paid for the search, and more for the find," the colonel declared.

Kurt's hand dived into his pocket, emerged with an envelope. "The doctor's name and our first payment, then."

The colonel slipped the envelope beneath the table's edge, counted, pursed his lips. "The first of many payments, if they are all of a size."

"No snippet of information can be too minor," Kurt told him. "We seek all possible details."

Hard eyes bore down. "It would help to know what you are seeking."

Kurt forced himself not to flinch. "Details," he repeated. "We are collectors of the minute, and we will pay the most for the most complete report."

CHAPTER
14

Because of the snow and ice and threat of more, Jeffrey and Katya flew from London to Frankfurt-am-Main, then took a train to Erfurt. Berlin would have been a marginally closer airport to Erfurt, but all the flights were booked solid by movers and shakers seeking to influence or lean on or sell to or feed off the new-old capital's massive restructuring.

The sky hovering above the German landscape was leaden gray, the clouds so close as to rest upon the undulating hills marking the old border country. There was little snow, but the midafternoon frost appeared permanent, unchanging, an eternal part of this heavy-laden landscape. Trees were bowed and motionless, their limbs burdened and hoary white. Even the grass beside their slow-moving train was frozen at icy attention.

They had their compartment to themselves, which was good. They needed the time alone to balance their love and their decision with the demands of business. They spoke of many things and left the most remarkable unsaid. The entire world seemed new, yet unchanged. Their conversation was casual, yet eternally serious, since now it was part of a lifetime they had agreed to spend together.

Jeffrey sat alongside Katya and watched her and spoke with her, and all the while he marveled at the fact that she was to be his wife. His *wife*. He could not help but smile. The word alone boggled the mind.

"Why are you smiling?"

He shook his head, unable to voice his thoughts just then. Instead he said, "Would you mind if I asked you how you came to faith?"

Katya looked at him a long moment, then asked in return, "Is that what you and Mama talked about?"

"Partly," he said, and felt an ease between them, a fluidity that could not be contained. His *wife*.

She sat beside him, very prim and proper in a dark-gray suit of softest wool. From time to time, however, one stockinged toe would emerge from her pumps to caress his ankle. There was a casualness to her motion that spoke of rightful intimacy. "It was probably very sad."

"It was."

"I don't want to hear about it right now, okay? But please tell me some other time."

"Whenever you like."

"My faith." She brought up one of his hands to give it a closer inspection. "I don't feel as if it's mine at all. It is a gift from the Father that I hold in trust."

"That's beautiful," he said softly.

"Mama was always strong in her faith, and I was raised to simply accept it as a part of life. As young as I was, I could see how much it meant to her in those tough times after my father left."

"You don't have to talk about this if you don't want to."

"It's all right. For me, growth in faith has always meant realizing that there's a lot I don't know, and probably even more that I don't have right. This keeps me from ever being too dogmatic about things, remembering times in the past when I thought I had it all perfect, only to discover later that it wasn't nearly as correct or complete as I imagined."

He moved back far enough to be able to see her face. "You sound so wise when you talk like this, Katya." He searched for some way to explain how he felt. "It humbles me."

She rewarded him with a brief kiss before returning to her story. "A few years after my father left us, we moved to England. As I grew older I kept looking for a healing faith in all the wrong places. I was sure I was going to find it in a church or in a person. Somebody who was going to sit me down and draw out this path and tell me where to put my feet and say, go from A to B to C and then you're home. But faith doesn't work like that.

"I think what I really wanted was somebody who would be my new daddy. Somebody who would be there when I needed him, who wouldn't leave me. It took a long time before I finally accepted that I really wasn't getting to know God at all, just another man—a preacher or a deacon or somebody in the church. They were substitutes, and sooner or later I was going to have to start looking for myself. Studying the Bible by myself. Praying by myself. Making contact directly with Christ, by myself. Making the relationship a *personal* one.

"When you grow up in the church, you know all the right answers. But that doesn't mean Christ is in your life. There are a lot of people who call themselves Christians and who hide from God when He manifests himself. In Genesis, it is not God who runs from people, but people who flee from God. Some things never change."

Katya bent over his fingers, sliding a feather-light caress around each in turn. "This lesson wasn't fully learned until I went for a semester as an exchange student to Warsaw. I went primarily to improve my Polish, but I also studied what they called History of Political and Legal Doctrines."

"Sounds positively riveting."

She settled his hand in her lap. "It wasn't so bad, really. And it gave me some incredible lessons in keeping my temper."

"I'm all for that," Jeffrey said.

"The class was taught by a staunch Party member. I mean a real flag waver. I was the only Westerner in the class, and he kept saying these things as though hoping I was going to explode. I never did, though. There wasn't anything to be gained by giving him the pleasure of seeing me lose it."

"What was the class about?"

"It was an exhaustive coverage of obscure Soviet bureaucratic Communist thinkers. Not Polish. Soviet."

"And the Polish students didn't complain?"

"Not in class. Not in hearing range of the professor. If a Pole made it as far as university, he had already learned to keep his mouth shut around Party members, especially when it came to complaining about the Soviets." Katya's eyes were frosty. "The Soviet theory of history is linear. That is, all events represent a class struggle and lead inevitably to socialism. This phrase is repeated ad infinitum—the *inevitability* of socialism. So all the studies concentrated on events that supported this perspective. Everything else was virtually ignored.

"History studies revolved around uprisings, strikes, workers' actions, and the cruelest possible examples of capitalist exploitation of workers. The thrust, the key, was always the ownership of production. Their basic principle was that until workers owned *all* land and *all* resources and *all* factories and *all* stores—through the central government, of course—these uprisings would continue. It was *inevitable*. Events so obscure they did not even deserve mention in a Western encyclopedia or textbook were treated as turning points on the path to Communism."

He made a face. "How could you put up with that stuff?"

"It was hard," she admitted. "But these are the lies that shaped Poland for over forty years. I kept reminding myself of that, and I studied the Bible harder than I ever had in my life. There, at least, I knew I could remember what truth really was. And when I finally returned home I knew that one reward of the journey, something I would treasure for all my days, was this coming to know a personal relationship with my Savior. Beyond the confines of any church or doctrine or earthly activity. He was my Lord, and He was my friend."

At the last stop before crossing the former border, the gray-suited West German train conductors gave way to a pudgy man with one wandering eye and a rail-thin girl with spiked blond hair. They wore uniforms of electric blue, replete with broad leather belts and shiny brass medals. They barked a demand for tickets, inspected them minutely. Katya asked them a polite question, received a smirk and several short words in reply.

"The conductors are much more imposing here," she said

when they departed. "Less discreet than the West German officials."

"I noticed," Jeffrey replied. "What did you ask them?"

"When we would arrive at the old border crossing. They said to watch out for the tank barriers."

Rolling hills gave way to a broad, flat expanse, a plateau that afforded a clear view in every direction of a frozen, silent winterscape. Soon enough the fields began growing a tragic crop of watchtowers and giant lights and crossed railings dug into metal-lined trenches. Although the barbed wire had been removed, the former dead man's zone remained marked by row after row after row of ten-foot-high concrete pillars. They stretched out to both horizons, endless lines of slender tombstones.

"Before the Wall fell, borders like this were a lot noisier," Katya told him, her voice subdued. "The dogs had vicious-sounding barks, especially at night. And the guards were always shouting, never just speaking."

Standing in the middle of the field was a single abandoned building, a vast multistoried structure washed to unpainted grayness by passing seasons.

"It must have been a prewar factory," Katya guessed. "It was in the fire zone; see the stands where they had the spotlights and the machine-gun placements?"

"I see," Jeffrey replied quietly.

"Look at the building; you can see how all the windows and doors on the first two floors are bricked up. It was probably too close to the Western border to let even the guards use; they might have tried to escape."

Their train swung around a bend, and the roadway border appeared. Tall stone and mortar guardhouses loomed over a point just prior to where the road diminished from four well-paved and brightly marked lanes to a narrow, rutted passage. The towers showed bare walls toward the east; all windows and gun emplacements and entrenched vigilance faced the other way.

Once beyond the border, barbed wire sprouted and grew everywhere. Everything was fenced—roads, train tracks, nearby houses, footpaths. The train slowed for another bend, and slowed, and slowed, and remained slow. The track became increasingly bumpy, the surroundings ever more grim.

"It's like another world," Jeffrey said.

"We've passed through a fifty-year time warp," Katya replied. "The price of Communism. One of them, anyway."

The houses were immediately older. Instead of Western double-paned windows, there were warped squares of hand-drawn glass set in flaking wooden panels. Shutters and doors and walls shed paint like old snow, if they were painted at all. Bricks stood exposed through shattered plaster, timbers bared ancient cracks. Bowed walls were supported by tree trunks stripped and replanted at an angle. Weeds grew waist high through cracked pavement. Cars turned tiny and plastic and sputtered smoky spumes.

At the first station after the border, the train ejected a steady stream of people. Most carried boxes and bales and bags and pushed strollers that contained not babies, but more boxes and bags. The people looked very tired. Exhausted.

"Shoppers," Katya explained. "There is still greater variety in the West, and the people trust the stores there more than they do the ones here."

Signs of renovation and new construction dotted the landscape like flecks of bright new paint on an old scarred canvas. Flashing lights and yellow construction trucks signaled roadworks almost every time a highway came into view. New, unfinished factories rose alongside structures built more from rust than steel. But despite the evident signs of change, the predominant color remained gray, the main impression one of deep fatigue. Bone tiredness of both the people and the land. That, and cold.

They arrived in Erfurt two hours late. Night had fallen hard on the city, engulfing it in almost total darkness. Occasional streetlights poured tiny islands of light into a sea of black. Here and there, apartment windows glowed in yellow solitude against the night. But the dominant feeling was of darkness.

Their hotel, the Erfurter Hof, was located just across a cement and asphalt square from the main train station. The centuries-old building had been redecorated in a bland Communist style, all hard edges and overly bright colors and

charmless prints of big-muscled men and women in determined parade. They were joined at the check-in counter by
a large group of weary businesspeople in rumpled suits and
dresses, all off the same train from the West as themselves.

Jeffrey collected their keys, joined the elevator's silent
throng, walked Katya down to her room. He saw his own
weariness mirrored in her face. "I don't understand how I
could grow so tired just sitting down all day."

"Travel does that," she agreed. She offered her face up for
a kiss. "I hope you sleep as well as I intend to."

His room was high-ceilinged and furnished with light-
wood beds and chairs and low tables screwed into the floor.
Jeffrey drew his drapes against the train station's constant
rumble and gave in to his rising fatigue.

CHAPTER
15

Erika paused on the Schwerin office building stairs to catch her breath and go over Ferret's instructions. It still rankled, this working at the beck and call of a half-finished man. He sat downstairs in her car, waiting for her to walk up and talk and go down and report. Then she had to smile. At least he had let her drive.

A taxi ride with Ferret was the most harrowing experience of a passenger's lifetime. Fear was an ever-present companion from the moment Ferret nodded his acceptance of the address and leveled his nose as close to the windshield as the steering wheel permitted. Ferret's vision was so poor he could scarcely make out other cars, especially at night, which was the only time he drove. He tended to stick to quieter ways and hope he would not meet anyone at crossroads. Traffic lights were seldom seen until the last possible moment. This meant he had the choice of standing on the brakes or shooting the intersection at blinding speeds. Either way, his passengers lost years.

Erika sighed, a sound she was making more and more these days, and walked down the hall. At least this work required a few of the talents she had garnered over the years. And though she did not understand what they were doing, it afforded her a small hope of moving on, of escaping this place where life as she knew it had disappeared.

For most Ossies, the nation of East Germany had been a prison, a landlocked cell without doors or hope of release. The slightest glimpse toward the outside world had been both forbidden and frightfully dangerous. If a child had happened to mention at school that his family watched Wessie programs intentionally beamed over the Wall, the entire family—children included—had faced arrest, interrogation, and a loss of job and hearth and home.

Ossies had responded by turning inward, especially in the smaller communities. Villages had become islands, struggling to provide barriers against a world that was beyond their control or understanding. Automatic suspicion of newcomers had kept Stasi infiltration to a minimum. Choosing brides and husbands from local stock had preserved local solidarity, even if communities were so small as to require inbreeding. Anything had been deemed better than letting in the dangers of the unknown, the outside, the secret, the hidden.

But for the keepers like Erika, the former system had provided security, sufficient wealth, and the thrill of life-and-death power over the masses. For them, the Wall's collapse had been the unthinkable brought to life, the subsequent investigations and trials beyond belief. Across the former country, worried conversations began and ended with the argument voiced by every defendant brought into court: We served our country as we were trained and ordered to serve. How can another country come in and fire us and put us on trial and accuse us under a different country's laws? How is this possible? Show us where we broke the laws of our own country! Show us!

Erika watched the unfolding drama from the relative safety of a new identity in a strange town and wished only to be away. Questions of guilt left her tired. As far as she was concerned, the difference between Stasi tactics and those of the West—such as the headline-grabbing 1982 alliance between Pope John Paul II and President Reagan to keep Solidarity alive after Poland declared martial law—was that the West had won the undeclared war. Safety did not rest in reason. These days, safety was possible only for those who could come up with enough cash to buy a new life.

Erika rapped sharply on the door, then pushed it open at the sound of a woman's voice from within. She entered a cramped office overflowing with books and ledgers, looked down on a middle-aged woman whose dark hair spilled over her face as she continued to peruse legal documents. Without looking up, the woman raised a nicotine-stained finger toward the chair across from her desk. Erika remained standing, waiting with patience born of a lifetime's experience.

The silence extended through another minute, then the woman slammed the tome shut and reached with a practiced gesture for her cigarette pack. It was only then that she raised her eyes and focused on Erika. With that first glance, her motions ceased.

Erika felt the faintest thrill of pleasure and a fleeting memory of a former world, when it had rarely been necessary even to show her badge to get total and unswerving attention. Badges had been superfluous for one accustomed to holding Stasi power. People had looked and seen and understood. Their freedom had depended upon diligent attention and absolute obedience.

Then the woman forced herself to relax, a conscious effort that cost her dearly. The shaking fingers that plucked out the cigarette told of her difficulty in casting aside the lessons of a lifetime. She lit the cigarette, dragged deeply, said with the smoke, "Yes?"

Erika felt the bitter disappointment of one robbed of her rightful place, and it grated into her voice. "Frau Reining?"

The woman nodded. "You are the woman who called for an appointment, Frau." She leaned forward, glanced at her calendar, said with evident skepticism, "Frau Schmidt?"

"Yes." Erika swallowed her bitterness. To stoop to such nonsense. Yet she knew how to follow orders, that much she still carried with her. She spoke as Ferret had instructed. "I represent a seller of an antique who wishes to contact a Western dealer. One who knows his business and can be trusted to offer a fair price."

"I see." Frau Reining took in almost a quarter of her cigarette in one drag. "And why come to me?"

"You are involved with several court cases involving compensation for stolen antiques. We had hoped you were in touch with people within the Western markets. Trusted people," she continued by rote from Ferret's own words, "who respect our need for confidentiality."

"We?" Frau Reining asked. "You are agent for the seller?"

"We will be pleased to pay a fee for this introduction," Erika evaded. "In hopes that it will help us avoid a costly mistake."

The woman showed no reaction to the offer, just as Ferret had predicted. And as he had said she would, Frau Reining asked, "It is a German piece?"

"No," Erika answered, more sure of her footing now that Ferret's strange-sounding predictions were proving accurate. An honest woman, Ferret had described Frau Reining. A freak of nature. One who couldn't be bought. Erika stifled a vague wish that things were still as they once had been, when she could have tested this ridiculous claim.

Erika had known a great many women to change their tune when faced with fear. Not just a little fear, no. A real fear. Of real pain. Pain promised by blood-spattered walls and a room filled with the stink of others' agony. Such women would enter a prison interrogation cell, see hopelessness painted on all the walls, and know there was only one hope, one escape—through utter submission. Through giving in to terror and doing exactly as they were told. At such times, fear stripped away strength and exposed principles for what they were—mere luxuries.

Once she had led a prisoner, a Christian caught handing out Bible tracts, into the cellar punishment chamber. The woman had taken one look around, and as her legs gave way she had spoken words Erika would never forget. She had raised her eyes to the gray-spackled ceiling and cried, *Oh, dear Father, protect me from the eater of souls!* Erika had no idea what those words meant, but she liked the ring of them.

But all she said to Frau Reining was, "The article we wish to sell resides in Poland." Which was another mystery to Erika, but here again Ferret had seemed both certain of his facts and unwilling to discuss them further.

"Poland." Reining showed surprise. "There has been a very unscrupulous history of antique dealing under the old regime. I have learned to be very cautious."

"Poland," Erika repeated, and continued as instructed. "It has been there since the war."

"I see." Frau Reining ground out her cigarette. "Normally I would not become involved in such a matter. But as the article is not in this country, I see no reason why I should not help you."

Erika reacted with stony silence, her thoughts and desires hidden behind a practiced mask.

Frau Reining reached for her notepad. "I will give you an address. It so happens that my contact is at this moment in Erfurt."

"We would prefer that *you* represent us," Erika replied as Ferret had instructed.

"Represent you how?"

"We wish to arrange a meeting on neutral ground. In Dresden. This week would be excellent." This moved up Ferret's time plan slightly, but the contact was nearby, and the little man had said to set up a meeting quickly. Within a week or so if possible, Ferret had told her, though why she did not know. They still had nothing to sell.

Erika handed over Ferret's typed instructions. "Please pass this on to your contact and confirm that you've done so by calling the number below."

Frau Reining was clearly unsure of herself. "I suppose I could—"

Erika slipped an envelope out of her pocket, set it on the desk. "This is a retainer. Let us know when further funds are required." With that she turned and walked from the room, glad to be done with this freakish woman and her foolish, unchallenged principles.

CHAPTER
16

Jeffrey awoke toward dawn to find that his heat had been cut off. The air was so cold that it poured through the hotel's windows as if they were open. The bathroom tiles burned his feet. He could see his breath. He put on clothes over his pajamas as well as a second layer of socks, stripped covers from the second bed, and piled everything on top of his own. Eventually he returned to sleep.

Breakfast was served in a plain, high-ceilinged hall so large the businessmen and their rattling papers were reduced to tiny, harrumphing dolls. Katya arrived looking incredibly fresh, and was followed to his table by every eye in the room.

He rose and said in greeting, "You look beautiful."

She kissed him twice. "One of those was for last night, in case I forgot."

He fought off a rising blush. "You didn't, but thanks just the same."

She ordered breakfast from the waitress, then said, "I called the antiques dealer, Herr Diehl. He is eagerly awaiting our arrival. He sounds like a very nice man."

Jeffrey nodded. "Was your room cold last night?"

"Freezing. And my bath water was brown."

"Mine, too."

"Rusty pipes," she said. "Probably there since before the war."

"In a first-class hotel."

"They haven't changed the radiators, either."

"I slept in both my sweaters last night."

"Good." She smiled. "You're learning to adjust to life in the glorious East."

Their way from the hotel to the Krämer Bridge took them down ancient cobblestone streets now used as pedestrian passages. Gradually the city was awakening from its long sleep, with a charm and heritage that even the depths of winter could not disguise. Some of the houses were minute, built for the smaller peoples of six and seven hundred years ago. Most buildings remained scarred from the old regime's determined neglect, yet everywhere there were signs of change— flashing store lights, cheerful window displays, enthusiastic street hawkers, new construction, fresh paint.

If Katya had not announced their arrival at the bridge, Jeffrey would not have known it. The line of old houses simply opened for yet another cobblestone way with ancient dwellings standing cheek-to-jowl along both sides. There was no sign of a river, no indication that they were stepping up and over a waterway. But a stone plaque attached to the first bridge-house stated that this was indeed the Krämer Bridge, built of wood in the twelfth century, then of stone two hundred years later. Closely packed houses lining the bridge showed chest-high doors, tiny waist-level windows, and bowed walls.

The *Haus der Glocke,* or Bell House, was a closet-sized shop halfway along the bridge. A cheerful little bell above the door announced their entry. They stood in the minuscule patch of free floor space and looked around. Gradually the shop's clutter took on a certain cramped order. Along the walls stood a glass-fronted display case for pocket watches, a glass-topped table for old ivory and meerschaum pipes, and another for rolling pins etched with household scenes from the last century. One corner cupboard held pewter, another antique jewelry. Higher up, decorative household items battled for shelf space with old silver serving pieces. Two wall cabinets displayed clocks, and a third showed off miniature oils in ornate cases. Hand-wound gramophones on ornately carved legs elbowed against antique dolls and horsehair footstools.

Katya looked around and declared, "This is a happy shop."

"Full of memories of better times," Jeffrey agreed. "Two of the clocks in that cabinet are museum-quality pieces, as well."

A slender man with thin strands of snow-white hair appeared from what Jeffrey had dismissed as a broom closet and now realized was the shop's office. "Herr Sinclair?"

"That's me. Herr Diehl?" Jeffrey shook hands. The slender fingers held a surprising strength. Katya exchanged a handshake and introductions with their host and translated for Jeffrey. "He is delighted that we have found our way to his little shop."

"Ask him if we are allowed to carry off those two clocks on the top shelf over there."

The spark of a dealer's heart showed in Herr Diehl's eyes as Katya translated. She told Jeffrey, "He is very glad to hear that Frau Reining was correct as to your eye for quality as well."

"As well as what?"

"Honesty is a most valuable commodity in such uncertain times," Herr Diehl replied through Katya.

"It's a good way to begin business," Jeffrey agreed. "On both sides."

Herr Diehl motioned for them to follow him. They skirted a narrow mirror-backed cabinet crowded with porcelain figurines and discovered a claustrophobic stairway that etched a passage along the house's back wall.

The stairs creaked and groaned under the dealer's weight. They were so narrow that Jeffrey found it necessary to turn sideways. The stairs emptied into a single cramped chamber floored with bare, ancient planking and a thick coat of dust. Lighting came from one bare bulb and a single tiny window. Yet the poor surroundings could not detract from the glory of the pieces awaiting inspection.

"I judged these to be of collector's quality," Herr Diehl said through Katya. "Articles that would require a larger showcase than what I could manage here in Erfurt."

"You judged correctly," Jeffrey agreed solemnly and approached the first piece, a secretary-cabinet constructed of solid walnut, with other light woods inlaid in a series of delicate floral patterns framed by mosaic swirls.

Lines tended to blur between lands and eras in Central European antiques. Wars and revolutions had redrawn national boundaries and allegiances, often with dizzying speed. With each change, woodworkers and silversmiths and ironmongers and jewelers had adapted anew to the tastes of those who could afford to buy. In the space of a century, therefore, the style of locally produced pieces had changed from Florentine to Russian, from Austro-Hungarian to Prussian, from French to Persian. This particular piece was German, probably from the eighteenth century, but executed in Italian Rococo style.

The second article was most likely eighteenth-century Austrian in design, as the Austro-Hungarian empire dominated much of central Europe at that time. The inlay was subtly crafted to suggest a patriotic figure within swirls of clouds. Done during an era of occupation, when overt patriotism to anything but the empire was punishable by death, it was a most ingenious piece.

There were three pieces from the Baroque period, the name given to the Renaissance in countries north of the Alps. One was a remarkable chest hand carved in the shape of a vase, narrow legs rising and expanding to a pair of drawers that both broadened and curved outward in gentle waves. The piece was made from wild cherry wood, the original fittings of dark bronze fashioned like draping sprigs of ivy. Another chest of drawers, also constructed of cherry, displayed the traditional Baroque curved front. Beside it was a late-Baroque commode with typically extravagant Rococo inlay in the form of Grecian urns. This piece, too, was solid cherry.

A great deal of cherry had been used in central European furniture around that time. Four hundred years ago, several royal decrees had ordered all roads to be lined with cherry trees. As the neighboring cities expanded and required larger roads, however, these trees had gradually been chopped down and fashioned into furniture. Cultivated trees like these were known for their smooth, long grain, as contrasted with the cramped, gnarled grain for wild cherry.

The final item was a woman's bureau, signed and dated 1809, and again carved from solid cherry. It was a piece made to stand alone, to draw the eye of everyone who entered the chamber. The finish was Empire at its best, simple and silken, accenting a wood so fine as to hold a jewel-like shimmer.

Jeffrey straightened from his perusal, released a breath he felt he had been holding on to for hours. "Magnificent," he declared.

The dealer showed a trace of anxiety and asked through Katya, "You would like to take them?"

"Every article you have here will be a valuable addition to our shop," Jeffrey replied flatly.

The man released a sigh of his own. "Then my own assessment was correct."

"I will need a second opinion on a couple of the more valuable items, and all of them will require a closer inspection before appraising," Jeffrey said. "But my first assessment is that you have brought together an excellent group."

"That is good news. Excellent news. You will make many people very happy." Herr Diehl appeared at a momentary loss. "You can perhaps accept more furniture?"

"Of this quality?" Jeffrey permitted himself a smile. "As much as you can deliver. No problem."

The dealer puffed out age-dappled cheeks, said, "You cannot imagine the difference between this discussion and those I have had with other Western dealers."

"Maybe I can."

"Yes, perhaps so." Through Katya he went on, "I have spent hours trying to fathom what on earth they were talking about as they inspected the undersides of drawers and ran their hands over nailheads and questioned provenance. Is that what you call it, provenance? The history of the owners."

"Provenance, yes," Jeffrey replied, and added, "All of that we will need to do as well, but not now. Yet even if the provenance proves questionable and it turns out we are looking at articles pieced together over several different eras, which I doubt, their quality is still enough to warrant a high price."

"Not according to your competitors."

"They were offering you a flat sum?"

Herr Diehl nodded. "And making it sound as if they were doing me an enormous favor."

Jeffrey gave silent thanks for his competitors' greed. "I'll have to get down on my knees before I can say anything for sure, Herr Diehl. But my first guess is that you've got well over two hundred thousand dollars in furniture up here. After commissions."

"So much," he murmured.

"I try to keep my first estimates conservative." Jeffrey weighed his alternatives, decided now was not the time to hold back. He pointed toward the Empire secretary and the cabinet with the dreamlike patriotic inlay. "There is a good chance those two pieces alone will fetch over that figure."

"If you can speak with such decisive authority, Herr Sinclair," the dealer replied, "then so can I." He extended his hand once more. "I shall look forward to doing business with you for years to come."

"Likewise," Jeffrey replied.

Herr Diehl then became the formal host. "My shop is unfortunately too cramped for us all to sit and talk comfortably. May I invite you to a nearby cafe?"

Jeffrey and Katya allowed themselves to be led back down the narrow stairs. Herr Diehl ushered them outside, locked up his shop, and started toward the bridge's far end. As they walked Katya said to Jeffrey, "He speaks a beautiful German. I wish you could understand it."

"Your translation sounds almost courtly." He motioned toward the ancient structures lining the bridge. "It fits the surroundings."

Herr Diehl beamed as Katya translated. "For a number of years, there was little with which I could occupy my mind, as the only work permitted me was hand labor. So I read. I read the Bible. I read everything I could find about antiques. It was an excellent way of immersing myself in times where troubles such as mine did not exist. I also read classical German literature, Goethe especially. There was a man who made heavy Germanic tones sound light and graceful as an aria."

"Frau Reining mentioned that it had been hard for you as a believer under the Communists," Jeffrey said.

"All Christians in this country had their own experience," Herr Diehl replied. "There were some imprisonments, yes, but in truth they were a minority. On the other hand, if you accepted Christ into your life, you *knew* what your lot would be. There was no question. You would lose your public name. You would never be granted a position that held any power of decision or authority over others. Promotions would be permanently blocked. You would wait weeks, months, years, for the simplest of government documents, even a driver's license. You would never be considered for new housing, no matter how many children you might have or how great was your need. Your family would suffer as a result of your action, from the eldest to the youngest, without exception. Your children would never be permitted to receive a higher education. Yet all this became, in a sense, normal for us. There was no question but that this would happen, you see. It came as no surprise. This was the way of life in our country for so long. You entered into such a decision with your eyes open.

"Under the Communists," Herr Diehl went on, "there were enough Christians in the cities for us to find comfort. The situation in the villages was far worse. A few women attended services, those who were too old or too insignificant for the Stasi to trouble over. Priests and ministers were barely tolerated by the local citizens, and they often went weeks without a friendly word from anyone outside the handful of believers. If asked, I suppose most villagers would have said that, yes, it was probably good to have a pastor around, for funerals and such. But not for them and not for now; they had to worry too much and work too hard just to survive in this life. There were frequent suicides among ministers, which the state made sure received nationwide publicity as a way to declare all who believed in God, even the preachers, to be mentally unstable.

"In the cities, with their larger populations of believers, the situation was different. The state gave us no choice but to get along, to form ourselves into a unified body. Minor disagreements over personality or style of worship fell into insignificance when faced with the issue of our very survival."

They arrived at the bridge's far end, which was anchored by a miniature church of ancient brick, so small as to appear a replica made for little children. "This is the Aegidien Church, erected in 1125 as a sanctuary for travelers and resident merchants alike." Herr Diehl led them to a cafe set slightly below the level of the bridge proper. "This was originally a small monastery, a standing invitation to the weary and the hungry and the fearful to turn from the world of money and peril and woes."

The door was narrow and little over four feet high, the stone walls almost three feet thick. Inside, the ceilings were arched and colonnaded, the floor stones sanded down by eight hundred years of use. Lighting came from ancient bronze torch holders adapted to electricity.

They selected a tiny alcove whose picture window overlooked the pedestrians. Herr Diehl ordered sandwiches and tea for them all. The waiter returned swiftly with a tiny saucer piled with a reddish dust. Katya and Herr Diehl shared a smile at the sight.

"What is it?" Jeffrey asked.

"Paprika and salt," Katya replied. "It's for our sandwiches."

"Why is that funny?"

"It's something from the old regime. Pepper was rare, especially in government-controlled restaurants where they couldn't charge for it. Pepper had to be imported. Paprika could be grown here, so it was often served as a substitute. I think it tastes horrible."

Herr Diehl spoke, and Katya translated it as, "These are lingering signs of what once was everywhere. We are able to smile at them now because the shadow is gradually drawing away."

Jeffrey asked Katya, "Do you think it would be all right to ask how he became a Christian? I don't want to offend him or anything, so please don't—"

In reply, Katya turned and spoke in a language made graceful by her lilting voice. Herr Diehl seemed genuinely pleased by the question and replied at length.

"Some stories are easier to end than to begin," he said. "I know that the ending arrives when I have opened the eyes of my heart and known the presence of the Lord. The beginning is somewhat more difficult, as it resides in the confusion that was everyone's life at the end of the war."

Jeffrey shook his head. "I love the way he talks."

"You should hear it in the original," Katya said.

"The crippling of my beloved Berlin began about two years before the Russians arrived," Herr Diehl told them. "I was two years old, and the year was 1943. Our home at that time was a large apartment building with an inner court-yard in the city center. Still today I remember the British and American bombing raids so well, so vividly. Still I can see the planes overhead, great, booming sheets of hundreds and hundreds of metal birds.

"Every night they came. It was all automatic after a few months of the bombing, our reactions. The sirens would start. I would rub the sleep from my eyes, and wait for my mother to come and take me from my crib. I had a little wooden toy car, green and gold, and I made it my responsi-bility to carry the car downstairs. My mother and my father had their packed suitcases and their little carry-sack of pro-visions. I had my little toy car.

"In the cellar we were twenty, maybe twenty-five. We heard the planes, we heard the piping sounds the bombs made as they fell, we heard the explosions come close, then closer, then shake us violently, then move away. We heard the tak-tak-tak of the antiaircraft guns. Then it grew qui-eter, and then the sirens called that it was over, and we went back upstairs to sleep. Sometimes it was already light when we came up, and we would go outside, and it was a different world! The windows were gone. The building next door had vanished. The street had great, gaping holes. Fires. Run-ning, shouting people. Great engines with different sirens trying to race around the holes and the rubble in the streets.

"A neighbor would come stand beside us and say that we had no electricity and no gas and no water. It was not so frightening for me, though. Either my father or my mother was always beside me, holding my little hand.

"The end of the war came at different times to the Ger-man people," Herr Diehl explained. "Like waves from several different storms crashing upon our little island. The Amer-ican troops moved fastest across our defeated nation, and we in Berlin kept hoping they would arrive first and rescue us from the dreaded Soviets. But they stopped just outside the city and waited for the Soviets to catch up.

"Refugees from the East brought horrible stories of what we could expect from the Soviets. I will speak about these refugees again in just a moment. Their true plight did not become clear until after the war ended, as the stream of homeless people struggling westward became a flood. At the time of the Soviets' approach to Berlin, they remained few enough for their faces to be seen as individuals, for their voices to be heard.

"I was four years old in 1945. I was what they called an autumn child; my father was fifty-five and my mother forty-nine. To say the least, my parents were not expecting me. When the Soviets arrived, we were living in South Berlin, a section perhaps a half-hour tram ride from the center city. Our home in the heart of Berlin had been totally destroyed in the bombing raids. It was our great fortune that the day our house was bombed, my mother and I were with my father in South Berlin where he worked on a company project. Everyone else in our apartment house died when the bomb took the front walls and the cellar away. Completely away. I will never forget going back and seeing our apartment. The back of the house stood, the front was gone. No rubble, no stone, nothing! Our home was dust. And yet the back rooms were still so complete I could see the pictures hanging in what had been my parents' bedroom. It made such an impression on my young mind, how the house had been split with a giant's knife.

"So we moved to this less-destroyed section, into a house owned by the company where my father worked, just as word came that the Russians were advancing. Our first night in this strange new home, we began to hear their guns booming in the distance. It sounded like thunder, and the light they made on the horizon looked like the first, faint colors of a false dawn.

"As a child, I thought the Russians were evil ghosts. I had never seen a foreigner, you see. Then one day my father, who had been too old to be a soldier, was gathered up and taken away with all the other old men who still had two arms and two legs. He was given bits and pieces of several uniforms, I remember the right sleeve had been sewn from a different jacket and was four or five inches shorter than the left, and there was a dark stain over the jacket's middle and a hole that had been sewn up in jagged haste. He was given only one weapon, a hand grenade.

"Four weeks later, he came back, dug a hole in the garden, stripped off his uniform, and buried it. Thirty minutes after that, the first Soviet soldier walked in. He stepped up to my father, who by then was dressed in his best suit and trying not to appear nervous, and asked what time it was. My father opened his pocket watch and answered, almost one o'clock. The soldier said, good, and took the watch. That was my first experience with a foreigner.

"South Berlin was a very dirty place. Filthy. Before the war, it had been the center for eastern Germany's coal-processing and steel works. My father had been born there and had sworn never to return. Now he was back, had been conscripted and sent off to fight in a losing war, then had returned only to greet the Russians and hear that they were to make our house the Soviet army's district headquarters. He was back, and living in the tiny, damp cellar while Soviet army boots clumped and thudded over our heads. But we did not complain overmuch. At least we had a roof.

"There was a park and a garden across the street. This became very important for us, because we raised vegetables there. It kept us alive, that park, us and our neighbors. We swiftly learned that our chances of survival were better if we could learn to live as an extended family.

"The Soviets were very bad, and most of the stories you hear of their atrocities are true. They took the last of our possessions—our clothes, furniture, carpets, jewelry, everything that had survived the war. But for me they often showed a different side, as many were kind to children, and sometimes they fed me from their kitchen. Even at that early age, I knew I was incredibly fortunate. I still had my mother and my father. There were few such complete families then. Very, very few.

"We survived those first two years with great difficulty. Those words do not describe the times, but no words would, so I will not try. My father had been an electrical engineer who worked for the coal and electrical combine. Before the war, all big German companies had their headquarters in Berlin. But now Berlin was no more. Destroyed. Leveled so completely that soldiers coming home from the fronts or the POW camps could not even find the *streets* where they had lived, much less their houses or their families.

"My father found work with a little coal company during the days, and at night he pedaled his bike to nearby villages and rewired the damaged electrical systems in cottages and farmhouses. He was paid in milk and vegetables and sometimes meat. He slept when he could. My mother sewed.

"Because my father worked for a coal company, we had heat. Others did not. Old people simply froze and died. The two winters after the war were *extremely* cold. The cities were hell, simply hell. People risked their lives to steal coal. There was no wood at all.

"Coal shipped by trains was sprayed with chalk over the top. When it arrived officials would look down on the train cars; a dark spot meant that some of the top coal had been stolen. The suppliers would then be penalized or sometimes jailed. So the suppliers hired very tough men to walk back and forth on these freezing trains and beat off people who raced up at crossings and tried to steal enough coal to keep their families from freezing.

"My father knew this for a fact, because sometimes he had to travel for the coal company and talk to the officials at the other end. There was no gasoline, of course, unless you were with the occupying forces. It took days and days for him to obtain the permits to travel by train, and then he was forced to sit on the coal wagons, atop little runner stations. In the open. He would sit like that for hours, wrapped in blankets my mother gave him. Once he traveled with the really privileged, inside an unheated boxcar. He never spoke of what he saw when he rode on the coal cars. Yet I could see how haunted his eyes looked when he returned from his travels, and hear how his sleep was disturbed by nightmares.

"There was no infrastructure in those early days. No cars. No trams. No streets sometimes. No resources. No food. The land was empty and barren and blown up and scarred, a landscape from hell. And the government was horrible in the east of Germany. Simply beyond description.

"The Soviets sent back German Communists who had escaped from the Nazis by fleeing to Russia and fighting with the Red Army. They came back to take over the new Communist government. And they *hated* the German people. They were merciless. The old people, the weak ones, the young, they suffered. And then they died.

"To make matters worse, much worse, there were refugees. *Millions* of refugees. Germans from the former eastern provinces—now part of Lithuania and Poland and Czechoslovakia and the Soviet Union, lands that had been part of Germany for centuries—all who could, fled to what was left of Germany. But when they arrived, starving and battered and stripped of everything of value, they found nothing left for them. No homes, no shelter, no food, no medicine, no heat, no sympathy. They came, they starved. They, too, died.

"Some months into that second year, I contracted typhoid. That was both very good and very bad. The bad side was how sick I became—very high fever, so high I almost died. This sickness stalked the city, with panic walking on one side and death on the other. At night I thought I was hearing ghosts, as screams and wails drifted through our little cellar windows, but later my mother told me they were real, the cries of mothers powerless to hold their children to this battered earth.

"Within a few days, the authorities gathered all the sick children who were still alive and placed them in a cinema. All the hospitals had been destroyed by the bombing raids, and this cinema was one of the few large halls that remained. It was something straight from my worst nightmares. There was very little medicine. There were not enough doctors or nurses, so most of the time I was left alone with my pain. The air was fetid, full of the smells of sick and dying children, too full of smells to breathe. The lighting was a dim, yellow glow, and there were frequent blackouts when the power failed.

"Every night children died all around me, their cries and choking gasps reaching out, threading their way through my fever to clutch at my life and pull it from my body and carry me off with them. And I was alone. More alone than ever in my life, before or since. We were not allowed visitors. I had not seen my parents since I was placed on the stretcher and carted away. I lay there in the putrid gloom and felt myself being consumed by the flames of my fever. And I cried, and I called out to a God I knew only through a child's prayers."

Katya choked back a shaky breath and reached for her glass. Both Jeffrey and Herr Diehl were immediately solicitous. Quietly she calmed the gentleman, then said to Jeffrey, "I'm all right. Really."

"We can stop now if you want."

"No we can't," she said firmly. "I have to hear the end. If I stopped now I don't know if I could ever go to sleep again. Just hold my hand, would you?"

He grasped it with both of his, tried to rub away the coldness in her fingers.

"As I lay there in my fear and my fever and my pain," Herr Diehl continued, "I felt something come upon me. I had not prayed for a healing, because I did not know what prayer was, beyond the words we spoke on Sundays and before meals and the little rhymes that sent me to sleep. I had simply called, and my call had been heard. That much I knew then, even in the midst of my fever-dreams. There was never any question that I had been heard, or that my call had been answered. A peace descended upon me, a love and a comfort that left me quietened and able to rest through that night and all the nights to come. It was only later that I could place words to the feeling. I had formed a solemn friendship, you see. The rest of my life, I have simply tried to hold up my side of the friendship that was forged on that dark and glorious night.

"That doesn't mean my life has been made easy, or even good. A good life does not exist for a Christian in a Communist land, especially one who feels led to tell his brothers the Good News. But never again did I face my trials alone." He paused and gave them both a gentle smile. "There was just one time when I did not share the miracles of my faith, at least not immediately. The day I returned home from the cinema-hospital, the Soviets moved out. My mother told me it was because they were frightened of infection.

"She was so happy to have both her son and her home back," Herr Diehl explained. "I could see no reason to argue with her."

CHAPTER
17

Kurt's car crawled toward Weimar along roads made treacherous by rain-dampened cinders. As he drove he was struck by the thought that this was the first winter he could ever remember not seeing bent-over old ladies carrying coal buckets up from black piles dumped in front yards, alleys, and street corners. Perhaps there was something to this progress after all.

Home to Goethe and Schiller and Thomas Mann, and former capital of the German Republic, Weimar had suffered badly during the Communist years. Now, with the new influx of capitalism, the city was gradually becoming two. Within the ring-road that encircled the central city, the old town saw renovation progress at a hectic pace. Outside the loop, however, life ground on as slowly as ever. People struggled to survive, and Wessie promises to lift their lives had little meaning.

Since the region produced soft coal, the Communists had ordered all buildings—offices, apartments, hotels, hospitals, museums, factories—to employ that cheapest, most easily available source of heat. The city, hemmed in on three sides by high hills, therefore spent long winter months under a fog of soft-coal soot. Roads became slush-covered, buildings eroded as though dipped in acid baths, paint disappeared in a matter of months, cars were lost under thick black coatings.

All the wealth and glory of Weimar had fallen victim to Communist homogenization, gradually fading beneath an ever-thickening layer of ashes and bureaucracy.

Approaching the ring-road at a snail's pace, Kurt decided he could make faster progress on foot and pulled into a parking space between two plastic Trabants. He opened his door and felt his shoes grind through a centimeter of cinders.

He followed his contact's instructions to what fifty years before had been the Gau Forum. It had been renamed Karl Marx Platz at war's end, and was now one of many nameless streets and squares awaiting new signs.

In the early thirties, the Nazis had taken a minor plaza at the outskirts of the city center and had transformed it into a gathering point for the new power brokers. The expanded eleven-acre square had become the Gau Forum, where Nazi parades drew hundreds of thousands of fanatics, reinforcing Nazi visions of fulfilling the Weimar Republic's lofty ambitions.

Buildings had been erected in stern Fascist style, with two long three-story arms extending down either side of the plaza from a central Nazi Party headquarters. Two balconies had been set at opposite midpoints; from these Hitler had often stood and incited the roaring mobs.

The Communists had converted the two arms into engineering and agricultural colleges and transformed the central building beyond all recognition. A modernistic glass-and-steel facade masked the original stone, and a fifteen-story office building loomed at its back. The clash of Fascist colonnaded stonework with Communist glass and steel, all surrounding a square of sooty-brown grass and stunted trees, gave the place a thoroughly grotesque appearance.

Kurt entered the main building's glass-walled annex to find himself in a sort of everyman's restaurant-cafe. Communist taste was stamped indelibly on everything—the orange globe lights, the fake-marble floors, the plastic ceilings, the cavernous size. Three or four hundred metal-limbed tables stretched out into the distance. The long side walls sported murals sixty feet long and forty wide, depicting strong-limbed Communist workers marching into a dull-red future filled with nightmarish Picassoesque ovoids and triangular three-headed sphinxes. The place was virtually empty.

Kurt walked to the window table where his contact sat peering into the depths of his coffee. Kurt asked, "Why meet here?"

The young man raised his head and inspected Kurt with glittering eyes. "Brings back memories, does it?"

"I didn't like such places before. I don't now."

"You should." The man's eyes were blue, yet shaded so dark as to be opaque. His hands were scarred black with oil and soot. "You built them. You and your kind."

"I didn't come for an argument. I need information."

"Have some coffee first. Go on, it won't break you. Costs only fifty pfennigs. One of the few bargains left these days."

The single cafeteria line served brown glop that appeared to have been cooking since before the Wall came down. Seven bored attendants sat around talking in loud voices that bounced off distant walls. Kurt stood and waited long enough to know bitterness over a life and a world made myth overnight before one of them slouched to her feet and took his order.

While Kurt waited, he glanced back toward the table where his contact waited, hunched over his own cup. Kurt shook his head. One part of his former life that Kurt did not miss at all was having to deal daily with such freaks.

The prostitutes, for example. His duties had included shaking down whores who pandered to the low-class hotels. Not the big internationals, no, those hustlers were specially trained and monitored by the international section, the glamour boys, the department Kurt would have given his right arm to be a part of. No. His lot had been the third-rate inns catering to low-rent tourists from other Warsaw Pact lands. The prostitutes had known he wasn't high up the power structure—otherwise he wouldn't have wasted time on them. They had treated him like dirt.

And the gays. All the fair-haired boys trapped and suffocating in little villages where their lives had been made pure hell by the local Party roughs. They'd sell their souls for a ticket to a big city, where they could get lost within a crowd of their own kind. They made Kurt promises of eternal devotion for work and resident cards, then forgot his name once they had developed their own contacts—especially the pretty ones, who would sidle up close to someone with *real* power and then could thumb their noses at the likes of Kurt.

And circus acrobats, like the young man waiting for him here, all of them with madness and mayhem in their eyes.

And the Christians. Kurt's last promotion had come in return for finding a Protestant minister and turning him. That is, he had found the man's flaw and widened the crack into a crevice. Kurt had learned the Stasi lesson well—to teach a man fear, to find out what he seeks to hide from the rest of the world, and then threaten to expose it. All men had at least one such secret, most men more. No matter how big or trivial or horrible the secret, the key lay not in its size, but in its capacity to inspire terror through having someone—spouse or family or business or village or congregation or whomever—find out. A well-functioning Communist regime made it their business to find out these secrets and then to exploit them mercilessly.

Kurt had been good at that. Very good. As the Protestant minister had discovered to his misery. The minister's failings would have been considered minor by anyone not bearing the weight of others' misfortunes, or souls, to use a word that Kurt had never understood. But neither superstition nor concern for the unseen had stopped Kurt from using what he had learned, confronting the man with his usage of church funds to supplant his own meager stipend and demanding that he help the Stasi cause by supplying the names of all new converts to this strange drug called religion.

The Protestant minister had dreaded Kurt and his power. The minister had lived in fear of him until the fear had become too much to bear and driven him to take his own life. Toward the departed minister Kurt had felt neither remorse nor sorrow, nor really even thought of him at all. By then Kurt's promotion had been official. Also by that time the minister's information had borne fruit; there were others within the church who had secrets to hide or families to protect and were willing to pay for their own protection with yet more information.

Kurt paid for his coffee and carried it back to where the

out-of-work acrobat waited. He sat down and asked, "Do you have what I need?"

"Let's see the money."

Kurt slipped the cash from his pocket and slid it across. The man lowered his cup, fanned the bills, and counted slowly. He held the bundle up and asked, "Where's the rest?"

"Half now, half when we're done," Kurt said. "Think maybe you could drop your hands a little?"

"Who's to see?" The man pocketed the bills. "Besides, it's not illegal anymore, is it? More's the pity, far as you're concerned. Before, you'd have just popped me into a hole somewhere and waited for me to cook, right?"

He was big and blond, very much of both. His flaxen hair hung down below his shoulder blades. Like a bushy foxtail, it was, when tied back as now. It sprung out from the rope knotted behind his head, the same rope thonged up and around his forehead, then twisted and tied at the nape of his neck. It was the man's trademark, the way he wore his hair in a loop of old rope, that and his strength. When released his hair fanned out like a rampant lion's mane. On him it looked natural.

He was dressed in the only clothes Kurt had ever seen him wear—tattered pullover, shapeless khaki pants, bulky pea jacket, filthy sneakers. But no amount of sacking could disguise the rock-solid bulk beneath. The young man was huge. Even his hands were oversized mallets. And he had strength to match his size.

The young man had been recruited fresh from training as an acrobat and promised a place with one of the major international touring circuses if he would both inform on his comrades and act as a courier for Stasi secrets. He had agreed and done a decent job, after a fashion.

Kurt had been the young man's contact, his keeper in Stasi jargon. Kurt had always thought the term especially apt with this man, with his lion's mane and his animal strength. He had remained surly and hard to handle throughout, giving Kurt the impression of facing a barely tamed big cat without benefit of chair or whip. When Kurt had mentioned to his superiors the young man's offer to break Kurt across one knee, they had smirked and shrugged and said, What do you expect from a performer?

Before the Wall came down, circuses had been one of East Germany's most famous exports. They had been small affairs by Western standards—one ring, a tent one truck could haul, three dozen animals at most, perhaps twice that number of performers and trainers. Everybody had worked to pitch and dismantle the tents. The boss had also been the bookkeeper, lions' feed had been cooked next to the acrobats' stew. They had toured the back roads and villages from Leningrad to Budapest, sometimes as far away as Peru and Mongolia and Cuba and North Africa. People in entertainment-starved Communist villages had sometimes waited in line for days.

Places in top schools for acrobats and performers had been more sought after than seats at the Berlin Medical Academy. Would-be dancers and stage performers and acrobats and mimes and many actors had seen the circus as their one hope for artistic expression, let alone foreign travel. The result had been a level of circus talent far surpassing anything seen in the West.

Now, with the state subsidies withdrawn from circuses and their schools, and with television and movies pouring in from the once-forbidden West, all the circuses were closing. And the dancers and performers and acrobats and mimes went hungry.

"Even half is a lot of money for a little information," Kurt said.

Huge shoulders gave a shrug. "Buy and sell, buy and sell. The law of the capitalist world, right? Besides, I need it for a ticket to Australia. Word is they're hiring acrobats." Blue-black eyes glittered. "And what I've got is not a little information."

"Tell me."

"Amazing what people will tell a day laborer," the young man replied, refusing to be hurried. "That's what I'm doing, by the way. Shoveling dirt in some forsaken hole, worrying night and day about losing my touch. Trying to fight off the bottle's call, though it's hard when I can't see a way to hope."

Kurt had debated long and hard before contacting this man. He was temperamental, hard to handle, often abusive. But he was the only contact Kurt still had who was in Weimar and available. "Tell me," he repeated.

"Got me a job on the digging crew, I did. Learned me a lot."

"You might as well get started," Kurt said. "I'm not paying you any more than I promised."

"Always a tight one, you were. Tight with money and tight in your mind. Like you wore a steel band wrapped around your head, always tightening it up and trying to squeeze the stuffings out. I always thought a good whap on the chin'd do a lot to loosen you up."

Kurt kept the queasy fear from his face. "There's still half your money left to earn."

The young man leaned back and smirked knowingly. "What's got you so interested in this?"

Kurt replied with silence.

"You're after Nazi treasure, aren't you?" When Kurt did not reply, he went on, "Well, you won't find it here."

Kurt searched the man's eyes for the first hint of gold fever as Ferret had instructed, found only the same barely controlled power. "Tell me what you found."

"Empty rooms. Dust. Tunnels with walls two meters thick."

"Artwork? Strange-shaped packing boxes?"

"Bones," the young man replied. "You know the SS used concentration camp prisoners to build the cellars."

"Yes."

The young man pointed at the floor. "Twenty meters below us is the Asbach River. When the Nazis started building their parade ground, they hollowed out a deep channel, filled it with concrete, and diverted the river. Then they put another layer of concrete on top and built a long cellar separated into little chambers by thick concrete walls. On top of that, another cellar. On top of that, a third. Then the plaza was set back in place. That's why trees don't grow big here, see. They're trying to dig roots into concrete reinforced with iron rods."

"Must be frustrating," Kurt probed. "All this work and nothing to show for it."

"The Wessies want to pay me to poke holes in Nazi walls, it's fine with me. Same with the others. The money's good, and jobs aren't easy to come by." The dark eyes glittered. "Lots of fools with money around these days."

Kurt let it pass. "How far down have you worked?"

"We break into the second level next week."

"Six months of digging and you're still on the first level?"

Muscles bunched as the man leaned across the table. "You think we just open a door and prance in?"

"Of course not."

"Listen, mate. It's like drilling into lines of coffins with walls thick as I am tall. Bones. Water to your waist. Rats, big ones. And every time the drill hits air on the other side, we're all standing there wondering if this is the one that makes those cursed rooms our own coffins." Huge hands bunched into killing fists. "Word is, the Nazis stored bombs down there, gas canisters and shells to keep out fools like me. You know what a bomb would do, going off inside a concrete coffin?"

Kurt nodded. He did, as a matter of fact. When he was still a child, one of his teachers had taken great delight in a story that had made headlines throughout East Germany. After conquering France, the Nazis had lined the entire Atlantic coast with massive concrete gun emplacements. These bunkers had proven to be far more difficult to dislodge than the German soldiers. The story had been told of a village on the southern coast of France that had finally come up with a means of ridding their beaches of these bunkers.

It seemed that the villagers had already tried and failed at drilling through the six feet of concrete poured around a webbing of inch-thick steel rods. Picking them up and hauling them off had proved equally impossible, as the bunkers weighed upwards of five hundred tons each and were not easily moved.

So the village had decided to load the bunker with all the remaining unexploded bombs left in a nearby Nazi munitions depot.

They had chosen a bunker fairly removed from the little town, filled it to the brim with bombs and grenades and mines, cleared out all the curious onlookers, and set the sucker alight.

The bunker had done its best to fly away, but its upward

progress had been hampered by the fact that there were two openings at ninety-degree angles from each other—the narrow entrance, and the even narrower cannon-slit. So, after rising a mere thirty feet off the earth, which admittedly was not bad for a bunker weighing almost one million pounds, it had turned into the world's largest whirligig. Before returning to earth with a resounding thud, it had stripped every tree within twenty miles of foliage, blown out all the village windows, and overturned the local train station. The bunker itself had been unharmed. Kurt's teacher, along with many other men across the war-torn nation, had taken great pride in this proof of quality German workmanship.

"So you don't think anything's down there," Kurt asked.

"What difference does it make what I think? But the boys with the charts and the maps and the ties, they're starting to talk like no treasures came any closer to here than Ulm."

The young man toyed with his coffee cup. "Story goes, when the Americans occupied here in 1945, back before the partition was worked out, they looked around here a little but didn't find anything. Then the Russians came in, and when they started rebuilding this place they found bombs and gas canisters. Thousands and thousands stored in a field where they built that office block out back. There's one old man working with me who remembers it, said the Nazis stored munitions here because Weimar didn't have any industry and wasn't being bombed. Rumor was, though, the Nazis buried treasure *under* the bombs. But the Russians dug around and didn't find anything. Then the Americans found the Ulm treasures, and everybody figured that was where it had all been stored."

Kurt knew the Ulm story. Every German his age did— how the Americans had needed over a hundred trucks to clear out the paintings and artwork and valuables stored in the Ulm depot, then spent years trying to track down the lawful owners. Finally what wasn't claimed had been parceled out among the victors and stuffed into museums around the world. The spoils of war.

Kurt decided he had enough. "I'll be back in a month or so," he lied.

"Anytime, at least for as long as it takes for me to earn

my one-way ticket." Dark eyes followed him as he rose to his feet. "Just don't come empty-handed. Information costs a lot these days, like everything else. We're all busy learning the capitalist tricks, even you and your old mates, right? Buy whatever you want, because everything has its price. New laws for a new world."

CHAPTER
18

Katya joined Jeffrey at the breakfast table with an announcement. "Frau Reining just called."

"Where's my kiss?"

She greeted the approaching waiter, ordered breakfast, said, "She wants us to go to Dresden."

"I asked you a question." He was only half kidding. "I can't get my motor started just with coffee anymore."

She leaned across the table, smacked him soundly. "You'll need to be awake for this one."

"I'm all ears."

She smiled mischievously. "Your mouth says one thing and your eyes another."

He kept his voice flat for the benefit of the waiter pouring her coffee. "Take your pick."

"I'd better not."

"What's that supposed to mean?"

She waited until they were once again alone, then opened her heart and confessed as much with her eyes as with her words. "I dreamed about you last night."

"Katya, I—"

"Don't say it." Pleading now. "I need your help, Jeffrey. I have to have it. I'm not strong enough by myself."

He nodded. The heat burned a dull ache in his belly.

She reached across the table for his hand. "I feel as if I'm walking along the edge of a cliff. Just the slightest push and I'll fall over."

A thousand arguments crowded for place in his mind. He struggled, fought, won he knew not how, and remained silent. He raised his eyes to find hers resting upon him, gently pleading, openly yearning, full of the same conflict he battled against. "I love you, Katya."

"Thank you," she said quietly.

He hid behind his coffee, waited while the urge subsided to a slow, dull ache.

"Did I tell you Frau Reining called?" Her voice was as unsteady as his own inner balance.

"I can't hold on to this for very long," he replied.

"I know," she sighed. Softer, "I can't either."

"What are we going to do?"

When she didn't answer he ventured another glance and found her looking very shy. "Did you want a big wedding?"

"No." Emphatic.

"Me neither." She hesitated. "I don't know if the girl is supposed to be talking about these things, but—"

"But why have a long engagement," he finished for her, and knew a surging thrill.

"I've always dreamed of being a June bride," she said softly. "If that's okay with you."

"Perfect," he managed, though from where he sat June seemed several lifetimes away.

Joy shone from her eyes. And something more. "I think I've just lost my appetite. Do you think there's time for a smooch upstairs before our appointment with Herr Diehl?"

He was already on his feet and reaching for her hand. Without really caring he asked, "So what's in Dresden?"

Katya almost skipped alongside him. "Nothing that can't wait."

Their business was swiftly concluded, aided by a mutual desire to see their new relationship grow into permanence. With another hour before their train departed for Dresden, Herr Diehl guided them from his shop, eager to play the tour guide.

"In old Erfurt," he told them as they strolled along the

bridge's cobblestone length, "the houses had names, not numbers. Before, my own shop was the city's bellhouse, as the name says in German. It was the only place licensed by the city to sell bells. The blacksmiths would bid for the privilege of making anything from cowbells to carriage bells to the great bells used in churches—but not by price. Prices were fixed by each guild, including the ironmongers' guild. So they could compete only on terms and quality."

"All houses were named after the people's professions?" Jeffrey asked.

"Not necessarily." He motioned toward a nearby shop, a bookstore, which had a hand-beaten copper sign of a stork hanging outside. "According to the old records, this was named the *Haus zum Storchen,* the Stork's House, because the family who lived here had forty-three children. They were weavers and embroiderers of fine linen, a very lucrative profession. It required a special training, one that was highly sought after because of its special combination of artwork and craft-training. No doubt the shrewd weaver decided the best way to keep his trained employees from leaving was to draw them all from his own family.

"There were sixty-two merchant houses along this bridge, all licensed by the king to do business with the international traders, and all carefully controlled. Then, as now, from no place could a passerby see the water. The houses formed continuous four-story walls along both sides. They sold and traded in the products of distant lands—pepper, sugar, saffron, soap, paper, silk, brass, bronze, gold, silver, jewels, ornaments, rare objects, illustrated manuscripts.

"For over five hundred years," Herr Diehl continued, "this bridge was a key destination along the Paris-Kiev trade route. It is hard for us to comprehend how vital these overland routes once were. There was no alternative, you see, none at all. The seas were pirate-infested and governed by unruly gods of wind and storm, and dragons were believed to lurk just beneath the surface. No right-minded medieval businessman would dare place his life or the livelihood of his descendants in such a precarious position. So he and his caravans traveled overland. If he was poor, he joined a group of other traders, praying they were trustworthy, and carried his wares on his back. With time and success and good fortune came first servants and donkeys, then horses, then wagons and armed guards."

The dealer nodded his head in time to his words. "Yes, these land routes dominated international trade until Christians once again chose that most dreadful path—arguing over how to worship the Lord of love with swords in their hands."

"The Reformation wars," Jeffrey said.

"What a name," Herr Diehl replied. "How in God's holy name could you ever reform faith with a sword?"

Jeffrey shook his head. "I don't know."

"The Catholics and the Protestants between them poured a tide of blood over the land," Herr Diehl went on, "and suddenly waterborne dragons seemed vastly more appealing than land-based madness. Many merchants began taking their wares to distant buyers by sea, and most of the land routes slowly shriveled and died.

"But before the flow of history was rerouted with a bloody and heretical sword, these very same land routes reigned supreme." Herr Diehl's voice lifted as he swept his hand to encompass all the shops along the bridge. "Imagine what the merchants of that day and age must have seen. Each voyage from Paris to Kiev, a distance of over two thousand miles, could take as long as one year. There would be rumors of wars and new borders and greedy tax officials up ahead, many of them formed from thin air by local merchants who sought to separate the travelers from their goods at panic-stricken prices. The shopkeepers who manned this bridge were the gatherers of news and gossip, and they spiced it with their own self-interest before serving it to footsore travelers."

Cathedral Hill dominated what once had been medieval Erfurt's central market. Herr Diehl led them across an ancient street and into the vast open market square. "After Martin Luther's proclamation sparked the rise of Protestantism," he continued, "Erfurt was one of very few cities that stubbornly refused to declare itself for one faith or another. The people and the ruling princes were so adamantly unified that they fought off the scalding rhetoric of both churches and clung to sanity."

The frigid air had a metallic edge that burned the nostrils. Katya's voice was muffled by the scarf she kept wrapped around the bottom half of her face. "The prince and people demanded that both churches, Catholic and Protestant, be allowed to coexist," Herr Diehl explained through her. "It balanced their power, you see, and kept either from dominating the government and private life. The ruling family, the government, and the royal court were all good Catholics. The tradesmen, farmers, guilds, and merchants were Protestants. As a result, during the unbounded horrors of religious conflict, all Christians were safe here. And Erfurt remained a successful center of international commerce long after the land routes began to decline and other merchant cities were either put to the torch or starved into legend-filled graveyards, inhabited by walking ghosts."

The vast plaza was lined with ramshackle stalls selling everything from hand-knit shawls to imported oranges. The throngs of buyers were surprisingly quiet, silenced by the effort of walking and standing and shopping in the icy air. Jeffrey and Katya followed Herr Diehl beyond the market to where a broad staircase rose up almost three hundred feet. At the summit, a pair of colossal churches stood side by side.

"The first church is the one on the left," Herr Diehl told them as they climbed. "It was erected in 1154 as a monastery and remained true to the faith, so the story goes, through kingdoms and centuries. During the Reformation, the monks ridiculed the Pope's political ambitions and refused to back his demands for a war against their Protestant brethren. In reply, the Pope commanded that a second church be built, close enough and big enough to dominate the original."

One church alone would have been majestic. The two together looked ridiculous. Both were vast structures whose spires reached heavenward several hundred feet. Vast swatches of stained-glass windows arched between flanking buttresses of stone and dark-stained mortar. Nearby four-story buildings were easily dwarfed by the twin churches.

"And so stands a warning to the church of today," Herr Diehl said. "A witness to what can happen when doctrine becomes more important than the straightforward laws of love given us by the simple Carpenter. Whenever one of us opens our mouth to condemn the way another worships, we set another brick in the wall of such a monstrosity. We offer our beloved Savior up to the nonbelievers as a point of ridicule. If we as the saved cannot agree to disagree in peace and love and brotherhood, what do we show the nonbelievers but the same discord and disharmony from which they seek to escape?"

When they arrived at the top, Herr Diehl opened his arms to encompass the two churches and their outlying buildings. The stone path between the central structures was as broad as a two-lane highway, yet the churches' sheer mass narrowed and constricted the way to a choking tightness. There was no divine relief offered here, no hope or lightness, only an overbearing weight and looming threat.

"The Stasi closed both churches and the monastery," Herr Diehl went on. "They took over all but the worship halls and made this compound the central headquarters for the region's security operations. They required no sign to remind the people of their presence. From this height they were seen by everyone who took to the streets of Erfurt."

He faced them and said solemnly, "I tell you this with the sincerity of a man who has sought to live the life of a true believer. It was a just punishment for the church's maneuverings in the ways of this world, and for the misery their worldly ambitions caused the men of their day."

The journey by train from Erfurt to Dresden lasted four hours and took them from the carefully tended farmlands of Thuringen through the industrial might of Leipzig and on into the old royal enclave of Saxony. Their entry into Dresden was marked by more of the same—tall, dilapidated apartment buildings, bleak forests of smokestacks, aged factories, and everything dressed a dreary gray.

They stayed in the Ship-Hotel Florentine. It was only after a dozen or so telephone calls, Katya told him, that she had found them rooms at all. Like all the other major cities of the former East Germany, Dresden had become a boomtown. The few decent hotels were so packed with industrialists that enterprising Wessie hoteliers had floated tourist ships down the Elba River to Dresden, where they were wharfed and used as floating hotels.

Jeffrey deposited his bags, then returned to meet Katya by the ship's ramp. "I'm paying two hundred dollars a night for a room the size of a packing crate."

"Every room is full," Katya replied.

He was not through. "My bed is exactly eighteen inches wide. And my bathroom is smaller than an airplane toilet."

"I heard the receptionist tell someone on the phone that they're taking reservations six months in advance." She smiled up at him. "We have two hours until our meeting. Would you rather spend it complaining or taking a look at the city?"

They walked down the riverside pathway with traffic thundering alongside. Beyond the road towered Dresden's medieval city walls, granting them an astonishing view into what Dresden once had been—a royal city, a seat of power and palaces and parliaments. With each breath, Jeffrey felt himself intoxicated by the scent of living history mingling with the diesel fumes and construction dust.

Only a small portion of the city remained intact after the Allied bombing during World War II. The surviving buildings now lay beneath blankets of grime and neglect, the tall roof-statues stained so black they appeared carved from coal. Yet they still bore witness to a city that once had been a treasure trove of art and architecture, of power and wealth.

They entered the wall through lofty gates built to admit mounted cavalry with lances raised in royal salute. Behind rose the skeletal remains of the Frauen Church, over seven hundred years old when destroyed in the war. They walked on, passing one of the five inner-city palaces that remained out of almost two hundred royal residences. Beyond them rose the royal opera house, erected from stones still blackened by the firebombs that had consumed it in 1944. The first act of the new city council had been to rebuild it as a beacon of reassurance to a cowed and battered populace. Jeffrey and Katya joined the quiet throng of German tourists who braved the cold to read the council's proclamation. It promised a future of hope, a city with renewed purpose, and opportunities for growth and improvement in their own lives. Jeffrey searched the faces around him as he listened to Katya translate the words and saw how deeply these grim-faced individuals wished to believe.

Everywhere were the signs and sounds of renovation—jackhammers and rumbling trucks and tall cranes, warning signs and dust clouds and great crews of men scrambling over war-torn surfaces. More ruins gave way to a palace that Jeffrey took for the grandest of all the old buildings until he caught sight of the one rising behind it. Beyond that loomed yet another. Each was grander and greater than the one before.

They escaped the snow within a street-side cafe. Jeffrey listened as Katya gave their order to a waitress who looked poured into her dress. He watched her walk away, wondering how she managed to breathe. He turned back to find Katya watching him. "Was I staring?"

"You know you were." Katya forgave him with a smile. "She's grown into that outfit. The shoes and dress are all pre-unification. See the dyed cork heels and fake-leather straps? Very Communist chic."

"She's kept the dress because she can't afford a new one?"

Katya shook her head. "Denial. It's a universal feminine trait. As long as she can get the zipper up, she's still a size eight."

When their lunch arrived, Katya nodded toward a young man seated at the next table. She told Jeffrey, "Buy him an ice cream, please."

The young man was small and slender to the point of evident hunger. Dark eyes were planted at definite slants in leathery skin. The face was all hollows and sharp angles. "What for?"

"Buy him an ice cream, Jeffrey. If you won't, I will."

"You'll have to, anyway," Jeffrey replied. "I don't speak the lingo."

Katya motioned to the waitress and spoke to her at length. The waitress gave them both an odd look, then moved away.

"He's a Russian soldier," Katya explained.

"How do you know?"

"Lots of things. The plastic belt. The quietness. He doesn't even move his eyes. When the waitress went to his table, he pointed to the menu to order, and when the waitress brought him a coffee he looked crushed. He couldn't read the menu and didn't know how to ask for something to eat. It's probably his only leave. And his only money. I read that the soldiers in some barracks are selling their boots for food. The officers are so ashamed they're keeping the enlisted men locked inside the compounds for weeks at a time."

The waitress brought over a large metal boat of ice cream; the young man made enormous eyes. Katya leaned across the gap between their tables and explained with her hands that it was a gift. The young man bowed almost to the seat and smiled openhearted thanks.

"Watch," Katya whispered. "Watch how he eats."

The man became totally locked into his ice cream. It *consumed* his attention. He ate each little mound in turn, taking tiny slivers with his spoon, making it last and last and last. Each time he felt their eyes he turned and gave them another genuine smile.

"That look makes me want to cry," Katya said.

"My little Samaritan," he said.

"I feel so sorry for him," she said, turning away. "He is hated here. He lives in a hell called an enlisted men's barracks, and when he leaves here, what will he go back to? What hope does he have?"

When they left the cafe, snow flurries opened to reveal frantic scurrying clouds, then closed into curtains swept sideways by the wind. They followed the example of others and huddled up against the nearest building as they walked.

The Semper Gallery, their meeting point, proved to be the last bastion of old Dresden. Beyond it was all garish modernism and broken pavement and traffic. Buildings were glass and concrete and steel and tasteless. The contrast to the Semper palace could not have been starker.

They crossed a wooden bridge over a swan-filled moat, then passed under a multistory arch formed as a gilded crown and colonnaded pedestal. Inside were acres of carefully sculpted gardens, all brown and empty and waiting for spring. Scaffolding covered two thirds of the surrounding ornate palace, over a thousand feet to a side. The sound of construction followed them everywhere.

Katya pointed through the falling white veil to where two leather-coated individuals watched them. "Frau Reining said they would be wearing red scarfs."

It was only when they were a few paces away that Jeffrey realized the second person was a woman. Her face was all angles and hard lines, her expression stubborn and suspicious.

Her pockmarked companion spoke with a voice roughened by a metal rasp. Katya translated it as, "He wants to know if you are the one."

"The one what?"

"Let me tell him yes, all right? I don't feel comfortable with this pair."

The uneasiness he felt from their gaze hardened into genuine dislike at the thought of Katya's fear. "Tell them the question is out of a third-rate spy movie, and it's too cold out here for games."

Katya hesitated, then spoke in a soft voice. The man stiffened, then turned and stomped off. The woman watched him go, then turned back to Jeffrey with a smirk and spoke a few words.

"I don't understand," Katya said.

"What did she say?"

"End of drama."

"This is ridiculous. Tell her we're leaving."

Before Katya could speak the woman held up her hand, pointed to where the pockmarked man reappeared through the colonnaded atrium. With him scuttled a little figure bundled within a shapeless greatcoat. On closer inspection, Jeffrey decided the man looked like the embryo of a giant mole.

When he spoke, the man had the gentle lisp of an ageless Pan. "I hear that you are an honorable businessman, Mr. Sinclair," the little man said in greeting. The act of translating those few words was enough to give Katya's voice a colorless tone.

Jeffrey bridled. "No one has said the same about you."

Katya glanced his way. "How do you know that he can't speak English?"

"I don't know, and I don't care. I don't even know what

we are doing here." He looked down at her. "Can we please get out of this snow?"

"Don't you want to know what he's got to sell?"

"Look at these people, Katya. Tell me how you think they came up with something of value."

Katya hesitated, then turned back to the trio and spoke in her lilting German. The strange-shaped man replied in sibilant tones. Katya translated, "This place is a most appropriate spot for our meeting, as the palace resembles greatly the former home of what I have to sell."

The pockmarked man's dull stare rankled almost more than Jeffrey could stand. He turned sideways and asked, "Is this guy all there?"

"I don't know, but his German is very precise, very educated."

"They give me the creeps."

Katya nodded, waited for his move. Snow dusted her hair with a faint, damp frosting. "Tell him he has one minute to get this over with."

The little man showed no irritation. "What we are selling is currently being sought by three different governments, all of whom believe it is in their territory—Lithuania, Russia, and our own German government. We know they all are racing down false trails. We know this for a fact, Mr. Sinclair."

"What is it?"

"We are not selling the article," the little man continued in tones as gray as his skin, "but rather the article's location."

Jeffrey took in the bottle-bottom glasses pinched onto the smidgen of nose, the peach-fuzz hair, the sloping forehead, and decided this was the strangest human he'd ever seen. "You want me to buy directions to an antique?"

"We will supply you with a sample of the merchandise, which will leave no doubt in your mind whatsoever," the other replied. "Payment will be required only after you have received the sample. We seek nothing in advance."

That slowed Jeffrey down. "You don't?"

"We are most serious in this endeavor, I assure you, Mr. Sinclair. We have unearthed a hoard of world renown. And for this we wish to receive a mere two million dollars."

Jeffrey laughed out loud. "Come on, Katya. Let's go back to the ship."

The man's lisping voice stopped him. "Naturally, we are leaving ample room for you to add your own percentage."

"Tell the man it's been swell," Jeffrey replied. "But I deal in antiques, not fairy tales."

The unlined, snub-nosed face remained expressionless as he spoke. Katya translated, "He wants to know if you have ever heard of the Amber Room."

CHAPTER
19

"What did they look like, these three?" Alexander asked.

"The little man looked like a skinless frog," Jeffrey replied. "Flanked by his and her linebackers."

Katya laughed out loud. "They did not."

"That guy with the pox," Jeffrey persisted. "If he was any dumber, you'd need to water him twice a week."

They were seated in Alexander's spacious living room, the night's bitter chill kept at bay by a carefully tended fire. Their return trip from East Germany the day before had been long and tiring but uneventful, their arrival most welcomed by Alexander. The gala was weighing heavily upon him. Together they had put in a full day's work on final details, then Katya had pushed aside the old gentleman's objections and insisted that he allow her to prepare dinner.

"The man wasn't dull," Katya replied. "He was careful."

"He was dumb," Jeffrey stated flatly. "Who would we be that he needed to go back, get the little guy, sneak him out."

"Habits of a lifetime die hard," Alexander observed.

"And he didn't have the pox," Katya said.

"Whatever. His face looked like somebody had drilled for oil. About a thousand times."

"You didn't like them," Alexander said.

"I didn't like any of it. This isn't antiques."

"But they wanted nothing up front," Alexander said.

Jeffrey shook his head. "I don't understand what they're trying to pull, but whatever it is, it smells."

"As soon as that man opened his mouth, you were angry," Katya said, smiling now. "If you had been a dog, you'd have broken your chain and gone for his face."

"I wish I had," he said, liking the image. Chase the guy down a few blocks, come trotting back with a mouthful of trousers. "I can't believe we went all the way to Dresden to meet those clowns."

"Yes, well, despite your impressions, there may be something to this," Alexander said. "In my experience, it is the offbeat character who takes the wild risk. He has nothing to lose, you see. All the normal channels for gain and ambition are closed to him. He walks along gray paths, neither legal nor criminal, skirting the edges, looking for those chances that others have missed."

Jeffrey thought that over. "But how could a trio like that come up with something hidden in Poland?"

Alexander's gaze snapped to full alert. "That is what they said? Why did you not tell me?"

"I thought I had."

"It wasn't them," Katya said. "Frau Reining said it when she called to set up the meeting."

"And what did she make of those people?"

"She only met the woman," Katya replied with evident amusement. "But she would have sympathized with Jeffrey."

"Why does that make you smile?" Jeffrey asked.

"It's so unlike you," Katya replied. "The suave and debonair man of the world with his hackles up and his teeth bared."

"I didn't know you thought I was suave."

She nodded. "Sometimes I can hardly believe you can be so polished and not let it go to your head. You—"

"Yes, well," Alexander interrupted, "this is all perfectly fascinating, but I am still not clear on how Frau Reining entered into this picture."

The touch of Katya's gaze lingered upon Jeffrey long after her eyes had turned away. She described Frau Reining's contact with the woman and finished with, "Frau Reining is positive the woman is Stasi."

"Former Stasi," Alexander corrected, not disturbed by

the news. "That might explain how they gained access to secret information. Did she say anything more?"

"I don't think she was very interested in knowing anything else," Katya replied.

"Yes, I can imagine it must have been an uncomfortable reminder of a world she thought lost and gone forever," Alexander agreed. "My dear, do you know of the Amber Room?"

"I've heard of it," Katya replied. "It always sounded like something from Ali Baba and the Forty Thieves."

"In this case," Alexander said, "I assure you, the legend is real."

"I have to see to something in the kitchen." Katya stood. "This is a story I want to hear from beginning to end. You have to promise to talk about something boring until I get back."

Alexander watched her leave, said to Jeffrey, "I don't suppose your making moon eyes at each other has affected business overmuch."

"I don't make moon eyes," Jeffrey replied hotly.

"My dear young man, lunar landings could be made upon the glances you cast at each other." Alexander sipped at his coffee. "But no matter. You are entitled to them."

"Moon eyes. What nonsense."

"Yes, but much of love to an outsider is seen as nonsense. Just as faith in the unseen must be to a nonbeliever."

Jeffrey looked at him. "You're still having questions?"

"Doubts, my boy. Let us call them by their correct name. Doubts."

"Me too," he confessed.

"Not that God exists, nor that I am now seeking Him." Alexander set down his cup. "Only whether I shall be able to find Him."

"I know what you mean," Jeffrey responded. "Did you talk to Gregor about all this?"

"I tried." Alexander showed irritation. "He positively refused to discuss it. His manner reminded me of a proud parent praising a baby's first steps."

"And he's usually so . . ." Jeffrey searched for the words, "pointed in what he says."

"Scathingly so," Alexander agreed. "But not in this instance. All he would say is that I should listen to the Master's words."

Jeffrey compared this with his own recent telephone conversation and came up confused. "Are you reading the Bible?"

"Every morning."

"Do you pray?"

"I do indeed, and with unceasing difficulty. I feel as though I am waiting for the arrival of something that I remain unable even to name." He shook his head. "I have had several discussions on this point with the bishop—he's agreed to attend our little event, by the way. The poor man is positively mystified by my disagreeable searchings and assures me that all is quite in order. But whenever I permit myself the least little bit of self-satisfaction, I find the image of Gregor's most sardonic smile dancing in my mind. And I realize that I must continue with my quest for the unseen."

"A quest for the unseen," Katya said, reentering the parlor. "What a beautiful way to put it."

"Please excuse an old man's ramblings, my dear."

"No discussion about a soul's honest yearnings could ever be described as ramblings," Katya replied, seating herself. "And if you will excuse me for saying it, I agree with Gregor. To acknowledge your heart's unquenchable desires is a great step."

"And what must I do now?"

"Wait," she said with quiet firmness. "Wait upon the Lord. You are called simply to prepare the vessel. It is the Father's task to fill it."

Alexander eyed her with evident fondness. "You do an old man's heart a great deal of good, my dear."

"And a young man's," Jeffrey added.

"Thank you." She clasped her hands before her and raised her shoulders like an excited little girl. "Can we please come back to your story?"

"But of course." Alexander settled back in his chair. "It was at the very dawn of the Russian empire that our story begins. Peter the Great, the first emperor of all Russia, ascended to the throne in 1682. He was determined to lift his country from the Dark Ages that had dominated since the Mongul hordes swept out of Siberia and laid waste Russia's heartland four hundred years earlier.

"Europe was the key, Peter knew. He intended to bind his great land to the heart of Christendom. To do this, he established a new capital alongside the Baltic Sea, the warmest waters within his empire and the closest to Europe. He reclaimed vast stretches of land from swamp and inhospitable tribes, named the new city Saint Petersburg, and declared his intention to make it the Paris of the east.

"As a wedding present to his new wife, Catherine Alexejevna, he gave her the estate of Saari, which lay twenty-six kilometers from Saint Petersburg—a most important distance, as you will soon learn. The succeeding emperors and empresses added to the initial buildings, until the estate had grown from its original palace of sixteen rooms to one that stretched over almost as many acres. Palaces of other royal family members sprang up nearby, along with those of princes and noblemen whose power and wealth bought them the right to summer with the ruler of all Russia. This vast village of palaces and riches became known as *Zarskoje Selo,* and its centerpiece was the Catherine Palace.

"We must now turn our attention to one of Peter's neighbors, the largest of the German principalities and by far the most aggressive in matters political and military. Frederick William I, ruler of the Prussian empire, was concerned about this newly unified behemoth to his east, but he was plagued even more by wars and rumors of wars from his northern neighbor, Sweden. Less than a century before, you see, tribes of ferocious blond giants had swept across a land weakened by the Protestant-Catholic wars and laid waste to almost half of Europe. Frederick William wanted to maintain good relations with Russia so that his strength and attention could be directed toward the clearest and most present danger—the one to the north.

"It was then, in 1717, that Frederick William decided to give Emperor Peter the Great the Amber Room.

"*Das Bernstein Zimmer,* as it was then known, had been designed by German and Danish craftsmen for Frederick William's own palace, the Charlottenberg in Berlin.

"Most amber came from the Baltic shores—what now is shared by Germany, Poland, Lithuania, and Russia, and then was dominated by the Prussian and Polish kings. But the amount of amber which this room required surpasses modern understanding. Nowadays we sell amber by the milligram. Records from 1944 tell us that the amber used in the Amber Room weighed in at *twenty tons*.

"Nowadays, amber is considered by most people as simply another semiprecious jewel. But it is not really a stone at all, rather the fossilized sap of pine trees. And just as there are a number of different types of pines, there are great differences in the colors and shades of ambers.

"The amber was fashioned as wood might be for inlay upon fine furniture. Where various tones of cherry or olive or satinwood might be used to design a floral arrangement and background, the amber was sorted by color shades. But where wood would be kept to razor-thin slices, the amber was carved at thicknesses of an inch or more. The carvings were then fitted together to form panels rising from floor to ceiling, depicting a vast variety of scenes—Grecian urns, cherubim by the hundreds, romantic landscapes, prancing stallions, royal emblems. Hundreds of thousands of amber pieces carved and polished and fitted precisely together, to cover the entire room.

"The gift of the Amber Room to Peter the Great marked the signing of a treaty of unending friendship between the two powers, and was intended to go in the Winter Palace in Saint Petersburg. But it was soon moved to the Catherine Palace at *Zarskoje Selo,* where it adorned one of the royal chambers.

"And such a chamber it must have been," Alexander went on. "Only one color photograph remains, taken toward the end of World War II. That picture shows a vast hall, perhaps sixty feet long and forty wide, with ceilings rising up twenty-five feet. Between each of the amber panels were wide mirrors with solid silver backing and solid gold frames. The three chandeliers were of solid silver, as were the hundred or so candelabras set into the walls. There was also a central table with vast silver and gold candelabras.

"Hundreds and hundreds of candles dancing and flickering on panel after jeweled panel." He smiled at the thought. "Those fortunate enough to view it gave it the name, Eighth Wonder of the World."

CHAPTER
20

Night gave way to dawn, the darkness not defeated but retreating grudgingly before a cloud-shrouded morning. Night left its shadows everywhere, on dank and sooty sidewalks, around corners of crumbling buildings, about the tired faces of early-moving people—silent reminders of its inevitable return. The cities of former East Germany were never far from the night.

The dwindling crowd within the Schwerin tavern had arrived at its lowest ebb. Conversations were muted and sentences seldom finished, words carelessly tossed out by mouths reluctant to make the effort. Eyes were dulled and distant from a night of little hope and the prospect of a bed with less warmth.

Erika chose that time to set her hands upon the table and stretch them out wide, as though clenching into the grain. Her nails were broad and flat, her hands very strong. She announced quietly, "My friend has found the man."

Kurt gave her an awful look. "You've been sitting here for almost an hour, and you just now decide to speak?"

"I've been trying to decide whether to tell you at all," she snapped back.

"What's that supposed to mean?"

Ferret raised his eyes from the aged yellow pages before him. "It means, Kurt, that she no longer is content to do our bidding. Doesn't it, my dear?"

"I've a right to know," she said stubbornly.

"Of course you do." The sibilant voice carried no sense of warmth and even less inflection. "You are a most valued member of our team, a full partner with every right to know all about our little quest."

"And how much," Erika replied. "Don't forget that bit."

"Of course I won't. The question is, where do I begin?"

"Begin by asking her if she can trust her contact to give us the right information," Kurt said. "We don't need just any address from an old Berlin telephone directory."

"I didn't say I had an address," Erika replied, her eyes on Ferret. "I said I had the *man*."

Ferret peered back at her through spectacles so thick they made his eyes appear to swim. "You are sure of this?"

Erika nodded. "You didn't tell me he had been posted in Königsberg, did you?"

"No," lisped the little man. "I did not."

"Colonel in charge of Division Transport, wasn't that right?"

"As I said," Ferret replied, "you have every right to know."

"Start with how much," Erika demanded. "I like to get the big things out of the way."

"As I said to our Western contacts, how would you feel about half a million?" Ferret asked. "Dollars."

Even Kurt showed surprise. "You really think they'll pay what you asked?"

"I should think two million dollars is not too much to ask for the location of the Eighth Wonder of the World," Ferret replied. "Would you?"

Erika recovered sufficiently to ask, "Who gets the fourth share?"

"I would imagine the man who remains yet unknown," Ferret replied. "He shall probably wish to have a share. If not, well, that would only mean more for us."

"Not to mention papers and travel," Kurt said.

"And my friend in Dresden," Erika added. "She's holding out the most important bits until we work out the next payment."

"There are many incidentals attached to our quest and

our escape," Ferret agreed. "But these we may leave for later. What matters now is that our lady partner has a wish to know."

"And a right," Erika added.

"Of course, my dear. Well, the story begins in 1717, when the world was shaped far differently from what we know today, and was even more unstable than these dark and uncertain times.

"As you know," Ferret went on, "Kaliningrad, as it is today known, was the capital of East Prussia before the war. Königsberg it was called then, a place full of palaces and wealth the likes of which we can only dream about today. Now it is Lithuania's main port, and little is left of its once glorious past."

His two listeners sat in utter stillness. Deadpan faces had long since lost the ability to react, but there was no masking the feverish glitter in their eyes. They remained blind to the cafe, the early morning, and all the new faces strange to their habitual nighttime crowd.

"During the war years Königsberg was ruled by a man called Erich Koch," Ferret went on. "His title was *Gauleiter*, which back then meant both Nazi Party leader and chief of the regional government. In effect, he had the power of life and death over all who lived there, and he ruled with an iron hand. On June 22, 1941, when the Nazis rolled the Blitzkrieg into Russia, Koch was also given the position of Kommissar over all Ukraine."

"A license to steal," Kurt offered.

"All completely legal," Ferret agreed. "As Gauleiter and Kommissar, he also carried the title of *Künst-Schutz Offizier*. In that capacity, as officer in charge of the security of treasures, he was entitled to 'relocate' all appropriated treasures to Nazi Germany.

"He robbed the treasure houses of Minsk, Pinsk, and Kiev," Ferret went on. His lisping voice did not require strength to hold his listeners fast. "But he had to hurry. There were many treasure troves, and only so many trucks and trusted soldiers could be spared. The Nazis surrounded Leningrad and began the famous siege, then continued on to their destiny and death on the icy Steppes before the Moscow gates. Koch, in the meantime, arrived at *Zarskoje Selo,* which held the treasure troves within the Catherine Palace and lay just far enough outside Leningrad to be within the Nazis' grasp."

"The Catherine Palace," Erika said. "All this is true?"

"Most well documented, I assure you, if you only know where to look," Ferret replied. "There are no complete records, however, on how much the Nazis transported back to Königsberg. The wealth in the Catherine Palace and the other royal summer residences was so great that it simply overwhelmed the Nazi record keepers. We do know that the transport required seventy trucks. Think of it. Seventy trucks brought together in the midst of the greatest siege in modern warfare, and simultaneous with the push across two thousand miles of enemy territory to Moscow."

"They must have found something special," Kurt said.

"So many things, so special, that they left behind *twenty thousand* treasures. We know this because that which remains now makes up the permanent collection of the Catherine Palace Museum, one of the greatest such exhibitions in all the world."

The morning sun poked through an opening in the clouds and glinted against the sweat-streaked window. Erika leaned far back in her chair so her face could remain in accustomed shadows.

"And these are the leftovers," Kurt said, shaking his head. "Amazing."

"Amazing is the right word," Ferret agreed, his voice barely above a whisper. "Amazing that among the treasures selected by the Nazis was an entire royal chamber with amber walls. Koch lost no time in stripping these jewels from their frames and wrapping the segments in cigarette paper. They must have been well aware of what they held, for the records pertaining to this one room are the most complete of the entire shipment. Upon each strip of paper was recorded the segment's place in the wall puzzle—quite a daunting task I would imagine, what with the pressure to complete this work and continue on behind the army's march to Moscow. Day and night, as guns boomed in the distance, the amber was rolled in wadding and packed into iron chests. Twenty tons of amber in all."

The Ferret spoke with scarce movements of his small bloodless lips, his lumpy body curved over the ever-present file, his pale, soft hands resting motionless upon the yellowed pages as though drawing sustenance from their ancient script. "Once the trucks arrived in Königsberg, unskilled hand workers and soldiers reassembled the pieces in a chamber of the central castle. Some amber was destroyed, one entire panel went missing and was never restored. Even so, this chamber became the single most popular museum exhibit in all Nazi Germany. And for good reason."

"For as long as it lasted," Kurt offered.

"It remained there for almost three years," Ferret replied. "Until July of 1944. One month after it was taken down and relocated, the expected waves of bombers arrived. The British carpet-bombed Königsberg for three days and nights, destroying almost half the city and leaving behind fires that burned for another five days before they were finally extinguished."

Erika shifted uneasily. "I've had enough of the history lesson."

"It is distasteful, I agree," Ferret said, "but an important part of our story."

"I don't see how," Erika said. "All that's better dead and buried."

"You asked for the scoop," Kurt snapped. "Button up and let him get on with it."

Erika flared, "I don't take that from anyone."

"Please, please," Ferret lisped. "Let us act as partners, yes? We have a long road yet ahead."

Kurt held her fast with his gaze, said to Ferret, "Get on with it."

Instead, Ferret stripped off his glasses, revealing surprisingly small eyes. They were a weak-looking, washed-out blue in color, and very red-rimmed. He pressed two childlike fingers to the bridge of his nose and said, "I really must insist on a truce here. We are seeking to unearth the hidden, do the impossible, escape with both freedom and the money with which to enjoy it. Such bickering must stop."

Erika leaned back in her chair, grumbled, "My old man used to get drunk and talk about the war and the bombings.

On and on he went. Then he'd start beating on anyone he could grab. Almost every night. It gave me the creeps then and it does now."

"My dad died in the war," Kurt said, subsiding. "I remember the bombings, though. Horrible, they were. Worse than horrible."

Erika looked at him, the makings of a cease-fire in her eyes. "You were a war child, too?"

He nodded. "Born in thirty-nine."

"You've five years on me, then. My old man, he said I was born in a bomb shelter and got covered with dust the minute I came out." Her tone now was conversational. "I never knew my mother."

"Me neither. I was a Young Patriot of the Great and Glorious Communist State," he said wryly, referring to the title given war orphans in the fifties.

Erika looked amused. "Fired with the true Communist spirit from the cradle."

"When young," he admitted. "Now I live for myself."

"The only logical course," Erika agreed.

"I knew all the right slogans, and I could shout with the best of them," Kurt went on. "But in truth I learned long ago to care for the State about as much as the State cared for me."

"I too lived the great lie," Erika said quietly.

They shared a look of understanding before Kurt repeated to Ferret, calm now, "Get on with the telling."

"With pleasure." Ferret refitted his spectacles. "The chamber was dismantled, as I said, in June of 1944. It was first placed inside the castle cellars, but after the British bombing leveled the castle, it was thought safer to locate it elsewhere. A temporary home was found in a local brewery, where it was walled into a disused storage room. The officials asked a local count if he would allow them to store it in his cellar, but he refused on the grounds that the cellar was too damp. So it was decided to transport the Amber Room along with other valuables in what proved to be the last recorded transfer of treasures before the fall of the Nazi empire."

Erika shook her head. "You sound so sure."

"I am."

"How can this be?"

"I have been searching," he replied, "for the pieces of a puzzle. Those who made this search before, the bureaucrats who were ordered to do so by their communist bosses, sought with logic. When logic failed them, rather than admit defeat, they declared that there was in fact no puzzle at all—that the treasure had been destroyed in the bombing. But this I know to be false. I have found what they were too lazy to seek out. Doors in the West have been opened to me that remained ever closed to them and their endless demands for secrecy."

Erika asked, "So what do you have instead of logic to solve these puzzles?"

"He lives with them," Kurt replied, the gleam strong in his eyes. "Don't ask me to explain it, because I can't. But I've been with him for almost fifteen years, and I know it for fact. Accept it."

"You must remember," Ferret said, "that many of the puzzles are indeed false, the treasures forever lost. More than many. Almost all. I have spent years and years walking upon paths which in truth no longer existed."

"But not this time," Erika demanded, hoping in spite of herself.

Ferret shook his head. "No. This time I am sure."

Erika thought it over, nodded her acceptance. "So a final transfer of the Amber Room was made."

"It left Königsberg in December of 1944," Ferret agreed. "The last available eighteen working trucks were loaded and placed upon flatbed railroad cars. There was very little gasoline left, you see. Certainly none to be had once they left territory controlled by their *Gauleiter,* no matter who signed and stamped their passes. In those last chaotic days, all remaining supplies were hoarded by the lucky and shared with none."

"A lot of treasure was left behind, I wager," Kurt said.

"More than was taken," Ferret agreed. "Room was made only for the priceless."

"Like the chamber," Erika said.

"Just so. The twenty tons of amber were stored this time in seventy-two steel chests, each so massive it took four men to shift. These cases took up three of the eighteen trucks. The train pulled out under cover of night, barely before the nemesis arrived."

"The Russians," Kurt said.

Erika smiled without humor. "You mean to say our saviors, don't you?"

"The invasion began on January 26, 1945," Ferret continued. "Königsberg fell on April 9. Between those two dates, the city was pounded into the dust. When the Russians finally entered the city, not a single building remained intact. Not one. The seven-hundred-year-old capital of the Prussian empire was totally obliterated."

With nervous gestures Erika fished a Russian cigarette from a crumpled pack. She spent a moment composing herself and pressing the paper-tube filter into various shapes. She finally lit it, drew hard, sighed with the smoke. "Cursed memories."

Kurt had the decency to look away. "But the chamber was already gone."

"Not according to the Soviets and their official story," Ferret replied, "I am happy to say. After searching for almost twenty years, they claimed that it was destroyed in the bombing and that the rest of the story was myth. But the Soviets have now fallen, and the new Russian government claimed that new evidence points a finger at cliffs filled with Nazi bombs."

"But you claim otherwise."

"I do not just claim," Ferret replied. "I know. I have had access to information which the Russians did not."

Kurt's eyebrows crept up. "The American quartermaster sergeant?"

"A mere conduit. But the records he gave us were invaluable."

"And the soldier who died in Siberia? The one whose records were supplied by the Russian colonel?"

"That is a bit of the puzzle overlooked by the logical plodders. They sought to do a job; their reward was security and nothing more. Finding or not finding the hidden treasures had no effect on their salary. Not a formula for stimulating independent thought."

"What about my trips south?"

"Doing away with possible loose ends," Ferret replied. "We had to be sure, you see. The caves at Jonastal and the underground bunkers in Weimar were intended as the collection point for all such treasures. The Königsberg shipment was supposed to have traveled there, just as Yeltsin said."

"*Supposed* to be there."

Ferret nodded. "No trace was found, no evidence that the trucks arrived."

Kurt waited, asked the expected question. "So where is the Amber Room?"

Ferret turned to Erika, who had managed to replace her stonelike visage. "You have the man's address?"

"My friend does. As of last year. He is old, and he may have died, but as of last year he still lived there."

"Let us hope that this essential thread remains within our grasp," Ferret replied. "I suggest we travel as soon as it is dark."

"Twenty tons of amber," Kurt said. "How much is that worth?"

Ferret blinked. "Nothing and everything."

"What is that supposed to mean?"

"It does not matter how much it is worth," Ferret said, "if we are not alive and free to enjoy the wealth."

"Let me see if I understand," Erika said. "We're going crazy looking for a treasure that isn't there—"

"Oh, believe me, it is there."

"—so that even if we do find it, we can't sell it," Erika finished. "That makes as much sense as one of Honecker's old speeches."

"Let him talk," Kurt said, but mildly. Erika shot him a glance, saw no rancor, subsided.

"As I said to our American contact, we do not sell what we cannot recover," Ferret explained. "We do not struggle to take what we could never escape with. There is no war to mask our efforts, no crisis to blind people to the unearthing and transporting of seventy-two heavy chests. No. We sell what is weightless, what can be packed in the smallest coffer and carried without being a burden to anyone."

"Information," Kurt said, nodding. "Smart."

"We will sell a treasure map," Ferret continued, "and leave the struggles over unearthing and the battles over ownership to the nations."

"While we make like the wind." Kurt smiled, exposing yellowed teeth. "We're in the pirate business. I like it."

"We will not be greedy," Ferret said. "We want the wealth of the fortunate, the ones able to enjoy the spoils. We will ask only so much that it is easier to pay than to give chase."

"Five hundred thousand apiece sounds like a fortunate number," Kurt agreed. "When do we leave?"

CHAPTER
21

"But twenty tons of amber," Jeffrey protested. "Seventy-two gigantic steel chests. How could anybody make something that big just disappear?"

It was two weeks since their return from Dresden, the day of the gala event. Despite the blitz of last-minute details, every free moment, every lapse in their work, every pause for coffee or food was spiced with reflection over the undiscovered.

"The war essentially turned much of Europe into the world's largest flea market," Alexander explained. "Priceless items were sold by the pound, and treasures were passed around like tourist mementos."

"That's hard to imagine." Jeffrey continued with his careful checking of place cards for the tables, grateful for the conversation to break the tedium of preparation.

"I understand. But this does not make it any less true. In Nazi-occupied territories, well-placed generals arrived for inspections with scores of empty lorries. Their hosts, the heads of the local military governments, offered roomfuls of treasures to remain in the general staff's good favor."

"Treasures," Jeffrey repeated, thinking of Betty.

"I realize it must sound strange to you, having never lived through such horrors yourself. But you cannot imagine how much was flooding the German-controlled markets, especially toward the end of the war. There was literally a sea of goods swept up by the German armies, mind-boggling amounts from cities and palaces stretching from Paris to the gates of Moscow. An entire world of treasures, carted off by the conquering armies. And then came defeat. And rout. Retreats planned in haste and executed in blind panic. With wave after wave of Allied bombers destroying roads and rails and airports. With few trucks that still ran and petrol scarcer than emeralds."

"So it wasn't just that records might have been lost," Jeffrey said. "Quite possibly, there were no records to begin with."

Alexander tossed his pen aside. "My dear Jeffrey, an entire castle could have disappeared into the morass of those final days with its going never noticed or recorded.

"Mind you," he went on, "this was not always the case. There were of course specialists on the German staff whose only job was to catalogue and ship the booty. Yet even at the best of times, when Germany was winning and the legendary German efficiency was in firm command, these people were worked to the point of exhaustion. In many documented cases, they only managed to view the tip of the iceberg. Most of these professionals were assigned to headquarters staff, used by the senior officers to catalogue what they themselves intended to hoard."

"Which left everyone else below them without expert assistance."

"Precisely. Officers in the field were laws unto themselves when it came to such matters, so long as a certain flow of goods continued to arrive at headquarters. This meant that much of the loot they happened upon was diverted to their own warehouses or parceled out to their men as rewards. And almost all of these items were catalogued by enlisted men, many of whom did not have a clue as to what they were handling. For example, I have seen records in which a Matisse, three Renoirs, and two Van Goghs were listed as 'six gilt frames with pictures.'"

Jeffrey strapped together the final dozen cards for the last table and announced, "That's done."

"Splendid. I am so grateful for your assistance, Jeffrey.

It would have been an impossible task to take on alone."

"It's been fun. Really."

"Yes, knowing that you share my enjoyment for both our profession and such events has been a reward in itself." Alexander glanced at his watch. "What time did you want to be off?"

"In a few minutes." The excitement that had been tugging at him threatened to spill over. He pushed it away with, "What do you think the room actually looked like?"

"Magnificent, without a doubt. I would imagine it to be as richly textured as a sunrise," Alexander mused. "That was undoubtedly the designer's intention, you know—to create an inlaid chamber fit for a king."

"An amber chamber," Jeffrey said for the thousandth time that week. "Incredible. Almost like walking inside a jewel."

"Oh, far more grand, I should imagine," Alexander replied. "Remember, the amber was of a hundred different hues, from the deepest topaz-brown to a fine white-gold champagne. Whatever the amber's shade, light transforms it into something that appears both molten and eternally still, a prism of softest hues. Imagine the color of sunlight through dark ale, or honey, or a fine white wine—this has always been amber's most appealing quality to me, its ability to take whatever light is cast upon it and transform it into something divine."

"But a *room* of it," Jeffrey said, awed by the thought.

"Yes, imagine." Alexander leaned back in his chair and said to the ceiling, "Hundreds of thousands of facets matched for both tone and texture, then carved like bits of a vast, room-sized puzzle. The result was a set of three-dimensional walls that appeared to flicker and flow."

"And all the light unsteady and shifting," Jeffrey continued, captivated by the thought. "Imagine what a cloud passing before the sun would have done to the walls."

"Exactly. The light of that era would have been splendid for amber. Vast floor to ceiling windows, all those chandeliers and candelabras, and tall mirrors reflecting the candlelight; the walls would take on a life of their own, flickering at hints of mysteries within their unfrozen depths. Yes, I would imagine that a chamber of amber would be the most mystical of earthly experiences. Especially at night, as its residents pondered vast affairs of state or read from ancient texts, or sought answers in the depths of walls whose very form appeared to flow with the power of thought."

Alexander rose to his feet, began gathering up the neatly stacked and bound place cards. "A famous Russian poet, a guest of the czar, was once invited to sit in the Amber Room. Upon his return to the more mundane realms, he wrote that when the sun shone in the room or the candles played over the walls at night, the room appeared to be *alive*. Every stone, every ornament, every single minute element of this timeless work combined to create a symphony of silent beauty."

Alexander closed his briefcase, snapped the locks, asked, "You will be meeting me at the prearranged time?"

"With Katya," Jeffrey said, rising as well.

"I do wish you would tell me what all the mystery is about. This is definitely not a night for further surprises."

"Everything we've been able to think of has been done," Jeffrey replied. "I went by at lunchtime, and the display cases and guards are all in."

"That was not what I was speaking of, and you know it. You have something up your sleeve for this evening, I've been catching wind of it now for several—"

"I've got to be going," Jeffrey interrupted, heading for the door. "See you at the Ritz."

Claridge's had no bar. Instead, hotel guests gathered in a parlor the size of a manor house's formal living room and furnished accordingly with overstuffed settees, graceful Chippendale high-backed chairs, Empire coffee tables, original oil paintings, crystal chandeliers, and positively the largest handmade rug Jeffrey had ever seen. Service was provided by footmen in brass-buttoned uniforms festooned with braid and buckles and ornamental finery. In the far corner, a quartet strung theater tunes together with light Strauss waltzes and Brahms melodies. The parlor's atmosphere was subdued yet grand, and reeked of wealth.

Jeffrey escaped the blustery winter damp by waiting in

the hotel's white-marble front lobby. He had time to check his dinner jacket for unnoticed stains, his starched shirtfront for wayward studs, and his silk bowtie for recent skews before he spotted Katya alighting from a taxi. The box in his pocket bounced against his side as he rushed for the door.

He paid off Katya's driver and ushered her back inside. She wore a dark gray overcoat with black velvet piping at arms and sides that ended at the cuffs in a curlicue of intricate handwork. Cloth buttons fitted within miniature matching designs formed double-breasted rows down the front. The velvet collar was high and stiff and rose to meet her shimmering black hair.

Jeffrey brushed at raindrops sparkling her locks. "You look like a Russian fairy princess."

She replied with a curtsy and "Thank you, my dashing prince."

He took her arm and ushered her into the hotel proper. "I'm sorry not to have picked you up, but I didn't have time to come out and still be with you here."

"That's all right." She stopped by the cloakroom and began unbuttoning her coat. "But why Claridge's?"

"I promised . . . No, wait, you'll see." He helped her with the coat. Underneath it, Katya wore an off-the-shoulder gown of emerald green silk, slit along one leg to reveal matching sheer stockings and high-heeled slippers. Her only jewelry was a tiny gold cross nestled in the base of her neck. His heart was squeezed tight by the sight of her. "Katya, I can't believe how beautiful you are."

She rewarded him with a sparkling smile. "When you look at me like that, I feel as if I need a fan to hide behind."

"Come on." He led her down the central hall, past the porter's desk, through the high portico, and into the formal parlor, conscious all the while that every eye in the hotel was upon them.

A liveried footman bowed a formal greeting and held Katya's chair. She made round eyes and whispered to Jeffrey, "What is all this?"

"Wait." He seated himself beside her and waited for the footman to depart. "I am doing this for all those who have helped to bring us together, Katya. May we honor them all our days with our love for each other."

"The way you say that makes me shiver." She looked at him for a long moment. "You sound so formal."

"I've thought about this moment for a long time," Jeffrey replied.

"What is it?"

"I'm not doing this for me," he replied. "Well, I am, but it's for others too. Especially why I'm doing it here. I promised someone."

"Jeffrey Allen Sinclair," she said sharply. "You positively may not make me cry tonight."

"I have something for you," he persisted. "It just arrived yesterday, and I know she'd want you to wear it tonight."

"Who?"

"My grandmother. When she became engaged to Piotr, my grandfather, Alexander gave her this and then took them here for dinner. She wants you to have this as her engagement present, and she asked if I would give it to you here, her favorite hotel in all the world. She asked me to tell you that she is very sorry not to be here, but her health won't allow it, so she hopes we will be traveling over to America very soon. She says that from what I've told her, she is sure you are a gift from above." He had to stop and swallow hard. "She also hopes we will be as happy as she was with Piotr, and that we will remember her and the love she holds—"

"Stop, Jeffrey. Please."

"The love she holds for us both," he finished. He brought the long, slender velvet box from his pocket. "This is for you, Katya."

"I can't."

"Please. I want you to have it. We both do."

Gingerly she accepted the box, pressed the little catch, swung open the top, gave a trembling sigh. "Oh, Jeffrey."

There were sixteen emeralds in all. Eight formed the necklace's first row, five the second, and a single gem twice as large as the others hung below in solitary splendor. Each was framed within a casing of yellow gold, and suspended upon a netting of intertwined red and white gold rope. The final two jewels were set as matching earrings and hung from little perches on the box's silk-lined top.

She reached over, asked, "May I have your handkerchief, please?"

"Here."

"Thank you." She dabbed at her eyes. "Am I a mess?"

"You are the most beautiful woman I have ever laid eyes on," he answered truthfully. "Would you like me to help you put it on?"

"All right." She swiveled in her seat to present him with her back.

He lifted the necklace, threaded it around her neck, fastened it, tasted her skin with his lips. "Turn around."

"How does it look?"

"Stop patting it for a second so I can see."

"Is this really for me?"

He nodded. "Do you want to try on the earrings, too?"

"Tell me how it looks, Jeffrey. Please."

"As though it were made for you. Truly." And it did. The jewels' shimmering green accented her skin's creamy whiteness and her eyes' sparkling depths.

She leaned forward to kiss him. "I don't think I can find the right words to thank you just now, Jeffrey."

"You don't have to say anything."

"Yes I do, and I will. But not just now." She rose to her feet, taking the box with her. "Now if you'll excuse me for a moment, I positively must go see this for myself."

CHAPTER
22

Unlike many great hotels, the Ritz carried the splendor of its lobby and public rooms into the main ballroom. A pair of liveried waiters flanked the double entranceway. Within these portals, the first guests milled about in the formal anteroom, itself much larger than many great-rooms. Beyond the polished-wood floors with their Persian carpets and valuable antiques stood yet another set of crested double doors, these leading into the ballroom proper.

Each of the ballroom tables was set for twelve and crowned with a vast floral centerpiece. Massive gilt chandeliers, nine in all, cast soft brilliance over the immaculate setting. In the hall's very center stood the display cases, of gray steel and security glass, holding the trio of precious Polish artifacts.

Alexander stood just inside the first set of doors, giving last-minute instructions to the obsequious maitre d'. The old gentleman was resplendent in well-fitting finery; the only mark of color to his severe, black-and-white evening wear was a small gold medal on watered silk that hung from his lapel. Jeffrey had never seen such a medal before, had no idea what it meant.

The old gentleman's eyes lit up at the sight of Katya. Alexander waved the maitre d' away and focused his entire attention on the young woman, pausing a very long moment before bowing and kissing the offered hand.

"My dear," he murmured. "You look absolutely exquisite."

Katya touched her free hand to her neck. "I believe I have you to thank for these."

"Tonight the past has come alive for me once more," Alexander replied quietly.

"I only wish Piotr and his wife were here for me to thank as well," Katya said.

Alexander looked at Jeffrey. "In one respect, they are. A part of them."

"A magnificent part," Katya said, looking up with pride at her husband-to-be.

Alexander nodded. "May I say how delighted and happy I am for you both."

"Thank you," she said, joy shining in her eyes.

"I suppose Jeffrey has told you of my engagement present."

"Not yet," Jeffrey replied.

"Then I shall. My dear, my first purchase as an antiques dealer was a ring. I have kept it long enough. I have asked Jeffrey if I might be permitted to offer it as an engagement ring, a mark of the affection I hold for you both."

Katya reached for Jeffrey's hand. "Please don't make me cry again."

"Very well." He clapped his hands. "Enough! I too shall be no good at all tonight if we continue. My dear, please be so kind as to go reassure the Count. He is over by the display case trying to convince himself that he has seen the chalice before. In Rome of all places."

"Of course," Katya agreed, and departed with a regal half-inch curtsy for Alexander and a brief hand-squeeze for Jeffrey.

They watched her gliding passage. "A magnificent young woman," Alexander said. "And a worthy mate for you, my friend."

"I only hope I can be the same for her."

"You will, you will. Of that I have no doubt." Alexander's manner became brisk. "I have reluctantly decided that you two must be separated tonight."

"All right." It was to be expected.

"You are both too valuable to keep together. I shall place Katya as hostess to a table of old Polish nobility. They will treat her like the queen she is."

"She'll like that," he said, missing her already.

"Your table will be a mixed lot. More males than females—there are several like that. Can't be helped, I'm afraid. But there is one gentleman in particular whom I have placed beside you, a photographer."

"He must be doing well to be able to afford tonight."

"Oh, he's here as the guest of one of our wealthier patrons-to-be. His name is Viktor Bogdanski. I'll introduce you when he arrives." Alexander patted Jeffrey's arm in parting and turned to greet new arrivals.

Jeffrey mingled as the room filled with wealth and power. Ignoring the uncomfortable sense that these people lived in a world where he did not belong, he greeted clients he had met in the shop, made polite noises as he drifted from circle to circle, kissed the air above innumerable age-scarred and bejeweled hands. Alexander was constantly pulling him before new faces, making sure that all present understood who he was.

Katya came over from time to time, to smile and share a few words before being pulled away once more. The Count had appointed himself responsible for ensuring that everyone met her. Yet no matter where Jeffrey was or with whom he spoke, he remained acutely aware of her presence. The brief glances they shared across the elegantly crowded room sparkled with an intimacy they knew was on display for all to see, and yet which they could not help but share.

Eventually Alexander led him to a small, neat man with a sharply trimmed beard who stood quietly in a corner, nodding and smiling slightly when attention turned his way. Jeffrey's first impression was of a man utterly content with his own solitude.

"Jeffrey, I would like to you to meet Viktor Bogdanski. Viktor, this is the friend I have spoken with you about."

Viktor offered his hand. "Alexander seldom speaks as highly of anyone as he has of you."

"I seldom have reason to," Alexander replied. "Now, I

shall leave you two to discover why I wanted you to meet."

Jeffrey watched the old gentleman glide back into the beautifully dressed crowd. "This is the most comfortable spot I've found all night."

"I share your sentiment wholeheartedly."

"So why are you here?"

"Ah." The man sipped at his drink. "I happen to believe in what is behind this charade. Events like this are a necessary nuisance. They are as close to real need as many of these beautiful people would ever care to come."

Jeffrey spoke of a concern he had carried since the project's onset. "Do you think perhaps the money should be going to something more, well—"

"Urgent?" The man shrugged. "I try not to judge the actions of others. I am also an artist of sorts, and I consider that there is more to the rebuilding of a nation than just filling bellies and healing physical wounds. Preserving a sense of national heritage is a most worthy endeavor." He smiled around his beard. "That is, I would think so if I were to judge such goings-on. Which I won't."

Jeffrey motioned at the sparkling throng. "The trickle-down theory at work."

"Exactly." Viktor examined him frankly. "Alexander tells me that you are new to the faithful fold."

"Newly returned," Jeffrey admitted. "Or trying to find my way back."

Viktor nodded approval. "It is good to know which way to turn when the wind blows."

"I am not all that sure I've got it clearly worked out," Jeffrey admitted.

"Toward the unseen sun," the photographer said emphatically. "You must remember where it was when you last saw it, and reach for it in hopes of its reappearing soon."

Jeffrey thought over the man's words as Alexander called the gathering to silence, welcomed them, repeated the night's mission, and invited them to find their assigned seats according to both the seating chart beside the doors and the place cards by each seat.

As they moved slowly toward and through the double doors, Katya came up and slipped her hand into his arm.

"Would the handsomest gentleman in the room be so kind as to escort me to my table?"

He looked down at her and said quietly, "I'm so proud of you."

Her violet-gray eyes shone at him. "I wish I could kiss you."

"Alexander told me to cool down the way we were looking at each other," he told her. "He said there were some hearts in this room too old for such vicarious passion."

"The Count put it differently," she replied as they entered the grand ballroom. "He said the sparks we were generating might set some of these varnished hairdos alight."

They arrived at her table. Jeffrey made the obligatory circle, exchanged stiff-backed bows with aged Polish aristocracy, kissed the hands of dowagers, held the back of Katya's seat, accepted a smile that touched him at levels he had not known existed, then walked to his own table.

The first courses were set in place. The glasses were hand-cut leaded crystal, the plates rimmed with gold leaf, the waiters swift and silently efficient. Jeffrey returned toasts and exchanged polite conversation with the others, wishing he felt more comfortable with such social chatter.

Viktor eventually pried himself free from the matron to his left, turned to Jeffrey, said, "I detect a yearning for a fare of greater substance."

"You're right there."

"Very well, I agree." He gave a sort of seated bow. "You begin with a question, and let us see where it takes us."

Jeffrey thought of Gregor and asked, "How did you come to faith?"

That brought a chuckle. "You do not act in half measures. I like that."

"If you'd rather—"

Viktor waved it aside. "Not at all. It is a most worthy question. What matters the surroundings to such as that?" He thought a moment. "I shall have to take us back to some rather dark days in my nation's heritage in order to answer you, however. It all took place during the early days of martial law in Poland."

Jeffrey nodded. "That's fine, but only if you want to."

Viktor's dark eyes turned inward. "I suppose there are many bad things to be during a state of siege, but among the worst is a photographer for the losing side. What my eyes saw, my camera captured. Thus was the moment preserved on my film and in my mind and heart for all my days. The bitterest truth and the harshest image.

"My life was my pictures, and my pictures sought to give life and reality to what otherwise could not be imagined. I sought to show the outside world the chains my country was seeking to cast off, the price my people had been forced to pay in carrying their weight for so very long.

"The date was December 11, 1981. I can't say that it was a typical evening. There was more excitement than usual, a tension throughout Poland that you could almost touch. I had captured some great material over the past several days. Massive demonstrations of workers. Students clambering on the shoulders of their fellows to look over the militia's riot gear and talk to them, shout at them, plead with them to wake up and remember who they were. A series of footprints in fresh snow forming the word *zwyciezymy,* which means 'We shall overcome.' Sympathy strikes by trainees in the fire department, who of course were seen as a great threat by the authorities, since firemen were officially part of the power structure.

"The clever activists among us, the ones who treated politics as a chess game, were speculating that a state of emergency would be declared. I would listen to such talk, but I seldom took part. My task, my life in those days, was simply to be the eyes for those who sought to see but because of distance or barriers could not. And yet I did listen, and much of what I heard made sense. The situation economically and politically was getting out of hand. There was no food on the shelves; everything had been diverted by the central authorities in an attempt to cow the people, force them by fear and by hunger into submission. The queues were unbearable, even for bread."

The room swirled about them in wafts of rich food and expensive perfume. Jewels glinted and flickered in the chandeliers' glow. Rich fabrics and starched shirtfronts and polished cuff links caught light and sent it spinning with each gesture and every word. As Jeffrey sat listening to Viktor's words, he felt a new dimension growing from the night. There was the world that he saw, and the world of Viktor's memories, and both held portents he could scarcely comprehend.

"We expected the decree might come in mid-December, when the Sejm, our Parliament, was to meet," Viktor continued. "Under the Polish constitution, only the Sejm has the power to decree a state of emergency. That evening, I was working on my photographs at the Solidarity press office in Warsaw, preparing a portfolio that friends would attempt to smuggle out of the country. It was a very good collection of images. As I was sorting them, our halls were suddenly filled with the militia's navy-blue uniforms. They said they had warrants for our arrest. We were accused of anti-government activities.

"Funny what you think at a moment like that. I was only worried about my camera. I looked over my shoulder as they led me from the room in handcuffs. They were going through my files of stills and slides and negatives. One of them picked up my camera, opened the back and stripped out the film, then with a casual motion swung it against the wall and smashed it. I felt as though I had lost a limb, and part of my life spilled to the ground with the little pieces of glass and metal."

Jeffrey felt a chasm growing between him and the room's glittering display as the man continued with his soft-spoken story. "Midnight Saturday they declared martial law. Sunday morning there were no phones, no radio, no papers—no one knew what had happened. All of this I learned later, from friends who had either gone underground and escaped the first sweep or were not listed by the police and remained free. My own story was quite different. But before I tell you what happened to me, first I shall speak of what my nation experienced.

"Later that day, Jaruzelski appeared in uniform on television. Jaruzelski at that time was Secretary of the Polish Communist Party and head of the armed forces—the first time one person had ever held those two posts. He announced that martial law had been declared. But it is important to note that the words in Polish for martial law are the same as for a state of war or a state of siege. You can imagine the reactions. Some said it was just the next stage of the argument between Solidarity and the government. Others lived that time in the terror of believing the Soviets had invaded."

Jeffrey glanced up and was astonished to find the entire table watching and listening. He inspected the circle of faces and sensed an unwavering quality to their attentiveness, a solemn sharing of what the photographer was saying. They listened with an intensity born of shared concern, a somber gathering who knew already of what the man spoke and yet listened with the patience of ones willing to allow the moment to live yet again. Jeffrey searched their faces, found a common bond and a collective strength rising from their love of the Polish nation.

"Monday came to those not arrested," the photographer went on. "For those of us in prison, the names of passing days meant little. People who were free went back to work and found that everything was much the same, yet altogether different. Everybody worked under much tighter control. Only one telephone line functioned in each factory, no matter how large the company. A stooge for the regime was placed in charge of the outgoing line. Every other hour, someone at Party headquarters would call to ensure that all was quiet.

"There was a curfew from ten in the evening to six the next morning. You were forbidden to leave town. You were forbidden to buy petrol. Train services were cut back, and a special Party permit was required to buy a ticket. Tanks were stationed on many street corners. Soldiers were everywhere. The military scrambled the army units. The central authorities did not want sons standing across the barricades from their sisters and mothers. So units were sent to distant cities—Cracow to Gdansk, Gdansk to Warsaw, Warsaw to Wroclaw, and so on.

"It was a very cold December, and on every street the soldiers kept bonfires burning in order to stay warm. Our cities remained shrouded by smoke from these fires throughout the cold winter weeks.

"Our cities lived a very oppressive life. People had no way of knowing what was happening. The papers said only what the government told them to say, which was the lie of convenience. Everyone on television wore uniforms. You could see how nervous the announcers were, how *terrified*. The authorities forced these reporters to dress up in military uniforms and read the Party line.

"The despondency was made very bitter because it arrived on the crest of hopes that Solidarity had ignited. Over all this loomed the constant fear that our friends to the east would arrive—that is how Soviet propaganda always described itself, Poland's friend to the east.

"That first Monday, everyone went into the stores and bought out everything they could find—all the flour, all the sugar, all the cans and boxes of preserved food. After that, no further shipments of food arrived. The shelves remained empty. Grocery stores remained open because they were told to do so, and yet they had nothing to sell except perhaps a few bottles of vinegar. Sales clerks just stood behind the counters. Then in the spring, when the first vegetables arrived, even the vinegar disappeared. People used it to pickle vegetables at home.

"Suddenly there were ration cards for everything—meat, alcohol, cigarettes, butter, cooking oil, flour, even cards for shoes and undergarments and little chocolates for the children. But the fact that you had a coupon did not mean you could buy the article. Usually the stores had nothing to sell. It simply meant you had the right to enter a store to ask.

"Rumors started then. People stood in line ten, twelve, fourteen hours just because of a word from a friend of a friend of a friend that this store *might* get a shipment of shoes or socks or sugar or bread.

"Basically, martial law was the latest brutal reminder of how Poland was manipulated by Russia. People lived under a constant cloud of depression, waiting, waiting, fearing the worst. They knew, whether or not it was spoken. International attention kept us from being annexed, but we were totally under the power of our friends to the east.

"I have talked to all my friends about this time, trying to fill in the gaps, seeking to close the void that my arrest caused in my life. I could not take pictures of that vital time, so I borrowed the images of friends. I remember only darkness and silence and cold. Over my absence of light and memories of bitter fear, I have set the recollections and photographs and experiences of others."

Waiters appeared in unison to sweep away the plates and set dessert in their place. The photographer's gaze was very bright, but he spoke in quiet tones; the people on the other side of the circular table had to lean forward to catch his words. Their table remained an island of intense silence in the swirl of evening splendor.

"My own glimpses of the fall of Poland's night came through a tear in the side of the army truck which carried us off that Saturday evening. We were not taken to the local prison. I heard a guard say as we were processed that the prison was already full. We were taken to an army barracks. I was led off alone and locked inside a cellar storage room. There was nothing in that room. No window, no heat, no water, no mattress, nothing. For light I had a single bulb strung from the ceiling. Hours later, two soldiers, an officer and an enlisted man, came in. They set down a blanket, a pail of water, and a slop bucket. I asked the officer how long I was to stay there. Until I have orders to release you, he replied. How long will that be? I asked. He did not answer, only shut the door and locked me in.

"There was no way of telling the passage of time. There was no day or night, only the bulb dangling from the ceiling. After a time, my fears began to take control of me. Food did not come regularly, or so it seemed, and I grew terrified that they would forget me and I would be left to starve. Then there was the fear that the bulb would burn out and I would be left in the dark. I spent several days fighting off sleep, terrified that I would wake up in the darkness and never see the light again.

"Weeks passed. I know that now. At the time it was an eternity, marked only by occasional meals handed to me by guards ordered not to speak, and by my growing fears. Then came a point when I realized I was going insane. That became my greatest fear of all, of losing my mind and my memories and my ability to give the world meaning through photographs. I decided I would kill myself in order to keep that from happening. But I did not know how. I was given no utensils with my food, I had no weapons or any other sharp article, and there was nothing in the seamless concrete walls from which I could suspend my blanket and hang myself. I spent hours and hours and hours searching for a way out of this man-made hell and finally fell asleep.

"I dreamed of a time as a very small child, so long ago that I was still in my crib. I recalled something I had not thought of for years and years. My mother used to come in as I was going to sleep, sit down beside my little bed, and say a rosary. I would fall asleep to the sound of the clicking beads and her murmured prayers.

"I awoke with a start, crawled to my knees, and prayed to a God I did not know for rescue. As I prayed, I had an image of something falling from myself, as though I were shedding an old skin. I did not know the Bible then, and I could not describe what was happening. All I could say was that I returned to sleep with a calmer spirit.

"And then I had a second dream. It was not of the past, but of a scene I could not recognize. I was looking out over beautiful green hills lit by very bright sunshine. In the valley below me was a small village of triangular-shaped thatched roofs—it was a very peculiar design. I was certain I had never seen anything like that place or those houses ever before. But it was not the scene itself which had an impact on me. I awoke with a sense of overwhelming peace, a feeling so strong that there was no room left in me for despair or doubt or even fear. I sat in my bare concrete cell and knew that I was going to be all right. I could not say how, or even if, I was going to be released. But the power of that peace was enough to make me know beyond doubt that I was not alone, that I was going to be all right."

A waiter appeared to collect the untouched dessert plates. The bejeweled matron seated beside Jeffrey waved the waiter away with a sharp motion. No one else at the table moved. All attention remained fastened upon the photographer.

"A short while later, an amnesty was declared. I was released, along with many others. It was night when I came out of the barracks. A friend was there to meet me, and he and his wife drove me immediately from the barracks to a place where I could rest and recover, a family cottage in the

Tartar Mountains, down on our southern border. By the time we arrived I was too tired to pay any attention to the surroundings. I went straight up to bed.

"The next morning I awoke, walked to the window, pushed open the shutters, and cried aloud. There before me was the exact same scene I had dreamed of in prison—the green slopes, the tiny village with the thatched cottages, the bright morning sunshine. And the feeling. It was there as well. The peace and the love and the assurance that I was not alone, would never be alone, that I was loved for all eternity."

CHAPTER

23

The man who answered the door at the Dresden address which Birgit had supplied to Erika was not an aging Nazi colonel; he was a middle-aged Wessie who looked at the trio on his doorstep with ill-concealed disdain. His family were now the sole occupants of the building, reclaiming the home that had been stripped from their grandparents when the Communists took power.

Even Ferret showed real emotion at that point, demanding in shrill anger to be told where the old man had gone. But the Wessie had never been taught to fear the authorities and replied with bored hostility. He had no idea where the occupants of the seven cramped apartments that the Communists had made of their home were now. Then he rudely ordered the trio away with threats and closed the door upon their fury.

The following two weeks were spent in helpless panic as Erika returned to her friend and Birgit returned to her records. They could do little then but wait—wait and worry and fret over the unknowns. What if the old man had moved away to another city? What if he had spent several frigid nights in the open, then taken his secret to an unmarked grave? Such questions left them tired and eaten with worry and snapping at each other. To be so close, so close, and then to—no, better not to say.

Then Birgit came through again.

The old man had done as any good Ossie would do, trained as they were from birth to follow any instructions from authority without argument or question; he had given his corrected address when accepting his monthly pension check.

There was an entirely different flavor to this second journey. They drove in grimly determined silence through a night turned treacherous by fresh snowfall. Not a word was spoken between Schwerin and Dresden. Not a word.

The address belonged to a two-room hovel, a place granted the name residence only because of the housing shortage and the lack of governmental control. It was a plywood shack set at the back end of garden plots stretching between an autobahn exit ramp and the railroad lines leading into Dresden. As in many European cities, sections of otherwise unusable property had been parceled out to the very poor, granting them a tiny postage stamp of earth where flowers and vegetables might be grown.

The shack stood at the garden's far corner, shaken by the man-made thunder of passing cars and trains. Smoke from a wood-burning stove poured from the tin pipe poking out of the roof. A pair of wires slumped down from a solitary pole, signaling that the shanty at least had electricity and perhaps the luxury of a phone. There was no indoor plumbing; a hand pump sprouted a long icicle in testament to recent use.

They sat in the car a very long moment, frozen into immobility by two weeks of worry. Finally Ferret spoke. "I will handle this myself." He waited; there was no dissent. "Very well. Let us begin."

The frail old man opened his front door and took an involuntary step back. The man and woman facing him were both of a size, as the saying went, solid and beefy and cloaked in knee-length leather trench coats. The starchy diet of the East had weighted them with undue pounds, yet their menace remained intact. The old man clutched his chest at their faces and the sweep of memories that accompanied the sight. He had seen many such faces through the years.

Then a third figure stepped forward, smaller and slighter than the pair, but no less menacing. "We have questions, Herr Makel," the little man said, his sibilant whisper matched perfectly to a face unmarked by age or emotion.

"I—I know no one by that name."

"We have not driven through nine hours of traffic and snow to stand in the night and talk drivel, Herr Horst Makel. We know who you are, and we are here for information."

"May I see your identification?"

"Of course not," the little man snapped. "And you will stop wasting my time with stupid questions."

The old man drew himself up as tall as years and arthritis would allow. "We are living in a democracy nowadays. The old days are gone."

"The new days have a lot of hunters out looking for Nazi criminals," the stranger replied.

"I have committed no crimes," the old man cried.

"Of course not. It was simply convenient to spend forty-seven years living under a false name, working as a tool-and-dye maker. *Nicht wahr, Herr Oberst?*"

The little man waited through a very tense moment, then stated flatly, "We are coming in, Herr Colonel."

He shouldered past the sputtering old man and entered the threadbare cottage. The silent pair walked in behind him and camped solidly by the door. That left the old man the choice of either arguing with a pair as pliant as two large trees or following the strange unfinished man into the parlor.

"I don't understand what this is all about, but—"

"Czestochowa," Ferret replied. He pronounced the name correctly, so that it sounded like *Chenstohova*. He then waited and watched as the old man deflated. "It has to do with Czestochowa, Herr Colonel."

"This is insanity," the old man replied, fainter now.

"It must have been agony to know all that wealth was just across the border, yet there was no way for you to get at it." Ferret selected the most comfortable of the chairs for himself and settled down with a sigh. "Was there, Herr Colonel? Always the risk that if you applied for a passport and someone checked the fingerprints, they would come up with things better left buried."

"I don't know what you're talking about."

"No, of course not. You don't happen to have a glass of schnapps, do you? It's been a long drive."

"I want you out of my house immediately."

"No, I suppose not." Ferret stretched out his short legs. "Well, to business. We've taken it quite far enough to have you turned over to the authorities. No doubt they'd be kinder to a former Nazi than the Ossies and their Russian comrades, especially once they caught the first whiff of riches. With the Wessies, torture has been outlawed, or so they say. Still, no doubt Spandau Prison would seem rather unpleasant if one were doomed to spend the rest of one's days there. I imagine that would be the fate for one with your record, no matter which authorities were in charge."

"Authorities," the old man spat.

"Our feelings exactly. Interlopers from the West out to buy us heart and soul. Everything for a price, especially loyalty. But we are not of them, and we come with a proposition."

"I have nothing to say."

"Not so fast, Herr Colonel. The night is young. Let me tell you what we have, and you might wish to sing a different song."

The old man groped for a chair, said nothing.

"You were commander of the Königsberg Transport Division at the end of the war." Ferret raised one gloved hand. "Don't deny it, Herr Colonel. We have proof. I assure you, I did not drive this distance on such a night to bandy hunches about. So. You were given a certain cargo to transport the last week before the Russians overran your position. An unlisted cargo, one so large it required three trucks. The trucks were carried by train as far as the rails remained intact, in order to save precious petrol, then you continued on by road, or what roads existed after the bombings.

"Strange, is it not, that a transport commander is ordered away from his post on the eve of a crucial battle and given three trucks and strings of petrol canisters, items which by that time were almost impossible to come by. Strange also that such a valuable cargo was granted no guards whatsoever, not even relief drivers. Stranger still is the fact that passes were issued, granting you passage through the entire Third Reich. It indicates, does it not, that this unlisted cargo was destined for somewhere so secret that only a handful of people ever knew of its existence."

"Less than a handful," murmured the old man.

Ferret nodded his satisfaction. "A *most* secret place. So

secret that your three trucks did not travel with the rest of the convoy, once they were off-loaded from the train. Perhaps not even you were informed of the destination, only the SS officer who accompanied you." Ferret leaned forward. "The one you shot."

The old man blanched. "I killed no one."

"Or had shot. It does not matter. What is important is that the driver who ran off into the woods, the one you shot and thought dead, was of that rarest of breeds, a patriot who survived. He described the scene to the authorities, Herr Colonel. Fortunately or unfortunately, as the case may be, it was to *American* authorities that he finally confessed. Interrogators in a prison camp, a lieutenant and two overworked sergeants, who paid no attention to the report of another dead SS officer. The driver died soon after, thus no one who might have pieced the puzzle together ever had the chance to question him."

The old man remained silent, his rheumy eyes turned inward on a scene he had replayed through ten thousand sleepless nights.

"The SS officer's demise took place at a crucial juncture in the road," Ferret continued. "As you well know. The right-hand fork took you south of Berlin, around Dresden, and on into the heart of the dying Third Reich. Or perhaps I ought to say, it *should* have taken you westward. Because you chose the left-hand fork, did you not? The one which led you south, around the remains of Warsaw, past Cracow, to the Czech border and then Austria and Switzerland and—"

Ferret leaned forward and gave his dead-eyed smile. "But there is no need to dwell on what did not happen, is there? Because it was in Czestochowa that one of the overloaded trucks finally broke down, burdened as it was by half the payload from the third truck. The truck for which you had no driver after the patriot fled into the night. Payload so valuable that you refused to leave it behind. By then you had opened one of the crates, had you not? You knew that your secret cargo was simply too precious to leave stranded in a driverless truck."

"Not a night goes by that I do not see it in my dreams," the old man murmured.

"It must have been a hellish night," Ferret went on. His

eyes held an intense gleam in the room's meager light. "The Russians were less than thirty kilometers away, weren't they, Herr Colonel? The line was collapsing; the road was choked with German soldiers streaming back from the front—those who could still walk, that is. And then what should happen but that you meet an officer more concerned for his wounded men than for your papers with all their fancy stamps and empty words. How cruel fate was, Herr Colonel, to curse you with two heroes within the same night."

"Fate," the old man grumbled. "There is no more wicked a word."

"The officer was not only patriotic," Ferret continued. "He was conscientious. He took your papers, as he promised, and handed them over to the authorities, along with the report of how he forced you at gunpoint to off-load your cargo and give him the truck for his wounded.

"The petrol he siphoned from the broken truck, along with the remaining canisters, was almost sufficient to see him across to the Americans as well. He was not only patriotic, this officer, but smart. He knew that there was less chance of a summary execution from the Americans than from the Russians. But in the end he failed. Despite the siphoned petrol, the truck died before he could reach the Americans' front line. He was held there by the love of his men, and he waited with the empty truck for the Russian tanks to catch up with him. You will no doubt be pleased to know that he ended his days in a Siberian labor camp. His men did not survive that long."

"Pleased," the old man muttered. "I'll be pleased to see him in hell."

"That can be arranged, Herr Colonel," Ferret replied quietly. "But we had hoped you would prefer to take your share of the wealth and disappear, as we intend to. We can even offer you a passport, and a ticket to anywhere in the world. America, even."

"Never."

"France, then. Or Australia. South America. Iceland, as far as I am concerned." The little eyes hardened to agate. "What concerns us, Herr Colonel, is that you help us."

Ferret rose to stand over the old man and demanded, "Now tell us, Herr Colonel. Where did you bury the Amber Room?"

CHAPTER
24

Jeffrey responded to Alexander's urgent fax by arriving at Heathrow Airport two hours before his Cracow flight was scheduled to land. The plane was delayed as usual, which meant that Jeffrey was fit to be tied by the time the customs doors opened to admit an Alexander burdened by more than his usual post-flight fatigue.

Jeffrey rushed forward, took hold of Alexander's overnight bag, demanded, "What's the matter?"

"Not just yet, please. Allow me at least a moment to recover my wits."

"Sorry." He directed them toward the car-park. "I decided to hire a car and drive you back myself. From the sounds of your fax, you had something to say that was for my ears only."

"A correct observation." Alexander showed confusion when Jeffrey stopped in front of a small stand selling freshly squeezed fruit juices at outrageous prices. "What is this?"

"Something Katya suggested. She said it would give you the stimulus you required and be much better for you than a quart of coffee."

"How kind of her to think of me. Very well, Jeffrey. Purchase the libation and let us leave this madhouse behind."

Jeffrey remained silent as he threaded the car through the parking deck's maze, paid the fee, and entered the aggressive stream of rush-hour traffic pressing forward at a snail's pace. For once, the slow speed bothered him not a whit. He was still far from comfortable driving a car on the left hand of the road, with the steering wheel on the right.

Once they were on the motorway and packed snugly between other cars and trucks on every side, Jeffrey asked, "How are you feeling now?"

"Much better, thank you. I do believe Katya was correct."

"Will you tell me what happened?"

"Yes, I suppose there is no reason to delay the news any further." Alexander settled back in his seat. "I arrived in Cracow yesterday afternoon and went directly to the Marian Church. As you well know, I wanted to be rid of the responsibility for the chalice as quickly as possible, and I returned it in person because I had accepted it personally from Karlovich. The curate was there waiting for me, I handed it over, thanked him as gracefully as I knew how, and departed. As far as I could tell, nothing was the matter.

"I proceeded directly to Gregor's—he has almost completed preparations for your buying trip, by the way. We took care of a few minor items and then I went to my hotel, had dinner, and went to bed. There was no good reason for my staying the night, except that the idea of two international flights in one day positively curdled my blood."

Alexander sighed. "The next morning, Rokovski arrived in an absolute panic."

•   •   •

Rokovski called Alexander's Cracow hotel room in a state of hysteria. He bluntly refused to allow Alexander to come down and meet with him in the lobby. Instead, he rushed into Alexander's room, absolutely beside himself—his tie loosened, his hair disheveled, his face creased with worry. He walked blindly past Alexander's outstretched hand and threw himself into the plastic-veneer chair by the window.

"I don't even know where to begin," Rokovski announced.

"What is it, old man? What's wrong?"

"I have some dreadful news. Dreadful. Karlovich called me first thing this morning, insisting that I come over at once. That man is not easy to deal with, I don't need to tell you." Rokovski mopped his brow with a crumpled handkerchief. "I went to his office immediately this morning, and said that he seemed most distressed on the telephone.

" 'Distressed! Distressed, indeed!' he told me, pulling on his beard and pacing the floor. He said, 'I am more than distressed. I am shocked. Horrified.' "

"What about?" Alexander demanded.

Rokovski held up his hand. "Wait, my friend. Wait. I want to lay it out for you just as it was presented to me. Hopefully our two heads will then be able to make some sense of this matter." Rokovski kneaded his forehead. "I asked him, 'What is it, the chalice? I know Mr. Kantor planned to return it yesterday. Has there been some damage?'

"Karlovich fell into his chair at my question. 'Damage?' he said. 'No. Damage can be repaired. But such damage as this is permanent.' "

"I am growing more alarmed by the moment," Alexander said.

"As was I. I demanded that he tell me what he was talking about. Karlovich fastened me with those great, glittering eyes of his and said, 'The chalice that has been returned to me is not the chalice I was good enough to lend.' "

"Impossible," Alexander exploded.

"That was exactly my reaction, but Karlovich was most insistent."

"How can that be? Did you see it?"

"Yes, of course. It was there in his safe. He pulled it out, still in the leather carrying case, set it on his desk, and motioned for me to take it." Rokovski pantomimed his movements. "I looked at it very carefully, placed it back down, and said, 'I don't know what you're talking about. This is exquisite. To think that this could be a forgery is, well—' "

"Positively absurd," Alexander finished for him.

"You will understand that I did not wish to say it outright, but that is what I was thinking."

"How could anyone have duplicated it in the short time that it was in our possession?" Alexander scoffed.

"My thoughts exactly. As you know, I have quite some experience in these matters, and this is what I told him. But the curate raised his hand and declared to me, 'As God is my witness, this is not the chalice from the Marian Church collection.' Then he said something equally remarkable."

"Go on," Alexander said impatiently.

" 'As I was putting the chalice away,' the curate told me, 'it struck me that something was amiss. I recalled the pattern of the signets around the central structure, and that two of the signets bore a different symbol. Yet with this chalice, there is the same letter in each of the faces. I wasn't sure, of course, but I was dreadfully worried. So I went through my records and found this.'

"My dear Alexander, you should have seen the mess about his desk. Stacks and stacks of books and drawings and portfolios with half-unrolled papers all over the floor behind his desk. A pile of dusty leather-bound tomes almost as high as his table. And on top was a very old portfolio. He opened it to a page, undoubtedly ancient, of museum quality itself."

"Get on with it, man," Alexander snapped.

"Yes, of course." Rokovski mopped his brow once more. "The page had detailed drawings of the chalice with explanations in Latin along the top and down both sides."

"You are certain it was a drawing for *the* chalice?"

"No, of course not. How could I be? And yet Karlovich was so sure, so completely certain. He pointed to that broad center section and said, 'You see, on this wreathlike portion surrounding the stem, there are two different emblems, just as I recalled, directly opposite each other. The other signets are all identical to those found on this chalice here. And yet what I did *not* know was that this central section contained a secret. One I discovered only when examining the description written here.'

"He stabbed at the writing on the left side of the page, and said, 'Our chalice had a secret compartment. By pressing these two opposing signets, one carved with alpha, the other with omega, the cup portion of the chalice detaches to reveal a small, hollow compartment inside the stem. If you will examine this particular chalice, you will find no such compartment.' "

Alexander mulled it over. "And you searched."

"Quite thoroughly, I assure you. No such symbols were

carved anywhere on this chalice, and I could find no compartment. And while I searched, Karlovich kept stabbing at the bottom left corner of this diagram and talking. He said, 'But the gravity of the matter does not hinge on the lack of the secret compartment. You cannot imagine how I shuddered with amazement and horror as I examined this small inset at the base of the drawing. This shows the contents, which now are also missing.' "

"And those contents are?" Alexander demanded.

"Mind you," Rokovski cautioned. "It is a legend only. There is no evidence save for an ancient drawing, one that no one has inspected in decades. Even centuries, perhaps."

"And save for Karlovich's insistence that the chalice I returned is not the one I received from him." Alexander shook his head. "To think that such a thing could happen."

"I, too, can scarcely believe this was taking place. While I sat in the man's office and examined what looked for all the world to be an ancient and valuable chalice, this gentleman began pacing back and forth amidst the scattered documents, bemoaning the loss. 'Of course I knew nothing about the compartment. Or that the chalice was also a reliquary. I would not have dreamed to allow such a sacred treasure to leave Polish soil. And now, alas, I make this dreadful discovery.' "

"The man sounds like a bad actor," Alexander retorted. "He actually called this supposedly missing chalice a reliquary? As if the compartment held some religious artifact?"

"He did."

"And did he also perhaps mention what that artifact was?"

Rokovski gave him a stricken look. " 'A small fragment,' he told me. 'One about the size of your thumb. A thorn, to be precise. From the final crown worn by the Son of God.' "

Alexander was on his feet. "You expect me to believe that such a relic could lie forgotten for centuries in a Polish crypt?"

"I expect nothing. I am simply telling you what was reported to me." Rokovski looked up in appeal. "Did you offend him in any way?"

Alexander thought it over. "No. Certainly not intentionally. Nor do I recall anything which might have indicated by look or word that he was offended."

Rokovski threw up his hands. "Then I don't know what to say."

"My dear Dr. Rokovski, I assure you—"

"Your reputation is one bound with an honor that goes back decades, Alexander. I do not know what the answer is here, but your honor is not in question."

"Yet the chalice is."

"According to Karlovich, yes."

"There must be some mistake."

"Perhaps. But I can assure you that the chalice you returned was not the chalice in his drawings."

"They differed only in this secret compartment and the signets?"

"And the contents," Rokovski added. "If the drawings are indeed of the chalice that he gave to you. If he was correct about your chalice's having those differing emblems."

"But why would the man go to such trouble?" Alexander ran frantic fingers through his hair. "I admit to being at a complete and utter loss."

"As am I." Rokovski hesitated, then said, "Alexander, I hate to ask you this, but did anyone other than yourself have access to the chalice?"

"Only about eight hundred guests at my gala." He shook his head. "No, forgive me. It was a feeble jest. Security there was impeccable. I had the chalice at my shop, which is most carefully secured and guarded, and then as an extra precaution it was removed to a vault at a leading bank."

"Well," Rokovski sighed. "I certainly am not going to make formal enquiries at this point. Whatever search we make must be done as discreetly as possible."

"So you do believe that the original chalice is missing?"

"What choice do I have? Why would this man lie to me?"

Alexander settled back into his chair. To that question he had no reply.

Alexander went directly to the Marian Church and found Karlovich awaiting his arrival, the chalice still on his desk. Alexander seated himself and examined the artifact, determined not to allow the curate's all-pervasive energy to force him into a hasty conclusion. After quite some time, he set the chalice back on the desk and declared, "This is absolutely extraordinary handiwork. I am virtually certain that this chalice is genuine gold and silver, and that the work dates back several centuries. Possibly more."

"Whether that is true or not," Karlovich replied coldly, "I as a simple curate cannot say. But what I can tell you is that this is *not* my chalice."

"Who else might know of this secret compartment of which you spoke to Rokovski?"

"I don't know. I would have thought no one in all Poland. No one alive, in any case. The cellar has been closed to the public and to most priests since before the war. Secrecy over our collection was the only insurance we had against its being stolen by either the Nazis or the Russians. In fact, this collection has been kept in virtual secrecy since the Austro-Hungarian invasion two hundred years ago. Even the existence of the crypt itself was a fact known only to a handful of people."

Alexander sat and listened intently to this dark-bearded, powerful man with the eyes of a zealot. The curate clearly felt he was telling the truth. "What do you intend to do?"

"What can I do? I certainly could not make a formal enquiry without losing my job for allowing the reliquary to travel outside Poland, not to mention perhaps causing an international outrage. And of course we must not scare the thief into some rash act. Clearly this was done with the intention of not being detected."

"I assure you that I am a man of honor, and that I shall do whatever it takes to right this situation. What do you wish me to do?"

"Find me my chalice," Karlovich replied. "But do not worry about your good name, Mr. Kantor. I am most willing to keep this entire matter very quiet. I understand the importance of your reputation, and I would not want to taint it with any hint of impropriety."

"You are most kind," Alexander murmured.

"And of course, your success in retrieving the chalice would depend upon secrecy."

"Rest assured I shall do everything in my power to unravel this mystery. Yet what if the chalice is not recovered?"

Karlovich spread out his arms. "Then perhaps you would consider arranging to have a suitable sum of compensation paid. Such money would of course be devoted to the most noble of church purposes."

"I understand," Alexander said quietly, wishing that were so.

"I have no idea when others might discover that the chalice you returned is not in truth the reliquary. I can only hope that my purpose in life has been accomplished by then, and that I have been called to my eternal home."

Alexander rose in confused defeat. "Please be so kind as to give me a few weeks. I shall come back to you, either in person or through Dr. Rokovski. I know the market in religious antiques quite well, and I shall try to draw out this piece by posing as a buyer. Failing that, I am of course most willing to offer some financial compensation, however meager it may be in comparison to your loss."

CHAPTER
25

The next morning dawned clear and bitterly cold. Jeffrey and Katya joined Alexander in the tiny alcove of the shop for coffee and commiseration, their conversation marked by numerous pauses and deep sighs.

Alexander stood and went for a mope about the shop, murmured from up by the front window, "How on earth did this happen?"

"It's not your fault," Jeffrey said for the hundredth time already that day.

Alexander chose not to hear him. "Forty years in the antiques trade, and here at the crown of my career I am confronted with accusations against which I have no defense."

"And when you were doing it for charity," Jeffrey added. "It wasn't even business."

Katya reached in her carry bag, brought out a yellow legal pad, and announced, "It seems to me that what we need most right now is clear thinking."

Alexander's tone was querulous. "How am I to defeat an accusation I cannot make public?"

"It's not just the chalice," Jeffrey agreed. "If this gets out, all our Polish sources are going to shrivel up like a dried prune."

"Not if," Alexander said, returning to the alcove and

dropping into his seat. "When."

"The way to defeat this problem is to solve it," Katya replied crisply. "We must outline all the possibilities. Everyone is a suspect."

"This is absurd," Alexander declared, but could manage no heat.

"We have to trace the line of possession of the chalice," she insisted. "We must examine every opportunity and motive for theft."

Jeffrey recalled her finding the Rubens in a crowded basement vault and felt a slight lift to his spirit. "What are you suggesting?"

"First, we have Karlovich," Katya said. "From the sound of it, he's not a totally stable character."

Alexander snorted. "You simply cannot go about accusing the curate of Cracow's central cathedral of being a thief."

"He accused you, didn't he?" Katya scribbled busily. "Then there's the three of us."

Alexander raised his hand at that. "Let us just say here and now that we trust one another, shall we? I don't care to see my world upset any more than it already is."

Katya nodded agreement. "So it was in your flat for one night—"

"Where no one entered," Alexander replied. "Not even the porter. Security in my building is meticulous."

"Then we have those people with access to the shop," Katya went on.

"There's the three of us," Jeffrey mused. "Plus the cleaning lady—no, she was off the week the chalice was here before it was moved to the bank. I remember because I had to vacuum and dust. Then there were our customers."

Alexander showed the first hint of renewed interest. "Did you ever allow a customer to be alone in the shop?"

"Not for an instant," Jeffrey replied emphatically. "Not ever."

"No, nor I. And I must say, I found myself especially vigilant with the chalice here, although I suppose we have several other items that approach it in value."

"What about when you were traveling back from Cracow?" Jeffrey asked. "Did you set it down?"

"Not in any place, not at any time," Alexander replied. "I shall not take you through the rather gruesome details, but suffice it to say that I suffered several indignities rather than part with the case for even a moment."

"We need to see if our security firm has any videotapes left of those days," Katya said, scribbling away. "Although they usually erase them once a week, I believe they told me."

Jeffrey looked at her. "You talked to the security firm?"

She did not raise her eyes from the pad. "This is my job now, Jeffrey. Security is a part of it. Okay. Could someone else have gotten into the shop?"

"In off-hours?" Jeffrey shook his head. "All Mayfair would have heard the alarms."

"No alarm system is foolproof, of course," Alexander responded, "but ours is very dependable. If someone did break in, it would have to be a very skilled thief. A professional. And no such professional would swap one valuable for another. And allow me to assure you, the chalice I returned to Cracow is unmistakably precious."

"He also wouldn't have left the shop's other valuables intact," Jeffrey agreed. "The same goes for entry into Alexander's flat. Some of his antiques are first-rate."

"Right." She continued writing and went on. "Then there was the photographer who shot the pictures for our invitation."

"I remained by the chalice throughout the session," Alexander replied. "I have also checked the photographs most carefully. All I can say is that the two signets facing the camera were identical. Five are not in view; of them I can say nothing at all."

Katya made swift notes. "That brings us to the transportation to and from the bank vault. Then you have the display. Then the return of the chalice to the church, and that afternoon until the discovery of the switch."

"Barclay's Bank is above question," Alexander replied. "Their reputation is certainly more valuable than the threat of scandal over one item."

"A king's ransom of valuables is stored in their Charing Cross vaults," Jeffrey agreed. "Why go to the trouble of switching just one item?"

"I positively concur," Alexander said. "And as for attracting the attention of international thieves, how did they come to hit on us so swiftly?" Jeffrey shook his head. "We only had the chalice for how long? Four weeks?"

"We did publicize it widely in magazines and publications," Katya pointed out. "Not to mention the three thousand invitations to the gala."

Jeffrey felt a sinking feeling. "What about Greenfield?"

"What are you saying?"

"I think we've got to include him. It was his idea to put the chalice in the bank's vaults."

"I certainly cannot confront the man directly," Alexander objected. "And unfortunately the bank won't tell us any details unless I give them ample reason, which would of course raise the threat of scandal. The question is how to speak with him without making this nightmare any more public."

"But could he have made a switch?" Jeffrey felt an inward cringe. The thought of a friend stealing from them sickened him.

"In the bank?" Alexander pursed his lips. "If there was an accomplice in the bank, perhaps. What might be more likely is in the arrangements regarding the display case."

"We were so busy with the gala details," Katya agreed.

"I can't think of any moment from the time the bank security people brought in the three treasures to when they were actually sealed in the cases that they were left alone." Alexander seemed to dim slightly. "But we were all so busy. It is possible, I suppose."

"I hate this," Jeffrey declared. "Greenfield is a friend."

"He is a somewhat distorted character, but I agree, he is indeed a good man at heart. I cannot imagine—" Alexander shook his head, sighed, "But I suppose we must."

"And the security people who guarded the display case in the ballroom," Katya added. "We'll need to speak with them as well."

Alexander regarded her gravely. "Painful as this exercise is proving to be, my dear, you have instilled in me a morsel of hope. For that I must thank you."

"The atmosphere has lightened in here a thousand percent," Jeffrey agreed.

"It's really nice," Katya confessed, "feeling a part of all this. Even in the middle of such a bad time, I truly feel fortunate."

"As do we," Alexander said gravely.

"Hang on," Jeffrey said, straightening in his chair. "Did whoever took the chalice know about the secret compartment?"

Alexander nodded. "I quite agree. We must also consider the fact that it was not an antique, nor silver and gold, which lured the thief. This may be the key. The replica of the chalice, or whatever it is that I looked at, is impeccable. To make a forgery like this would take a tremendous amount of preparation."

"And time," Katya agreed.

"And effort," Alexander continued. "I examined the chalice in the curate's office quite carefully, I assure you. If it was a forgery at all, the work was remarkable, the materials first-rate. I would have staked my reputation that I was looking at a product of fifteenth-century craftsmanship."

"So the thief was possibly after the fragment," Jeffrey agreed. "But who would have known about it?"

"We also have to ask ourselves who would be willing to go through all this trouble for such a relic," Katya urged.

"Even Karlovich didn't know about the secret compartment until two days ago," Alexander protested.

"He *said*," Katya replied.

"I can't see why he would allow such an item out of the country if he knew about the relic," Jeffrey said.

"There were too many other items in the collection to choose from," Alexander agreed.

"Unless he had a reason," Katya said.

"Let's not allow ourselves to become carried away," Alexander said. "Karlovich is a bit off-balance, there's no question about that. But we can't go along blaming him. The fact is, we are responsible. What we have to come to grips with, assuming we all trust one another, is that we let the chalice out of our protection and our control—either when we sent it to the bank vaults or at some other moment along the way."

"So what do we do now?" Jeffrey asked. "The police aren't of any use to us."

"Quite the contrary," Alexander agreed. "But perhaps, just perhaps, greed will work on our behalf."

"What do you mean?"

"Suppose that we pose as buyers of ancient religious artifacts and let the thief or his accomplice come to us."

"You're going to pay to get it back?"

"I am certainly prepared to do so," Alexander replied.

"But why would anyone who stole something from you try to sell it back to you?"

"Not us in person, of course. We shall have to utilize the services of a front. We shall make other arrangements. Much more discreet." Alexander leaned forward. "Now here is my plan."

CHAPTER
26

Kurt settled the last of Erika's suitcases in the trunk of the car, paused, and looked down at the compartment's contents. There were four cases made of battered cardboard and vinyl, two for Erika and two for Ferret. Little enough to show for a pair of lives. Kurt shut the lid with a solid thunk and felt a curtain come down inside himself.

His attention fastened on a newly erected billboard that towered above the road and the colonel's shabby cottage. It proclaimed in giant letters and bright colors the wonders of a certain washing powder. He smiled without humor, compared the capitalist slogan with those of his Communist days. The colors and words were different, but the intent was more or less the same as far as he could see—to convince the unbeliever that something was true. Were they lies? Kurt kicked at the icy ground, remembered a lesson from his early training—the easiest lie to sell was the one wrapped in a covering of truth.

"We're Building the Germany of Our Dreams." That one had been a favorite during his teen years. For a time it had been plastered almost everywhere. The propagandists had slapped it across acres of buildings. They had competed over who could erect the largest billboard, all in red and white and fiercely, angrily proud. Then had come "There Is One Germany and We Are All Working for Her Development."

As prophetic a statement as he had ever heard, although perhaps not in the form the propagandists had intended. The year before the Wall fell it had been, "Our Ambition Is a Strong and Unified Socialist Germany." Take out the word socialist, and the ambition had come true.

Ferret scuttled from the cottage. He nodded to the colonel leaning against the doorpost and said something Kurt could not hear. The colonel made no response. Ferret turned with a minute shrug and hurried down the muddy path. A battered overstuffed briefcase was clasped up close to his chest like a child with a favorite toy.

Ferret approached the car, stopped, and peered up at Kurt through the over-thick lenses. "You know the plan," Ferret said. It was not a question.

"We have gone over it a dozen times," Kurt replied. "More."

"At this stage, I prefer repetition to mistakes." Bundled within his oversized coat, Ferret looked more than ever like a bespectacled mole. "You will stay here—"

"And await your word," Kurt interrupted, boredom fighting for place with irritation. "You will call if the amber is found."

"When," Ferret corrected. "When the amber is found, and when the agreement is made. Until that moment, you will not allow the colonel out of your sight."

"Then I shall contact the Schwerin lawyer as we discussed, and then travel to Poland." Kurt cast a sideways glance back to where the old man hunched in the house's shallow doorway, out of the bitter dawn breeze. The colonel's shanty stooped and swayed beneath its burdens of neglect and age.

Kurt watched the Ferret bundle himself into the passenger's seat. He shut the door, nodded a farewell. Then he turned to where Erika waited by the hood of her car, the little plastic taxi sign now permanently removed. He said, "The final departure."

"I never thought this day would come," she replied. "After Birgit found the man, I still could not believe it was real. Even now I wonder."

"That was her name?" Kurt asked. "Birgit?"

Erika had a momentary start, then saw his smile. "You made a joke."

"A poor one."

"It does not matter what you know now. We shall not return."

"No," Kurt agreed. "Any regrets?"

She looked out over the icy landscape, admitted, "Some."

"I was not necessarily speaking of the departure," Kurt said.

"Nor I." Erika's gaze returned to him. "Some nights I wonder if anything will ever come of all this."

"Nights are the time for me to wonder how it will be to live the life of an alien."

It was Erika's turn to smile. "We have been that since the Wall's collapse. It is our fate. The place we choose to reside no longer matters."

He walked her around to the driver's side, opened the door, said, "I also find myself wondering about our new residence."

"Where do you think we shall go?"

Kurt pointed with his chin toward the waiting Ferret. "He likes Argentina. They've fifty years of experience in burying German records."

"Nazi records, you mean."

He did not deny it. "Ferret and I, we had contact with them once. Trying to get hold of old documents in another treasure hunt."

"They did not help, did they?"

Kurt shook his head. "We kept the contact, though. The man let us know he could be used for buying other papers."

"He said that?"

"Passports, drivers' licenses, even birth certificates if the price was right." Kurt lifted his eyes to tree boughs slumped beneath their loads of snow and ice. "At the time, of course, we saw no need for such things—"

"And never thought you would," Erika finished, a wry bite to her words.

"And I suppose you had perfect vision when it came to such events."

Her good humor remained. "Naturally. That is why I'm here."

He subsided. "I suppose Buenos Aires would be an acceptable place to have been born."

"Now that our own homeland is no longer," Erika agreed, climbing in and starting the car. She reached for the door, said, "You know, I think I might just learn to like being rich."

CHAPTER
27

Andrew opened the door for a heavily laden Jeffrey and Katya, then led them through his shop to the back office area. "This the lot?"

"Nineteen books on the crucial subjects," Jeffrey said, setting down his load next to the oversized art books he had brought by the week before. "Katya's box has some prints and imitation artifacts."

"To add a bit of atmosphere," Katya said.

Andrew gave her a look of mock injury. "Atmosphere? And what does my little world have now?"

"A beautiful feel," Katya replied. "Truly."

"You know the way to a man's heart," Andrew said. "Pity about the choice you've made. Choice of men, that is."

"I think I did rather well," Katya replied smugly.

Jeffrey was too frantic to share in their banter. "You understand these books are on loan?"

"Not part of the fee, I take it."

"Not on your life. A couple I had to borrow, several I haven't been able to read yet myself. And some of these have been out of print for over a century."

"All right, lad," Andrew replied easily. "Speaking of fee, we haven't gotten around to discussing that."

"Alexander said to tell you that he is doubly in your debt," Katya said. "First for trying to assist us, and second for doing so confidentially."

Andrew thought it over. "Coming from the old gent, I'd say that's not bad, not bad at all."

"You can add my gratitude to his," Jeffrey said. "For what it's worth."

"Ah, well, seeing as how I disagree with the run-of-the-mill lot and their comments, I'd treat that almost as highly as the other. Maybe even a notch above, seeing as how you're the up and comer."

"Thanks, Andrew. I won't forget this."

" 'Course you won't. I'm not aiming on letting you, now, am I?" Andrew reached into an overstuffed drawer, came up with a set of clippings, passed them around. "Here's the copy and bills for the first set of ads. Cost you a packet, especially the daily rags. The Times wanted eight hundred quid per day."

"We've got to move ahead as though there were big money behind it."

"Right you are, then. Here, have a gander at how the lucre's being spent."

The ad was a standard four-by-eight inches, framed in double black lines. The text took up less than half the space and simply read: "Major international collector seeks to acquire pre-seventeenth-century religious art and artifacts of the first order. Sellers of second-quality items need not apply. Paintings, manuscripts, altars, reliquaries, ornamental works, and other items will be considered. Utmost discretion and confidentiality guaranteed. Payment may be effected worldwide. Interested parties should contact," and below was given Andrew's name and shop address.

"Perfect," Jeffrey declared. "Can I keep this one?"

" 'Course you may, lad. You paid for it."

"I'm leaving on a buying trip next week. I don't suppose—"

"You'll be hearing from me the instant I pick up the first bit of news, lad. The very instant, don't you worry. As to timing, that's out of our hands, now, isn't it."

Jeffrey nodded glumly. "Alexander's really taking this hard."

"Only on account of the weight you two put on reputations and the like." He caught the look in Jeffrey's eye and added,

"Just kidding, lad. Of course he is."

"You don't speak any other languages, I guess."

"No, but I understand Yank fairly well. And Sydney Greenfield works in Kentish, which I can get around in."

"I don't think it's Greenfield."

"You've said that half a dozen times already. And I've told you I agree with the lady here—we've got to look everywhere. All the same, I do believe you're right. This doesn't look like something our man would be up to. Did I ever tell you he was decorated in the Korean War?"

"Sydney Greenfield?"

"Goes against the grain, doesn't it. But there you are. Ruddy great gong it was, too. Pinned on his chest by the head honcho himself. Said it was for bravery and valor beyond the call of duty, or some such."

"Are you sure we're talking about the same guy?"

"Hard to believe, I admit. Had a rough time getting the man to speak of it at all. I heard rumors about it for years and finally cornered him at the local. Wouldn't let him go until I had the scoop."

"What did he say?"

"Told me he didn't remember what he'd actually done," Andrew replied. "Scared blind, he was. Honest. One minute he was there on the sand, the next he was two miles inland, sitting by a bombed-out farmhouse having a quiet smoke with the boys. Still, they gave him the VC when it was all over. Told me he stood there and let them pin it on his chest, didn't have a clue what all the fuss was about. That's the way to go to war, I told him. Just skip over the nasty bits."

"I've always liked Sydney," Katya said. "Did Jeffrey tell you he was completely honest about his dealings in the repaired furniture?"

"Yes he did. Glad to hear it too, I was." He clapped Jeffrey on the back. "Don't look so glum, lad. From the sounds of it, nobody's actually said Alexander stole the piece, am I right?"

"The implication is enough."

Andrew nodded. "Yes, and that's why I'd take your word of a debt over a lot of other people's checks. You're a strange one for this trade, though, you and your boss both."

"Thanks, Andrew." Jeffrey tightened his scarf. "Now, remember, the most important thing at this point is to retrieve the chalice."

"Or reliquary," Katya corrected.

"Or whatever it is, right. But we'd be interested in looking at anything of really top quality that comes in, especially if its origin is central European."

"For this cause your boss has gotten himself involved in?"

"If the chalice is recovered," Katya explained, "we'll have substantial funds available both from the gala itself and promised by new patrons specifically for expanding the Polish religious heritage collection."

"If it's not," Jeffrey added, "then paying for such pieces out of the firm's pocket should buy us some breathing space. And time."

"Hopefully we'll be hearing from the thieves or their fences before long," Andrew said. "As to this other matter, in such a case as I come up with a few class articles, I imagine I'd be splitting the commissions with you."

Jeffrey shook his head. "They'd all be yours."

"That's a good sight more than fair." Andrew ushered them back to the front. "Any time you feel a touch of the nerves setting in, feel free to give me a call. But best you not be seen around here for a time, in case they're having the premises watched. And don't you worry, lad. You'll be hearing from me the instant I catch wind of anything."

CHAPTER
28

The waiting was hard. Waiting always was. The word alone meant that control and action and power had slipped from his hands. Kurt had never been good at waiting, and the seven days hung heavy on his hands.

The old colonel moved about his own home like a silent wraith. Kurt wondered about that whenever the old man slipped in and out of view. The colonel carried with him a thoroughly defeated air. He had been so since their arrival, as though telling his secret had robbed him of his final reason to live. He sat now, the strength and ramrod straightness with which he had confronted them upon their arrival a thing of the distant past. He awaited his fate with a helpless air, stooped and old and tired and sad.

The phone call came on the seventh evening at the pre-arranged time. Even though he had awaited it anxiously, the bell caused Kurt positively to leap from the earth.

"You found it, then." Kurt felt his voice was disembodied, spoken by another—one whose knees had not gone weak at the news and whose heart was not hammering like thunder.

"Did I not just say that?" Erika permitted herself a chuckle. "Though I had to stand and gaze for quite a while before believing it myself."

"How did it look?"

"Rats," she said. "Big ones. And bones. Our colonel left no tongues alive to tell tales."

"I meant the—"

"Don't say it," Erika warned.

"I was simply going to ask about the merchandise."

"Unimpressive. Covered in mud. And other things."

"But you're certain?"

"Ferret is positive. I have come to trust in our little man's judgment. That surprises me almost as much as our find."

He repeated, "How did it look?"

This time she answered him. "Fistfuls of dark glass, carved with weird designs, covered with the filth of ages. Ferret only let me clean a few, he says each piece was wrapped in tissue paper—"

"Covered with the place-code for putting it back together," Kurt finished for her. His heart was beating so hard it was difficult to get the words out. "I remember him saying it."

"Yes, well, for that reason he did not let me clean but a few. And those . . ."

"Well?" Kurt urged.

"I do not wish to sound absurd."

He bit off the remark that came first to his tongue, said, "Tell me."

"Great jewels," she replied. "Glass vessels full of molten gold when held to the light. All the shades of a bronze rainbow. Like nothing I have ever seen in my life."

"An amber rainbow," Kurt said. He thought he heard the old colonel stir behind him, give off a ghostly sigh of defeat. But his attention remained fastened upon what he himself would never see.

"I told you it was absurd."

"You did well," Kurt replied. "After all, the only glimpse I shall ever have is through your eyes."

"Perhaps not. I am hoping to convince Ferret that we should keep a few mementos."

"With one for me, I hope."

"How not?" She spoke in muffled tones to someone in the room, came back with, "Ferret says now is not the time for idle chatter. He says to contact the lawyer and set up the meeting. Not by phone. It is possible that there are still listening ears."

"Tomorrow," Kurt said, the excitement making his voice rise. "I will travel back to Schwerin at first light. There is too much ice on the roads just now to risk driving at night."

"Tomorrow is fine."

"She will give those antique dealers the when and where as we discussed." Kurt continued talking now simply to hold on to the contact. "At the city whose name I cannot pronounce."

"Czestochowa," Erika replied. "You will wait until we have confirmed it all went smoothly."

"And then travel to Poland."

"Where we shall not meet."

"As was agreed," he said. "It is safer, and yet I worry."

"By the time you arrive, we will have gone on to Switzerland to await the transfer of funds." Again the muffled talk, then, "Ferret says that you can trust us."

"I have no choice."

"No." She paused. "But in any case you can. You have my word."

"It is enough." And to his surprise, it almost was.

"Ferret says, do you remember where to go upon your arrival?"

"For the hundredth time, yes."

"We shall call you once the money has been received and pass on the remaining details." A smile came to her voice. "Palm trees."

"What?"

"Your dream. Beaches of white sand. Does Argentina have beaches?"

"And coconuts," Kurt replied, and suddenly wanted to laugh out loud. "And all the rest."

"You will hear from us," Erika said.

Kurt hung up the phone and turned back to where the colonel sat in his lone and ragged chair. Kurt looked closer, realized that the old hands were motionless. Kurt moved forward, saw how the jaw had fallen slack. The old colonel's eyes stared sightlessly at the feeble fire. Kurt bent to place one ear next to the frail chest, wondered idly if he should not list the cause of death as a broken heart.

CHAPTER
29

"Regular as clockwork, you are," Andrew said when he realized it was Jeffrey calling. "Still off on your travels this week?"

"Tomorrow," Jeffrey replied.

"Won't do me any good to ask where, will it?"

"Not a bit."

"No, didn't think so." Andrew gave a jolly sigh. "Have to tell you, lad. I'm having the time of my life reading about all these lovelies. Something I didn't know the first thing about before."

"A whole new world."

"That's it exactly. Not to mention the three buys I've made so far. Good bit of brass, they were."

"Alexander says to tell you they're all really first-rate."

"Yes, I thought so myself." His tone sobered. "Nothing on the chalice, I'm afraid."

Jeffrey did not try to hide his disappointment. "I can't stop hoping."

"No, nor I. I did come across something rather interesting, though. Found a description and a sketch of what looks like the chalice in question."

"The one we brought from Cracow or the one we took back?"

"The only one I've seen, whichever one that is. I assume

the one you're looking for, I ruddy well hope so, seeing as how that's the one I've got my eyes peeled for. And from what you've said, on the surface there isn't much difference between the two."

"Sorry. Stupid question."

"Yes, it was. No matter. Case of nerves does that to a body. Anyway, it says here, hang on, let me see if I can lay my hands on it." The phone was dropped, then Jeffrey heard the sounds of rummaging. Andrew returned with, "Yes, here it is. Found it in one of the old tomes you brought by, dated 1820. From the looks of it, the book hasn't been opened in over a century. Says that in 1475 a chalice was designed by this goldsmith called Bertolucci for the Holy See. What a name, the Holy See. Sounds like some great marble bath with a dozen gilded cupids spouting scented water. Anyway, one chalice was made in silver and gold with a secret compartment as a reliquary, while two others were produced at the same time *without* this compartment, so that the reliquary could be secured in the Vatican vaults while a similar chalice was used during Mass and other religious ceremonies."

Jeffrey felt a peal of hope pick up the pace of heart. "Very interesting."

"Yes, isn't it just."

"I don't know what it means, though."

"No, nor I. Perhaps you ought to run this lot by the old gent, see what he can make of it. Tell him it appears to me that the thick plottens, or whatever it is they say in the spy flicks."

"I'll do that."

"Pass on my regards while you're at it."

"I will, thanks."

"Don't mention it. This favor I'm doing, turns out it's loads of fun. Not to mention the odd commission."

"You're a big help, Andrew."

"Not yet, I'm not. But there's always hope."

Jeffrey hung up, turned back to where Katya and Alexander waited. "Andrew's found something."

"So it sounded," Alexander said.

"One of the older tomes described what appears to be our chalice, and provided a small sketch. Interestingly enough, three chalices were made, only one of which had the secret compartment for the relic. Apparently they were made in Rome. For the Vatican."

"Rome," Alexander said. "Our dear friend the Count will be most pleased to hear that he has been vindicated after all."

Jeffrey nodded. "He was so sure he had seen it before."

"The man has a positively incredible memory. People take him for a fool all too often, but behind that clownish exterior rests a brilliant mind, one that has lofted him up from obscurity to immense wealth."

"And his interest in antiques is borderline fanatic," Jeffrey added.

"What was it he said," Katya asked, "something about having seen the same chalice in Italy?"

"I don't have to remind you," Jeffrey mimicked, "of the exclusive circles I travel in while visiting Rome."

"Let's take this one step at a time," Katya suggested. "We've learned that there is definitely a chalice with a secret compartment and two other chalices very similar to it."

"And the chalices were made in Rome for the Vatican," Alexander added. "Or at least so this book has declared."

"We need to follow up on this," Jeffrey agreed.

"Indeed. Do these chalices exist, and is one of them still in the Vatican collection? That's what we need to know next," Alexander said.

"I know my way around the university libraries," Katya offered. "I could check to see if this reliquary is catalogued anywhere in the official Vatican collections."

"Splendid," Alexander declared. "Jeffrey, when we arrive in Cracow tomorrow, while you begin your work on the next shipment, I shall make my report to Rokovski."

"Not Karlovich?"

Alexander shook his head. "The less I see of that man, the better. There is something about him which I find positively disagreeable." He looked at Katya. "My dear, I shall need you to assist Mrs. Grayson from time to time in the shop."

"And to spend every possible moment in the library stacks," Katya added for him.

"Precisely. I shall return the day after tomorrow. Unless your research requires more time, the following day you shall travel out to assist Jeffrey."

"I'll start first thing tomorrow morning," she assured him.

"Excellent." Alexander patted his knees with evident satisfaction. "This is most reassuring. I was positive that the crafting of the piece I returned was so exquisite as to make it impossible for it to be modern imitation."

"And now there are three," Katya said.

"Perhaps." Alexander nodded. "If so, it explains the situation at least in part."

Jeffrey asked, "But why would anyone have switched them?"

"That," Alexander agreed, "is a question we must diligently pursue."

•   •   •

Jeffrey rented a car upon their arrival at the Cracow airport. The driver Alexander had used in the past was now working daily for Gregor, either transporting purchased antiques or aiding with one of the numerous children's projects. Alexander acted as navigator on their drive into the night-darkened town, guiding him through streets whose names had been rendered out-of-date by the demise of Communism.

"Good evening, Alexander," Gregor said in greeting when they arrived at his minuscule apartment. "Welcome back."

"Hello, Cousin," Alexander replied wearily, returning the formal double kiss. "You are looking well."

"Thank you, I am feeling marvelously fit for a winter's eve." Gregor turned to Jeffrey and smiled warmly. "My dear young friend, what a joy it is to see you again. Come in, come in."

Once they were seated and the formalities of offering tea were completed, Gregor turned his attention to Alexander. "Tell me how you have been, Cousin."

Alexander made a visible effort to push aside the flight

fatigue. "We continue to receive an excellent response from the gala, I am happy to say. A number of new patrons have joined our cause."

"That was not what I was asking, but I am glad for you nonetheless."

Alexander looked at him sharply. "Why do I detect a note of condemnation in your voice?"

"I do not seek to condemn," Gregor replied.

"Criticize then. It is there clear as day."

Gregor sipped at his tea before replying quietly, "We are told in Proverbs not to boast about the day. The Hebrew word is *hellal,* which means praise when applied to God, but boast when applied to man. Do you see? When we place ourselves in the spotlight, we assume a strength we do not have. We are indulging in self-worship, or self-praise. We have robbed the Master of what He gave to us only on loan, and claimed it for ourselves."

"I do not think I seek to praise myself," Alexander protested, his voice lacking its customary strength. "And neither does the bishop. I have spent considerable time with him recently. He is a most admirable man, and he speaks of God in terms which are much easier for me to follow than those of others whom I do not care to name."

"My dear cousin," Gregor replied. "I seriously doubt that the Lord will deem to speak to your heart through the bishop."

Alexander looked genuinely peeved. "Why on earth not? Besides you and Jeffrey here, the bishop is the person with whom I feel most comfortable discussing this whole affair."

"Precisely for that reason do I think He will select another."

Alexander showed alarm. "You don't suggest I contact one of those glossy television pundits, do you?"

"I think you should do away entirely with the thought of finding God through those who have achieved worldly fame."

"And pray tell, why should I? I am simply seeking to meet people in keeping with my own nature."

"It is not your nature that we are discussing here."

Alexander swatted at the words. "I will have none of your vague hints and mysterious wanderings."

"All right, then. What if God has something else in mind?"

"Why should He? The bishop speaks a language I can understand."

"What if God chooses to use a different voice?" Gregor persisted. "The cry of a lonely child, for instance. Will you hear that in a bishop's chamber? Or what if He speaks through a woman of the streets? What if He calls to you from the bitter cold of an old man's empty hearth, or the shameful solitude of a prison cell?"

Alexander shifted uncomfortably. "Why is it that your questions tear at me, Gregor?"

"Perhaps because God may choose to speak through me just now, though that is only something you and He can tell. In any case, I hope it is not just me behind these words."

Alexander gave his cousin a hard look. "I suppose the next thing you'll be saying is that I should tell others about this mystery called faith."

Gregor gave him an easy smile. "Where would you be today if someone had not told you about Christ?"

Alexander remained silent for quite some time. Finally he stood, turned toward the door, and said over his shoulder, "I shall think upon what you say."

"Search for your answers within God's Word," Gregor said. "And in prayer. Remember it is His voice you should be listening for. His word to you is something only you will hear, and only within the depths of a hungry heart."

Jeffrey waited to speak until he could hear Alexander's measured tread upon the lower floor's landing. "I feel so uncomfortable sitting here while he talks with you like that."

"Don't let it trouble you," Gregor replied. "He needs you just now, you see, especially when meeting with me. He is afraid of facing the Lord alone. He needs a friend. Someone he can trust. Someone who will share the quest with him."

"I like to think I'm his friend," Jeffrey said.

"Of that you need never doubt," Gregor assured him. "Alexander himself speaks of you in those terms, and he is not one to bandy such a word lightly about."

"I wish I could help him more."

"Always remember that the very nicest compliment you

could pay my cousin is to declare him a patriot," Gregor replied. "He is struggling with the utterly alien concept of a faith that calls for him to trust in the unseen, and he is trying to place it into terms that he can fathom. So, he is seeking to reach God through actions tied to his patriotism and his desire to rebuild the artistic heart of his homeland."

"I don't think I'll ever understand you," Jeffrey declared. "You praise Alexander for making the same mistakes as I do, or at least that's how it seems. Then you turn around and tell me to reach for the stars."

"I urge you to reach higher than my beloved cousin," Gregor replied calmly, "because that is the call I hear within my heart. I look at Alexander and see a man doing all that he can to come to grips with his newfound faith."

Jeffrey asked dispiritedly, "And what do you see when you look at me?"

"Once a mason showed Michelangelo a block of marble and said, it's of no value; there's a flaw right the way through it. Michelangelo replied, it's of value to me. You see, there's an angel imprisoned in it, and I am called to set the angel free." Gregor's eyes shone with a burnished light. "When I look at you, my friend, I see a man striving to grow wings."

Once at their hotel, Jeffrey bade Alexander a good-night, only to call his room an hour later. "Sorry to bother you, but I've received an urgent fax from Katya."

"Wait a moment." There was the sound of Alexander sitting up and turning on the light. "All right. I'm ready."

"I'm not sure I understand what she's saying," Jeffrey began tentatively.

"Then let us apply two heads to the problem," Alexander replied.

" 'My research has turned up important information pertaining to the chalice,' Jeffrey read. " 'Nothing conclusive, but it is perhaps another piece in the puzzle.' " He paused, not sure of Alexander's reaction to the remaining portion.

"Is that all?"

"No," he said slowly. "There's a little more."

"Well, read it, Jeffrey, read it. It is far too late for dramatics."

" 'I have received a call from our lawyer colleague in regard to the room decorations which we recently discussed. It appears that events are developing at a rather rapid pace. Because of what she said, I have moved my departure up to tomorrow morning. Perhaps you would prefer to postpone your own meeting until after we have had a chance to speak.' "

"She was right to be discreet," Alexander said, fully awake now.

"Is this about—"

"It must be. There is nothing else that might justify such a move on her part. Thank you for this little gift, Jeffrey. I shall certainly repose with a lighter heart, thinking that perhaps I might have some good news to pass on to Rokovski tomorrow."

"She said it was not conclusive," Jeffrey reminded him.

"I was not speaking of the chalice," Alexander replied. "Good-night."

CHAPTER
30

Winter's fierce grip held the morning in a blanket of frigid stillness. Jeffrey walked alone through the darkness of a late-coming dawn. He took a longer way despite the cold that bit hard through his clothes, savoring the solitude and the alienness of this medieval city.

The warmth of Gregor's building came as a welcome relief, as did the old gentleman's smile. "Look at the frost on your scarf. How long have you been out there?"

"Long enough to need a glass of tea," Jeffrey replied. "I hope I'm not too early."

"My dear young friend, I have been up for hours."

"Me, too."

That brought him back from the kitchen alcove. "You did not sleep well?"

"I never do, my first couple of nights here or in eastern Germany," Jeffrey replied. "There's so much hitting me."

"A new world," Gregor agreed. "And a world of new challenges." He returned behind the curtain, asked, "What do you do with your time, then, during those sleepless hours?"

"Read," Jeffrey replied. "Think. Pray. Or try to."

"Your perspective on faith remains unchanged?"

"Far as I can tell."

Gregor limped back into view bearing two steaming glasses. "Here, my boy. That should put the warmth back into your bones."

"Thanks." Jeffrey accepted the bell-shaped glass and held it carefully around the upper edge. As with most glasses used to serve tea and coffee in Poland, the glass had no handle. Curving thumb and forefinger around the rim, above the level of the steaming drink, was the only way he could keep from scalding himself.

"Tell me, Jeffrey." Gregor eased himself down. "Do you still doubt the existence of God?"

"No, I don't guess so. Not anymore."

"And yet you have failed to find whatever it is that you search after. How can you therefore hold on to this newfound assurance that God is truly there for you?"

"There's too much going on that I can't just explain away." Jeffrey took a gingerly sip from his glass, sighed a steamy breath. "I look back over these past five or six months, and I see changes I could never have made myself. A relationship more peaceful and filled with love than anything I've ever had in my life. A job that absorbs me and brings me satisfaction. A sense of purpose. An honesty with things really deep inside myself, facing up to things I've always run away from before."

Jeffrey lifted his glass, sipped carefully. "Things are changing. I can't stop and say that this minute, this hour, I feel God's presence. But if I look back over the past weeks and months, I can feel something there. It's as though an invisible hand is guiding me toward something. What, I don't know. But I do think I can see God at work in what is happening."

Gregor shook his head. "My boy, if only you could hear your own words. They are such a declaration of the path you have chosen."

"You make it sound simple."

"No, I make it sound straightforward. There is a very great difference. As the blessed Mother Theresa once said, it is not how God calls you that is important, but rather how you reply."

"But now that I've recognized this need in me, I'm *afraid*. I'm afraid of making a mistake, of doubting too much, and maybe of doubting too little as well."

"Afraid not to find and afraid to find," Gregor murmured.

"Both prospects can be terrifying."

"Everywhere around me I see signs of how this new religion has redesigned my life."

"Not religion. Call it by its true name."

"Faith, then," he conceded.

Gregor nodded. "Religion is external, faith is internal. And it is not the external that calls for change, but the internal."

"But change for what? Where am I going? I'm looking for something, and I can't find it. I don't even know what to call what it is I'm after."

"What do you truly want?" Gregor demanded. "An explosion? Do you seek a thunderbolt? What if God chooses to come to you in a whisper, or a soft call to a listening heart spoken with the first breath of a new dawn breeze? What then? If your ears are tuned only to the great and brilliant, will you miss the beauty of a tiny songbird, a whisper of divine joy meant only for your own questing heart?"

Jeffrey remained hunched over his glass. He sipped, waited, sipped again, taking the words in deep. "All my life I've worried about finding something that mattered enough to really care about having it and keeping it. Now that I've found it, or at least I think maybe I have, I don't know where to look."

"If you don't know where to look, don't keep searching," Gregor replied. "It is that simple. Wait and let it come to you. Learn the strength of patient expectation. Learn the joy of knowing you are a cup for God to fill, a vessel intended to bear His divine fruits of life and love to a thirsty world. Be patient and know He will find you."

Gregor paused for a silent moment before adding, "And He will, my boy. He will."

Jeffrey returned to the hotel so that he and Alexander might go out together to meet Katya's plane. She greeted Jeffrey with a fierce hug and the older gentleman with, "I hope you're not upset that I changed my plans without asking."

"My dear young lady," Alexander replied, "anything that might even possibly inject a hint of good news into my meeting with Dr. Rokovski deserves to be shared without delay. This is why I insisted on imposing upon your reunion."

"You're not imposing," Jeffrey and Katya said together.

"Thank you both. So let us return to our vehicle and hear what you have to say."

Once beyond the airport grounds, Katya said, "I suppose you want to hear about the chalice first."

"You are correct."

"I don't have anything certain," she began, "and Andrew reports nothing new on his front."

"Then let us hear what you do have, so that we may draw our own conclusions," Alexander said, pointing. "Left here, Jeffrey."

"The university library has a fairly extensive historical arts collection."

"More than extensive," Jeffrey added, skirting around a pothole of unknown depths, pulling back sharply to avoid losing his door to a barreling truck. "Vast is a better word. I've gotten lost in their arts section half a dozen times. More."

"I searched their records of the Vatican collections and found a picture of the chalice," Katya reported. "It is claimed to be a reliquary."

"In the Vatican," Alexander said. "How fascinating."

"I thought so, too. So I called the cultural affairs department of the Vatican embassy in London and told them I was a student doing research."

"All true," Alexander murmured. "And all brilliant, I should add."

"Thank you. I said I was just wondering if such an item had ever been loaned out, or might be. The man was positively shocked. Certainly not a reliquary, he replied. It would never leave the vaults beneath the Vatican. No reliquary has ever been released. Never. It has been centuries since any outsider has viewed a fragment from the crown. All such reliquaries are most carefully guarded, very seldom shown, and *never* allowed outside the Vatican."

Save for Alexander's directions, silence reigned through the remainder of their drive back to the hotel. Jeffrey pulled into the parking lot, turned off the motor, declared, "This doesn't add up."

"I quite agree," Alexander said, opening his door. "Come, we shall be much more comfortable pondering the impossible inside."

They selected Alexander's room as a gathering point once Katya had checked in. When the old gentleman opened his door to permit them entry, Jeffrey said, "The curate must have made a mistake."

"Come in, both of you." Alexander stood aside. "Please forgive the lack of space. My dear, take that comfortable chair in the corner. Would either of you care for tea?"

"No, thank you."

"The drawing he showed you was for the Vatican's reliquary," Jeffrey persisted. "Not the chalice he gave you."

"That is certainly a possibility," Alexander replied, settling onto the second straight-backed chair. "However, I am not convinced."

"The curate was very certain," Katya said.

"Precisely. The man was absolutely positive that the chalice he gave me was not the one he received in return."

Jeffrey shook his head. "You're saying the Vatican only *thinks* it has the reliquary?"

Alexander leaned back and mused to the ceiling, "If they were to discover its absence, they certainly would be keen to have it back."

"Wait, wait," Jeffrey protested. "How did it get to Poland in the first place?"

"As to that," Alexander said, still speaking to the ceiling. "I have no answer. And to many other questions besides."

"I discovered something else," Katya announced.

"My dear, your researches have been indeed phenomenal."

"Just by chance," Katya went on, flushed by the praise. "Eleven years ago, Pope John Paul made an announcement that, in celebration of the beginning of the third millennium, the Vatican's reliquaries would all be placed on display."

Alexander sat up straight. "What?"

"The exhibit is scheduled to begin in the year 2000," Katya went on. "And to last for three years."

"If the reliquary had indeed found its way to Poland," Alexander said, "this would put extreme pressure on the Vatican curators to see it returned." He was on his feet. "You must excuse me. Rokovski needs to hear about these findings."

"And Gregor has business for us to attend to," Jeffrey added.

Alexander looked down on Katya. "My dear, you have done excellent work. I thank you. From the depths of a despairing heart, I thank you for the work you have accomplished."

She raised a timid hand. "There is one thing more."

"The other item in your fax," Jeffrey remembered.

She nodded. "Frau Reining called. The people Jeffrey and I met in Dresden are ready to deliver the sample."

Alexander slowly sank back into his chair. "When?"

"The day after tomorrow."

He pondered the news, then shook his head. "Tempted as I am to remain, this you must do yourselves. We do not have evidence that these findings about the chalice are anything more than simple conjecture, and Andrew should not be left without an immediate contact. I shall therefore report this possible development to Rokovski and urge him personally to accompany you to, where did you say this meeting was to take place?"

"Czestochowa," Katya replied. "At a hotel near the Cathedral of the Black Madonna."

CHAPTER
31

Winter appeared to vanish with the dawn. The sun rose in a pristine sky and banished the bitter cold as though it had never existed.

"A glorious morning," Gregor said in greeting. "Let us hope it is truly the arrival of spring."

"Katya said that I should wish you a happy Name's Day," Jeffrey said. "She is only giving us a couple of minutes alone. She is impatient to see you herself."

Gregor ushered Jeffrey inside. "There is a saying that when it is pretty on Saint Gregor's morn, winter has been banished to the depths of the sea, and spring has truly begun."

"When you talk about things like the saints, it makes me feel as if I'm coming from a totally different world." Jeffrey accepted his glass of tea with a nod of thanks. "Does it bother you that I'm a Baptist?"

"My dear boy, the only thing that concerns me is whether or not Christ will know you when the day of reckoning arrives." He sat and straightened his back in the slow way of one who is aware of possible pains. "We shall someday stand before the throne to be judged for our reward. I am speaking about believers here. From my own studies of the Scriptures, I understand that there shall be a second judgment for non-believers. A truly terrible thing. Too terrible to even contemplate. No, I speak here of the judgment of believers. When we stand before His throne, I do not think the majestic Lord will ask us to which denomination we belonged. I believe He will ask us how well we have *loved*."

"I don't feel I know Him at all," Jeffrey confessed.

"You will," Gregor replied with utter certainty. "For the moment, take heart in the fact that He knows you. His knowledge is perfect. Just come to live by that and you'll do fine."

Jeffrey gave a dispirited shrug. "I guess I need to have a better handle on religion."

"As I said yesterday, the *last* thing you need is religion," Gregor replied emphatically. "Religion won't ease your restlessness. Christ entering your life, my dear young friend, *that* is the answer. Not the laws, not this or that sect, not any certain form of worship. The answer is found in knowing Jesus Christ. The solution is being filled with the Holy Spirit. The Lord has said, I will let my goodness, my graciousness, my presence pass before you. And He will, Jeffrey. Open yourself, and He will do as He promised."

"So, how should I worship?"

Gregor smiled. "My favorite definition of worship is to turn toward and kiss."

"Turn toward what?"

"Yes. That is the endless question of those whose thirst remains unquenched. You must open yourself and let *Him* show you where to turn. Seek Him with the eyes of your heart, not with the eyes and mind of material man."

Jeffrey allowed a fragment of his frustration to surface. "That sounds more like poetry than an answer I can use."

Gregor gazed at him fondly. "Those same words could have been said by your grandfather," he replied. "In a different tongue, but with the same honest spirit. He would be very proud of you, my boy."

"For searching in vain?"

"No. For searching in *honesty*." He shifted painfully. "Could you please be so kind as to set one of those cushions behind my back? Ah. Much better. Thank you. Now then, pay attention to me, Jeffrey. When Peter stood on the mountainside and witnessed the Lord's divine majesty unveiled during the Transfiguration, what did he do? He did as most of us would have done. He wanted to jump up and set up tents and build stone monuments and move around and *do*. And the Lord said to him, Stop. Be still. Relax. Don't strive. *Receive*. My young friend, I share with you this same message. Take the single solitary step of being open, and let the Lord work the miracle before you."

"You're saying that I shouldn't be so ambitious," Jeffrey said.

Gregor looked dismayed. "Is it so easy to misunderstand me? The Good Book is full of calls for us to be ambitious. The key is what we are to be ambitious *for*—ourselves, or Him. I cannot imagine that the Lord would endow so many of us with this focused power and then have us call it sinful. That is in my mind utter nonsense."

"That's a relief," Jeffrey said. "I could see changing my ambition to suit His need a lot faster than I could see getting rid of it completely."

"It is an unfortunate human trait to call qualities that we ourselves do not have a sin in someone else. We wish to be comfortable with where we are and who we are, and therefore we do not see that someone else may be driven to *greater* heights, to *greater* service, through a quality that is bestowed by our Maker.

"Paul himself calls us to make service our ambition. The word used when First Thessalonians was written was *philotemesti*. It means to hasten to do a thing, to do it quickly, to exert yourself to the fullest while doing it. It says that we must consider the focus of our ambition to be a vital action, and we must therefore expend whatever energy is required to do this thing."

"It sounds, well, thrilling."

"Of course it does." His eyes shone with a light that humbled Jeffrey. "Take the one essential step, my boy, and then wait. He in His own good time will come, will enter you, will fill you. Not because you've been good. No. Not because you deserve it. You're too honest to suppose that. Rather, because He is the God of unfailing love, and He has been waiting for you to turn and invite Him in."

"But I've asked Him," Jeffrey said plaintively. "At least

I've tried. But when I say it, I can't even do that right."

"You can do it perfectly," Gregor replied. "With God's help. He has built up an expectation within you. A longing. A thirst. He wants your life to be aggravated and restless with longing for what only He can give."

"That's it," Jeffrey said, immensely relieved to be understood. "Like an itch I can't scratch."

"In the second chapter of Acts," Gregor told him, "a group of people witnessed the effects of the Holy Spirit for the very first time. Before their very eyes, the invisible was made visible. And they questioned it. They asked, is this truly of God? For remember, my young friend, these people considered themselves to be believers. At the same time, those who were honest with themselves must have found God to be extremely distant, a power on high rather than an integral part of their inner lives. Certainly they lacked this personal contact with a living Savior, and the Spirit that was His gift to believers.

"I find myself looking back across the incredible distance of these two thousand years and living the experience with them. I see myself being forced to choose—do I remain with the acceptable and the visible and the traditional, or do I reach into the invisible and recognize the hunger that gnaws at my heart? I stand with these baffled witnesses, ignited by the yearning within me to search the unseen realm. Yet I am anchored by the calls of this world, afraid of choosing, knowing that I must choose, realizing that not to choose is in itself a choice.

"Yes," the old man continued, "I can very easily see myself standing with this crowd, terrified by the changes demanded by my empty existence, seeking some way to ignore the call and remain with what is comfortable, what is defined by the elders and the leaders and the people in power.

"But I cannot. I am called by the voice of my heart to turn toward the unseen and accept the Holy Spirit. I am called to dance with the joy that such madness brings."

The buzzer rang, startling them both. Jeffrey stood and released the downstairs catch, then waited while Katya climbed the stairs. She arrived slightly breathless and very excited. "Hello, Gregor."

"My dear young lady, what a joy it is to see you again. Come in, come in. How was your trip?"

Katya accepted his invitation for tea and watched him bustle about the cramped apartment with his listing gait. Once the water was boiled and tea served and Gregor seated, Katya lifted her package. "I brought something for you."

"My dear child, how thoughtful."

"It's nothing, really." She watched him unwrap the package with shy eyes. "Just something I saw that made me think of you."

"There could be no greater gift than your thoughts and prayers." He lifted up the frame. "Marvelous. I am deeply touched."

He turned the antique frame around. The yellowed parchment was decorated top and bottom with brilliantly hand-colored pictures depicting two of Christ's parables—the shepherd returning the lost sheep to the fold and the man finding a pearl beyond value. The center contained a hand-lettered verse. Jeffrey read the delicately scrolled words, "Teach me, Lord, in the ways of the wise."

"Jeffrey took me to my very first antiques fair a few weeks ago," Katya said. "I found this, and I thought of you."

Gregor pointed to the empty wall at the end of his bed. "I shall hang it there, where it will be the first thing I shall see upon rising each morning. Thank you, my dear."

"Those are two of my favorite parables," Jeffrey said.

"Do you know what a parable is? A heavenly truth clothed in an earthly body. It is a way to make the unknowable clear, the unseen perfectly visible." He smiled at Katya. "I am deeply touched by your thoughtfulness."

"Has Jeffrey told you that we are traveling to Czestochowa tomorrow?"

"Is that so?" Gregor was clearly delighted. "May I impose and accompany you? I have long wanted to make another pilgrimage to the Cathedral of Jasna Gora."

"It wouldn't be an imposition," Jeffrey replied. "But I thought pilgrimages went out with the Middle Ages. Something you only find nowadays in books that make fun of the old practices."

"Our modern world is too swift to criticize what it does not understand and to condemn what it finds the least bit uncomfortable," Gregor replied. "A pilgrimage is nothing more than a prayer with feet."

"I think it would be great to have you along," Jeffrey said simply.

"I've heard about this place all my life and never been there," Katya said. "My mother has a copy of the picture in the church, the Black Madonna, on her bedroom wall."

Gregor asked, "What time is your meeting there scheduled?"

"Lunchtime."

"Do you think it might be possible to arrive in time for the eleven o'clock Mass?"

"Sure. I'll just call Rokovski and ask if we can meet him there." Jeffrey stood and signaled to Katya with his eyes. "We have to be going."

"Indeed you do. Business is waiting." Gregor pushed himself erect and saw them to the door. "You know where the Russian market is?"

"I have found it on a map," Katya replied.

"Splendid. Until tomorrow, then."

A continuing thaw left Nova Huta's Russian market swimming in a sea of mud. Visitors paid it no notice, except to walk on tiptoe through the deepest puddles. When Jeffrey and Katya arrived, the sun was shouldering aside clouds and casting an unfamiliar light upon throngs who jostled good-naturedly among the acres of stalls and peddlers. They joined the crowds strolling, gawking, pointing, laughing. They listened to people arguing prices in a mishmash of Polish and Russian and Ukrainian.

The slender young man whom Jeffrey had last seen in a Cracow apartment with two valuables strapped to his thighs spotted them first. He shouted them over with the underhanded come-hither gesture of the East. Beside him stood a young-old girl in her twenties dressed in layer upon layer of sweat shirts, her unkempt dark hair tied back with a length of ragged cloth. Her face was as hard and unflinching as her eyes. Before the pair of them were piles of wrenches and crowbars and hammers and hacksaws and nails and screws and manual drills.

The Ukrainian nudged his companion and spoke to her in a Russian singsong. She spoke in turn to Jeffrey and Katya in Polish, her mouth barely moving in the rock-hard face.

"He says their profit from the last trip was enough to go into business," Katya translated to Jeffrey. "At least, I think that's what he said. This girl's Polish is horrible. I can barely understand her."

"Buy-sell," the man shouted happily in an English so heavily accented as to be barely understandable. "Valuta."

"Valuta," Jeffrey agreed, liking him. "Tell him I'm glad things have worked out so well."

Their conversation attracted attention from nearby stall-holders and patrons. The gawkers and gossipers began to gather and watch and listen and point and talk words that needed no translation. Look, an Englishman speaking with another woman—listen to her Polish. And how do they know this pair from the other side?

The young man waved his hand proudly over his wares, said through the dual translators, "Even after bribes to the border guards on both sides, a good day brings enough to keep both our families alive for a month."

By now the crowd hemmed them in on all sides. The woman spoke a warning; the young man grinned and jerked his head for them to follow. He clapped the next stallholder's shoulder in passing, said something that was answered with a grunt and a shift of position by the man's thick-set wife.

Jeffrey and Katya followed the pair by stalls selling everything from tatty sweaters to sheets to pocket watches to aspirin to Russian fur-lined gloves and hats. Most of the sellers were women, hard-faced and very large and older than their years. The stalls were rudimentary in the extreme, waist-high blocks of poured concrete with wavy plastic roofs supported by rotting timbers. The entire market lot was surrounded on all sides by multistory Communist-built apartment bunkers.

They crossed a mud-swamped parking lot and stopped

beside a thoroughly trashed and battered Soviet Lada. The young man opened the trunk, tossed out sacking and roof-ropes, and pulled out a single remaining wooden crate.

"On the black market the dollar sells for two hundred and ten rubles and it's going up every day," he said through the laborious process. "Prices shoot up fifty, maybe a hundred percent each week. Pensioners get enough money each month to feed themselves for three days. There is trouble brewing."

"So why don't you get out?" Jeffrey asked as he watched him gingerly unwrap multiple layers of padding.

"Family," he answered briefly. "Parents and uncles too old to move. And where would I go, what would I do? There at least people come to me and say, sell this, help me, bring me valuta so I can feed my family another month."

The box held three individually wrapped parcels. The young man tossed back the final layer of matting in one to expose a pair of delicate porcelain "Easter eggs," so named because they were often given by royalty as gifts at the end of Lent. These were painted with minute yet beautifully accurate pictures of the Sansouci Palace of Potsdam. Jeffrey squinted more closely, made out people no higher than a pinhead moving across a graceful bridge. He knew from his reading that they had been painted with a magnifying glass and a brush made from one single horsehair. Each egg represented a month's work by a skilled artisan. They bore the stamp of Meissen, dated 1710. Museum quality.

Next emerged a case the size of a small paperback book. The outside covers were of engraved silver, framing a solid block of ivory. Gingerly he accepted the case from the grimy hands and opened it to find a *Diptyque*; on each block of ivory, two carvings, one above the other, depicted scenes from the life of Christ. Cases such as this one had once adorned the private chapels of late medieval royalty. From the formation of the carved figures and the surrounding decorative motif, Jeffrey guessed that the piece dated from the fourteenth century. Possibly earlier.

Reluctantly Jeffrey handed back the item and accepted the third. His initial disappointment faded when he realized that he was not holding a painting as he first imagined, nor an icon, but rather a seventeenth-century *Adoration*. The frame took the form of an altar, with Doric columns of ebony and silver holding up an ornate frieze and a cross inlaid with polished semiprecious stones. The centerpiece was a painting on what appeared to be a sheet of lapis lazuli. The stone's deep blue had been used to depict a starlit sky from which a finely painted cloud of angels sang hosannas over Mary and the Christ-child.

Jeffrey looked up. "These will feed a family for a lot longer than a month."

The young man answered his unasked question with grave words. Katya's tone matched his as she translated, "In 1917, when the Communists began taking control of the countryside, some of the villages heard what was happening in the cities, churches looted and desecrated or burned to the ground. Priests handed the church heirlooms to devout families, as they knew that most of their brothers in the cities were vanishing without a trace. The villagers were sworn to guard these treasures and to return them to the church once the Communist threat had passed. But now the villages are starving, and the sick are dying untreated. The priests are giving dispensations to sell off what treasures survived."

Jeffrey looked back at the treasure in his hands. "Your village will eat well for a long time to come if this is authentic."

"I am an honest man," the man said strongly. "A good man. I take a little and give most back. This is not for me."

"I believe you," Jeffrey replied. And he did. But he explained, "There are a lot of fakes coming out of Russia just now. All this will have to be carefully authenticated."

The young man nodded. "But the last shipment, they were real?"

"Yes."

"Then take my word." He waved an arm covered to the elbow with grime and grease. "Genuine and old."

Jeffrey cast another lingering glance over the items, nodded agreement. He thought so, too.

"You can buy icons? Good ones, old. Silver frames. Some gold."

"I don't know," he said doubtfully. "There's a wall of icons now in one London antique store."

The young man was not surprised by the news. "But if I bring you ones as special as these?"

"Then I can buy them. I don't know the price, but I will buy any of this quality." He traced the pattern of the blue-veined sky. "Definitely."

"For a lot of people and villages, the only thing of value they have left is the icon. Stored away since the Revolution. Now they either sell or starve."

Jeffrey inspected the young man. "Things are that bad?"

"Come and see," the man replied, his animated face turning as flat as his companion's. "Some things you have to witness to understand."

"Maybe I will."

"You come see me first here, I'll take you to the *real* Ukraine. And more things to buy. Real treasures."

"Maybe this summer," Jeffrey said, liking the idea of a new adventure.

The woman lost her patience, snapped at her companion and started to move away. The Ukrainian smiled, held her shoulder, and gestured with evident pride at her spirit. He soothed her with a few words and said something more which was translated as, "Five thousand dollars now. It is a lot, but I must have it now. The rest you give to your priest, along with word on when you can come with me across the border."

Jeffrey felt the thrill of stepping out into the unknown. "Gregor is not a priest."

The young man shrugged. "The honorable man, then. In a world like this, which is harder to find?"

CHAPTER
32

"The Baroque era in Poland," Katya said as Jeffrey drove them out of Cracow the next morning, "was a golden age in more ways than one. During that period, the nation entered into years of relative stability and vast political power. So long as far-flung powers did not ignite the flames of war, as sometimes happened—"

"Too often," Gregor murmured. "For century upon century, war was seen as a valid arm of everyday politics."

"This stability brought unbridled economic growth to Poland," Katya continued. "And with this growth came phenomenal wealth to the ruling classes. Poland's location made it a bridge between empires—the Ottomans to the south, the Swedes and the Prussians to the north, the Muscovites in the east, and the tottering Holy Roman Empire to the west. For much of this period, the Polish-Lithuanian empire was the only one of these powers that was not at war."

"A bridge of culture, and a bridge of trade," Gregor agreed. "For seven months a year, ice closed off all the northern seas, so that the only way to arrive to the new empire of Muscovy was overland. The only safe overland passage, with decent roads and stable government and security against brigands, was through Poland."

"And every time a cargo came through the empire, a bit was left behind in the form of taxes and payments and trades," Katya finished. "Since there were fewer wars to drain the coffers of either government or commerce, the gentry grew rich."

"Incredibly so," Gregor said. "Sadly, the wars that swept through this land afterward left little evidence of what Poland possessed. But believe me, my dear boy. Poland once set the definition of what it meant to be wealthy."

"A will dated 1640 tells of one woman's estate," Katya said. "She left *five thousand* diamonds and emeralds to her daughters. And she was not a princess nor a queen, Jeffrey, simply the wife of a wealthy landowner. Another landowner of this same period left his children a cloak woven of solid gold thread, embossed with eight hundred rubies. Yet another deeded to just one of her children over eight thousand pearls."

The hills lining the new four-lane highway to Czestochowa were speckled white with old snow. The lower reaches nestled beneath a gently falling mist, the sky descending to wrap distant hills in ghostly veils. Ancient castles and hilltop monasteries emerged from the haze-like painted apparitions before melting from view. Jeffrey decided he had never seen a more beautiful winter landscape.

"When the pillage of this great land began," Gregor said, "the stories that circulated spoke of wealth beyond the greediest of imaginations. Warlords swept in like packs of wolves following the scent of a fresh kill. One country estate contained so much art that the Swedes required one hundred and fifty wagons to cart it away. Another castle, which fell to the Austrian army, listed over seven thousand paintings in its archives."

Tree-lined rivers appeared from time to time, impressionist glimpses that flowed into the white-shrouded distance. Carefully tended farms gave way to forests of silver birches, tall and graceful and otherworldly in the floating mists.

"But during the period of stability," Katya went on, "this outward display of wealth was carried over into how Poles worshiped. By this time, the Polish Catholic church was referred to simply as 'our church.' Rome was scarcely granted the time of day. The Vatican was so embroiled in trying to keep the Holy Roman Empire from scattering to the winds that little more than passing complaint was made. At least the name Catholic was kept."

"Keep in mind as well," Gregor added, "that the tide of Protestantism swept much of Europe at the onset of this era. While wars scarred the face of many countries, Poland opened its arms to all sects, including many that even the Protestant church considered too heretical."

"I love it when you two do this," Jeffrey said.

Gregor showed genuine surprise. "Do what?"

"Trade off on each other. Tell a story together."

Gregor looked at Katya in surprise. "Were we doing that?"

"I don't know," Katya replied.

"Yes you were, and it's great," Jeffrey assured them. "Please continue."

"Very well," Gregor agreed. "Where was I?"

"Heretics."

"Ah, yes. Thank you. Calvinists formed a very large colony here under the protection of the king. Lutherans dominated several regions, converting even the ruling princes. Aryans, who were condemned by every other church body in Europe, populated several cities. There was even a point when a majority of the Sejm, Poland's parliament, was Protestant. In the almost two centuries that religious terror and oppression swept through the rest of Europe, only seven people were sentenced in Poland for religious crimes, and five of them were Catholics convicted of burning down a Protestant church. When a Papal envoy arrived to complain, the Polish king was heard to say, 'Permit me to rule over the goats as well as the sheep.' At a time when other countries, Protestant and Catholic alike, were torturing people before burning them at the stake just for reading the wrong book, upholding the cause of human rights like this was extraordinary."

"Many historians feel that it was precisely because of this liberal attitude that Poland eventually returned to the religion of its heritage," Katya went on. "In any case, by the middle of the eighteenth century, Catholicism was again the predominant form of worship, and churches in wealthier regions reaped the benefits of their princes' and patrons' riches."

"Regions such as Czestochowa," Gregor added.

Katya nodded. "One patron decided such an important painting of the Madonna and Child needed to be clothed in robes of more than just paint and so gave a cloak of woven gold and encrusted diamonds. Another donated a cloak of gold and emeralds. Another of silver and rubies. Yet another had an embossed metal plate designed and covered with a sheet of hammered gold, then set in the wall to slide over and protect the painting when it was not being viewed."

"So what is so important about this painting?" Jeffrey asked.

Katya glanced at Gregor, who smiled and nodded. "After you, my dear."

"It's hard to separate fact from legend," Katya began. "All that can be said for sure is the original painting is at least one thousand five hundred years old."

"What?"

"That is the minimum," Gregor confirmed. "But being an incurable romantic, I prefer the legend."

"So do I," Katya agreed.

"Which is?" Jeffrey pressed.

"That it was painted by Luke on the tabletop from the holy family's home in Bethlehem," Katya replied.

"Luke, as in the writer in the Bible?"

"There is much to argue that the story might be true," Gregor said. "Legends and early historians both agree that it is so. There is also another image of Mary and the Christ-child in Florence, Italy, which authorities insist was also painted by Luke. The two paintings are remarkably similar."

"This one was reportedly taken from Jerusalem by the Roman Emperor Constantine around the year 300," Katya continued. "Constantine stopped Rome's persecutions of Christians when he himself was converted. He is said to have placed this painting in his own chapel, where it remained for over six hundred years. By that time, the eastern Holy Roman Empire was collapsing. Constantinople was warring with enemies on every side, including some of its own provinces. Allies were desperately needed. In return for an oath of fealty, the painting was given to Prince Lev of Rus, as the lands to the north were then known. Prince Lev moved it to his own palace at Belz, where it remained until 1382, when his descendant Prince Vladislaus decided to relocate it to a new monastery he was starting in Czestochowa."

"All of this is carefully documented, I assure you," Gregor added. "From the gift of the painting to Prince Lev in the year 900 to today, the deeds of authentication still exist. The only question is whether it was truly painted by Saint Luke."

"In 1430 the monastery was attacked by bandits," Katya went on. "The painting was shattered by sword blows. The king ordered it restored no matter what the cost, but painters were unable to make their colors hold fast to the old picture."

"We know now that the reason was that very early painters made their primitive colors hold true by fusing them onto the wood with a wax coating," Gregor explained. "But at the time it was an international calamity. There are records within the monastery of letters from all over the civilized world, asking for reports on the progress of repairs."

"So the painters put a new coating on the repaired tabletop," Katya said, "and then painted the picture again. They kept to the original as exactly as possible, except for one thing. On Mary's face they painted in a long jagged scar, to show for as long as the painting existed that it once had been desecrated."

Czestochowa proved to be, in effect, two cities in one. The outlying town was the same collection of dreary buildings flanking pitted and crumbling streets they had seen everywhere in Eastern Europe. The inner city, however, the hill of Jasna Gora, was something else entirely.

The hill was separated from the rest of the city by a broad expanse of gradually rising green, bordered by a series of glass-fronted restaurants and gift shops. Beyond their covered ways, a number of enterprising capitalists had set up suitcase-stands; several dozen competing boom-boxes blared out a cacophony of religious music, while other sellers let postcards and picture books flutter in the breeze.

The hilltop was buttressed with red-brick fortress walls; these descended far below the footbridge that crossed from the paved walkway to the first of three vast ornamental gates. The hill took a swooping dip down into a grass-covered canal before joining the fortress at the base of what once had been a very deep moat. Small, barred windows rimmed the brick facade above the ancient, mossy waterline.

Beyond the first wall came a second and beyond that a third, each marked by guard towers and high stone gates crowned with royal seals. And past the third gate rose a village from another era, lined with narrow cobblestone streets which wound amidst ancient buildings and stone fountains with time-sanded facades. Windows wore hand-drawn panes that flowed downward with the patience of centuries.

At one end of a cobblestone plaza rose the church, where a steady stream of people made their way through high arched portals. Jeffrey stood far enough inside to be protected from the wind while Katya and Gregor bought books from nuns at a glass-fronted stall. He watched the faces that passed. Over and over he found himself inspecting hardened features with eyes that showed a surprisingly gentle light.

The painting was not in the main church at all, but in a side chapel that could be called small only when compared to the central hall. It was reached through a series of three other chapels, each of which could easily have held a thousand people. Each had a multitude of naves and alcoves and doors leading to still more chapels and prayer rooms. All these ancient halls had been renovated several centuries ago in lavish Baroque style. Distant ceilings bore ornate and gilded frescoes surrounding religious paintings, with these in turn encircled by cherubim heralding the King's return on long, silvered trumpets.

After this parade of wealth and glitter, the painting's chapel was positively plain. There were no marble-pillared side chapels bearing massive paintings, nor giant gilded angels, nor rising ranks of candles, nor elaborate chandeliers. Mosaic floorings, tapestries, and ceiling pictures had no place here. The floor was hard granite worn smooth and grooved by six centuries of pilgrims' feet. Jeffrey passed through the ancient oak door, looked around the small entrance portico, and wondered what all the fuss was about. Then he turned the corner, entered the chapel proper, and saw the nave.

The church's front section was protected by floor-to-ceiling iron bars, connected by a gilded, hand-wrought pattern of leaves and vines. Great double doors were swung open, and chairs were set in cramped rows up to the banister and communion table.

The altar reached up almost to the distant ceiling, a massive structure covered with intricately detailed scenes. The apostles gathered to either side, life-sized bas-reliefs whose hands held scrolls and books and lifted them up to the angels on high. And in the center was the painting of the Black Madonna.

She was not black at all, but rather had an olive-skinned complexion that could have been called dark only by light-skinned medieval folk who never in their lives had seen a southerner. Her face had the stiffness and lack of expression Jeffrey had seen in very early religious mosaics. Her eyes were slender as tears and slanted upward. The Christ-child in her arms was a miniature rendition of his mother. Whatever the actual date of the painting, one thing was utterly clear in that first glimpse; it was very, very old.

The painting was gilded like an icon and hung above the chapel's central cross and altar. Penitents made circles around the front chamber on their knees, murmuring prayers in time to those who sat in the front rows. Jeffrey followed Katya to the last row of seats and sat down beside her. An older woman moved forward; he stood and offered his seat. He then backed up against one of the central pillars, not at all sorry for the chance to look around.

Perhaps six hundred people were standing and kneeling and sitting in the chapel, and this was a midweek morning of no special importance. Jeffrey bowed his head and said the Lord's Prayer. As he spoke, he had the fleeting impression of all their softly murmured voices melting together to form one great prayer sent lofting upward, all joined as though spoken from one great heart.

Hearts. He opened his eyes, looked around the chamber, and saw that the old stone walls were not quite so plain as he had first thought.

Tiny silver hearts were hammered into the walls, hundreds of thousands of silent witnesses presented by believers who wished to testify that prayers had been answered. Jef-

frey looked out across the chamber and found himself bound
to the six hundred years of believers who had come and worshiped within these same walls. How many had known the
questions he faced? How many had yearned for more understanding, more wisdom, more knowledge of the Lord? How
many had come and stood and thirsted?

Mass began. Katya was too caught up in her own prayers
and the priest's message to come back to him and translate.
Jeffrey did not mind. It was enough to stand and listen to
words he did not understand, surrounded by people he did
not know, and yet somehow be filled with the feeling, the
knowledge, that he was not alone.

Here in these foreign surroundings was a flavor of something he could not explain. Jeffrey stood by the ancient pillar
in an alien church in an alien nation and was filled with an
absolute certainty that he was in the presence of something
greater than himself. He stood and inspected his heart and
yearned for a greater knowledge of his Savior.

His mind touched on concepts that he only half understood. His heart knew the longings of one not yet fulfilled,
yet in some strange way the act of honest searching brought
him joy. He was aware of a contentment that came not *despite*
his lack of wisdom but rather *because* he hungered for more.
He watched the others with eyes that searched inward, and
he realized that always before he had seen his hunger as a
fault, a failing, when in truth it was a gift. It forced him to
continue walking, keep searching, keep struggling to throw
off his burden of isolation from his Lord.

His eyes were drawn back to the walls and their silent,
shining testimonies, and he somehow felt a kinship with the
centuries of thankful messages. One alcove was given over
to crutches—tiny ones for children, ivory-tipped canes for
the elderly, crutches of every size and make and description—rising up the trio of high walls and covering every inch
of space. Two other alcoves were full of crosses and rosaries
and medallions bearing prayers of thanks in a multitude of
languages.

But the majority of space was for the hearts. None larger
than his hand, some as small as a fingernail, they covered
half a dozen alcoves, each with three walls ninety feet wide.
A silver sea of thankful hearts.

CHAPTER
33

As they emerged from the church into the damp chill, Gregor patted Jeffrey's arm. "Thank you for allowing me to be a part of this. And thank you both for the Mass."

"I hope it wasn't too boring for you," Katya said, taking hold of Jeffrey's other hand.

"I enjoyed it," Jeffrey replied. "I learned a lot."

Katya smiled up at him. "And what did you learn from a sermon given in Polish?"

"I don't know if I can put it into words."

Gregor nodded his understanding. "The most valuable of lessons are seldom those that can be restricted by man's puny tongue. Especially at first."

They descended the hill and walked to the city's one large hotel, a glass and steel structure designed in the best of Communist sixties style. While they shed their coats and scarfs and gloves at the cloakroom, Jeffrey glanced into the restaurant. "These places all look the same, don't they."

Katya did not need to turn around to understand. "All such hotels were built around the same time. All the menus were printed by the central supply office for all restaurants. All the chairs and tables and plates and glasses for all Polish restaurants were manufactured by the same factories."

"All very boring."

"Stimulation of individual tastes ranked low on the list

of Communist priorities," Gregor said, opening the restaurant door and ushering them inside.

A swift glance assured him that Rokovski had not yet arrived. Jeffrey followed the others to a table by the window, inspected the plastic-bound menu, listened as Katya passed his order to an attentive waiter, then turned and gave in to the pleasure of people-watching.

Food arrived at the next table over, and all conversation halted as if a switch had been thrown. The intensity with which the people ate was something he rarely observed in the West.

Katya saw what had caught his attention. "You never see people picking politely at their food here," she told him quietly. "If they do, they are foreigners. A Pole has been hungry too often to play at eating. If food is put in front of him, he *eats.*"

A newcomer waddled in and took the table across from them. The man wore his triple chins with a nervous air. He was too small to be called fat, yet every inch of his little frame was padded to the point of absurdity. He was all bone, fat, and skin, from the looks of it, with no muscle at all. His flesh shivered with every step. Everything about the man was gray—gray suit, gray and white striped shirt buttoned to a neck that folded over and swallowed his collar, gray shoes, gray eyes, gray pallor to his skin. His lips were buried in a tight little grimace that brought his chin almost into contact with his pudgy little nose.

Jeffrey leaned toward Katya, asked, "How do people allow themselves to get that way?"

She responded like a mother teaching a child something that he could not have yet learned, but should know. "Maybe because he's lazy. Maybe because he hasn't had any choice. You don't find many sports centers in Poland. These are not an exercising people. Either you are a professional athlete or you maybe play a little soccer on vacations, or you do nothing. Maybe it's because life requires so much hard work of them. Maybe food was so hard to find when they were young that it would have been foolish to use up more calories than necessary. Or maybe they have never been taught to think that, after a certain stage in life, personal appearance is still important."

Jeffrey spotted Rokovski entering the restaurant and rose to greet him. The others stood with him.

"My dear Jeffrey," Rokovski walked over with hand outstretched. "How wonderful to see you. I hope you haven't been waiting long."

"Not at all. You remember my fiancée, Katya Nichols."

"But of course." He bowed over her hand and continued. "Alexander informed me of your betrothal during his last trip. May I add my own congratulations and best wishes."

"Thank you. And this is Alexander's cousin, Gregor Kantor. Dr. Pavel Rokovski."

"It is indeed an honor to meet Alexander's illustrious cousin," Rokovski said formally.

Jeffrey showed surprise. "You know of him?"

"There are not so many who have forsaken the chance for both wealth and position to aid the needy that they would go unnoticed," Rokovski replied, holding fast to Gregor's hand, "or their name remain unspoken in the highest of circles."

"You do me great honor," Gregor murmured.

"On the contrary," Rokovski said, "it is you who do honor to both your name and our nation."

As they resumed their places the waiter appeared. Jeffrey asked, "Would you join us for lunch?"

"Thank you, perhaps a bite of something." He waved away the menu, spoke briefly, then turned back to the table. "You have heard from them?"

"Nothing."

"So we are to wait, then." He did not seem troubled. "A small price to pay for the return of such a treasure."

"We don't know that for sure," Jeffrey warned.

"Our dear Alexander took the greatest of pains to explain the situation," Rokovski assured him. "Several times now, in fact. I am well aware of the unknown factors, but I must say I agree with him that there is at least a shred of hope. To make such an offer of evidence without payment in return suggests that they are indeed serious."

"You haven't met them," Jeffrey muttered.

"I beg your pardon?"

"Jeffrey is not overly impressed with them," Katya explained.

"Ah, yes, Alexander mentioned that as well. I find it good to have reservations when entering into such affairs," Rokovski replied easily. "Although my enthusiasm runs away with me from time to time, I must confess. So it is good to know that someone else will remain my anchor, should that be the case here."

Over lunch the dreaded subject arose. "I don't suppose you have any word of the chalice?"

Jeffrey shook his head miserably. "Nothing at all."

"That's not true," Katya protested.

"Yes," Rokovski agreed. "Alexander discussed with me your remarkable findings. I found them to be of the greatest interest, although I could not successfully fit the pieces together."

"We're missing some crucial element," Jeffrey said.

"My sentiments exactly. For that reason, I have placed two of my best researchers on the matter. Already they have come up with what might be yet another fragment."

"Which was?"

"As you may know," Rokovski said, "there was a point in our history when Poland and her church stood calmly and watched as much of Europe went up in the flames of religious conflict."

"The Reformation Wars," Jeffrey said. "We were just talking about that this morning."

"Indeed. Well, Poland's church became very independent-minded during this period. Rome was unable to complain very loudly, for at least the wealth and power of Poland remained Catholic, even if they did refuse to join the battle against the Protestants." Rokovski shook his head. "My country has committed a number of very foolish acts in her long past. Yet here stands one of the shrewdest moves in all European history, one country who retained its senses through two hundred years of religious insanity. I wish words could express how proud I am of the rulers who forged this dangerous path.

"In any case, the Polish kings found it much wiser to appoint their own bishops than to risk having Rome bring in someone who would ignite the fires of battle. They sent messengers to Rome informing the Pope of their decisions. This policy was a matter of great distress to Rome.

"In the midst of all this turmoil, with diplomatic missions and Papal letters going back and forth, an emissary arrived from Rome. He stated that the Pope wished to have a particular cardinal appointed, someone he could trust. A man who would be a voice for Rome in the midst of the Polish empire's growing might. The emissary arrived bearing gifts, gestures of goodwill, and so forth. One of these gifts, or bribes if you like, was a golden chalice."

Jeffrey leaned forward. "*The* chalice?"

Rokovski shrugged. "That we have yet to confirm. But the dates do correspond."

He pushed his plate aside and leaned both elbows upon the table. "I must tell you something else, something that should not go beyond this table. I do not trust Karlovich. I have been forced to spend quite a bit of time with him as this investigation has progressed, and I have grown more and more concerned over the man."

"In what way?"

"Nothing specific. He simply gives me the sense of being overly enthusiastic. In a number of questionable directions, I might add. There is a very fine line between passion and fanaticism, and one great danger of fanatic belief is the feeling of infallible judgment."

Further conversation was halted when Katya stiffened and pointed. "They're here."

All turned to see a large blond woman in a black leather trench coat enter the restaurant.

"Perhaps I should wait outside," Gregor said, not rising with the others.

"Nonsense," Rokovski replied, not taking his eyes from the woman approaching their table. "We shall simply consider you as Alexander's honored emissary. Which you are."

She stopped before them, gave each of them a blank stare. Her eyes met Rokovski's, where they remained. She set a pair of battered plastic-leather suitcases down at her feet and said a few words in German that Katya translated as, "You have five days."

"That should be adequate," Rokovski replied. "How—"

She spoke again briefly, drew an envelope from her pocket, and placed it on the table. Katya translated, "Two million dollars are to be deposited in an account in Zurich, Switzerland. Details are listed here."

"We will need some form of guarantee," Rokovski said. "Some promise that we will actually receive the remainder of the treasure after payment is made."

The woman had clearly been expecting the question. Immediately after Katya finished her translation, she responded with, "One of our number will check into this hotel in five days. He will deposit with you his passport. He will remain for twenty-four hours after you have received the location details. In return, you will deposit with him a guarantee of safe conduct to Switzerland on the evening of the sixth day." Eyes turned hard as agate. "No tricks."

"No tricks," Rokovski repeated. "It is agreed."

•　•　•

"Rokovski is over the moon," Jeffrey reported to Alexander that evening by telephone.

"He thinks it is genuine, then."

"He won't say anything, but you should have seen his eyes when he opened the cases."

"What did they contain?"

"Amber," Jeffrey replied. "Pieces about the size of my fist, mostly."

"Splendid," Alexander said, his enthusiasm growing.

"All different shades. White as powder to golden to a dark tea shade. Carved with designs on one side and left flat on the other. They looked sort of like puzzle pieces." Jeffrey paused. "I wish you could have been there."

"My dear boy, thank you for saying so. But I am quite content to live the experience through you."

"There were bits of yellowed paper stuck everywhere on the amber."

"The wrapping," Alexander said definitely. "There were always rumors that the Nazis had placed the amber in tissue paper that contained markings for how the walls were to be fitted back together again."

"That's what Rokovski thinks too. He's having the paper

tested now. He says that will be the clearest assurance that the pieces are genuinely from the Amber Room."

"Although he already believes it to be so," Alexander finished for him. "As do I."

"He says some of the whitest amber isn't even available anymore."

"Bone amber," Alexander said. "Extremely rare."

"There are pieces six or seven inches wide of the stuff," Jeffrey said, remembering the light in Rokovski's eyes when he picked up the first piece, carved in the shape of a blooming rose.

"The Amber Room. I can scarcely believe that it might indeed be within our very grasp."

"Don't get your hopes up too soon."

"My dear Jeffrey," Alexander replied, "I shall indulge myself as I please on this account. It makes up for the distress over this other matter. Almost."

CHAPTER
34

"Tell me," Gregor said the next morning, once Jeffrey had been settled in the apartment's most comfortable chair, and tea had been served. "Have you spoken with others about how they came to know the presence of the Almighty?"

"Some," Jeffrey admitted. "I was just thinking about that this morning. I read that part in the Bible, you know, where Jesus says that you have to die and be born again. It seems as if they were all brought to a point that made them look to something more than their own human strength."

Gregor gifted him a look that illuminated the reaches of his heart. "My boy, I shall make a prediction. A time will come when you shall make a wonderful teacher for our Lord."

He had to laugh. "You've got the wrong man."

"If only you could hear the growing wisdom in your own voice or recognize the hunger in your breast for being the gift that it is." Gregor smiled at Jeffrey's discomfort. "Enough of that. Being broken, as this experience is also known, is another name for facing a need greater than yourself. I find it most wonderful that our Lord promised that we as believers would never, ever face such an overwhelming defeat again. The trials we encounter, once the turning has been made, shall never break us. I find that truly beautiful. Once the path has been found, we are given a shield for all our remaining days."

Jeffrey cast a glance at Gregor's own twisted form, then looked guiltily away.

"I did not say we would not face trials," Gregor told him softly. "I said we would always be given the strength and the protection and the guidance to see us through."

"Sorry."

"My dear boy, why should you be? You didn't cause this." He sipped from his glass. "Now tell me. If these people with whom you spoke about the experience of faith did so in fullness, they shared another trait. An event equally as important as being broken. Can you see it?"

"I'm not sure."

"Remember. It is there, I assure you. Can you see it?"

Jeffrey felt as though he was being pointed directly toward something, but was unable to identify it. He shook his head.

"Someone told them about faith. Ah, yes, now you see. Excellent. Yes, it is important for all believers to remember that faith is always teetering on the verge, always just one generation away from total extinction. There is only one way for faith to continue."

"It has to be passed on," Jeffrey said.

"Exactly. Someone has to plant the seed. The gift of witnessing has to be offered. A believer must stand and by his or her life show the power of the invisible at work." Gregor offered a smile. "And this brings us to what I would suggest as your next little exercise, my young friend. I would ask you to go out and practice illogical witnessing."

"Do what?"

"Choose the absolute least likely person you can find. Make sure it is someone who leaves you utterly unsettled. If possible, somebody whom you positively loathe." He examined Jeffrey. "Am I getting through?"

"How about another assignment?" Jeffrey asked.

Gregor shook his head. "This one fits perfectly."

"No it doesn't. I'm positive about that."

"I feel utter harmony with this notion."

"So you do it. Just the thought makes my skin crawl."

Gregor beamed. "Wonderful."

Jeffrey shook his head. "Anything but."

"Listen to me, my brother in Christ. Here is the key. There is positively *no one* on earth whom God does not love. You need to begin to see yourself as an instrument of this love, someone through whom Christ may live and love and save. You must accept this as a part of your daily life and stop trying to keep it at arm's length.

"You want something that makes sense. Something that you can analyze and fit into a comfortable little box. My friend, God's salvation is intended to explode *every* box, to shatter *every* myth in your life. Including the one you continue to hold out in front of yourself as a shield. Do you know what that is?"

Jeffrey motioned his denial. "I'm not sure I want to know."

"Of course you do. You're upset because I speak of what you both want to hold on to and desperately seek to let go. It is the old and the new struggling for central place in your life. The myth you cling to is that you are unworthy, is it not? You fear that you are not good enough to receive God's love, to be filled with His gift of the Spirit. The mirror of your newfound faith is confronting you with the multitude of your faults and your sins, and you are wondering at how an all-knowing, all-seeing, all-powerful God can truly love someone such as you. Is that not it, Jeffrey? Is this not the question you are afraid to bring out into the open and admit to yourself and to God?"

Jeffrey remained silent.

"Listen, my brother. Your fear has power because it contains truth. It is both true and not true. True, because you are *not* worthy of God. But not true because He has sent His Son to cleanse you, to clothe you anew, to *make* you worthy. It is the greatest gift of all history, both what has been written and what is yet to come. So when you stand before this person you loathe and witness to him, I want you to remember this ultimate and undying truth. That not only is this other person eternally worthy, if only he or she will open their hearts to the truth, but *so too are you.*"

●　●　●

Their first meeting that morning took place at the Forum Hotel, a vast structure of over four hundred rooms, situated across the Vistula River from Cracow's old city. The seller was an eye doctor, in town for a symposium on new ophthalmological equipment. He was a tall, slender man going prematurely bald, his face was as bland as his voice, his hands the only expressive part about him.

The doctor led Katya and Jeffrey through the foyer and down a hall transplanted from any big-city Hilton—marble floor, veneered walls, decorative modern art displayed for sale, flower shop, hair salon, travel agent, Hertz. The change from the world outside could not have been greater.

The symposium took place in a hall that looked to seat five or six hundred and was filled to standing room only. Outside the hall were smaller rooms filled with displays of the latest Western equipment. The doctor led them toward a stand of microscopes mounted on what looked like a cross between a robot arm and a crane.

Through Katya he said, "This is what I want. A surgical microscope. Fifty-four thousand dollars the cheapest one costs, when I add up the diagnostic equipment here and here. I want you to see this and understand that I am perfectly serious. I must have this much money. Otherwise I do not sell. Do you understand? I do not sell unless I can buy this for my practice."

With the same hurried calm that Jeffrey knew from Western doctors, he led them back down the hall, through the main foyer, and into a waiting elevator. He talked the entire way, Katya using his brief pauses to translate for Jeffrey.

"Until the fall of Communism, private practice and physician-owned equipment was illegal. The only items I was allowed to use in my own office were those things abandoned by a hospital. You cannot imagine the battles we had among the hospital doctors over machines that were barely more than scrap. Even if we couldn't use them, there was still a certain status associated with having your own equipment.

"Now all this has changed, and private practices are allowed. Doctors can charge clients for their services, which before was also illegal. And now doctors want to work at Western technological levels. Myself included."

He led them out of the elevator and down the seventh floor hall to his room, still talking. "This is becoming urgent, because the hospitals are sliding into chaos. The social system has broken down. People keep going to the hospitals, but the government has no money for funding. The poor are now waiting *days* in hospital lobbies for an appointment with a doctor. I will not make you sick by describing what our emergency rooms look like. When patients are finally seen, they are inspected with equipment that has broken down and treated with drugs that are out-of-date. There is a desperate lack of needles and syringes and even the simplest of bandages. People who can afford it are going to private clinics for everything."

He opened his door, ushered them into a room fitted with standard Western hotel furniture, and waved them toward the two seats. He perched on the end of his bed and continued. "If you're retired, you get free medicine. Everyone else pays thirty percent for local, Polish-made pharmaceuticals. If you can afford it, however, you purchase drugs made in the West, and for them you pay the full price. The problem is, you see, there is a *huge* difference in quality."

He went to his closet and pulled out two heavily strapped cases. "The government ran out of money to pay for medical treatment, which means that the pharmacies have not been reimbursed for the drugs they distributed free of charge or sold at subsidized prices. So what happens? The state-run pharmacies are cutting back on the number of drugs they keep and dispense to match the amount they received from the government the month before. Many of the poor are going without, or having to spend what to them is a month's salary for one dose of imported antibiotics at an international pharmacy."

The doctor opened the first case and began unfolding multiple layers of burlap wrapped around an ornate silver tureen chased in gold leaf. Jeffrey took the opportunity to whisper to Katya, "Do you remember our talk about tithing together and doing something for the people here?"

She turned and gazed with eyes that drank him in. "I remember," she said quietly.

"I have a feeling this is it," he said. "Could you ask him for an introduction to a hospital that's in trouble? Maybe one that treats kids?"

CHAPTER
35

There was another snowfall that night, so the next morning they decided to take the train for their visit to the children's hospital. A thaw had set in by the time they left for Wroclaw, which was good, because the heat on the train was truly feeble. It was an old Polish train, with PKP stamped on the side of each green smut-stained wagon.

The trip took seven endless hours. Jeffrey worked through all his notes, talked with Katya until the jouncing fatigue silenced them, watched landscapes roll by under a flat gray sky. He walked the passageway, saw young and old huddled under coats or swaddled in quilts and blankets, sitting with the patience of those who knew that however long the voyage took, it would take longer still.

With each stop, the compartments and passageways became more crowded. The train went from comfortable to overstuffed, with all seats taken and people standing in sardine-packed confinement in the passageway.

"It used to be like this all the time," Katya said. "Train tickets cost pennies, and there were always delegations traveling everywhere. Even a visit to another factory was done by committee. Delegations meant extra eyes were open and watching."

An hour outside Wroclaw, Katya told him, "Many Poles still consider this region to be a part of Germany. It didn't belong to Poland until 1945. After the war, the Allied powers agreed to redraw Poland's boundaries. The Soviet Union annexed almost a third of Poland, which was then attached to its border. In compensation, a slice of Germany, including parts of Silesia, was given to Poland on this side."

"No one complained?"

"Who listened to a defeated Germany? As for Poland, the Soviets made sure no one made an official complaint. A lot of people, like Mama, protested with their feet. They moved West in hopes of escaping the spread of Russian troops. A few managed to escape. Most did not."

She pointed out the window at a passing small village. "The architecture is very German here. You won't find structures like this anywhere else in Poland."

"Like what?"

"Wait until we arrive in Wroclaw. It's easier to describe when you see a city."

The ring of factories marking the outskirts of Wroclaw left the air tasting bitter. Within the city proper, the streets showed a hodgepodge of building styles. Communist highrises mingled with prewar apartment and office buildings that would have looked at home in Paris or Vienna if only they had been painted. Lacy iron grillwork wove its way around breakfast balconies fronting tall French double doors. Walls were festooned with plaster bas-reliefs and stone gargoyles. Wrought-iron streetlamps from the age of gas and candles still stood guard over many street corners.

The station itself was tall and curved and walled in with glass, as were many European stations remaining from the steam-driven Industrial Revolution. The air smelled dry. Metallic. Sooty. It sucked the moisture from Jeffrey's eyes and mouth and throat.

"Now it's mostly Poles who live here," Katya said as they walked through the echoing terminal. "The Germans left in waves of hungry refugees. Then Stalin forcibly resettled many families here from eastern Poland, which was incorporated into the Soviet Union after the war."

They stepped out into a wind-driven mixture of sleet and slushy rain, and settled into a taxi that stank of the driver's Russian cigarettes. After Katya had given him directions,

Jeffrey asked, "What happened to the Poles who didn't make it out of those eastern lands?"

Katya gave her window a tiny shrug. "From one day to the next, all contact was lost. I remember asking the family I stayed with in Warsaw that same question. They had relatives still there, or so they thought. But no communication was allowed. Now we know that some survived, but many were lost. Most, perhaps. Stalin sent wave after wave of those Poles to Siberia, never to return. He wanted to make those lands totally Soviet, to silence any former claim those people might have made for their homeland."

The children's hospital of Wroclaw was a grim, square-faced building stained gray by years of soot. It was fronted by what once had probably been a formal garden and was now a parking lot paved with cinders. Grimy windows gave way to prim cleanliness within as they passed through the entrance. The waiting area was lined with hard-backed benches and filled with parents and children waiting in patient silence.

Katya gave their names to the receptionist, and they were soon joined by the chief pediatrician, Dr. Helena Sova, an attractive blond woman in her mid-thirties. "Dr. Mirnik called from the opthalmologist's conference to say you were coming," she said in greeting. "He has been very kind to consult here when our small patients have eye troubles. Please come this way."

She was very trim, very stately, with a happy face framing a pair of huge sad eyes. "We have seventy beds for children from birth to eight years," she said, leading them down a very old yet absolutely spotless hall. She spoke excellent English with a most appealing lilt, her voice brisk and slightly breathless at the same time. Jeffrey noticed that her presence brought a smile from everyone they passed—doctors, nurses, parents, children. All smiled, all spoke, all received the blessing of a few quick heartfelt words. The process was so natural and continuous that it never interrupted their conversation.

"Our main problem is lung disease, as the air pollution is extremely bad. Poland, you see, is the most polluted country on earth, and we stand at the edge of the most polluted region in Poland. From Cracow to Katowice and up to the edge of Silesia, that area is known as the Triangle of Death." She gave them a smile in direct contrast to the look in her eyes. "Rather dramatic, don't you think?"

She ushered them into her office, made the formal offer of coffee or tea, and continued. "In the sixties and seventies, the government borrowed billions from the West, gambling that they would be able to launch Poland into the future. They constructed massive factories, with absolutely no consideration whatsoever to the environment. They were desperate, you see, to use all this capital for output."

"You heard such words everywhere," Katya agreed. "Output and productivity and five-year programs."

The doctor gave Katya a closer inspection, then spoke to her in Polish. Katya's reply brought a new light to those sad, intelligent eyes. They conversed gaily for a few minutes, then Dr. Sova turned back and said, "Your fiancée speaks an excellent Polish."

Fiancée. It was still a new enough thought to send shivers up his spine. "So I have been told."

"As I was saying," the doctor continued, "the government built these industrial behemoths all through Poland, but many were concentrated in this area because the Germans left behind an excellent infrastructure—roads, power stations, waterlines, and so forth. These factories were both extremely dirty and extremely inflexible, so large that they could not be adapted to a changing environment."

"And out-of-date before they were built," Katya added.

"Many of them," Dr. Sova agreed. "Poland was forced to buy Russian technology at vastly inflated prices. The Russians simply told us what we were to purchase, and what the price would be, and that was all. But in some areas, such as steel and chemical production, the industries that are concentrated in this region, the technology dated from before the First World War."

"There was a total disregard shown for worker safety and health," Katya explained, "and the consequences are just now being understood. In the Nova Huta steel works outside Cracow, the *average* time a worker holds employment in the factory is four years. The major reasons for departures are accidents and lung disorders."

Dr. Sova gave Katya the welcome look of a kindred spirit. "Such information has been released only in the past two years. Under the Communists, studies of this kind were outlawed, because they feared public reaction if the truth were ever known. But we knew. We saw the result of their attitude toward pollution here in our children."

"This region has forty times what is considered to be the maximum safe level of dust in the air," Katya told him, "and sixty times the level of lead in both the air and the water. Half of all rivers in Poland are so polluted that they are not even fit for industrial use; their water will corrode the intake pipes. Almost two-thirds of Cracow is without any sewage treatment at all; everything is simply dumped into the Vistula River. New studies show that the level of chemicals in the air has reached critical levels."

"Sulfur dioxide," Dr. Sova recited. "Carbon dioxide, carbon monoxide, heavy metals, iron, and just plain soot. This region has one *ton* per square meter of dirt fall from the sky each year, the highest on earth."

"The effect on people's health must be devastating," Jeffrey said.

"Especially the children," Dr. Sova agreed. "Within this region, *ninety percent* of all children under the age of five suffer from some pulmonary disorder at one time or another. One half of all four-year-olds suffer from some *chronic* disease, two-thirds of all six-year-olds, and three-quarters of all ten-year-olds. Again, these figures have only in the past six months become collected. Under the Communists, all records of our children's health were classified top secret, and no such collation of data was permitted. All we could tell you was that too many of our children were ill for too long. Far too long."

She stood and motioned toward the door. "Now that you have heard a bit of the background, perhaps it is time to show you the result."

Reluctantly Jeffrey followed her into the hall. The walls were institutional orange and yellow, the floors mismatched strips of various linoleum shades. The air smelled faintly of disinfectant and soap.

"As I said, lung diseases are our single greatest problem,"

she said, walking them by glass-fronted rooms filled with cribs and children of various ages. "Babies are born with symptoms inherited from their mothers, such as extremely irritated mucus membranes. This makes it very hard for them to draw breath. It also makes them vulnerable to infections, especially bronchitis and pneumonia."

Many of the rooms also contained beds for adults. "This is a very new program for us," she explained, pointing to where a father assisted a nurse in bathing his child. "Under the Communists, parents were not allowed into children's wards at all. Nowadays we encourage it for all of our non-critical patients. We feel both the children and the parents are helped by being together."

She passed by two rooms whose glass walls fronting the hallway were painted over. "Cancer ward here, and next to it leukemia," she explained curtly. "I do not think we shall stop in there."

"Thank you," Jeffrey said quietly.

She glanced at his face. "This is hard for you?"

"Very."

"And yet you wish to help us?"

He felt tender relief as Katya's hand slipped into his. "If we can."

"I have discussed it with my superiors, and we have decided that it would be best if we pinpoint one particular area of need—that is, if you are in agreement."

He nodded. "Where did you learn your English?"

"Here and in America. I was able to do a year's residency at Johns Hopkins." She smiled wistfully. "It was very hard to leave there; so many new and exciting things were taking place every day. But I felt that I was needed more here."

She pushed open a door at the end of the hall. "And here you see exposed the wound to my nation's heart."

The ward held a number of tiny cribs and glass-covered incubators. Dr. Sova marched purposefully toward one, unaware of the difficulty Jeffrey and Katya had in following her. When the incubator's occupant came into view, Jeffrey felt the air punched from his chest. Katya responded with a very small cry.

"This baby is now in her thirtieth week," Dr. Sova said,

the professional briskness unable to hide her concern for her tiny charge. "With premature births we count from gestation, as you do in the West. This is now what we call an old lady, because she has survived the first critical ten days, and her weight is up over three pounds."

"She's so small," Jeffrey whispered.

Dr. Sova's smile was tinged with sadness. "This is a very big baby. Very healthy. She's almost ready to go home. We have many premature births with weights at seven hundred grams, or about one and one-half pounds. Those are the ones who cause us the greatest worry."

The baby was more than tiny. She was so small as to appear incapable of life. A rib cage smaller than his fist. A head that could have fit within the palm of his hand. Incredibly fragile arms and legs and hands and feet, like the limbs of a tiny china doll.

"The problem is not just one of survival," Dr. Sova went on. "The problem is the *quality* of survival. Cerebral palsy. Blindness. Mental ability. All of these are unanswered questions with premature babies at this stage of their development."

Wires and needles were taped to the baby's head and abdomen and wrist and ankle. A tiny tube was taped inside her nostril. Monitors standing on a bedside table and hung from the wall hummed and beeped and drew electronic pulses.

"Today, one in five babies born in this region are premature. In the West, the rate is less than one in twenty. Here, placentas are affected by air and water quality—this is now documented fact."

She placed a hand on the thick plastic incubator cover and stroked it, as though touching the baby within. "We are still using incubators that are extremely loud for the baby— their ears are very sensitive at this stage. Some of those from Russia, the only ones we can afford, risk cooking the child because the temperature inside is not always the same as what is registered on the thermometer. We need new ones that both monitor the child's safety and let it grow healthily through this dangerous period.

"Some of my patients who were preemies like this one are now children of seven or eight years of age. I've watched them grow, and I love them as my own. I want to give all these children not just the gift of life, but the gift of a *quality* life. If they wish to be violinists, I want to be sure that their ears are intact and their muscle coordination is precise enough to allow them to play as a virtuoso."

"You need new incubators," Katya said.

"We need *everything*," Dr. Sova replied. "Our financial problems are crippling. We hold our doctors' salaries to two hundred dollars a month and pray that they will not be stolen away by offers from the West at twenty times that amount. With the government's finances in such disarray, we find our budgets being cut daily, while everything we require grows steadily more expensive. Light, coal, repairs to buildings and equipment—every week we wonder if next week we shall have enough to do what is required. One day we lack needles, the next syringes, another day something else, but up to now we have lost no child because of our lack. Of this we are very, very proud."

Dr. Sova guided them around the ward and its tiny occupants. Everywhere were signs of a world far removed from the wealth of the West. The cribs were prewar metal types, heavy and painted white and sided with bars that rose and lowered with screeched protests. The bed sheets all bore hand-stitched repair jobs, as did most of the blankets Jeffrey saw. Machines and wirings wore heavy bandages of silver tape. In the corner station, two nurses were using their break time to crochet miniature bonnets and booties for their patients.

"Basically we need to outfit an entire new ward," Dr. Sova explained. "We need Western-type incubators, which will ensure a stable environment for our little ones. IV pumps, monitors, X-ray machine, lung ventilator and compressor—all of these are desperately required."

As she walked them back down the hall toward the main entrance, Dr. Sova told them, "Across the border in East Germany, before the Wall fell, they had a policy very different from ours. We heard it from doctors we met in conferences. In their heavily polluted cities, all babies weighing less than a kilo were drowned at birth. The authorities decided to spend their scarce resources on patients with a better chance of survival, you see. We have struggled with the problem in a different way, but so long as the culprit remains, so long as pollution levels continue to climb, such horrors are a real possibility in poorer lands."

She pushed open the doors, shook hands, smiled them out and away from the problems locked within those doors. "Poland has never faced so great a threat as it does now from air and water pollution," Dr. Sova said. "This I believe with all my heart. The future of this very generation—the one being born today, not several decades from now, but today— lies in the balance."

CHAPTER
36

"It's the Amber Room," Jeffrey announced to Alexander the next evening by telephone. He made no effort to mask his own excitement. "Rokovski is absolutely certain."

"And, no doubt, most ecstatic."

"He did everything but climb the walls while we were with him," Jeffrey confirmed. "He's had three top experts examine the stuff. They've found tracings of old ink on the tissue around each piece."

"Instructions for fitting the puzzle back together."

"That's what they think," Jeffrey agreed. "And he says there is no doubt whatsoever that the amber fits the descriptions of old documents."

"They haven't made their find public in this search for authentication, I hope."

"Not on your life."

"That is good. If this truly is the Amber Room, two million dollars is a paltry sum to pay."

"Not for them," Jeffrey replied. "Rokovski is frantic with worry over how to gather together that much money without going to the central authorities and running the risk of word getting out."

Alexander was silent a long moment, then, "And he is certain that the carvings are not forgeries?"

"Rokovski estimates the suitcases' contents alone are

worth over a third of what they've requested," Jeffrey replied. "He said the carvings are exquisite. That was his word. Exquisite. Like nothing he has seen in modern times."

"A lost art," Alexander agreed. "There is no longer a world of kings and queens and dukes and princes who can afford to sustain the expertise of carving jewels into entire chambers."

"He's worried that if he doesn't come up with the money soon, they may search out other buyers."

"And rightly so. Now that this German group has its hands on it, there is an enormous risk that they will either try to move it or to up the price completely beyond Poland's reach." Alexander paused, then decided. "Jeffrey, I want you to call Rokovski for me. Inform him that if he is willing to use the remainder of the funds we have in his special account, I shall lend him the balance."

Jeffrey felt a surge of pride and affection. "He wasn't expecting this. I'm certain it hadn't even occurred to him."

"Yes, Pavel is that sort of man. Nonetheless, this is my decision. Tell him no papers will be necessary. His word will be sufficient." His tone darkened. "It is the least I can do, under the circumstances."

"Speaking of which," Jeffrey replied. "He said he has to travel to Rome the day after tomorrow."

"In relation to the chalice?"

"He didn't say exactly, but I'm pretty sure. I hope so, anyway." Jeffrey hesitated, then continued. "There's more, but maybe it should wait until you get here."

"What on earth do you mean by that?"

"I don't want to get your hopes up unnecessarily."

"My dear Jeffrey. I have seldom given you a direct order, but I shall do so now. Tell me everything Pavel said."

"His researchers have turned up another item. Do you remember his talking about the Vatican emissary who came bearing gifts?"

"Of course."

"Well, they have found records of a legend. That's what Rokovski called it, a legend. The emissary was a powerful member of the Vatican and traveled through lands totally devastated by the Reformation Wars. There was not a sense of safety nor an absence of starvation until he passed over the Polish borders. Then he arrived in Poland in time for the summer harvest, the only harvest that was still intact in all of northern Europe. All of this convinced him that it was absolutely imperative for Rome to have a man in this powerful kingdom, a man they could fully trust."

"Go on."

Jeffrey took a breath. "The legend is that the Polish king was willing to accept the Pope's man as the new cardinal. But then he told the emissary that he had heard there was a reliquary in the Vatican's possession which contained a segment from the crown of thorns. He wanted it for his kingdom in return for this agreement."

"And the emissary accepted?" Excitement crackled over the line.

"Rokovski says there are two versions, both of them written down about two hundred years ago, over a century after all this took place. In one, the king backed down and accepted the cardinal without further payment. In the other, the emissary made a *second* trip to Poland. A *secret* one. He traded the original chalice that the Pope had intended as the gift for the reliquary which the king demanded. The emissary then returned to the Vatican with news of the king's acceptance of Rome's cardinal."

"So the reliquary did find its way to Poland after all," Alexander exclaimed, "and without Rome's formal approval."

"Perhaps," Jeffrey cautioned. "At least, as far as this second legend is concerned. A few years later, the Vatican supposedly discovered that the chalices had been switched. They approached the king of Poland and said there had been a mistake, that the reliquary had been given without the Pope's permission. They requested that it be returned to its rightful place at the heart of Christendom. The king replied that there had been no mistake. Poland had hundreds of valuable chalices, he said, but no such symbol of Christ's suffering and dying for mankind. The only reason he would have considered granting the cardinal the appointment was in return for this priceless gift."

"I wonder what happened to the emissary," Alexander murmured.

"Rokovski said he asked the same thing. His researchers told him there was never any further mention of him or his family's name. Not anywhere. It was as though he had never existed."

"Yet the Vatican could not complain too loudly," Alexander mused. "There was too much at stake, and the ties with Poland too tenuous."

"It appears that polite enquiries were made every ten years or so," Jeffrey replied. "With each new cardinal or king, the question was raised. How would it appear in the eyes of the world if it was learned that such a relic were no longer in Rome? In time, though, as Poland's preeminence continued, an agreement was reached. What was important to Cracow was that they had the relic. What was important to Rome was that the people thought it was still there. So without actually saying as much, Cracow agreed never to make public the fact that the chalice they had was indeed the reliquary."

"And in the more than three hundred years since the switch was made, there has been time for the secret to be forgotten," Alexander concluded. "And now that the millennium approaches, there is pressure to bring the reliquary back to Rome."

"Again, all this could be true only if the second legend is the valid one," Jeffrey went on. "But I think it is, and so does Rokovski. At least, he said it was worth pursuing to the end. It also appeared that he was on to something else. But it was only half worked out, and Rokovski refused to tell me what he was thinking. All he would say was that he hoped to have something positive to report to you upon his return from Rome."

"This indeed is a night filled with good news." Alexander's tone sounded lighter than it had in weeks. "Find out from him when he expects to return to Cracow, if you would. I shall be there myself to greet him."

"I'll call him first thing tomorrow morning."

"Splendid. Now tell me, how are your other activities proceeding?"

"Business is great. We've picked up some excellent new pieces."

"Not new in the strictest sense, I hope."

"No," Jeffrey hesitated, then told him about Katya and his visit to the hospital and their decision to work on equipping a new premature birth unit.

When he stopped, Alexander released a long sigh. "My dear Jeffrey, I find myself deeply touched by your act."

"It was Katya's idea, really."

"Do not do yourself a disservice. Already you two are beginning to join in true union. The idea of one is given life by the actions of both." Alexander's voice softened. "And such actions. Yes, you have given me great food for thought, my friend. So. You shall speak with Rokovski and then call me tomorrow? Splendid. Then I shall bid you a good-night."

CHAPTER
37

"It has taken me over a day to obtain this connection to Schwerin," Erika declared once she had Kurt on the telephone.

"I would far rather fight with operators than have to do what I have done," Kurt replied. "Which is sit on my hands."

"Waiting is pure agony," Erika agreed.

"Especially when there is nothing but doubt for company."

"I told you I could be trusted."

"Yes, you did that."

Erika paused, acquiesced, "Were I in your place, I would feel no different."

"Your honesty is most reassuring."

A muffled voice spoke from the distance. "Ferret is reminding me again."

"No doubt."

"To business, then." She kept her voice brisk, determinedly calm. "The transfer has been made."

Though expected and hoped for, the news brought with it an electric stab. He had to stop and breathe before asking, "All of it?"

"So many zeros," Erika replied. "You cannot imagine how it feels to stand in such a place, one of the grandest banks in the world, and look at a number that large."

Kurt searched as far inward as he ever allowed himself, found only doubt and worry and fear. "And here I stand," he said bitterly. "My passport is in the hands of others, and there you are, looking at all those zeros."

"It boggles the mind."

"No doubt," he agreed. For a moment, he felt the fear give way to a certainty of ruin, and in that brief instant Kurt felt a bonding with the old colonel and his tired, defeated air. "Never have I felt more helpless, or more alone."

"Such a confession," Erika said.

"At least you have the decency to act surprised."

"I am surprised because it is exactly as Ferret predicted," she replied. "He has arranged a suitable reply. Do you have pen and paper?"

"What for?"

"Do you have it?" A little sharper this time.

"Wait." Then, "All right. Go ahead."

"Write this down," she said, and proceeded to give him a bank's name and a Zurich address, followed by a telephone number, then two longer numbers.

"Do you have it?"

"What is it?"

"Our bank. The first set of numbers is your account. They have been instructed that you will either call or fax and request confirmation of a deposit."

"A what?"

"A deposit. A large one. Very large. Your share of the proceeds, to be exact. You are to give them this second number, which is your access code."

The flood of relief left him utterly weak. "You have done this?"

"Deliver the treasure map to Poland," Erika replied. "Then come to Switzerland. It is time to begin your new life."

CHAPTER
38

Before traveling to meet Alexander at the airport, Jeffrey accompanied Katya on a stroll through Cracow's old city to the Marian Church. A placard of postcards for sale stood beside the church entrance, staffed by a smiling rheumy-eyed woman in a gray-wool dress and head-kerchief. The pictures were of Polish winter scenes—a heavily laden horse cart, children walking a snowy forest path, icicles growing from an ancient thatched farmhouse, mountain passes, descents into steep ravines, sunset forests lit like a stained-glass chapel. In the center was a handwritten card, the script shaky and uneven as from a very old hand.

"What does the card say?" Jeffrey asked.

"If you allow," Katya read, "every experience will become part of the path that leads you to God."

Jeffrey stared into the face of the old woman and found a light in her ancient, teary eyes, a force and a sureness that left her untouched by his stare and his silent questions. She was content to stand and stare back and allow him to feed on her gaze.

"We need to go now," Katya finally said, "if we're going to have time to pray before your meeting."

Reluctantly Jeffrey followed. As he entered the immense eleventh-century oak doors, he turned to find the crone still watching him. She withdrew one hand from the folds of her wrap and pointed a twisted finger toward the card.

Katya was waiting for him just inside the church. She asked, "Could we go sit up there?"

"No, you go on ahead."

She inspected his face. "Is everything all right?"

"I'm fine," he replied. "I just want to stand here for a while."

"I'll be near the front," Katya said quietly, and left.

Although the church was ringed by vast expanses of stained glass, fifty years of soot and grime considerably dimmed the light permitted entry. The murky quality of this illumination was in keeping with the interior's darkened confines. Brilliant gilt work had faded over the centuries. Ceiling mosaics, once glimmering with a hundred different hues, now lay in a half-seen distance. The central cross, rising up a full seventy feet above the nave, seemed to float of its own accord. Through the gloomy light, the Christ figure gazed out and down across the eight hundred years since it first was raised.

As the afternoon faded, low-slung chandeliers were lit. Jeffrey watched people come and go, their hands clasped before them, their faces set in repose made gentle both by inward thoughts and soft lighting. The church's higher reaches became lost entirely. Jeffrey craned and searched and caught sight of lofty shadows and half-seen images, glimpses of a heaven close only to believers, visible only to the eyes of a love-filled heart.

Even in the slow afternoon hours between Masses, the church remained almost half full. Silent prayers charged the atmosphere and heightened the sense of mystery. Candles flickered before the three dozen altars tucked in side alcoves, and within stands surrounding the vast pillars. Penitents stood or knelt or sat, hands entwined in rosaries or still in laps or supporting burdened foreheads.

Jeffrey searched the faces that came and went, wishing he could somehow capture in paint the beauty he found there—their intensity of concentration, their histories of suffering, their peace, their joy. Young and old, men and women, entered and knelt and spoke to the Invisible whose Spirit filled Jeffrey's heart as he watched. In that moment he loved

them all. And with the flood of caring came the realization
that the love he felt was not his own.

In time, he walked forward to join Katya in prayer.

"I've never seen a church so full except for services," he
said upon their departure.

"People have no place else to pray," Katya replied. "They
live crammed together in apartments meant for half their
number, as many as three generations in three rooms. In
some families there is no quiet time, in others there is only
one believer who is not given space for prayer, not even a
closet. Some are scoffed at and ridiculed. The church is their
island, their refuge, their place to come and sit in peace and
talk to God."

Alexander arrived, showing his normal post-flight blues.
When Jeffrey started to tell him that Rokovski had arrived
back the day before, he waved the words aside, saying that
the situation was too important to waste upon a mind that
was not yet functioning. Jeffrey bore the burden of his news
in suffering silence all the way back into town, deposited
Alexander in his room, and wore a track in the downstairs
carpet until the appointed hour. He and Katya arrived at
Alexander's room just as the secondhand ticked into place.

Alexander opened the door with a flourish. "Excellent.
The tea has just been delivered. Come in, come in."

He was wearing a neatly pressed dark suit, a starched
white shirt, a discreetly striped silk tie. His color was excellent. "I hope you will excuse my concern for privacy, but I
find public rooms to be no place for such discussions."

"You are looking extremely well," Katya said, taking the
offered chair.

"Thank you, my dear. I must say, I am feeling better than
I have in weeks. Perhaps you would be so good as to pour."

Once tea had been served, Alexander gave Jeffrey a brief
smile. "You had best deliver the news before you burst."

"We leave for Czestochowa at four o'clock tomorrow morning," he announced.

Gray eyes sparked with interest. "The key to the mystery
has been delivered, then."

"It better have," Jeffrey replied.

"Rokovski is laying his professional life on the line for this," Katya explained. "If the treasure isn't there, the best he can hope for is a posting to some provincial backwater."

"You both have seen him?"

"Yesterday late afternoon and again this morning," Jeffrey said. "He hasn't slowed down since his return from Rome."

"Speaking of which," Alexander said, "did he mention what he discovered while there?"

"Only that it was good news," Katya replied, "and that his feelings about Karlovich were confirmed."

"He prefers to tell you himself," Jeffrey said. "He asks that you please have patience until after this other matter has been settled."

"But he did say that the time for worry was over," Katya added, "at least so far as the chalice is concerned."

"So there was a reliquary," Alexander said, leaning back in visible relief.

"It looks to me as if Karlovich knew there was one all along," Jeffrey said.

"I would wager that at any odds," Alexander agreed. "He was probably one of very few people alive in all Poland who did. A keeper of secrets passed down from curate to curate over three centuries."

"We played right into his hands, didn't we?" Katya said.

"Indeed we did," Alexander replied. "Our request to have a selection of Polish religious art for the gala, coming as it did through the proper channels, was the perfect way for the reliquary to depart from Poland."

"You mean Karlovich already had some deal worked out with the Vatican to return the reliquary?" Jeffrey asked.

"That would certainly appear to be a possibility," Alexander replied. "Though only Rokovski shall be able to say for sure."

"And they made the switch in London?" Jeffrey continued.

Alexander shook his head. "I very much doubt it. I would imagine that yet another emissary from Rome appeared some time ago, one who did not share the current Pope's

Polish heritage, and who wanted the relic returned to its rightful place."

"Maybe even at the request of Karlovich," Katya suggested.

"That would be my guess," Alexander agreed. "A man in his position would no doubt have numerous contacts within the Vatican museum structure."

"Not priests," Katya said.

"Most certainly not. A curate such as Karlovich would consider himself a man apart and would seek people of like station and mind. No, the emissary on this occasion would probably have been the equivalent of a Vatican civil servant, puffed up with his own importance, a petty power seeker intent on furthering his own career by announcing the completion of such a coup." Alexander sipped his tea. "It is probably a very good thing for my soul that I shall never have an occasion to meet this person face-to-face."

"So the curate and the emissary met and discussed the millennium event," Jeffrey said. "And then, just as they're trying to figure out a way to get the reliquary back to Rome, up we pop. What do you think was Karlovich's motive?"

"Money," Katya decided.

"Most likely," Alexander agreed. "You see, Jeffrey, a curate is a man without power, yet charged with weighty responsibilities. He manages the church cleaning staff. He pays all bills. He handles all supplies. He arranges for all day-to-day operations such as cooking and feeding and housing the priests. He must effect all necessary repairs to the church. And a church of this size and age, neglected as it has been for over five decades, must be in desperate need of major repairs. So here we have a man facing financial pressures, with no one in this new capitalist regime to whom he could turn." Alexander shrugged. "And who knows? Perhaps he felt his first loyalty was to Rome, and decided that here was a means of killing two birds with one stone. So he called a colleague within the caverns burrowed beneath the Vatican, met with him and discussed the reliquary, and then waited for his chance."

"There are probably records kept of all visiting emissaries," Katya presumed.

Alexander gave her an approving nod. "Which Rokovski's researches no doubt uncovered. I would imagine that he has had an interesting time in Rome."

"Not half as interesting as what's happened since he got back," Jeffrey replied. "Oh yes. He asked me to tell you that he will not even attempt to thank you for the loan."

"Ah, yes. The other matter." Alexander sighed luxuriously. "Such a moment comes seldom to mortal lives, my dear friends. Savor this experience, I urge you. Drink your fill. Allow it to be firmly anchored in your memories, so that you may return to it in darker hours. Here is the anticipation of triumph, the risking of it all upon a hope, a struggle, a decision to seek and if possible to *achieve*. And it is done for that most important of reasons, the type of purpose which gives meaning to the grayest of lives."

"A cause," Jeffrey said.

Alexander's strong gaze rested upon him in solemn approval. "A cause shared with friends, a quest taken on for a higher purpose. That, my young friends, is an essence strong enough to make the blood sing in your veins."

CHAPTER
39

Jeffrey always thought of it as the dawn raid.

Rokovski arrived to pick them up three hours before sunrise, as tired and frantic as a man could be after two days without sleep. He greeted them with, "You cannot imagine the problems I have had."

Alexander stood on the hotel's top step and surveyed the mass of men and equipment stretched out in front of him. "I am sure I don't want to know."

There were a trio of cars for Rokovski, Jeffrey, Katya, Alexander, two beribboned officers, a stranger in a quiet gray suit, and Rokovski's three assistants. Beyond them were two police trucks filled with silent, sleepy uniformed figures. Behind these stretched an additional half dozen open-bed trucks bearing shovels, portable lights, pitchforks, drilling equipment, ladders, rubber knee boots, parkas, ropes, and bales of canvas wrapping.

"I do not wish to leave whatever we discover there for one minute longer than necessary," Rokovski explained. "I therefore decided to bring out all the reinforcements I could think of."

"My friend," Alexander declared, "you have worked a miracle."

"I have fought many battles," Rokovski countered.

"And no doubt lit a number of fires under moribund backsides," Alexander agreed.

Rokovski managed a tired smile. "Bonfires. With blow-torches. A number of my illustrious colleagues will work standing up for weeks to come."

"And you have kept this quiet?"

"I found an ally at the highest level," Rokovski explained, leading them down to the waiting convoy. "One who has not yet decided whether to keep the entire Amber Room as a part of our own national heritage, or trade a portion of it in return for vast sums."

"Perhaps even to rid our nation's soil of the pestilence of Soviet troops," Alexander murmured.

Rokovski opened the car door for Alexander. "I see that great minds think alike."

He walked around to the other side, slammed his door shut, motioned for the driver to be away, and continued. "I have resigned myself to perhaps being permitted to keep only a few of the panels. This is to be expected. In return for allowing the politicians to place portions of this room upon the chessboard of international politics, however, I shall gain immense conditions."

"If the amber is there," Jeffrey muttered.

"I no longer have the freedom," Rokovski replied gravely, "even to permit such a doubt to surface."

Czestochowa was wrapped in sleepy silence as they ground their way down dimly lit streets. They followed the directions that Rokovski had translated and typed and kept fingering and reading and perusing. They stopped before the series of shops fronting the broad Jasna Gora lawn, where two additional police cars awaited them. Rokovski and one of the uniformed officers traveling in the second car walked over. The waiting officers snapped to attention. Papers were exchanged and examined, salutes traded. Rokovski turned and motioned for them to alight. The officers went to organize their men.

"We must act as swiftly as possible," Rokovski stressed quietly. "There are too many conflicting lines of interest, both with the treasure and with the place they chose for depositing it."

"It would be far better to inform all concerned of an act

already completed," Alexander agreed.

"Exactly." Rokovski cast a nervous eye back to where the unloading of equipment brought the occasional clatter. He waved back into the dark as an officer softly called out, "Please go back to where my colleague waits. All of you will be equipped with rubber boots and flashlights."

When they returned he inspected them briefly, spoke into the darkness where dozens of lights flickered and bounced and wavered up the hillside. An answering call came quietly back. "Very well," Rokovski said. "Let us begin."

They walked up the lawn alongside the cobblestone path. But where the battlements marked the road's passage through the first high portico, Rokovski motioned with his flashlight for them to descend to the base of the empty moat. "Careful here. You will need to use the ropes and proceed cautiously. The ground is very slippery."

One by one they grasped ropes held by soldiers and reversed themselves down the icy grass-lined slope. Jeffrey helped Alexander as he landed clumsily, then turned and assisted Katya, smiling at the excitement in her eyes. Rokovski was already reaching up and inspecting the barred windowlike openings, each about four feet square, that once had delivered the medieval city's sewage and rain runoff into the moat. Suddenly he gave a muffled cry, dropped his flashlight, reached up with both hands, and wrenched at one iron-bar frame. Swiftly other hands arrived to assist; together they lifted the heavy bars free and settled them on the ground.

No more light was needed to show the fervor that gripped Rokovski as he called softly up into the darkness, then waited for a ladder to be slid down the embankment. It was propped into position, then Rokovski signaled to Alexander. "My friend, if you wish, the honor is yours."

"It is enough simply to be here," Alexander replied. "Go, my friend. Go."

Rokovski counted out several people who were to follow him, then positively leaped up the rungs and disappeared into the hole. The leading officer half bowed toward Alexander and motioned him forward. After him came Katya, then Jeffrey. The excitement was electric as he climbed the rungs and entered the dark, dank space.His feet hit ankle-deep water as he slid into the low tunnel. Rokovski was already proceeding down the depths, his flashlight illuminating tiny cantering circles of slimy ancient wall. One by one they followed him in a stooped position, craning to keep his bobbing light in view.

The floor gave an unexpected drop, and filthy water began pouring in over the top of Jeffrey's boots. He heard the squeaks of tiny animals—rats or bats or both—in nearby crevices, but had time neither for worry nor discomfort. Nor did his companions. They hustled forward as swiftly as caution and the mucky liquid would permit.

Without warning the tunnel joined with another and rose high enough to permit them to stand upon dry land. The ceiling became lofty, arched in stone and age-old brick. They paused long enough to empty their boots, then pushed on.

Another turning, yet another muffled shout from Rokovski. They rushed forward, saw him standing before an opening recently hacked from what before had been a crudely finished corner of the turning. Heaped in a half-hidden alcove were an uncountable number of human remains, now little more than bones and rags. Rokovski stood and shone his light upon them for a long moment, then raised his eyes to the waiting group and spoke solemnly in Polish. Katya translated his words as "I cannot avenge their death. But I can seek to give it meaning. On my honor, their tale will be told, and panels of what they died to keep hidden will remain in Poland, as testimony to those who come after."

"On my honor," Alexander agreed solemnly.

Rokovski bent and stepped through the opening, then emitted a long sigh. The group crowded in behind him. Jeffrey clambered through the opening and straightened to find himself facing row after row of coffin-like chests. They were stacked five and six high, lining the aged bulwark. It was possible to see in the distance where the false wall that the slain workers had been forced to build joined with the ancient original.

One chest lay open and spilled at their feet, its corroded and dirt-encrusted surface battered with shiny streaks from a recent fury of hammer blows. Fist-sized blocks of amber, still flecked with bits of yellowed paper and rotten matting, lay scattered in the grime of centuries.

Rokovski raised his arms up to gather in the multitude of chests and spoke in a fierce whisper that Katya translated.

"Behold, my friends. Behold, the Amber Room!"

CHAPTER
40

They waited in the darkness just beyond the light surrounding the Cracow airport. Every breath he and Katya took sent plumes of white into the star-studded night. Jeffrey shivered, partly from the cold, more from what he knew was to come.

One moment they were alone, the next the man with the pockmarked face was standing before them. His eyes continually scanned the night as he thrust a gloved hand outward and spoke in a voice as dead as his eyes.

"He wants his papers," Katya said quietly.

Silently Jeffrey handed over the man's passport. He caught a flicker of surprise, as though the man had not expected it to be so easy, to come without a struggle. He riffled the pages as though unsure of his next step, then turned and started for the airport.

Jeffrey knew he was going to do it, had known since Gregor had first spoken the words. Even before perhaps, though this he could not explain. What Gregor had told him to do was mirrored somewhere deep within, and the willingness to recognize this fact had shattered him. Left him unable to refuse. To do anything but what this new heart budding within his chest was quietly demanding.

Which was to speak. "Katya, tell him I have something else to say."

Reluctantly the man turned back toward them. Katya looked at Jeffrey in confusion, but for a brief moment he could not speak. The instant was so short as to outwardly appear as only a hesitation. But for him, in that instant, Jeffrey felt the realization rush up and up and up from a heart suddenly filled with a blinding white power that *demanded* release. With the words, "Tell him that there is an answer to his every need, to his every doubt and fear and worry." He took a breath, finished, "And that answer is Jesus Christ."

Katya hesitated before beginning the translation. When he refused to drop his eyes to hers, a small hand shivered its way into his grasp. But there was no room just then for more than a comforting squeeze. The moment was locked in stillness. The seed was being planted. The call was being made.

When she had finally spoken, he continued, "You need to confess that your ways have been the wrong ones, and that neither answers nor lasting peace have been found. You need to turn to the giver of peace and ask Him into your life."

Katya spoke, stopped. The man did not move, his gaze showing nothing but the same perpetual hostility.

In the silence of that eternal moment, Jeffrey felt his entire being struck by invisible lightning. He heard the voice of his heart well up with the power of unspoken wisdom. The power cracked open the lies of his existence like the shell of a bird now ready to emerge, and grow, and fly.

Jeffrey stood and saw the man's self-centered darkness, the dull, lightless world of suspicious eyes, the utter ugliness of all he was and thought and did. And in those eyes and in the world behind them, Jeffrey saw himself. With this moment of recognition came the gift of eternal truth, the realization that he, too, was loved. Not for what he had done, nor for the struggles he had made, nor for the searchings. Nor was he to be punished for all the missed opportunities and wrong turnings and false hopes and empty days. Or sins. All the sins of his life that were reflected in the man's empty eyes.

He was simply loved for the promise of who he was and who he could be. An eternal child of God. A man made clean and whole.

In the angry bitterness of a wounded, hateful man, in this pair of empty eyes was the answer Jeffrey had been seeking all his life. He found assurance that the Lord's offer was made to *everyone*. None were too far from the fold. None were unworthy. Not even himself.

And with this realization came the ability to love. To give, to accept, to be lost in a moment that reached out in all directions with a force that left him unable to remember what about this man had angered him before.

"As far as the East is from the West," Jeffrey said, and the calmness was not his own, nor the quietness that left him steady despite a furiously beating heart. A truth pressed upward from the deepest fiber of his being, yearning for the release of giving, the gift of passing on what was not his, yet his forever, to another in need. "That is how far you can be from all the troubles and sins in your life if only you will give yourself to Jesus Christ."

The words were more than sounds of the mouth and thoughts of the mind. They were the only way he could give purpose to the love welling up in his chest. Not love for this man. Love. Without direction and without claim and without a need to be confined or measured or given against expected return. Love.

Jeffrey listened to Katya translate his words with a voice made small and shivery by more than the cold. He gazed into eyes that squinted back in undisguised hostility. And he felt the love pour out and say with a clarity that went beyond all words, all doubt, all worry, all fear, all unworthy feelings— he stood and looked and *knew* that here was just another brother his Lord yearned to call home.

And he was too full of newfound truth to feel the slightest scarring as the pockmarked man sneered and snorted and turned away.

Instead, Jeffrey reached out an open hand and called to the retreating back, "I will pray for you!"

CHAPTER
41

Kurt arrived in Zurich a very angry man.

The corridor leading from the satellite terminal to the main hub of the airport was almost a quarter of a mile long. It ran beneath several runways, a gently curving tunnel of spotless white stretching ahead as far as he could see. He did not need to walk. A smoothly running automatic walkway sprang lightly beneath his feet. Classical music played soothing strains along the entire distance. Instead of windows, enormous backlit displays advertised all the things that before had remained beyond his wildest dreams, and which now were within his grasp. All of them. From the gold watch to the lakefront resort to the mountain ski holiday to the luxurious clothes to the rented sports car to the private helicopter service. All of it could now be his.

And yet all he could think of was that strange American and the insanity of his final words. It *consumed* him.

He felt like pounding his fists against the gleaming white walls.

Just when he should have been readying himself for the good life, a barb had been wedged in his flesh at heart level. With every step he came closer to losing control, to shouting his unexplained rage to the unseen heavens. Try as he might, he could not shake off the words. They rang in his head over and over and over, lancing at his reason in ways he could neither understand nor stop. He felt helpless, caught up in something that made no sense to him at *all*.

The tunnel's end appeared in the distance. Kurt picked up his single valise and marched forward, shrugging hard at the resounding pressure in his mind and heart. He would leave this barbed message behind, it and the messenger both, and enter the new life that awaited him. The life he had always dreamed of. The life he *deserved*.

Wait until he told the others about the crazy American.

CHAPTER
42

When Jeffrey arrived downstairs the next morning on his way to Gregor's, he was surprised to find Alexander up and waiting for him. "I was wondering if you might permit me to accompany you this morning."

"It would be an honor," he replied.

Together they exchanged the hotel's stuffy warmth for a bracing dawn breeze. Clouds scuttled overhead through a sky touched with the first faintest hues of the coming sun. A silver moon hung calm and peaceful upon the horizon, touching all the world with silver mystery. "Katya does not mind your traipsing off each morning on your own?"

"A little," Jeffrey admitted. "But she knows how much it means to me, and she doesn't complain."

"An act of wisdom far beyond her years," Alexander replied. "You are most fortunate in your choice of mates, my friend."

"I'm not sure how much I had to do with it," Jeffrey said. "It's always felt like a gift from above."

"Yet who was it who endured the difficult beginning, who sought answers beyond what was evident?" Alexander strode forward with a light heart. "Who made the choice to abide despite pain and emotional hardship? Who loved in defiance of logic? Who sought answers beyond the known and the comfortable?"

"You do me great honor," Jeffrey said quietly.

"None that is not deserved. I am most proud of your endeavors, both with the young lady and with your work." He pulled his scarf up around his neck. "As for myself, I seem to learn my greatest lessons in the loneliest of hours."

"Me too," Jeffrey conceded. "Some of them, anyway. I hope it's not some unwritten requirement for being a Christian."

"Oh, I think not. In my case, it is a need that I force upon myself. So long as all is well in my world, I feel little urge to struggle with uncomfortable questions." He glanced Jeffrey's way. "I have found myself comparing my own searchings with yours. I wish I had your strength of purpose."

Alexander stopped further conversation by taking a sprightly step up Gregor's front stairs and pressing the buzzer. The latch released; he pushed through, held the door for Jeffrey, then proceeded up the stairs.

Once tea had been served and Gregor was settled back in his bed, Alexander confessed cheerfully, "Your unspoken lesson has come through loud and clear, Cousin."

"It was neither my lesson nor my voice," Gregor replied mildly. "And you should not belittle the gift by failing to recognize the Giver."

Alexander remained silent for a time, sipping at his tea. Then, "Why do I have such difficulty in accepting that I have heard God's silent voice?"

"Because you are human." Gregor smiled with genuine warmth. "You continue to surprise me, my dear Cousin."

"Not nearly so much as I surprise myself."

"No doubt." He reached over to pat Alexander's shoulder. "Nothing you might say could please me more, nor make me more proud of you."

"A compliment." Alexander showed mock surprise. "I do hope you are not suffering from a fever, Cousin."

"You go against all of your worldly heritage to ask such a question," Gregor replied. "Now tell me what lesson you have learned."

"My lesson. Yes, well." Alexander sipped from his glass. "I have spent numerous sleepless hours watching helplessly as my reputation was threatened, my life's work torn asunder. And all because of a chalice that was not mine, for a gala I took on for others. Or at least, so I thought."

"Such honesty." Gregor smiled. "Go on, dear Cousin."

"I have found the hours before dawn to be a powerful mirror," Alexander said. "Most powerful. I have seen how much of what I did was for selfish pride, and pride alone."

"You cannot imagine how your words stir the soul," Gregor told him.

Alexander turned sharp gray eyes Jeffrey's way. "And then a certain young friend tells me of a project he and his fiancée have begun in a nameless children's hospital, out of sight of all publicity, in a crumbling corner of a region so polluted it is known as the Triangle of Death. He does not tell me with pride. No. He is embarrassed. Moved so deeply by the need he has discovered in an alien land that he is ashamed of his feelings. He tells me because he wishes to share his discovery with a friend. Yet he does so with shame for his own emotions, and with fear that I may scoff. He does not say so, but I hear it in his voice. And what he does not know, what he cannot imagine, is that he shames me. He *humbles* me. He *teaches* me. Not with words. No. Such a lesson cannot be taught by any means save example. He stands before the altar and honors the Father with a gift made with no expectation of receiving anything in return."

Alexander nodded solemnly. "I listened to my young friend heed the call of his Lord, and I learned. I realized that the missing chalice was part of a lesson. I understood that I might also grow through the gift of humble, nameless service. Out of the light of publicity. Away from the adulating crowds. In the lonely reaches of others' needs. Where the Father's voice might be more clearly heard."

CHAPTER
43

"My friends! Come in, come in!" A jubilant Pavel Rokovski ushered Alexander, Jeffrey, and Katya into his office. "Champagne is called for, but perhaps at this hour you would prefer tea."

"Tea would be splendid," Alexander replied for them all.

"One moment, then." He soon returned and served them. "So much to tell, so very much. Where on earth to begin?"

"With the chalice," Alexander replied. "Please tell me that the mystery is solved."

"More than solved! Providence has been at work here, my friends." Rokovski pulled up a chair, asked, "You heard of my discoveries?"

"About Karlovich, yes. But only that you discovered you were right to distrust him."

"That man." Rokovski shook his head. "He deserves to enjoy his retirement within a prison cell. He was in contact with a Vatican emissary—not a priest, however. What is the English word for *niebieski ptaszek?*"

"Literally it translates as a little bird," Katya replied, and exchanged glances with Jeffrey. "But it really means a peon, a scoundrel. Someone who lives off the importance of others."

"Thank you. Yes, we made several fascinating discoveries about this mysterious Vatican *aparatchik,* and these were what prompted me to travel to Rome. There, I had a most interesting visit with a certain Signor Buracci, the highest official within the Vatican museum system who is not a cleric. He answers directly to the cardinal. I asked him if he might shed light on a most curious set of circumstances."

"I do wish I could have been a fly on the wall for that discussion," Alexander murmured.

"I explained to him of our careful records," Rokovski went on. "And I asked about certain things that surprised me no end. My attitude was one of requesting information, asking questions, seeking guidance."

"Most politely."

"And humbly," Rokovski agreed. "These discoveries we have made were most confusing to a simple mind such as my own, and I simply sought his lofty guidance."

"Including the confusing matters surrounding a certain curate."

"Well, yes. That was one of my questions. Why was it, I asked, that our Mr. Karlovich traveled twice to Rome in the past year, and that a certain emissary, one Signor Danilo Disertori, visited Cracow three times? The first was two months before Karlovich loaned you the chalice, the second three days after it left for display in England, and the third the day after it was returned."

"And discovered to be a fake."

"I had a further question," Rokovski continued, "about the transfer of funds from the Banco Sao Paolo to Karlovich's account here in Cracow of fifty thousand dollars. The Banco Sao Paolo, as you may know, handles the Vatican's commercial transactions."

"About this time," Alexander said, "I would imagine the good gentleman is finding his collar most constricting."

"He did appear to have great difficulty in speaking," Rokovski agreed.

"You didn't involve the Pope."

"Of course not," Rokovski answered, hugely satisfied. "It was not even necessary to suggest that I would do so."

"Everyone knew," Katya offered.

Rokovski smiled her way. "And positively trembled at the thought."

"So," Alexander nodded, the sparkle back in his eyes. "What happens now?"

"Now there will be a vast public announcement of Poland's magnificent gift, which will be displayed at the millennium celebration in Rome. It will then be returned with great fanfare to become the centerpiece of our new Museum for Religious Artifacts in Cracow, which will be officially opened in time for its arrival." Rokovski's gleam turned hard. "While all these mysterious documents will remain locked in a very safe place, and certain individuals in Rome and Cracow will be urged to consider an early retirement."

"I shall not miss them," Alexander declared.

"No, nor I," Rokovski agreed, and his vast good humor returned. "There is more. In this great central hall will be displayed three outstanding paintings, loaned by the Vatican for an indefinite time, to commemorate this wonderful new museum. A Raphael, a Da Vinci, and a Michelangelo."

"Magnificent," Alexander proclaimed. "A worthy recognition of our nation's new renaissance."

"You know, of course, what will adorn the galley leading to this chamber."

"Panels from the Amber Room," Jeffrey breathed. "What an awesome place this is going to be."

Rokovski nodded his agreement. "There is still more."

"How so?"

"It appears that in their haste," Rokovski explained, "our mysterious treasure hunters miscounted the number of chests."

"Miscounted?"

"There happened to be seventy-three." Rokovski watched their reaction with immense satisfaction. "Yes. And since no one outside my office knew exactly how many the Amber Room required, this last chest remains a secret known only to me and my most trusted allies." The gleam in Rokovski's dark eyes was blinding. "This extra chest, my friends, was filled with gold and jewelry and ornaments."

"A treasure chest?" Alexander was at full alert.

"Much of secondary quality," Rokovski replied, "at least from an art collector's standpoint. Chosen in haste, no doubt, by one with an untrained eye who selected on the basis of their weight in gold and the size of the stones. There is very little that we shall want to display, but the remaining items would fetch a handsome sum on the open market. If only we might find a dealer in the West willing to represent us in the utmost confidentiality."

"We accept," Alexander replied with alacrity. "It will be an honor."

"Splendid. The proceeds shall first go to repaying your most generous loan." Rokovski stood. "Of course the personal debt shall remain with us always."

"There is no debt," Alexander replied. "Not between friends."

Rokovski nodded his understanding and extended his hand. "Or patriots."

Acknowledgments

My habit of writing rather lengthy acknowledgments has grown from my desire to recognize the many people who have given generously of their time and of themselves in the development of my books. From the idea stage through research, writing, editing, and promotion, the most valuable aspect of my work is the personal contact with people willing to share, and teach, from the heart. I would like to express my sincere thanks to all those who have contributed to my books in so many ways.

In this regard, I must extend a special thanks to the readers of my books. Writing can be a rather solitary pursuit, especially in a foreign country. Your cards and letters, as well as our brief meetings at promotional events, brighten my days and encourage me more than you may know. I am absolutely thrilled to learn a particular passage has touched you deeply, or that you learned a valuable lesson, or even that you lack sleep because you proverbially "couldn't put it down." I know from you that you even read the fine print in the back of the book, the acknowledgments section, to learn how the book was developed, to seek advice from the suggested counselor, or to contribute to a named cause from helping the homeless to combatting pornography.

If you would like to write to me, please do so care of Bethany House Publishers. I do try hard to answer all my letters, but being a professional writer is much like running a small business; I always have more to do than I have hours in the day. It takes about two weeks for a letter to be forwarded to England, so please be patient. I will try to respond as best I can.

As with *Florian's Gate,* this book has been enriched by the open-hearted support of my wife's family in Cracow and Warsaw. I will refrain from mentioning all of them a second time, yet a few must be remembered for a special reason. Marian and Dusia Tarka, together with Olek and Halinka Tarka, went out of their way to help me at every turn. They offered their usual hospitality and made me feel part of their extended family. Regrettably, I arrived in Cracow to do research on this book having been struck by food poisoning in Dresden earlier that week. My suffering later proved to be a liver disorder. Not only did they do their utmost to nurse me back to health, but they also took it upon themselves to become additional eyes and ears and arms and legs, helping me with much work that I was too weak to do myself. I am deeply indebted to them for this invaluable support.

Thanks must also go to Isabella's aunt in Warsaw, Dr. Teresa Aleksandrowicz, chief surgeon at one of the city's hospitals, who saw me back to a level of fitness that made traveling back to London possible. Jan and Haluta Zorawski opened their home to us during this difficult period, and laced their concern with a splendid sense of humor. Laughter truly is the best medicine.

As for all my books based within Eastern Europe, my wife's assistance has been absolutely indispensable. I remain humbled by her ability to give with such loving patience, by her wisdom, and by her love. Thank you, Izia, for enriching both my life and my work.

Much of the information that went into developing the Solidarity photographer came from my wife and her family. Isabella was traveling from Warsaw to Cracow the morning that Martial Law was declared in December of 1981, and became caught up in the heart of the army-imposed darkness. Members of her family, as all Poles, each had his own story to tell. For their patient sharing I am truly grateful.

The story of the vision within a prison cell, however, came from a businessman with whom I worked several years ago. As managing director of a major Italian confectionery company, he was kidnapped by Red Brigade terrorists eighteen years ago and held for ransom. His prison was an extremely cramped tent, erected in a dark closet, from which he was not permitted to move for almost three weeks. Three days before his release, as he was battling a despair similar to the photographer's, he had a vision of a place he had never seen before, and a gift of God's peace. The remainder of his story mirrors that of the photographer, except the vision he had was of the Island of Capri seen from the window of a friend's house on the Bay of Naples—a place he had never before visited.

Dr. Wlodzimierz M. Borkowski is the Director of the Pediatric Division of the Narutowicza Hospital in Cracow. Dr. Grazyna Gabor is a pediatrician in this department. They provided a detailed overview of both their own hospital and the general state of children's care in Poland. The conversation held during Jeffrey and Katya's visit to the children's hospital was the same one I had with the doctors during my own visit. I was most impressed with their kindness and their dedication.

Dr. Borkowski was also one of the leading authorities filmed in the BBC's "State of Europe" program on the dangers of pollution in Eastern Europe. He shared with me a copy of this program; it provided a wealth of background information that went into forming this story.

The situation within the children's hospitals in the region of Poland known as the Triangle of Death is just as it is described in this book. Premature births and pollution-related illnesses place severe pressures on their already limited financial resources. The equipment described in this book is urgently required. If any reader knows of a hospital that is upgrading their children's ward and has surplus used equipment available, *please* be so kind as to let us know. Assistance with the cost of air freight would also be greatly appreciated, but we can help arrange the required transport documentation. Anyone who feels a call to assist financially with these desperate needs is welcome to send any size donation. Every cent will go to the purchase and shipment of medical equipment, supplies and medicines—nothing will be used for hospital salaries or administrative costs. Tax deductible donations may be sent to:

> Full Gospel Businessmen's Fellowship, Int.
> P.O. Box 7046
> Naples, FL 33941

The grisly stories about the former secret police in East Germany and its current status are based on true accounts and recently released German exposes. Gary Johnson, the publisher at Bethany House, suggested blending some "missing Stasi spy files" into what was then just an idea for the sequel to *Florian's Gate*. As ever, I am indebted to our many friends and colleagues at BHP.

Lupold Von Wedel, former Director for Eastern Europe of the Matuschka Investment Group in Munich, has in recent months been appointed managing director of a multi-billion dollar heavy industries conglomerate in former East Germany. Lupold was born in the area of Poland known as Upper Silesia. He is a good friend, and has been most kind in relating both the circumstances of his early childhood and the trauma of leaving behind a war-torn Poland. I am also most grateful for his current assessment of the economic and political situation in Poland and the former East Germany.

Barbara Beck, Press Attaché with the German Embassy in London, was most helpful with background information on the search for the Amber Room. She also supplied contacts in both Erfurt and Weimar.

H. Reichmann is the new Director of Art Union Gmbh, the antique store on the Erfurter Bridge which was used as the antiques store in this novel. I am indeed grateful for his detailed chronicle of his own shop, the other nearby buildings, and the bridge itself.

Dr. Schleiff is Director of the *Erfurter Landesamt für Denkmalpflege,* which translates literally as the "Erfurt city authority for the care of memories," and means essentially the preservation of monuments and buildings. He offered very valuable insight into the current search for the Amber Room.

Joachim Vogel is Press Attaché to the Lord Mayor of Weimar, and while maintaining a professionally detached view to the whole affair is passionately interested in the Amber Room and all the interconnected mysteries. He was most kind in assisting with general information and valuable contacts.

There is only one color photograph of the Amber Room in existence today. A copy of this was loaned to me by Weimar resident Hans Stadelmann, who is involved in the current probe into the Nazi bunkers beneath Weimar's Karl Marx Platz (the former plaza for Nazi Party gatherings, soon to receive its third name change in four decades). I am indeed grateful that he offered me this picture, from which this book's front cover was painted. Poring over stacks of yellowed documents and blueprints, he provided an extraordinary account of the Amber Room's passage from the Catherine Palace in Russia, to Königsberg in Germany, and from there into the mists of unsolved mystery.

Joachim Gommlich is currently Managing Director of Wilhelm Glaudert Gmbh in Düsseldorf. He was born in Berlin and escaped two days before the Wall was finally sealed; by this time the Russian soldiers were no longer permitting people casual passage to the West, so Joachim kissed his mother and father goodbye, and with their blessings took his camera and some pocket money and walked over the border, telling the guards he was on a school photography project. It was the last time he ever saw his parents. The war-end recollections of the Erfurt antique dealer are based on those of Herr Gommlich. I am indeed grateful for his recounting these early memories.

Reverend Seyfarth, the head of the evangelical seminary in Schwerin, granted insight into the faith of the East German people, which proved most valuable in the structuring of both this book and *Florian's Gate*.

To the numerous antiques dealers who have assisted me with both of these books, I extend my heartfelt thanks. All of you have shown remarkable patience with my never-ending stream of questions. I have been truly fortunate to meet so many people who not only know their business but love it as well.

Just as Jeffrey goes through personal and spiritual struggles in this book, so do many others who feel that their own problems are too difficult to share or their questions too unworthy of being asked. This simply is not the case. We are, every one of us, both unique and uniquely important in God's eyes. Anyone who feels he or she needs a listening ear or advice from a man of God is most welcome to write:

> Reverend Paul McCommon
> %Bethany House Publishers
> 6820 Auto Club Road
> Minneapolis, Minnesota 55438